image comics presents

THE WALKING DEAD™

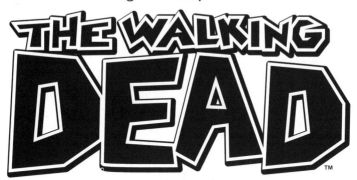

ROBERT KIRKMAN
CREATOR, WRITER

CHARLIE ADLARD
PENCILER, INKER

CLIFF RATHBURN
GRAY TONES

RUS WOOTON
LETTERER

CHARLIE ADLARD
&
CLIFF RATHBURN
COVER

SINA GRACE
EDITOR

SKYBOUND™

For SKYBOUND ENTERTAINMENT

Robert Kirkman - CEO
J.J. Didde - President
Sina Grace - Editorial Director
Shawn Kirkham - Director of Business Development
Tim Daniel - Digital Content Manager
Chad Manion - Assistant to Mr. Grace
Sydney Pennington - Assistant to Mr. Kirkman
Feldman Public Relations LA - Public Relations

FOR INTERNATIONAL RIGHTS INQUIRIES,
PLEASE CONTACT SK@SKYBOUND.COM
WWW.SKYBOUND.COM

IMAGE COMICS, INC.
Robert Kirkman - chief operating officer
Erik Larsen - chief financial officer
Todd McFarlane - president
Marc Silvestri - chief executive officer
Jim Valentino - vice-president

Eric Stephenson - publisher
Todd Martinez - sales & licensing coordinator
Jennifer de Guzman - pr & marketing director
Branwyn Bigglestone - accounts manager
Emily Miller - administrative assistant
Jamie Parreno - marketing assistant
Sarah deLaine - events coordinator
Kevin Yuen - digital rights coordinator
Tyler Shainline - production manager
Drew Gill - art director
Jonathan Chan - design director
Monica Garcia - production artist
Vincent Kukua - production artist
Jana Cook - production artist
www.imagecomics.com

PRINTED IN THE USA

ISBN: 978-1-60706-559-3

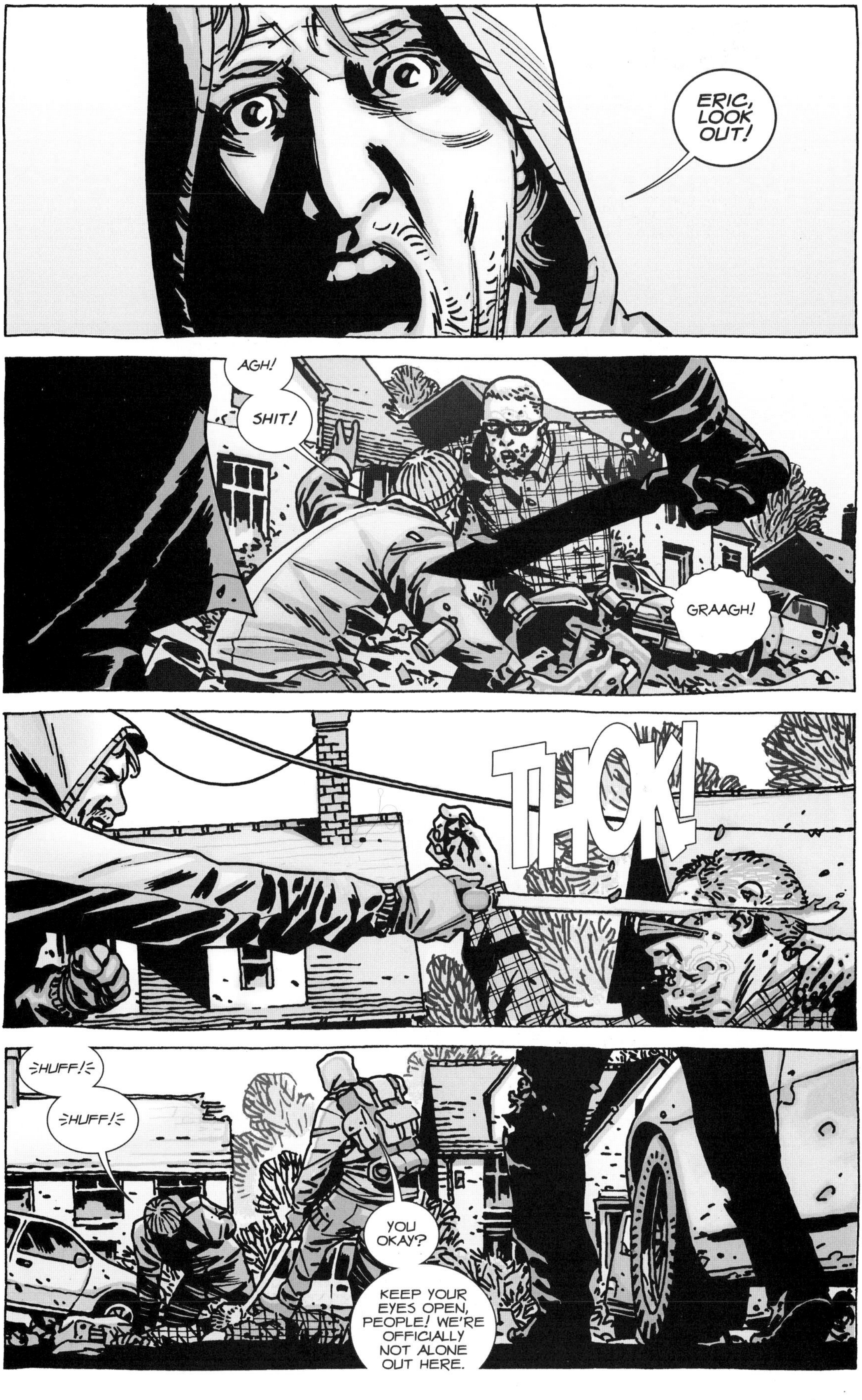
ERIC, LOOK OUT!
AGH!
SHIT!
GRAAGH!
THOK!
HUFF!
HUFF!
YOU OKAY?
KEEP YOUR EYES OPEN, PEOPLE! WE'RE OFFICIALLY NOT ALONE OUT HERE.

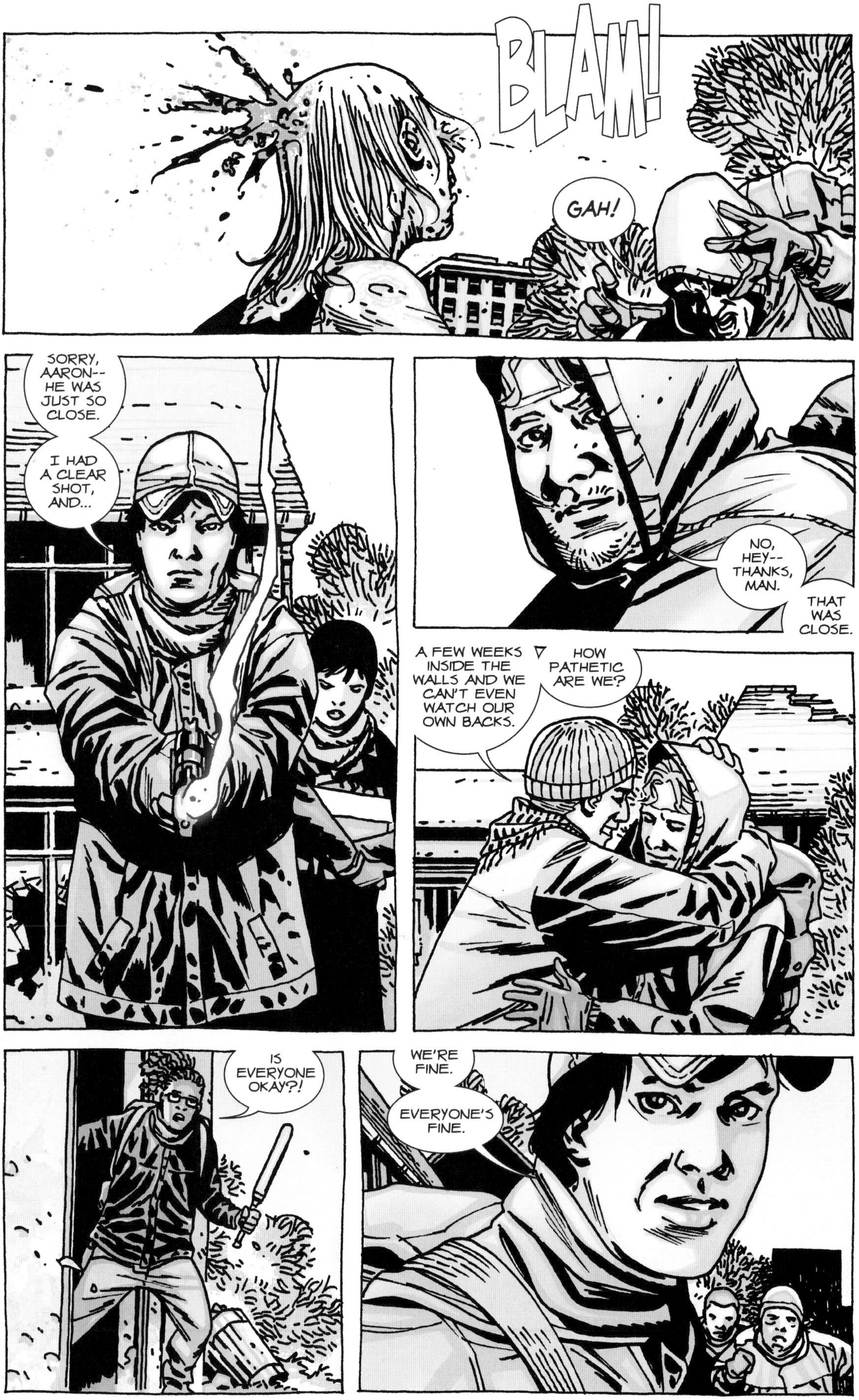
BLAM!
GAH!
SORRY, AARON-- HE WAS JUST SO CLOSE.
I HAD A CLEAR SHOT, AND...
NO, HEY-- THANKS, MAN.
THAT WAS CLOSE.
A FEW WEEKS INSIDE THE WALLS AND WE CAN'T EVEN WATCH OUR OWN BACKS.
HOW PATHETIC ARE WE?
IS EVERYONE OKAY?!
WE'RE FINE.
EVERYONE'S FINE.

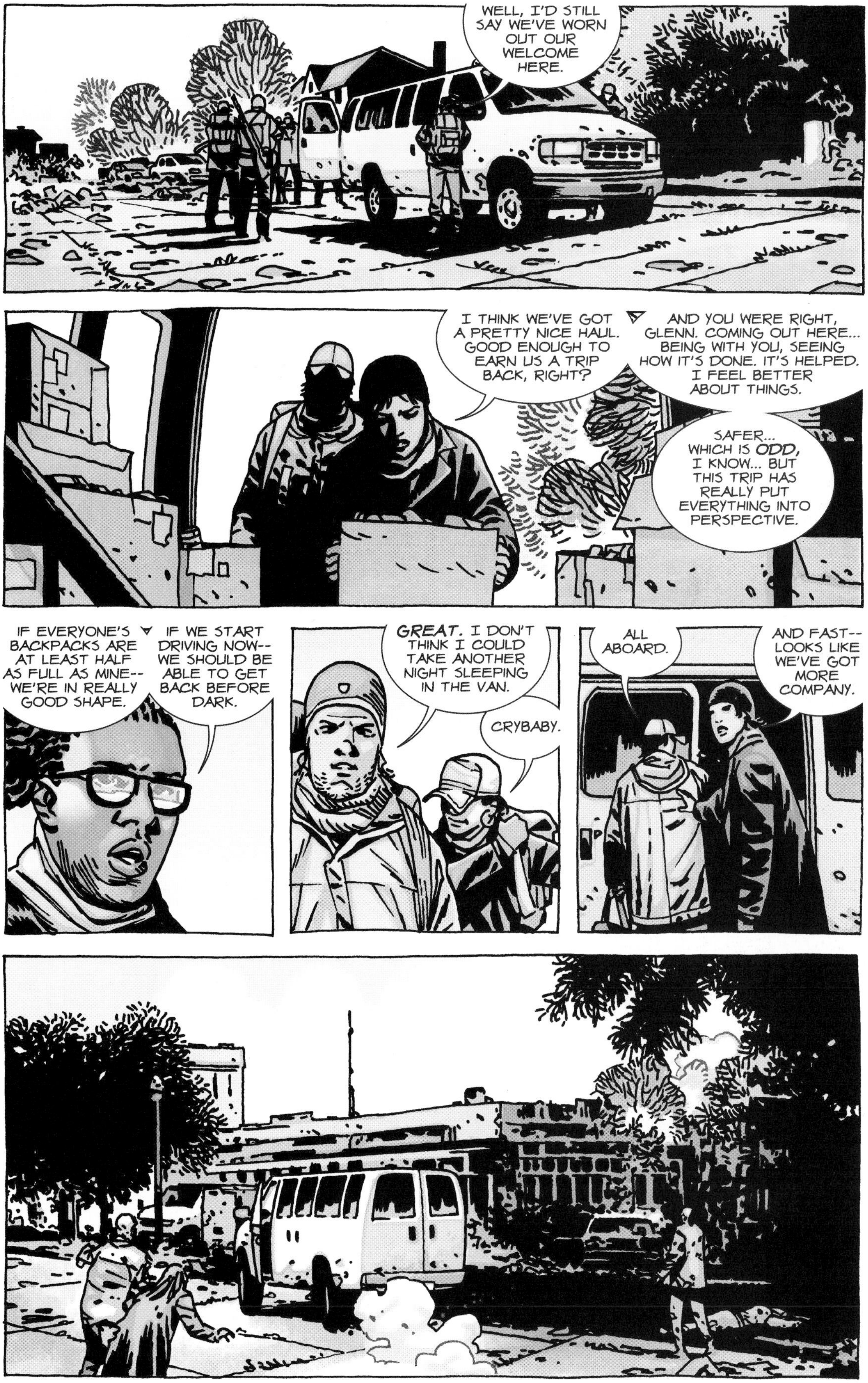
WELL, I'D STILL SAY WE'VE WORN OUT OUR WELCOME HERE.
I THINK WE'VE GOT A PRETTY NICE HAUL. GOOD ENOUGH TO EARN US A TRIP BACK, RIGHT?
AND YOU WERE RIGHT, GLENN. COMING OUT HERE... BEING WITH YOU, SEEING HOW IT'S DONE. IT'S HELPED. I FEEL BETTER ABOUT THINGS.
SAFER... WHICH IS ODD, I KNOW... BUT THIS TRIP HAS REALLY PUT EVERYTHING INTO PERSPECTIVE.
IF EVERYONE'S BACKPACKS ARE AT LEAST HALF AS FULL AS MINE-- WE'RE IN REALLY GOOD SHAPE.
IF WE START DRIVING NOW-- WE SHOULD BE ABLE TO GET BACK BEFORE DARK.
GREAT. I DON'T THINK I COULD TAKE ANOTHER NIGHT SLEEPING IN THE VAN.
CRYBABY.
ALL ABOARD.
AND FAST-- LOOKS LIKE WE'VE GOT MORE COMPANY.

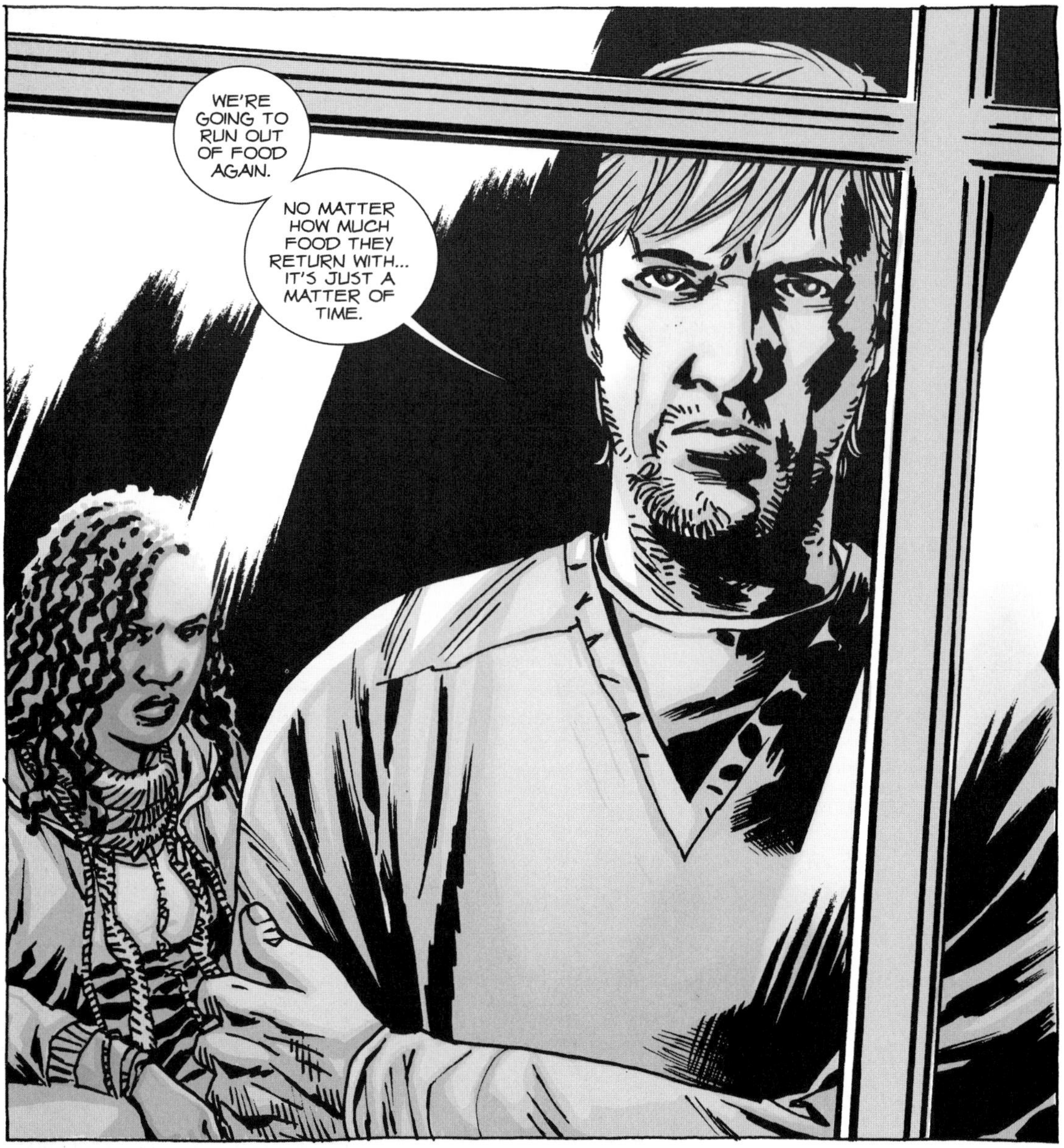
WE'RE GOING TO RUN OUT OF FOOD AGAIN.
NO MATTER HOW MUCH FOOD THEY RETURN WITH... IT'S JUST A MATTER OF TIME.

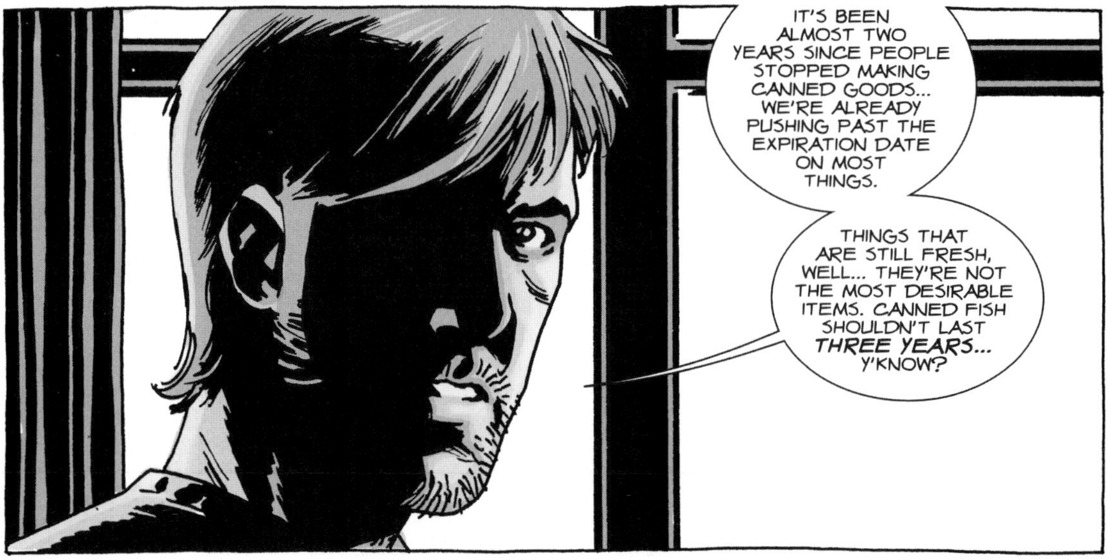
IT'S BEEN ALMOST TWO YEARS SINCE PEOPLE STOPPED MAKING CANNED GOODS... WE'RE ALREADY PUSHING PAST THE EXPIRATION DATE ON MOST THINGS.
THINGS THAT ARE STILL FRESH, WELL... THEY'RE NOT THE MOST DESIRABLE ITEMS. CANNED FISH SHOULDN'T LAST *THREE YEARS...* Y'KNOW?

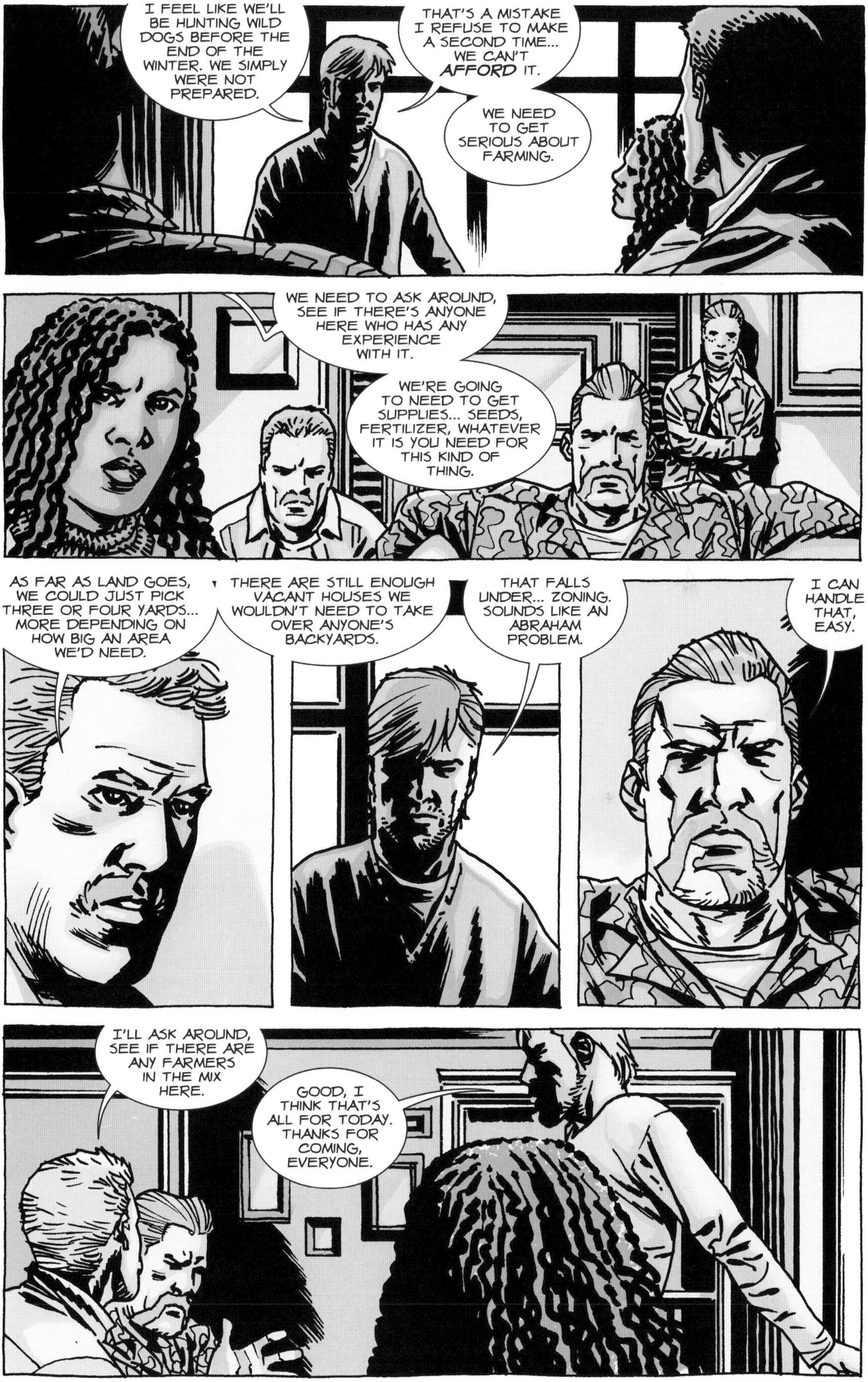
I FEEL LIKE WE'LL BE HUNTING WILD DOGS BEFORE THE END OF THE WINTER. WE SIMPLY WERE NOT PREPARED.
THAT'S A MISTAKE I REFUSE TO MAKE A SECOND TIME... WE CAN'T AFFORD IT.
WE NEED TO GET SERIOUS ABOUT FARMING.
WE NEED TO ASK AROUND, SEE IF THERE'S ANYONE HERE WHO HAS ANY EXPERIENCE WITH IT.
WE'RE GOING TO NEED TO GET SUPPLIES... SEEDS, FERTILIZER, WHATEVER IT IS YOU NEED FOR THIS KIND OF THING.
AS FAR AS LAND GOES, WE COULD JUST PICK THREE OR FOUR YARDS... MORE DEPENDING ON HOW BIG AN AREA WE'D NEED.
THERE ARE STILL ENOUGH VACANT HOUSES WE WOULDN'T NEED TO TAKE OVER ANYONE'S BACKYARDS.
THAT FALLS UNDER... ZONING. SOUNDS LIKE AN ABRAHAM PROBLEM.
I CAN HANDLE THAT, EASY.
I'LL ASK AROUND, SEE IF THERE ARE ANY FARMERS IN THE MIX HERE.
GOOD, I THINK THAT'S ALL FOR TODAY. THANKS FOR COMING, EVERYONE.

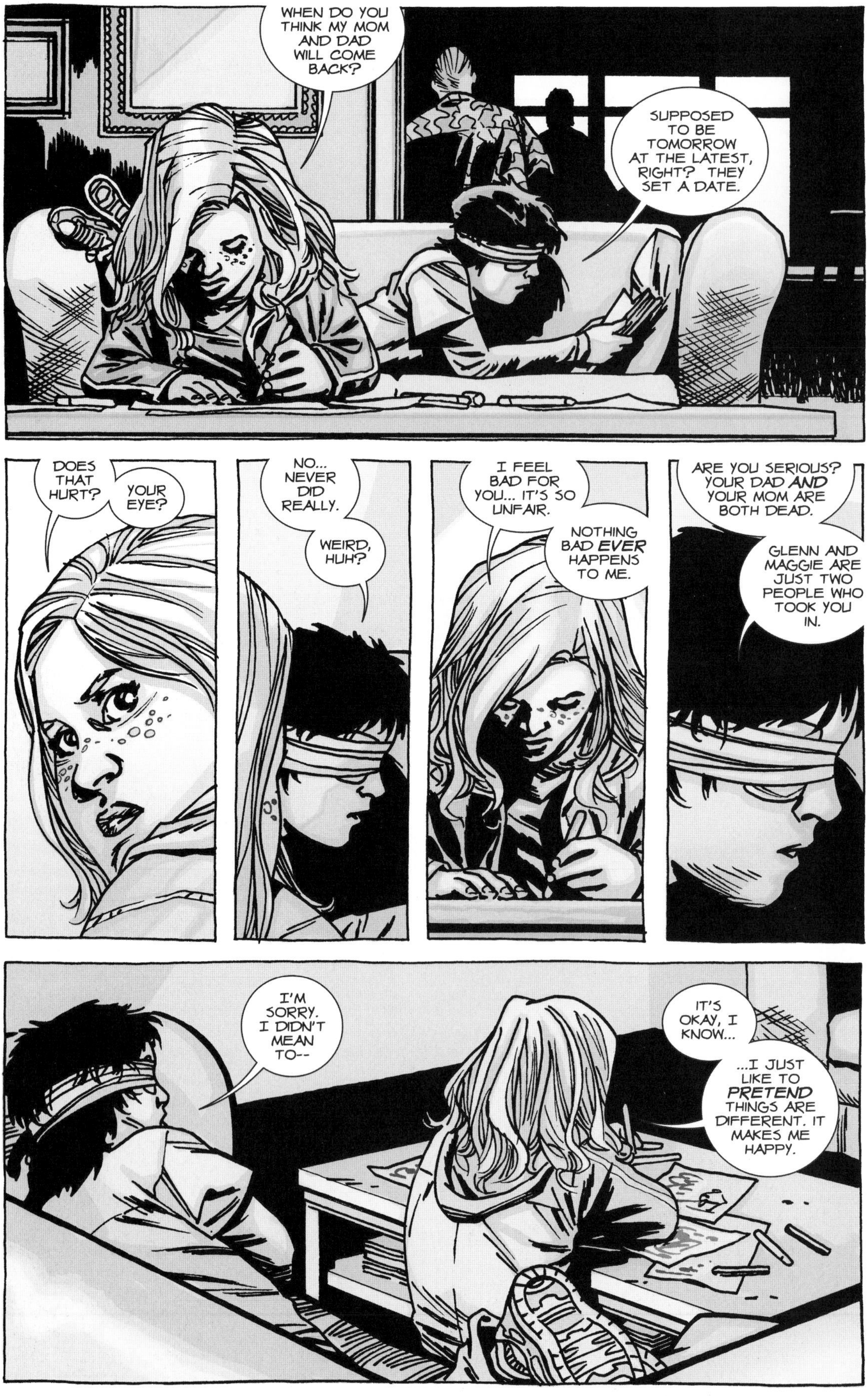
WHEN DO YOU THINK MY MOM AND DAD WILL COME BACK?
SUPPOSED TO BE TOMORROW AT THE LATEST, RIGHT? THEY SET A DATE.
DOES THAT HURT?
YOUR EYE?
NO... NEVER DID REALLY.
WEIRD, HUH?
I FEEL BAD FOR YOU... IT'S SO UNFAIR.
NOTHING BAD EVER HAPPENS TO ME.
ARE YOU SERIOUS? YOUR DAD AND YOUR MOM ARE BOTH DEAD.
GLENN AND MAGGIE ARE JUST TWO PEOPLE WHO TOOK YOU IN.
I'M SORRY. I DIDN'T MEAN TO--
IT'S OKAY, I KNOW...
...I JUST LIKE TO PRETEND THINGS ARE DIFFERENT. IT MAKES ME HAPPY.

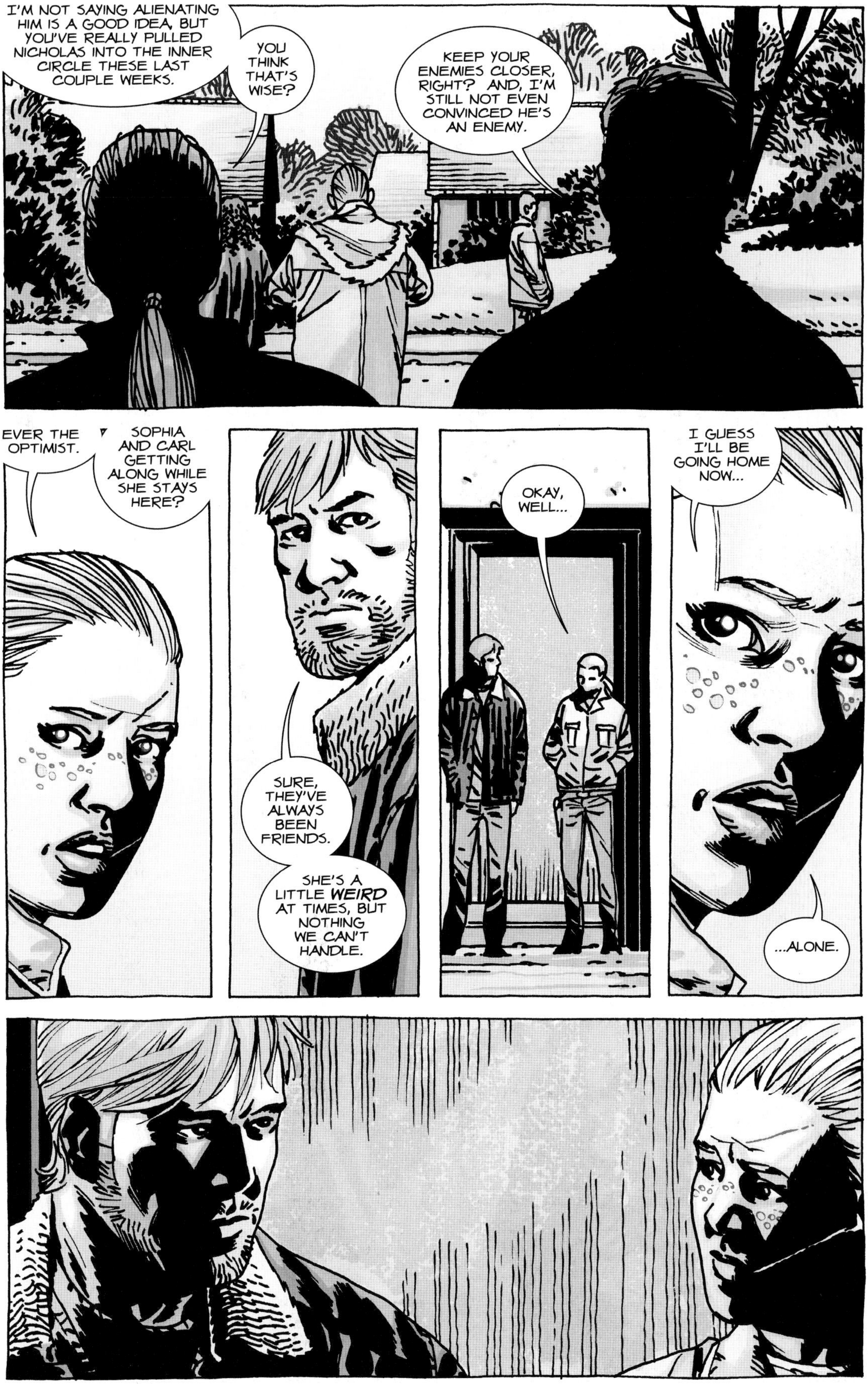
I'M NOT SAYING ALIENATING HIM IS A GOOD IDEA, BUT YOU'VE REALLY PULLED NICHOLAS INTO THE INNER CIRCLE THESE LAST COUPLE WEEKS.
YOU THINK THAT'S WISE?
KEEP YOUR ENEMIES CLOSER, RIGHT? AND, I'M STILL NOT EVEN CONVINCED HE'S AN ENEMY.
EVER THE OPTIMIST.
SOPHIA AND CARL GETTING ALONG WHILE SHE STAYS HERE?
SURE, THEY'VE ALWAYS BEEN FRIENDS.
SHE'S A LITTLE WEIRD AT TIMES, BUT NOTHING WE CAN'T HANDLE.
OKAY, WELL...
I GUESS I'LL BE GOING HOME NOW...
...ALONE.

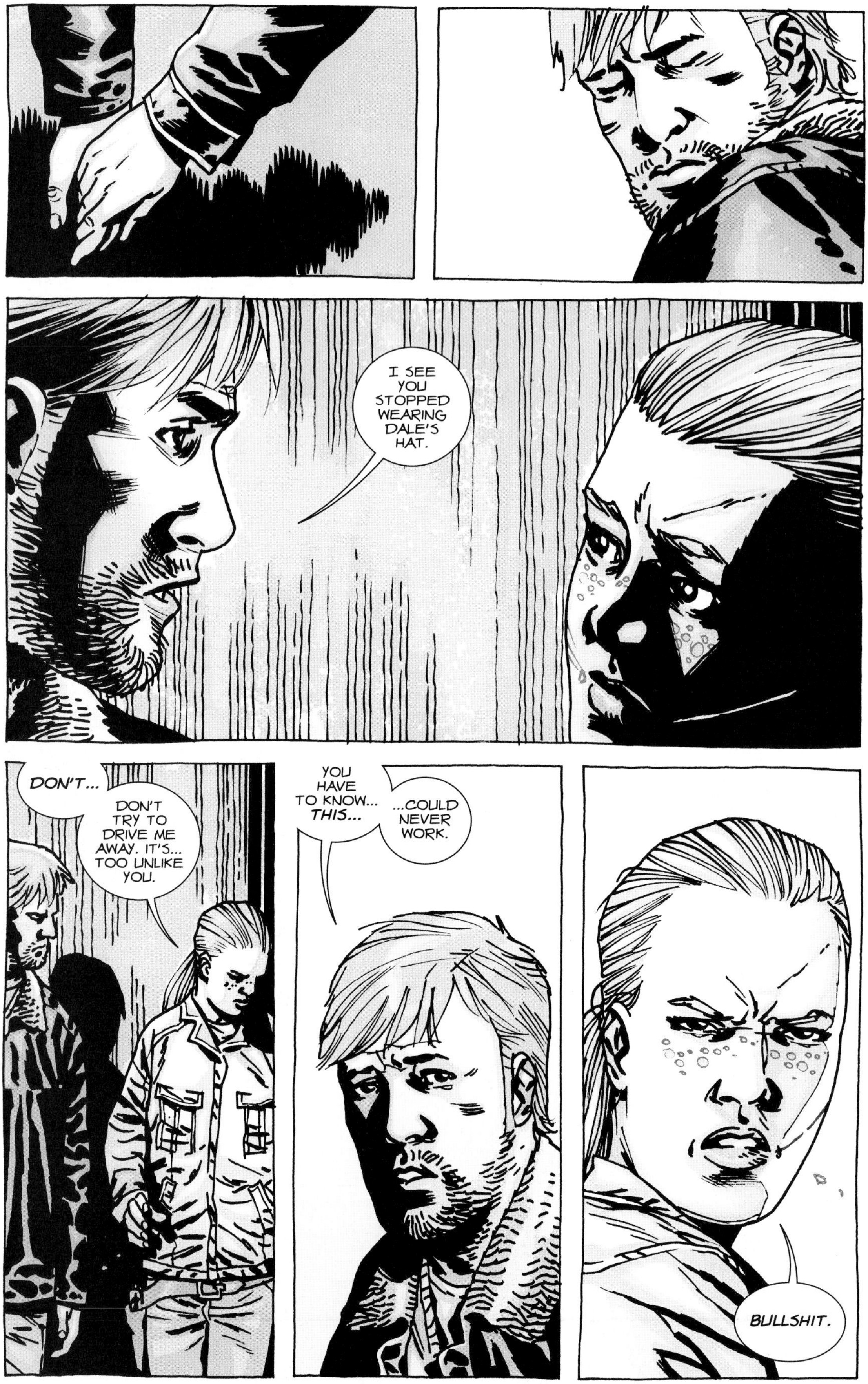
I SEE YOU STOPPED WEARING DALE'S HAT.
DON'T...
DON'T TRY TO DRIVE ME AWAY. IT'S... TOO UNLIKE YOU.
YOU HAVE TO KNOW... THIS...
...COULD NEVER WORK.
BULLSHIT.

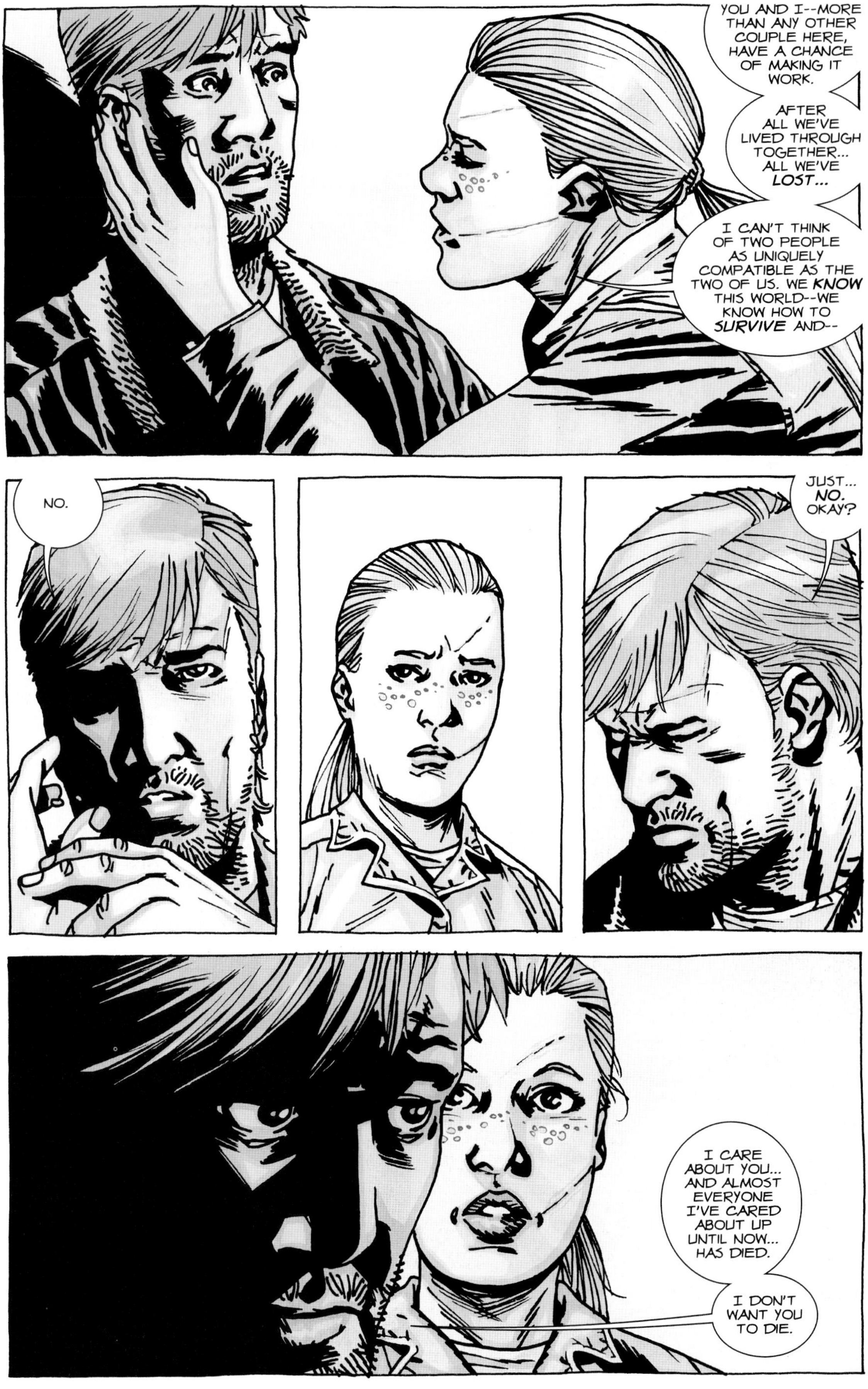
YOU AND I--MORE THAN ANY OTHER COUPLE HERE, HAVE A CHANCE OF MAKING IT WORK.
AFTER ALL WE'VE LIVED THROUGH TOGETHER... ALL WE'VE LOST...
I CAN'T THINK OF TWO PEOPLE AS UNIQUELY COMPATIBLE AS THE TWO OF US. WE KNOW THIS WORLD--WE KNOW HOW TO SURVIVE AND--
NO.
JUST... NO. OKAY?
I CARE ABOUT YOU... AND ALMOST EVERYONE I'VE CARED ABOUT UP UNTIL NOW... HAS DIED.
I DON'T WANT YOU TO DIE.

GOOD, RICK'S GETTING REALLY GOOD AT BOSSING EVERYONE AROUND.

HOW'D THE MEETING GO?

NO COMMENT.

OH, STOP IT.

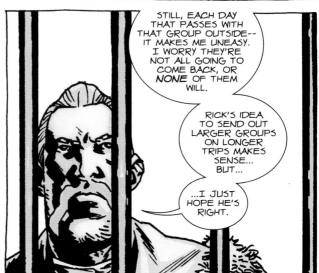

STILL, EACH DAY THAT PASSES WITH THAT GROUP OUTSIDE-- IT MAKES ME UNEASY. I WORRY THEY'RE NOT ALL GOING TO COME BACK, OR *NONE* OF THEM WILL.

RICK'S IDEA TO SEND OUT LARGER GROUPS ON LONGER TRIPS MAKES SENSE... BUT...

...I JUST HOPE HE'S RIGHT.

COME ON-- YOU CAN'T STAND HERE ALL DAY.

THERE'S WORK TO BE DONE...

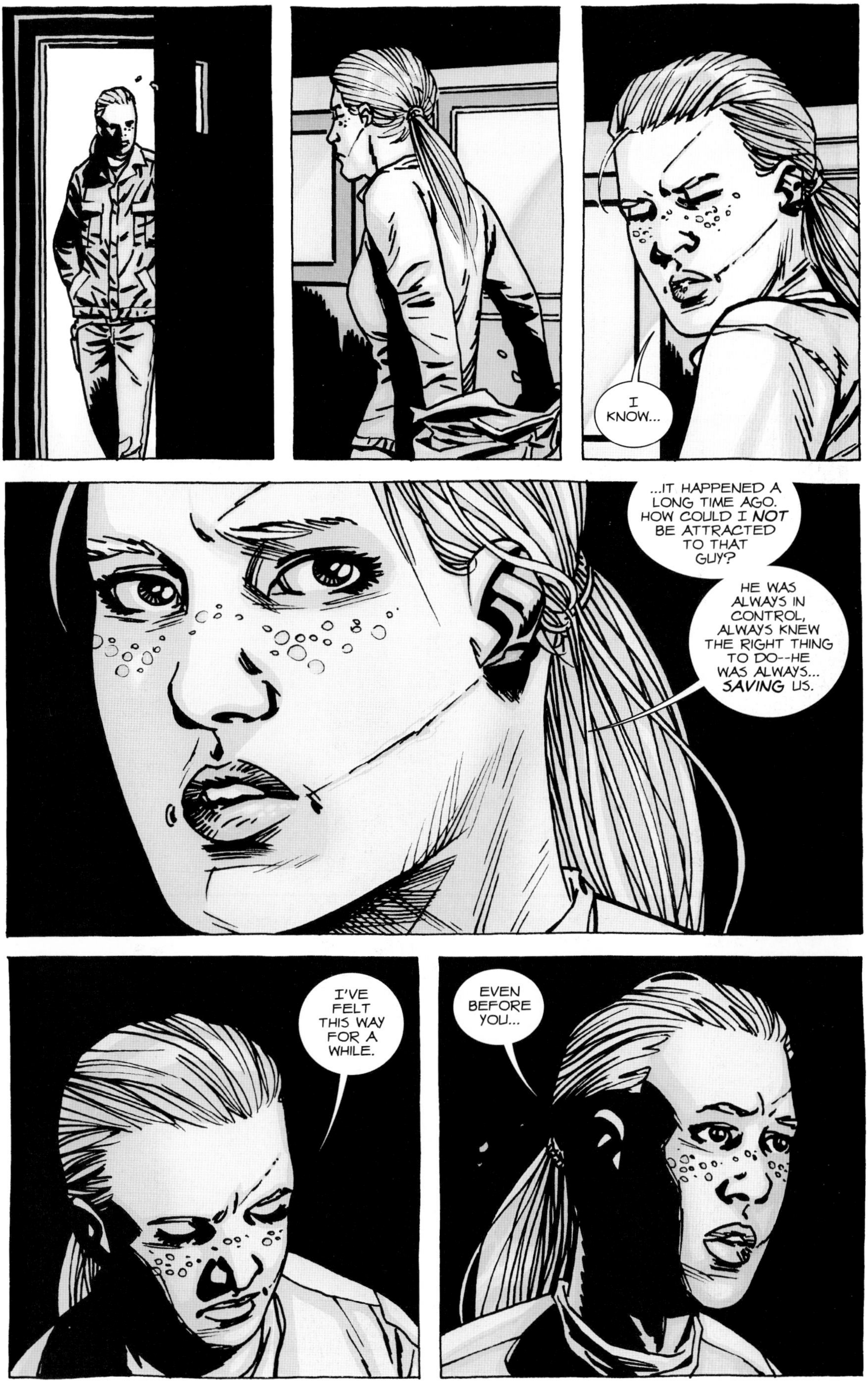
I KNOW...
...IT HAPPENED A LONG TIME AGO. HOW COULD I NOT BE ATTRACTED TO THAT GUY?
HE WAS ALWAYS IN CONTROL, ALWAYS KNEW THE RIGHT THING TO DO--HE WAS ALWAYS... SAVING US.
I'VE FELT THIS WAY FOR A WHILE.
EVEN BEFORE YOU...

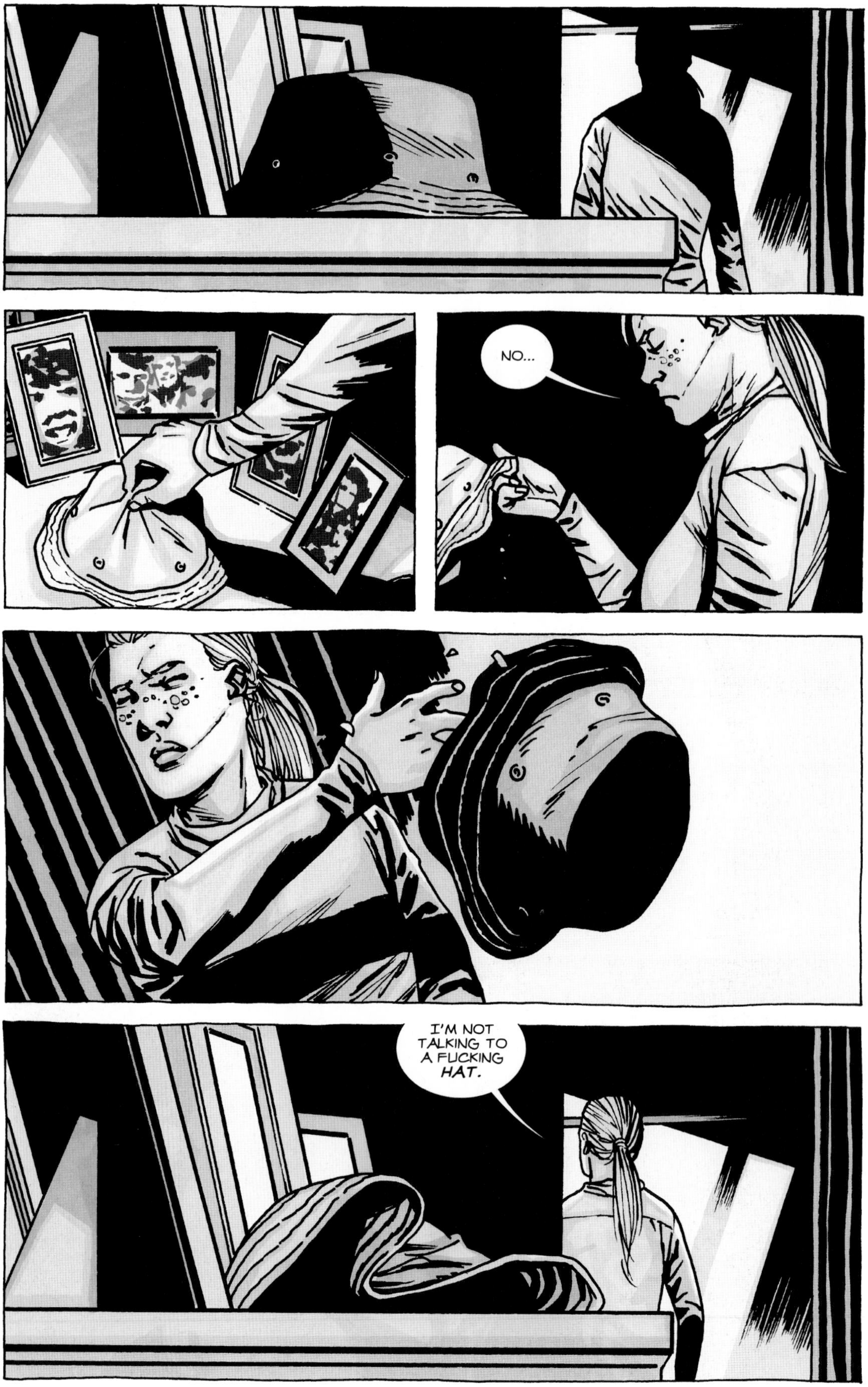
NO...
I'M NOT TALKING TO A FUCKING HAT.

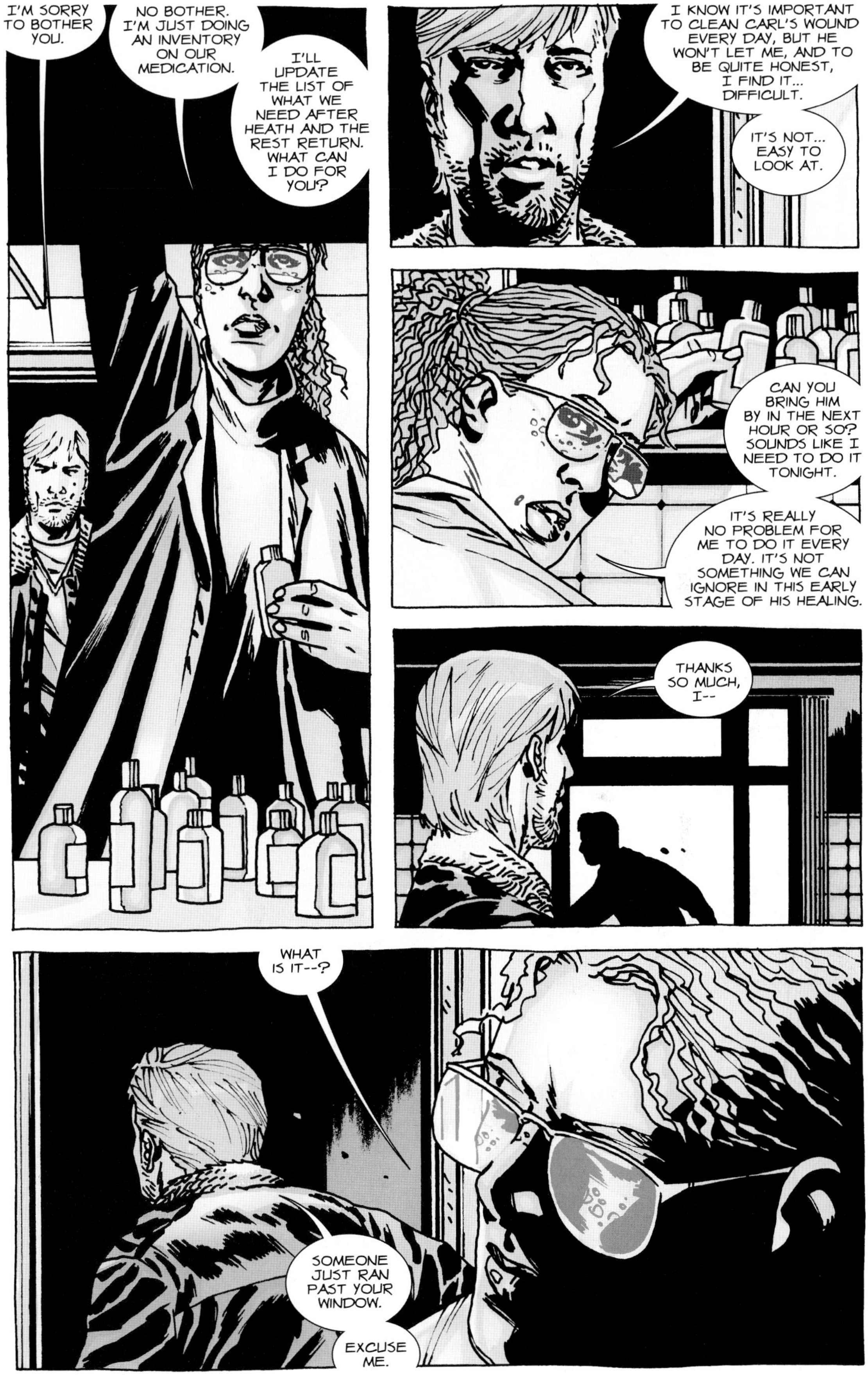
I'M SORRY TO BOTHER YOU.
NO BOTHER. I'M JUST DOING AN INVENTORY ON OUR MEDICATION.
I'LL UPDATE THE LIST OF WHAT WE NEED AFTER HEATH AND THE REST RETURN. WHAT CAN I DO FOR YOU?
I KNOW IT'S IMPORTANT TO CLEAN CARL'S WOUND EVERY DAY, BUT HE WON'T LET ME, AND TO BE QUITE HONEST, I FIND IT... DIFFICULT.
IT'S NOT... EASY TO LOOK AT.
CAN YOU BRING HIM BY IN THE NEXT HOUR OR SO? SOUNDS LIKE I NEED TO DO IT TONIGHT.
IT'S REALLY NO PROBLEM FOR ME TO DO IT EVERY DAY. IT'S NOT SOMETHING WE CAN IGNORE IN THIS EARLY STAGE OF HIS HEALING.
THANKS SO MUCH, I--
WHAT IS IT--?
SOMEONE JUST RAN PAST YOUR WINDOW.
EXCUSE ME.

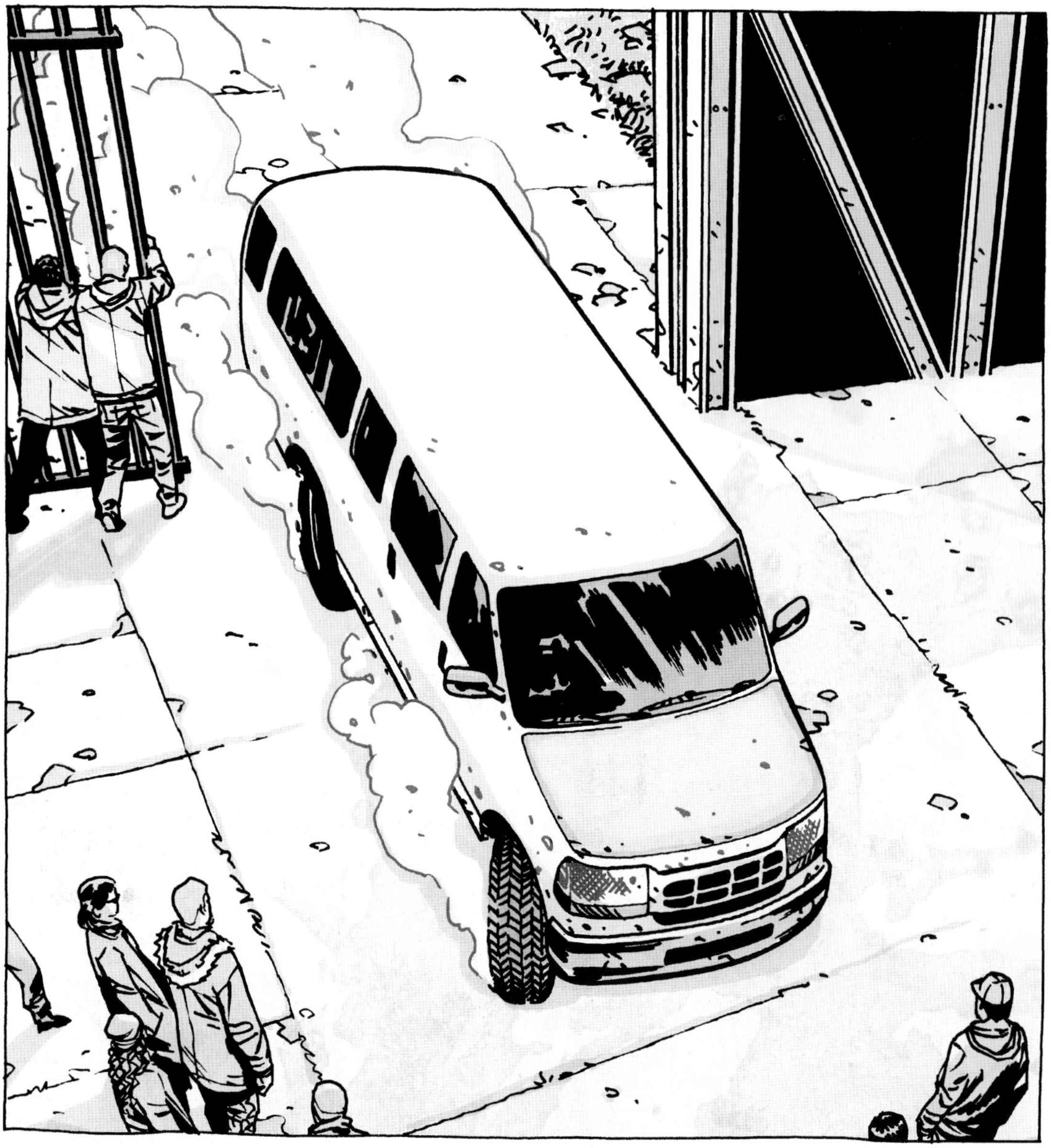

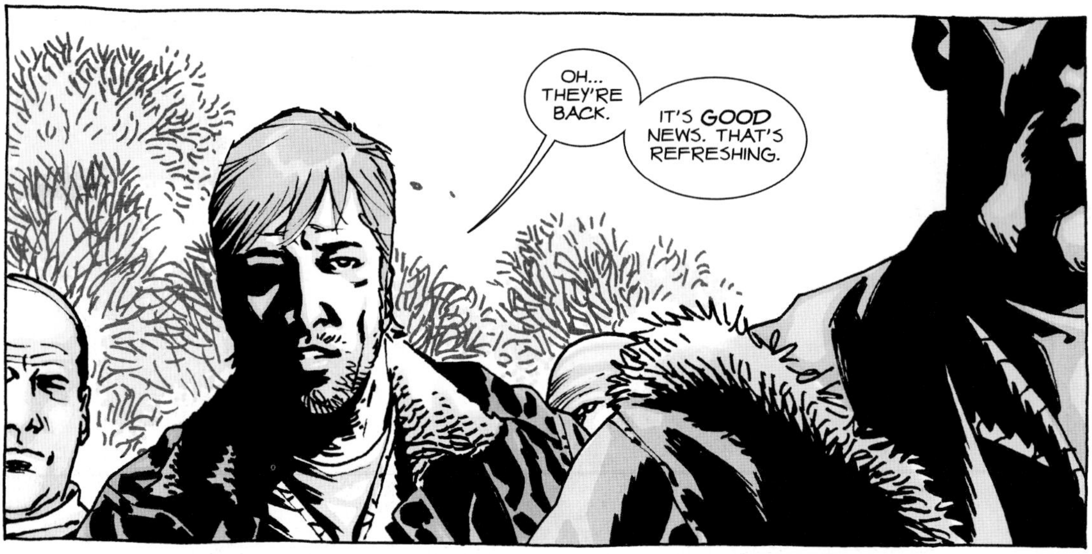
OH... THEY'RE BACK.
IT'S GOOD NEWS. THAT'S REFRESHING.

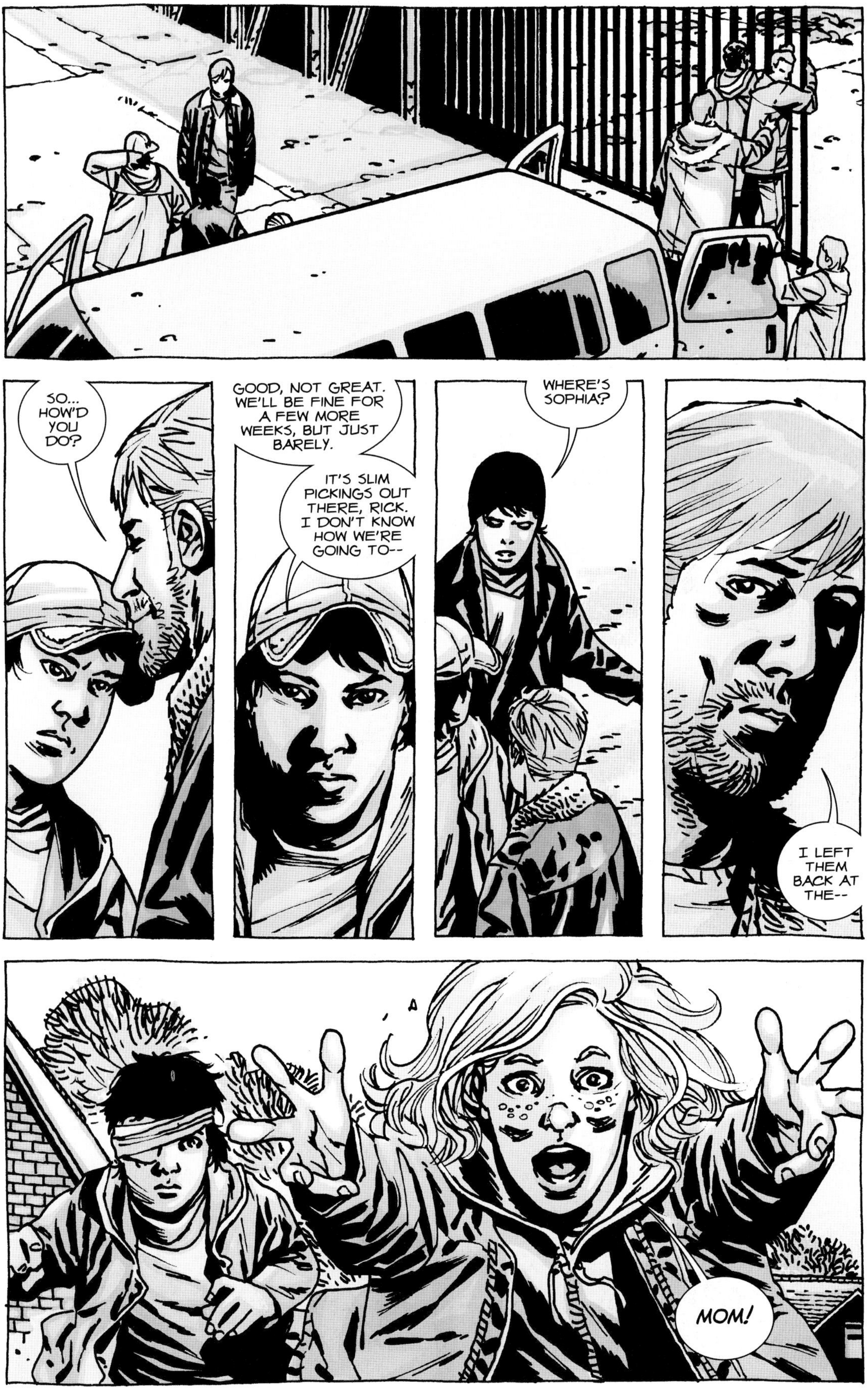
SO... HOW'D YOU DO?
GOOD, NOT GREAT. WE'LL BE FINE FOR A FEW MORE WEEKS, BUT JUST BARELY.
IT'S SLIM PICKINGS OUT THERE, RICK. I DON'T KNOW HOW WE'RE GOING TO--
WHERE'S SOPHIA?
I LEFT THEM BACK AT THE--
MOM!

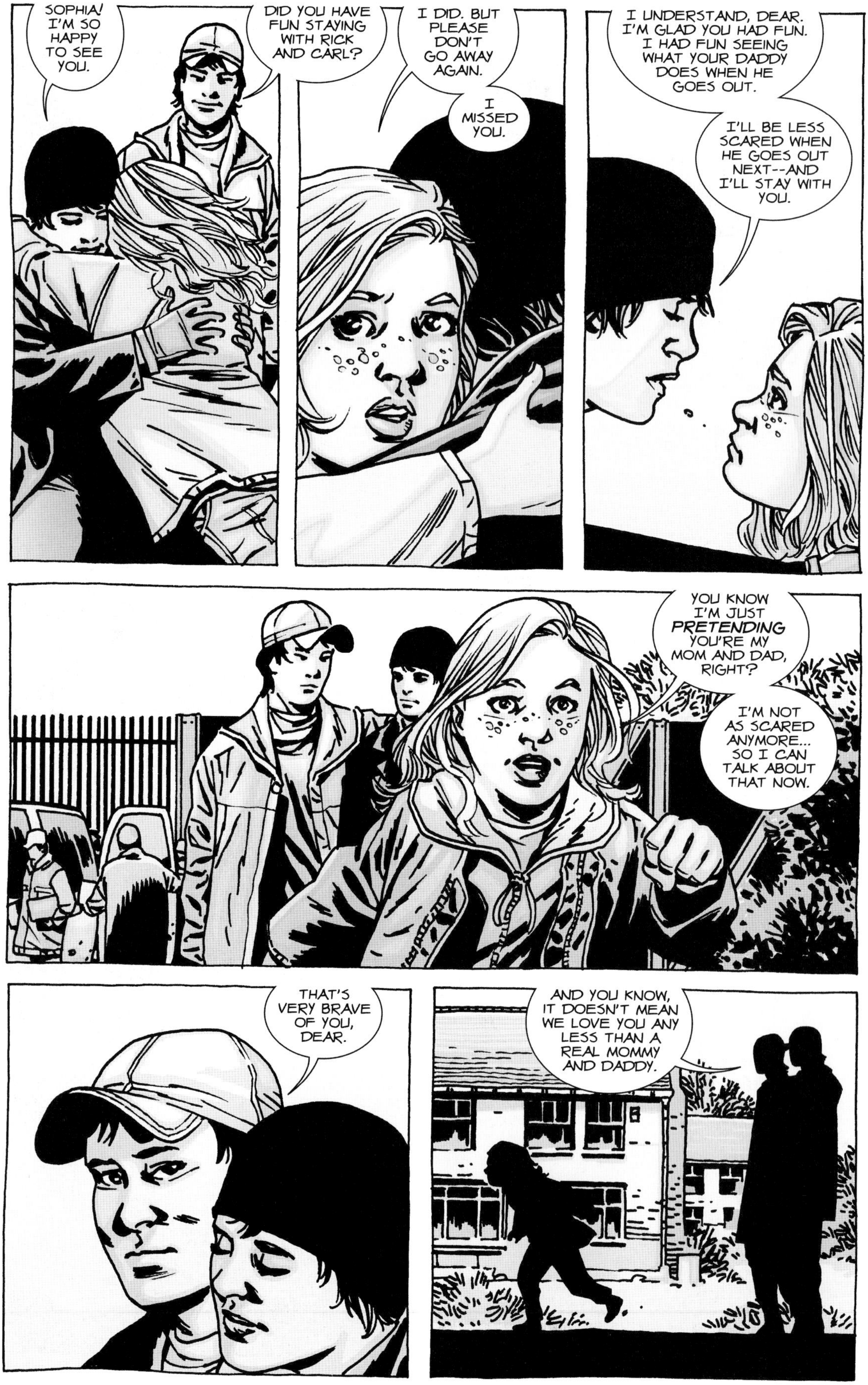
SOPHIA! I'M SO HAPPY TO SEE YOU.
DID YOU HAVE FUN STAYING WITH RICK AND CARL?
I DID. BUT PLEASE DON'T GO AWAY AGAIN.
I MISSED YOU.
I UNDERSTAND, DEAR. I'M GLAD YOU HAD FUN. I HAD FUN SEEING WHAT YOUR DADDY DOES WHEN HE GOES OUT.
I'LL BE LESS SCARED WHEN HE GOES OUT NEXT--AND I'LL STAY WITH YOU.
YOU KNOW I'M JUST PRETENDING YOU'RE MY MOM AND DAD, RIGHT?
I'M NOT AS SCARED ANYMORE... SO I CAN TALK ABOUT THAT NOW.
THAT'S VERY BRAVE OF YOU, DEAR.
AND YOU KNOW, IT DOESN'T MEAN WE LOVE YOU ANY LESS THAN A REAL MOMMY AND DADDY.

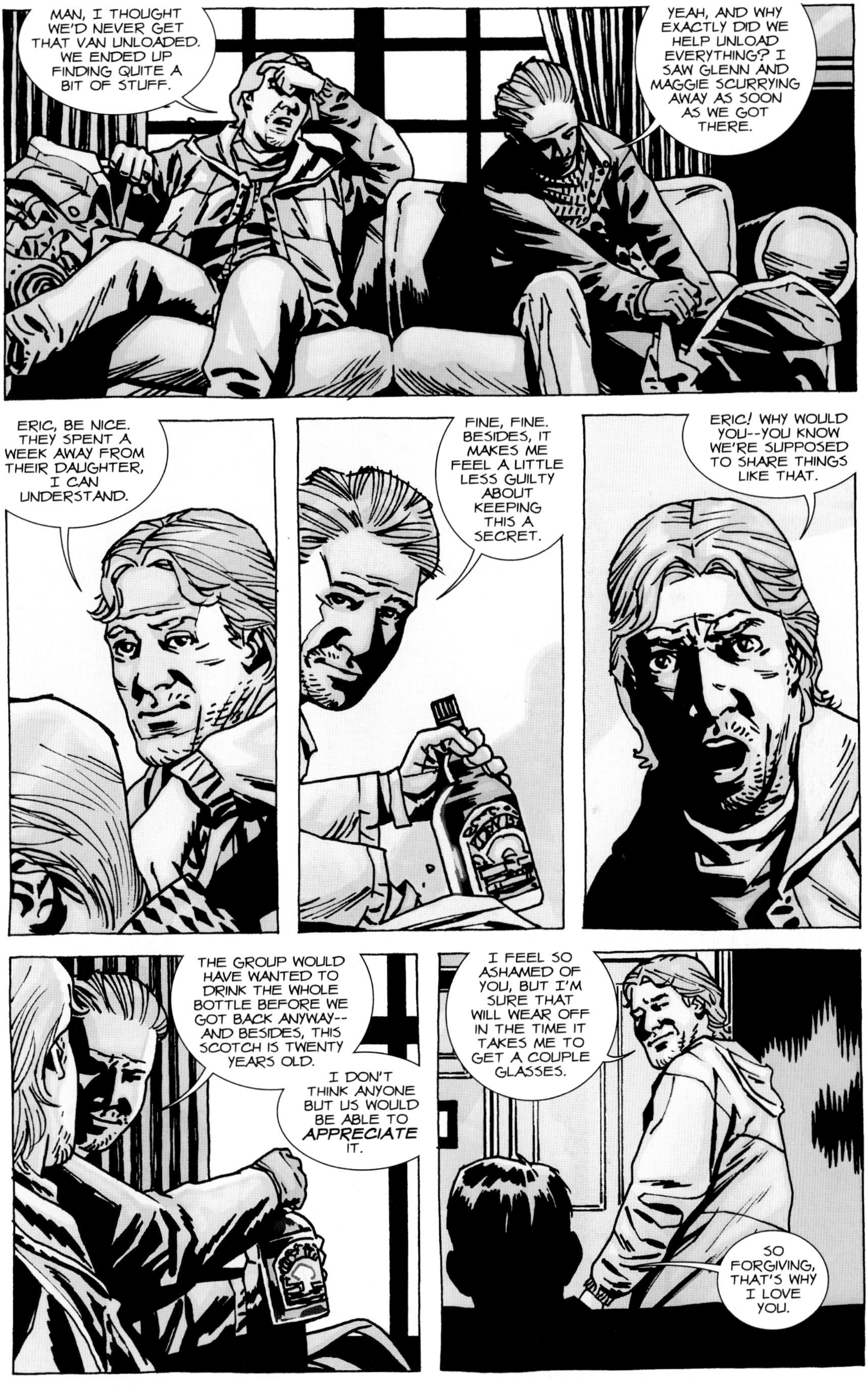
MAN, I THOUGHT WE'D NEVER GET THAT VAN UNLOADED. WE ENDED UP FINDING QUITE A BIT OF STUFF.
YEAH, AND WHY EXACTLY DID WE HELP UNLOAD EVERYTHING? I SAW GLENN AND MAGGIE SCURRYING AWAY AS SOON AS WE GOT THERE.
ERIC, BE NICE. THEY SPENT A WEEK AWAY FROM THEIR DAUGHTER, I CAN UNDERSTAND.
FINE, FINE. BESIDES, IT MAKES ME FEEL A LITTLE LESS GUILTY ABOUT KEEPING THIS A SECRET.
ERIC! WHY WOULD YOU--YOU KNOW WE'RE SUPPOSED TO SHARE THINGS LIKE THAT.
THE GROUP WOULD HAVE WANTED TO DRINK THE WHOLE BOTTLE BEFORE WE GOT BACK ANYWAY--AND BESIDES, THIS SCOTCH IS TWENTY YEARS OLD.
I DON'T THINK ANYONE BUT US WOULD BE ABLE TO *APPRECIATE* IT.
I FEEL SO ASHAMED OF YOU, BUT I'M SURE THAT WILL WEAR OFF IN THE TIME IT TAKES ME TO GET A COUPLE GLASSES.
SO FORGIVING, THAT'S WHY I LOVE YOU.

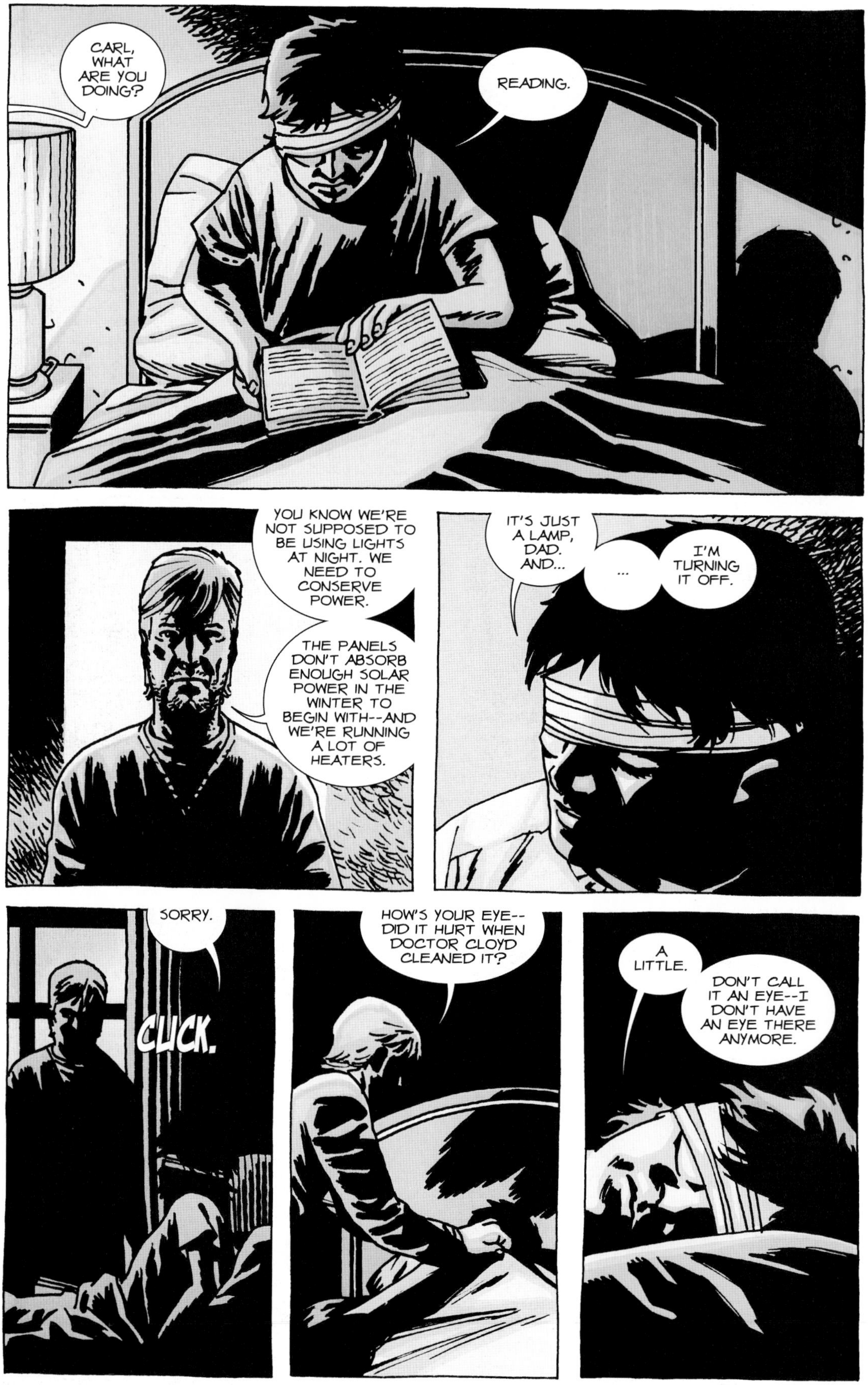
CARL, WHAT ARE YOU DOING?
READING.
YOU KNOW WE'RE NOT SUPPOSED TO BE USING LIGHTS AT NIGHT. WE NEED TO CONSERVE POWER.
THE PANELS DON'T ABSORB ENOUGH SOLAR POWER IN THE WINTER TO BEGIN WITH--AND WE'RE RUNNING A LOT OF HEATERS.
IT'S JUST A LAMP, DAD. AND...
...
I'M TURNING IT OFF.
SORRY.
CLICK.
HOW'S YOUR EYE-- DID IT HURT WHEN DOCTOR CLOYD CLEANED IT?
A LITTLE.
DON'T CALL IT AN EYE--I DON'T HAVE AN EYE THERE ANYMORE.

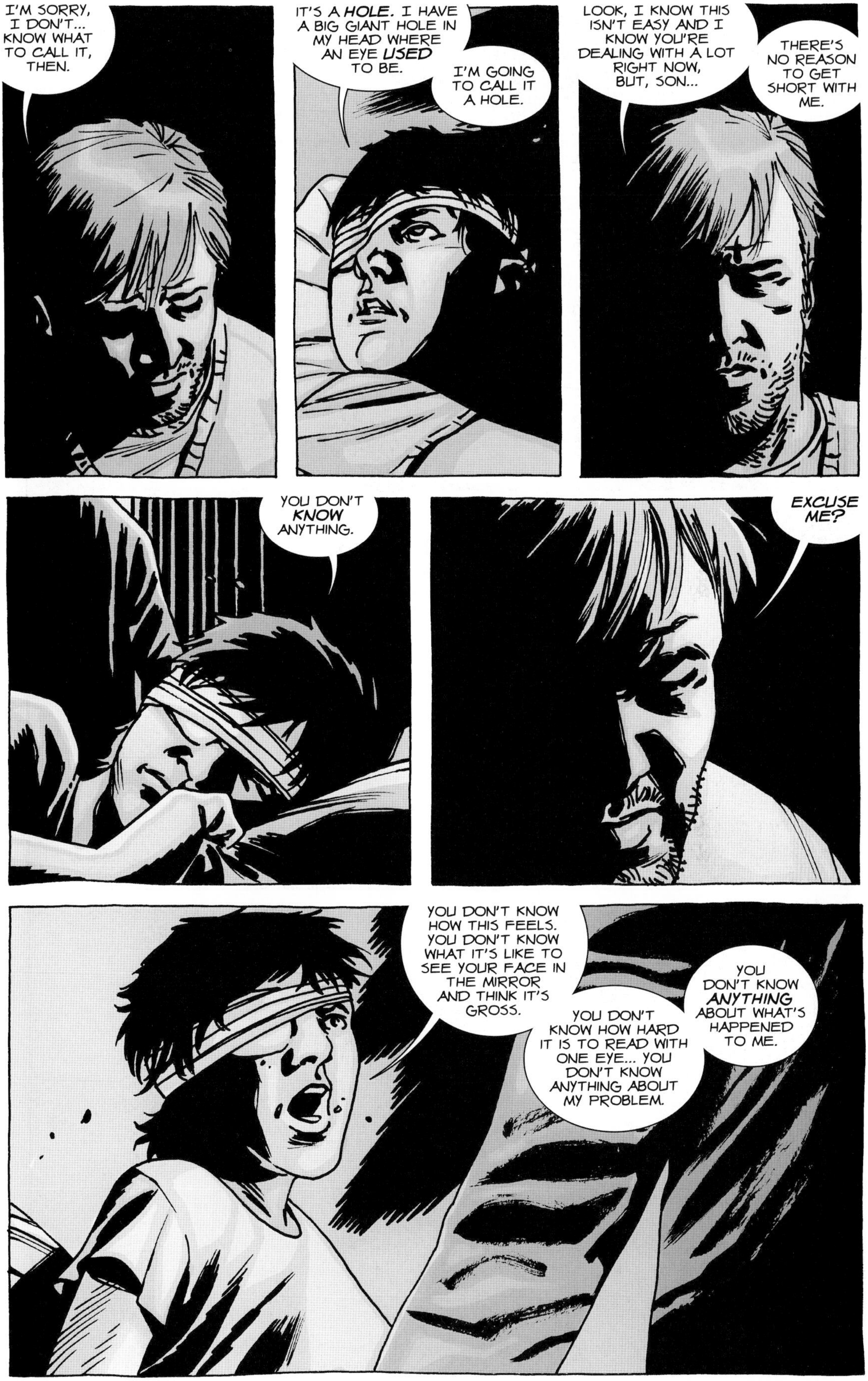
I'M SORRY, I DON'T... KNOW WHAT TO CALL IT, THEN.
IT'S A HOLE. I HAVE A BIG GIANT HOLE IN MY HEAD WHERE AN EYE USED TO BE.
I'M GOING TO CALL IT A HOLE.
LOOK, I KNOW THIS ISN'T EASY AND I KNOW YOU'RE DEALING WITH A LOT RIGHT NOW, BUT, SON...
THERE'S NO REASON TO GET SHORT WITH ME.
YOU DON'T KNOW ANYTHING.
EXCUSE ME?
YOU DON'T KNOW HOW THIS FEELS. YOU DON'T KNOW WHAT IT'S LIKE TO SEE YOUR FACE IN THE MIRROR AND THINK IT'S GROSS.
YOU DON'T KNOW HOW HARD IT IS TO READ WITH ONE EYE... YOU DON'T KNOW ANYTHING ABOUT MY PROBLEM.
YOU DON'T KNOW ANYTHING ABOUT WHAT'S HAPPENED TO ME.

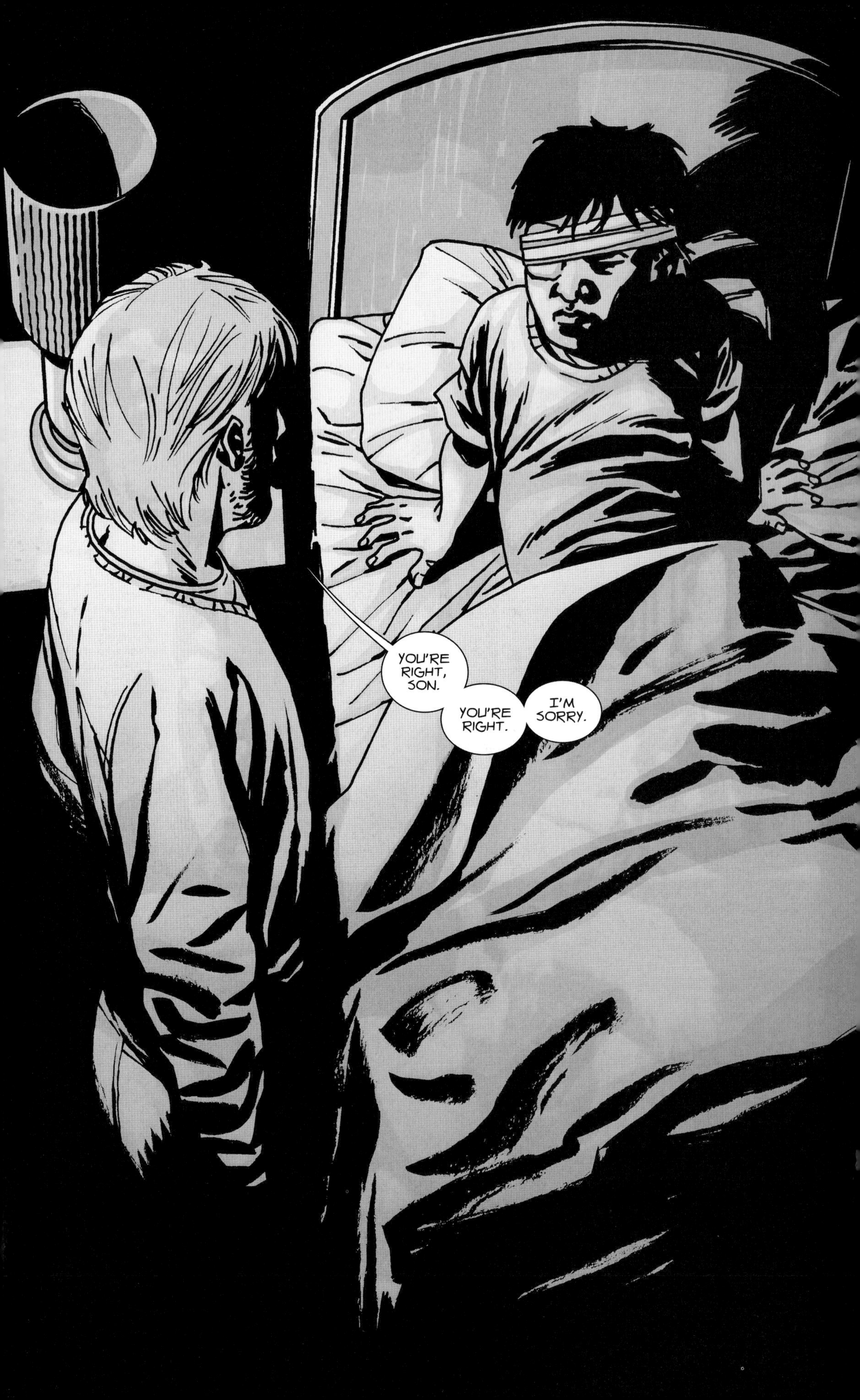
YOU'RE RIGHT, SON.
YOU'RE RIGHT.
I'M SORRY.

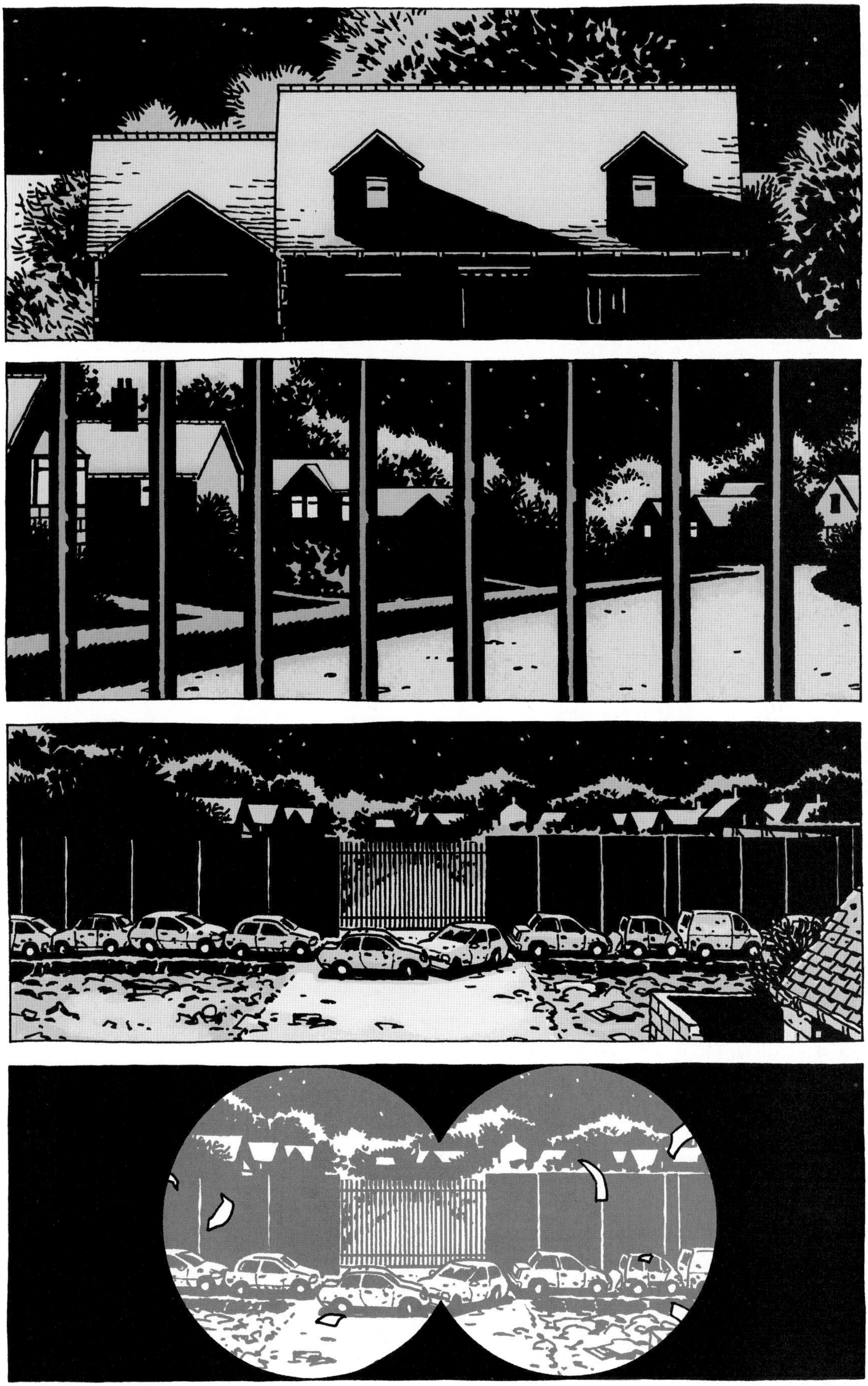

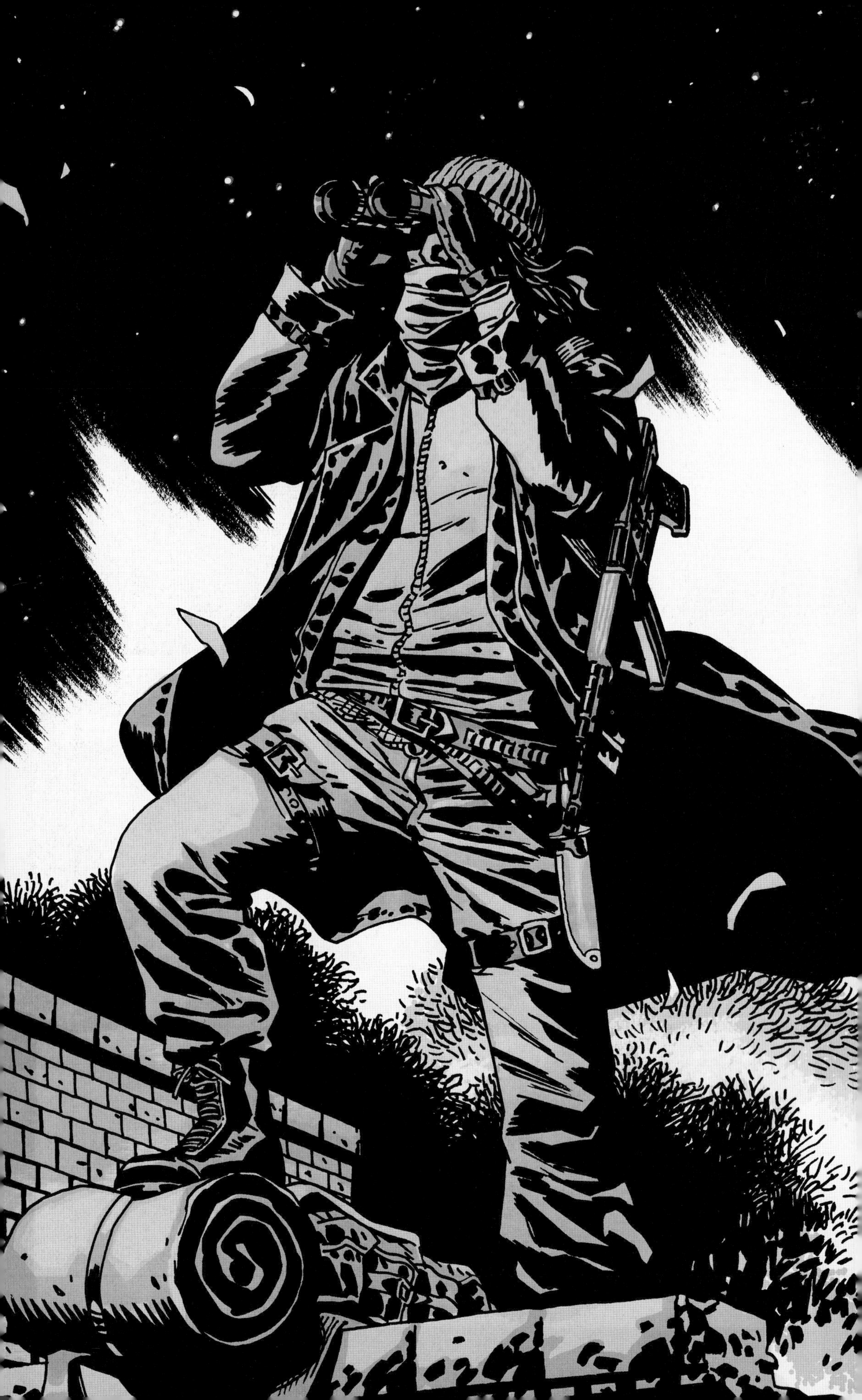

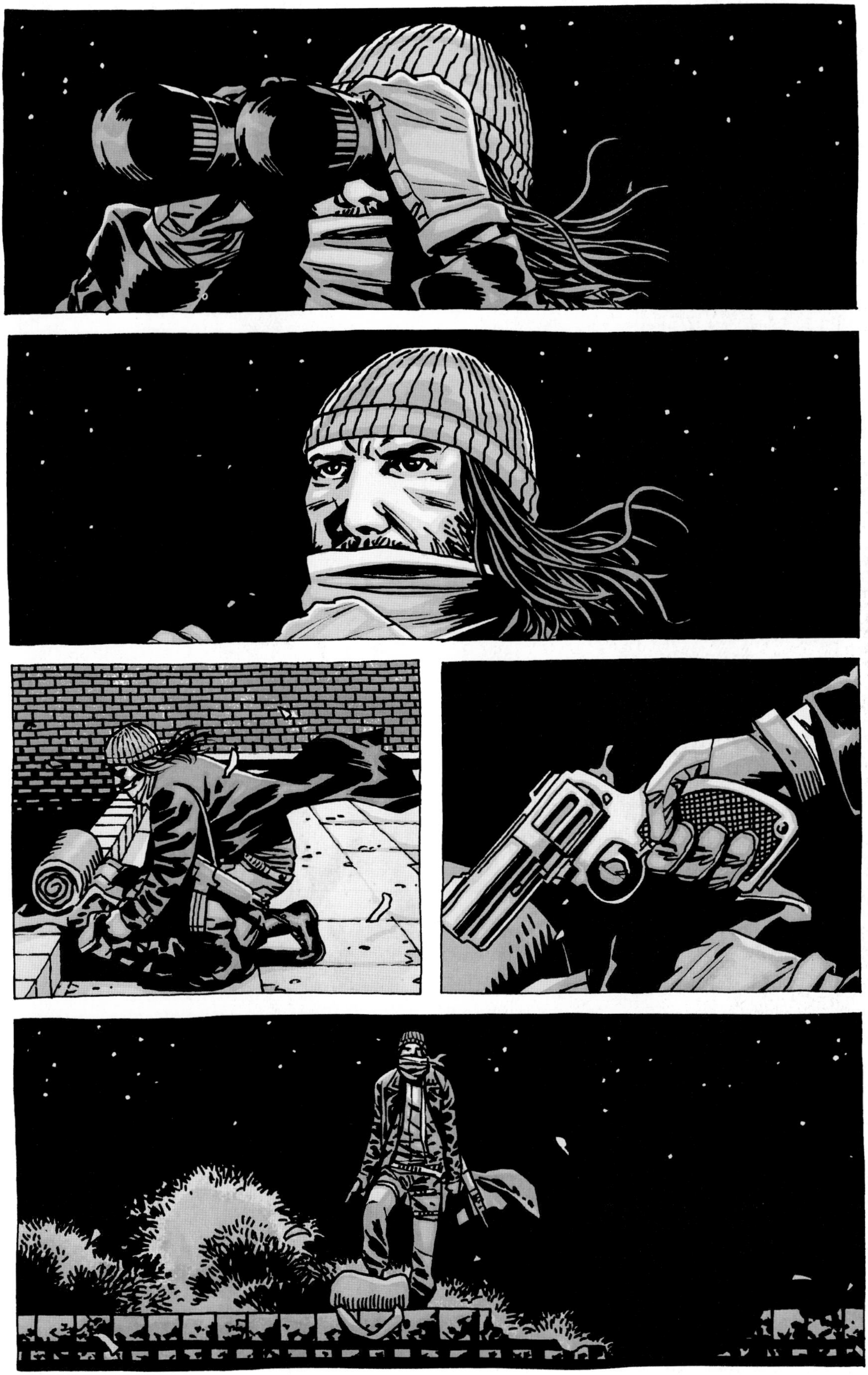

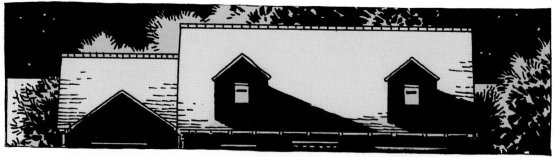

AAGH!

CARL?!

WHAT HAPPENED?

I... HAD A BAD DREAM.

IT'S OKAY, YOU JUST STARTLED ME THERE.

IT WAS *HORRIBLE*, DAD.

THERE WAS THIS BOY... AND HE WAS YOUNGER THAN ME...

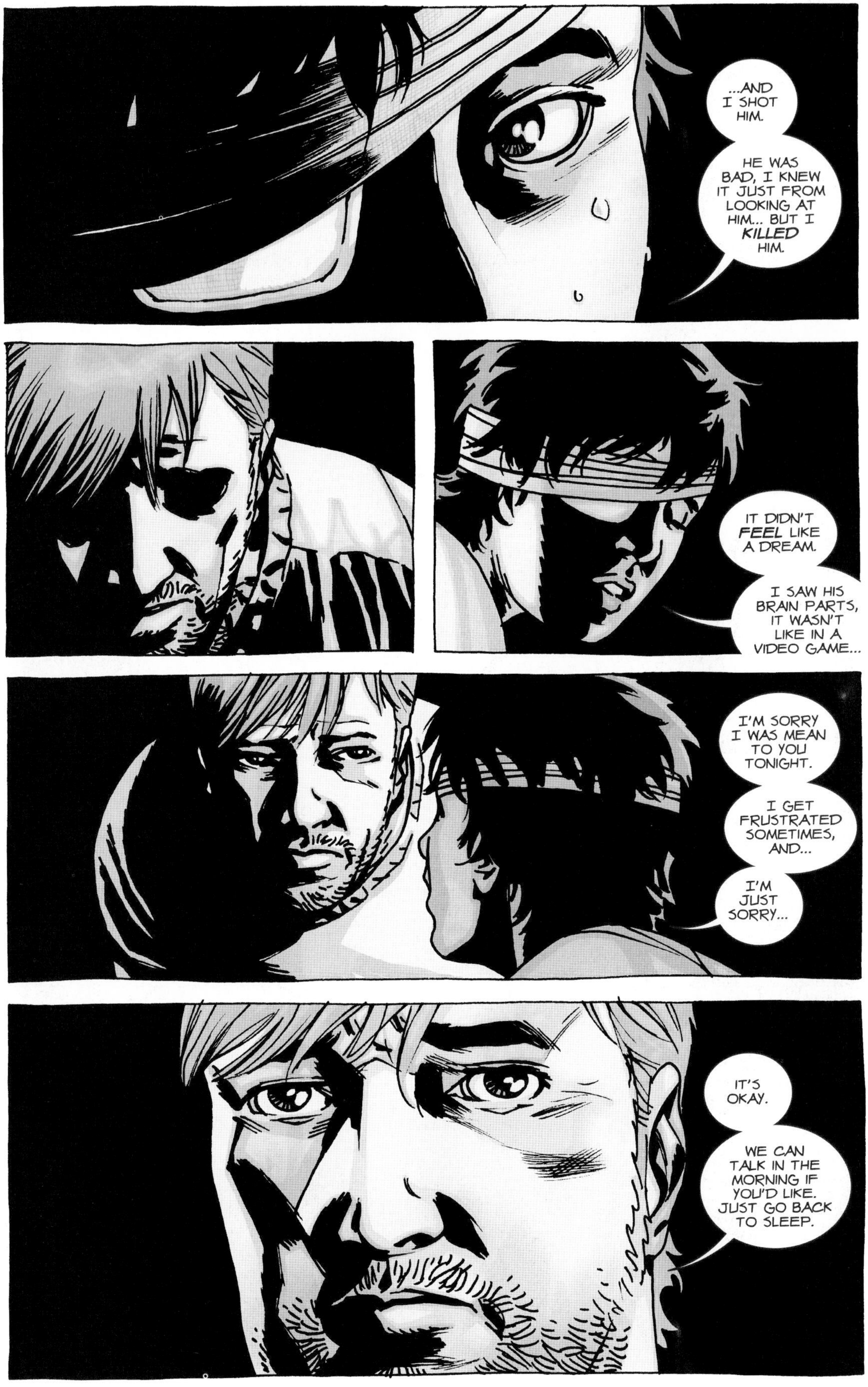
...AND I SHOT HIM.
HE WAS BAD, I KNEW IT JUST FROM LOOKING AT HIM... BUT I ***KILLED*** HIM.
IT DIDN'T ***FEEL*** LIKE A DREAM.
I SAW HIS BRAIN PARTS, IT WASN'T LIKE IN A VIDEO GAME...
I'M SORRY I WAS MEAN TO YOU TONIGHT.
I GET FRUSTRATED SOMETIMES, AND...
I'M JUST SORRY...
IT'S OKAY.
WE CAN TALK IN THE MORNING IF YOU'D LIKE. JUST GO BACK TO SLEEP.

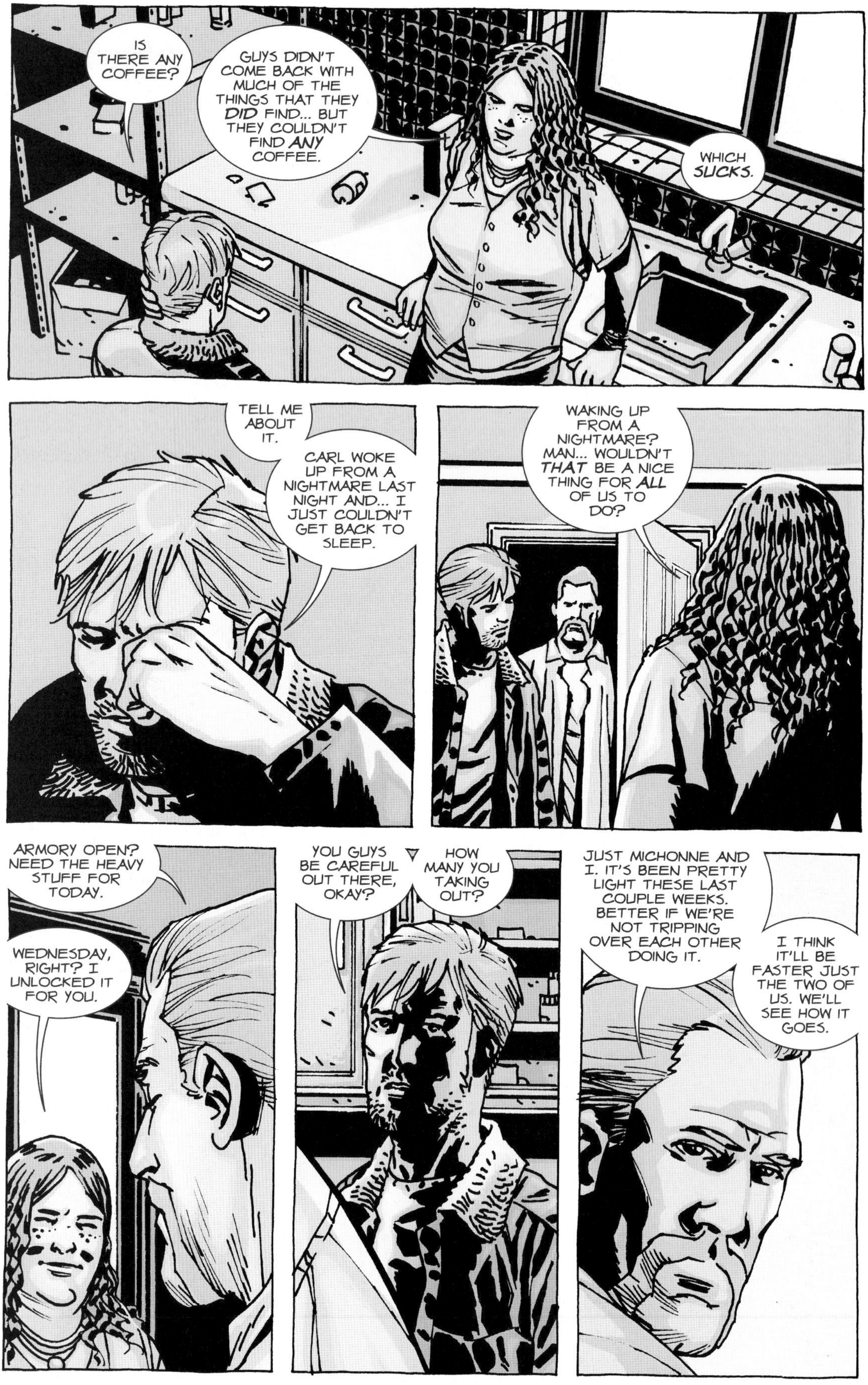
IS THERE ANY COFFEE?
GUYS DIDN'T COME BACK WITH MUCH OF THE THINGS THAT THEY DID FIND... BUT THEY COULDN'T FIND ANY COFFEE.
WHICH SUCKS.
TELL ME ABOUT IT.
CARL WOKE UP FROM A NIGHTMARE LAST NIGHT AND... I JUST COULDN'T GET BACK TO SLEEP.
WAKING UP FROM A NIGHTMARE? MAN... WOULDN'T THAT BE A NICE THING FOR ALL OF US TO DO?
ARMORY OPEN? NEED THE HEAVY STUFF FOR TODAY.
WEDNESDAY, RIGHT? I UNLOCKED IT FOR YOU.
YOU GUYS BE CAREFUL OUT THERE, OKAY?
HOW MANY YOU TAKING OUT?
JUST MICHONNE AND I. IT'S BEEN PRETTY LIGHT THESE LAST COUPLE WEEKS. BETTER IF WE'RE NOT TRIPPING OVER EACH OTHER DOING IT.
I THINK IT'LL BE FASTER JUST THE TWO OF US. WE'LL SEE HOW IT GOES.

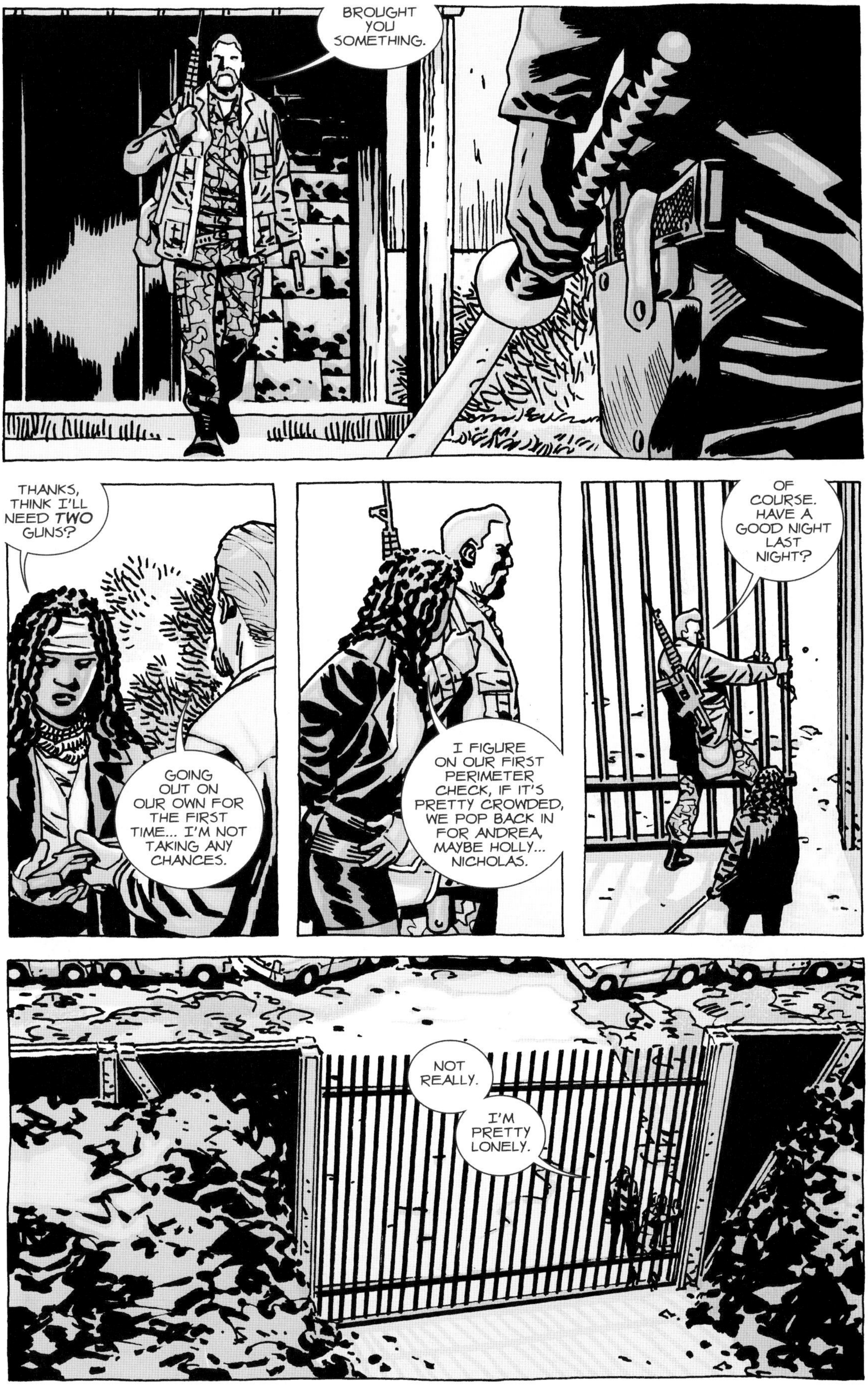
BROUGHT YOU SOMETHING.
THANKS, THINK I'LL NEED *TWO* GUNS?
GOING OUT ON OUR OWN FOR THE FIRST TIME... I'M NOT TAKING ANY CHANCES.
I FIGURE ON OUR FIRST PERIMETER CHECK, IF IT'S PRETTY CROWDED, WE POP BACK IN FOR ANDREA, MAYBE HOLLY... NICHOLAS.
OF COURSE. HAVE A GOOD NIGHT LAST NIGHT?
NOT REALLY.
I'M PRETTY LONELY.

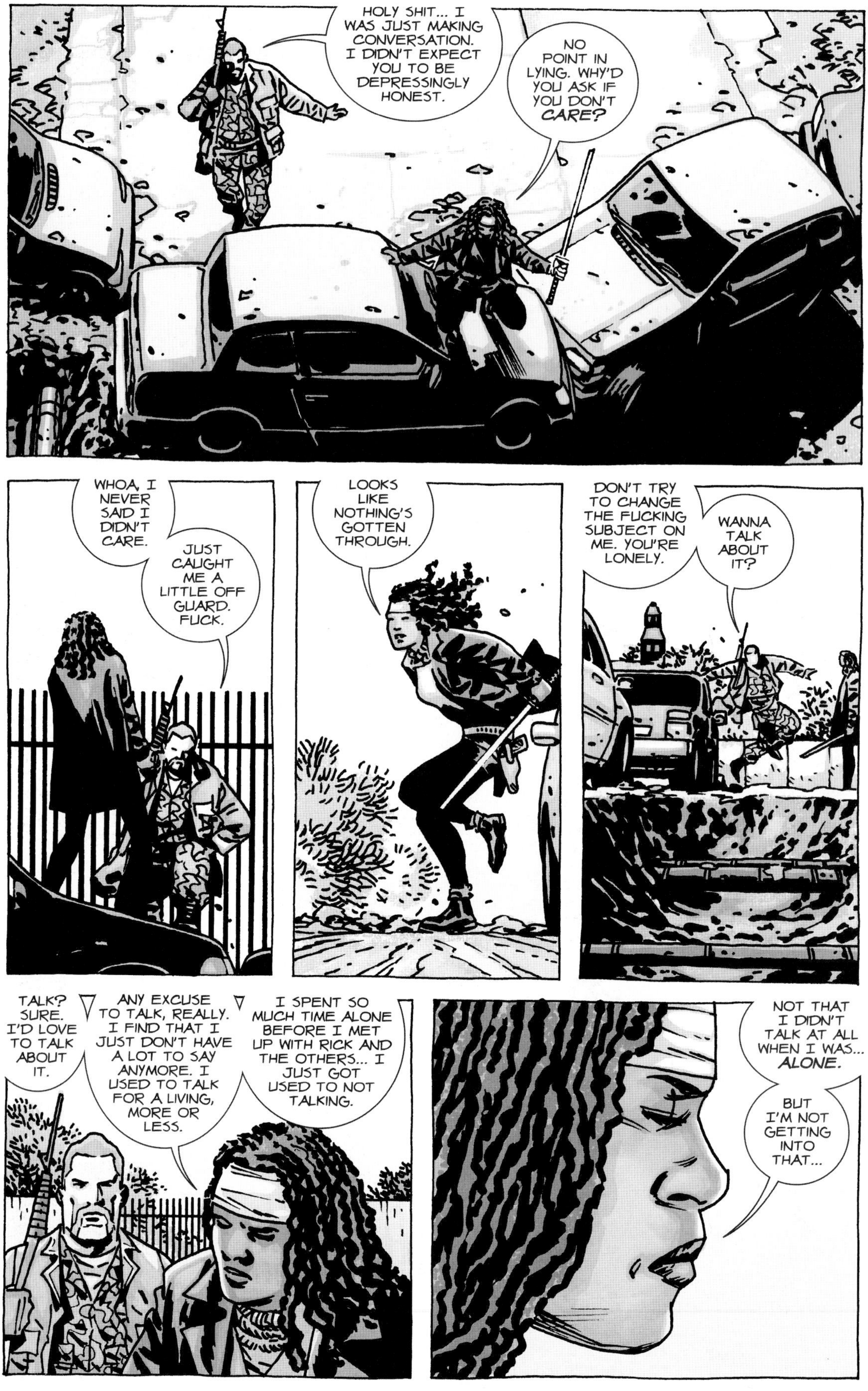
HOLY SHIT... I WAS JUST MAKING CONVERSATION. I DIDN'T EXPECT YOU TO BE DEPRESSINGLY HONEST.
NO POINT IN LYING. WHY'D YOU ASK IF YOU DON'T CARE?
WHOA, I NEVER SAID I DIDN'T CARE.
JUST CAUGHT ME A LITTLE OFF GUARD. FUCK.
LOOKS LIKE NOTHING'S GOTTEN THROUGH.
DON'T TRY TO CHANGE THE FUCKING SUBJECT ON ME. YOU'RE LONELY.
WANNA TALK ABOUT IT?
TALK? SURE. I'D LOVE TO TALK ABOUT IT.
ANY EXCUSE TO TALK, REALLY. I FIND THAT I JUST DON'T HAVE A LOT TO SAY ANYMORE. I USED TO TALK FOR A LIVING, MORE OR LESS.
I SPENT SO MUCH TIME ALONE BEFORE I MET UP WITH RICK AND THE OTHERS... I JUST GOT USED TO NOT TALKING.
NOT THAT I DIDN'T TALK AT ALL WHEN I WAS... ALONE.
BUT I'M NOT GETTING INTO THAT...

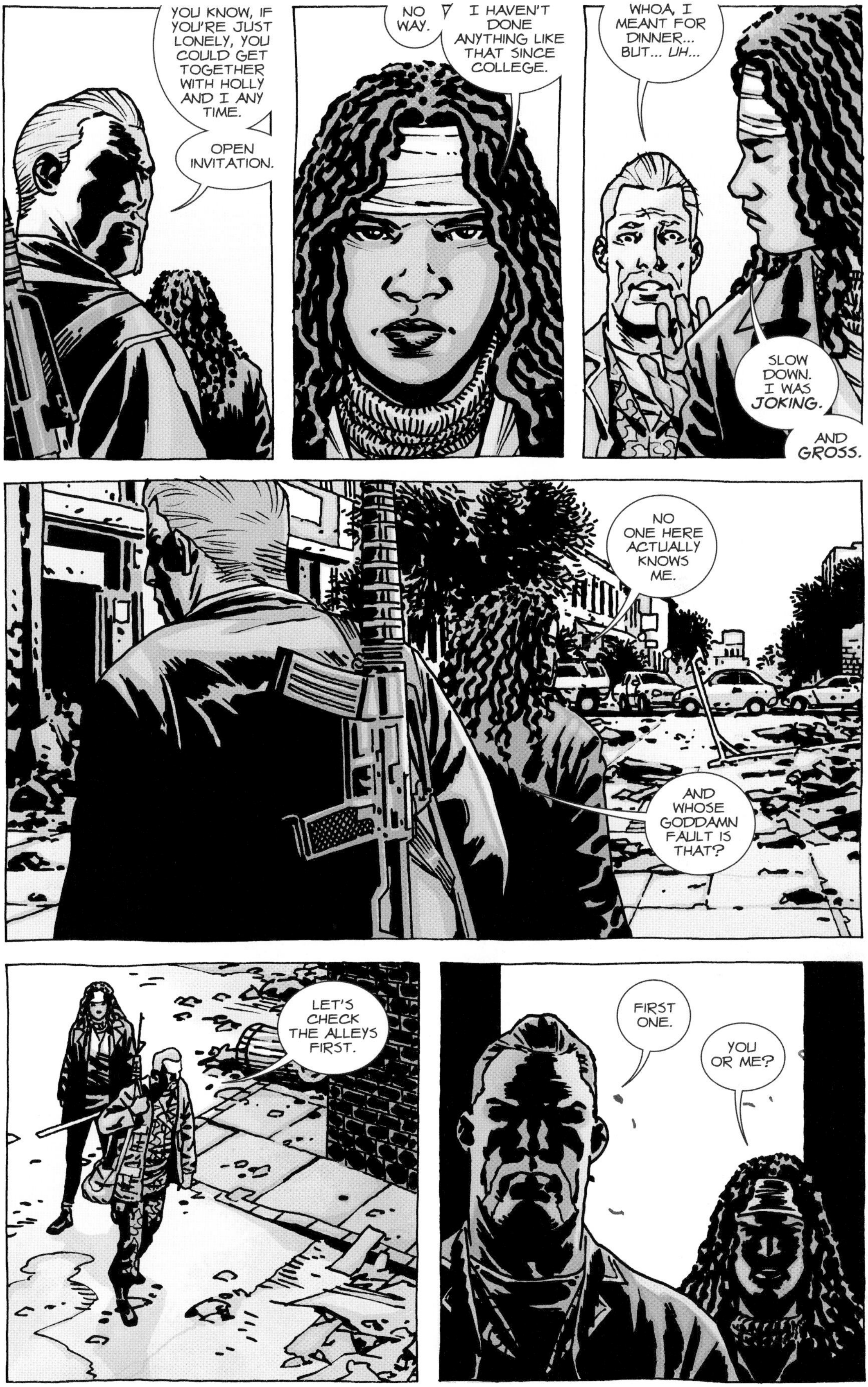

YOU KNOW, IF YOU'RE JUST LONELY, YOU COULD GET TOGETHER WITH HOLLY AND I ANY TIME.
OPEN INVITATION.
NO WAY.
I HAVEN'T DONE ANYTHING LIKE THAT SINCE COLLEGE.
WHOA, I MEANT FOR DINNER... BUT... UH...
SLOW DOWN. I WAS JOKING.
AND GROSS.
NO ONE HERE ACTUALLY KNOWS ME.
AND WHOSE GODDAMN FAULT IS THAT?
LET'S CHECK THE ALLEYS FIRST.
FIRST ONE.
YOU OR ME?

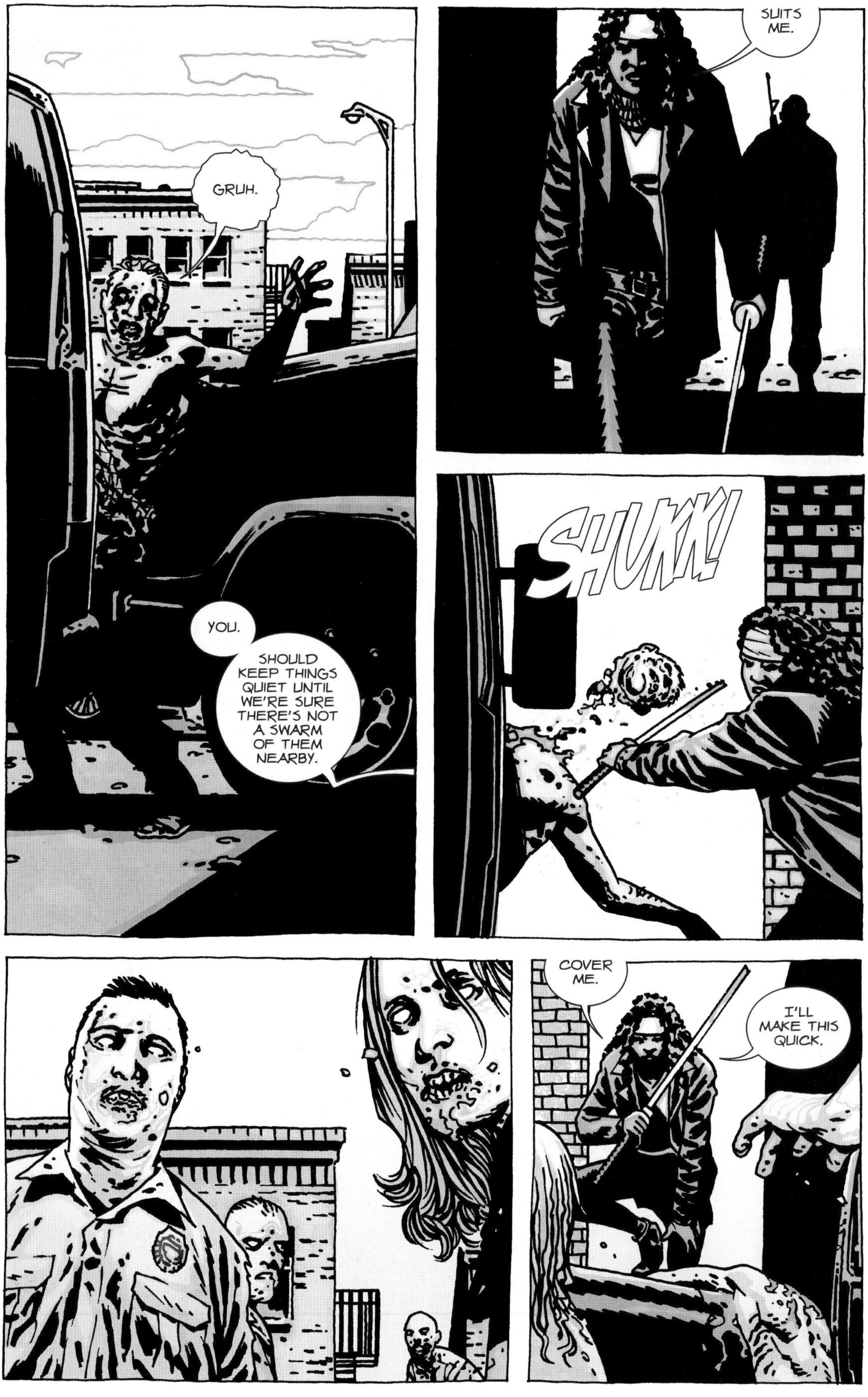
GRUH.
YOU.
SHOULD KEEP THINGS QUIET UNTIL WE'RE SURE THERE'S NOT A SWARM OF THEM NEARBY.
SUITS ME.
SHUKK!
COVER ME.
I'LL MAKE THIS QUICK.

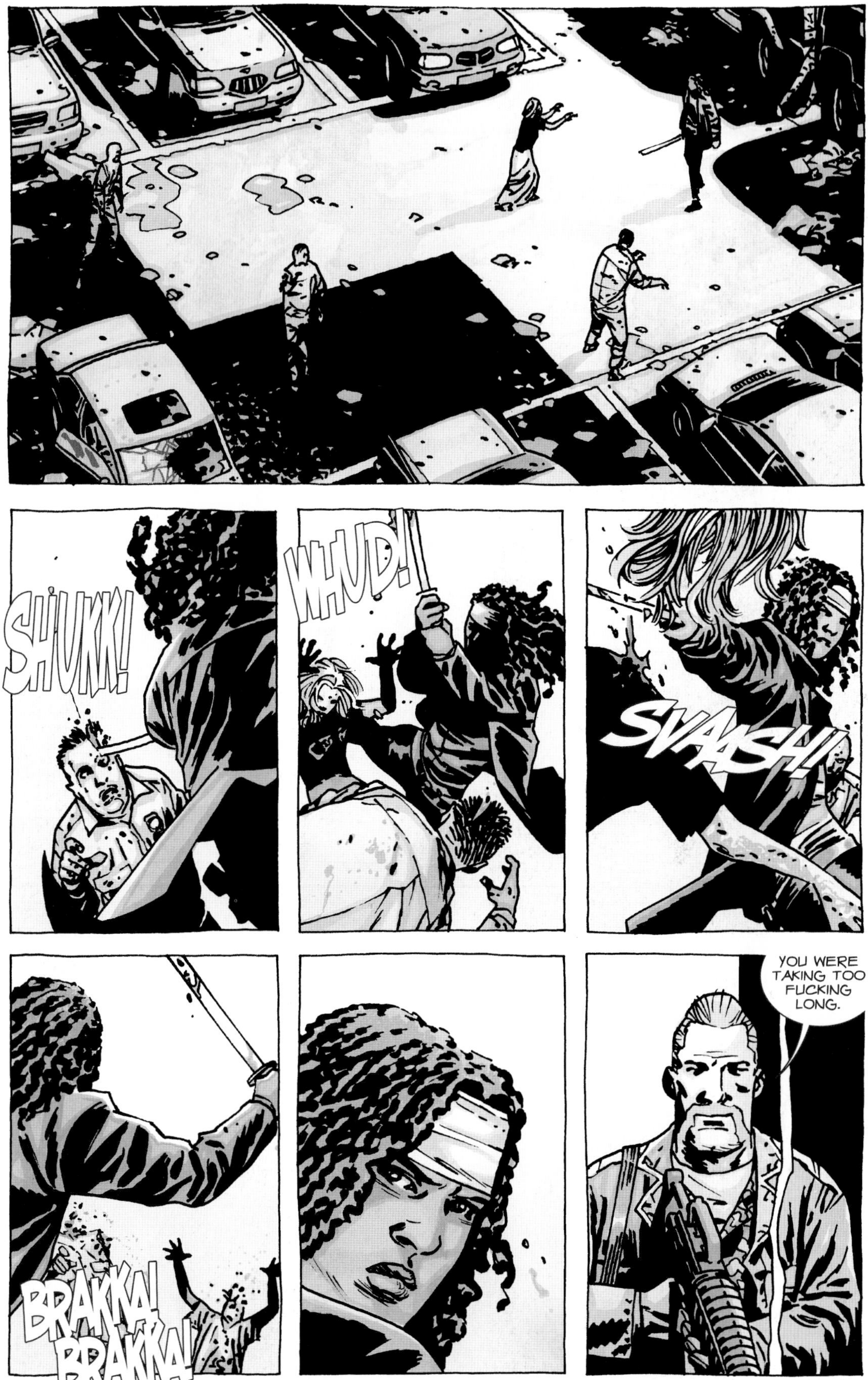
SHUKK!
WHUD!
SVASH!
BRAKKA! BRAKKA!
YOU WERE TAKING TOO FUCKING LONG.

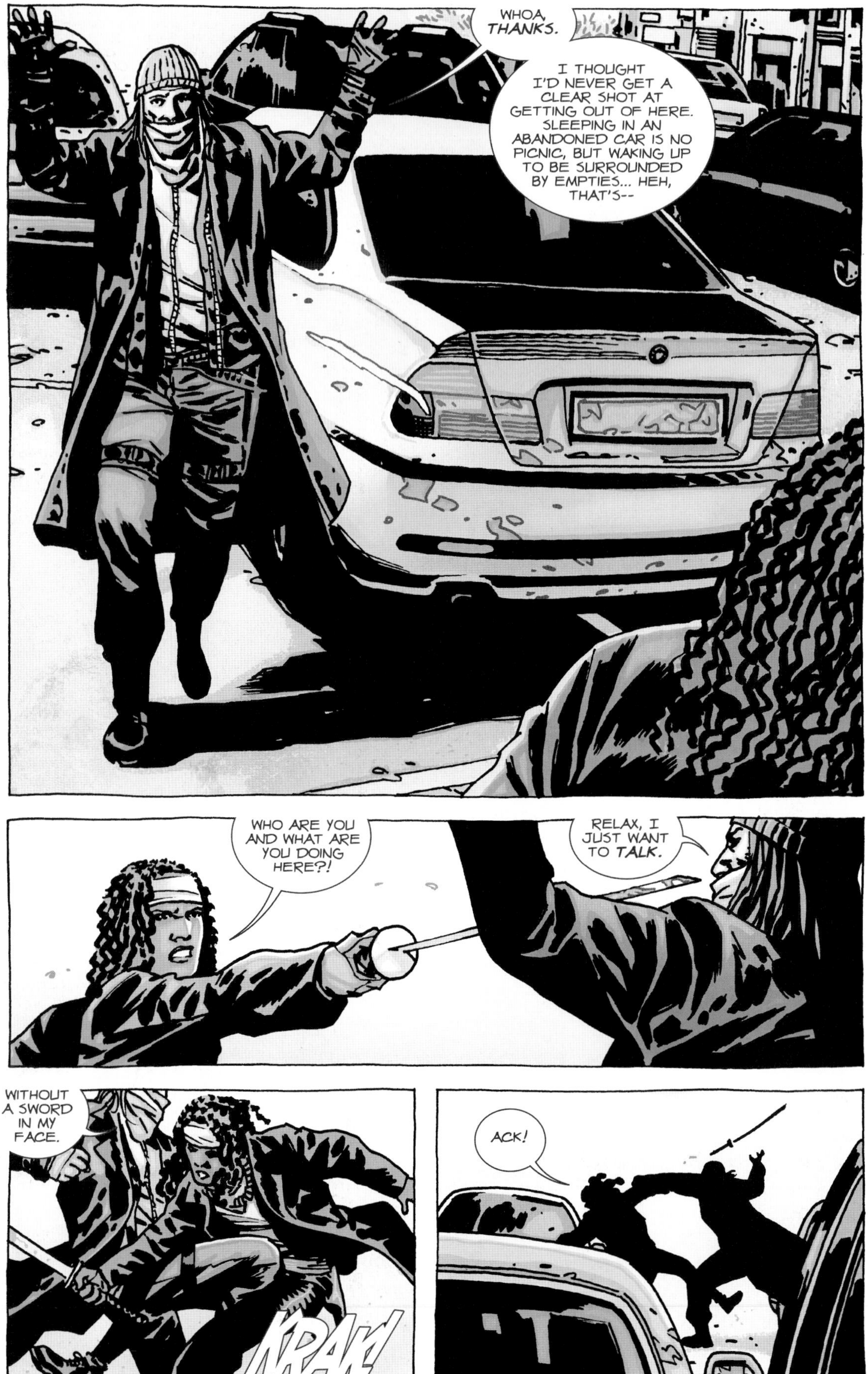
WHOA, THANKS.
I THOUGHT I'D NEVER GET A CLEAR SHOT AT GETTING OUT OF HERE. SLEEPING IN AN ABANDONED CAR IS NO PICNIC, BUT WAKING UP TO BE SURROUNDED BY EMPTIES... HEH, THAT'S--
WHO ARE YOU AND WHAT ARE YOU DOING HERE?!
RELAX, I JUST WANT TO TALK.
WITHOUT A SWORD IN MY FACE.
KRAAK
ACK!

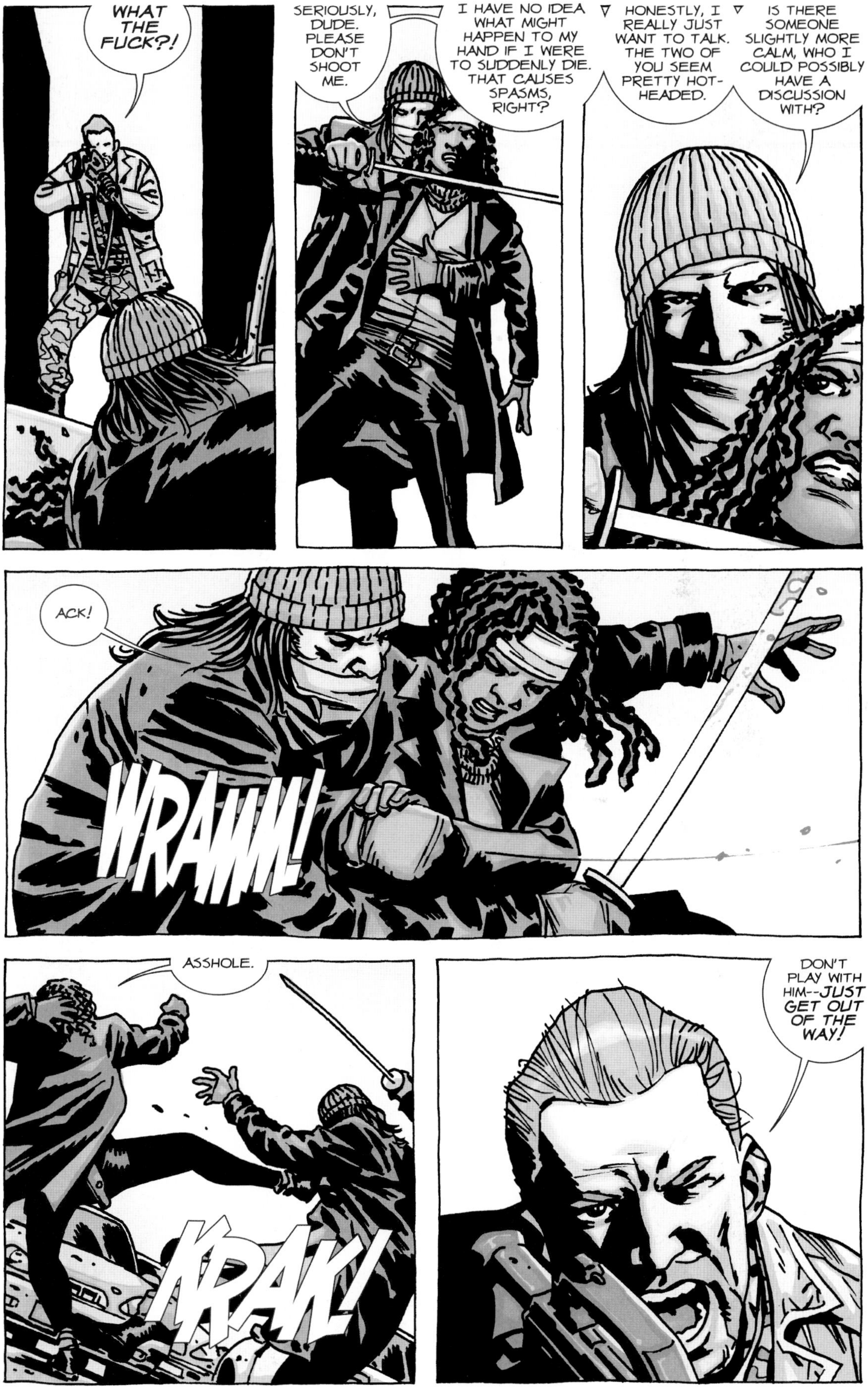
WHAT THE FUCK?!
SERIOUSLY, DUDE. PLEASE DON'T SHOOT ME.
I HAVE NO IDEA WHAT MIGHT HAPPEN TO MY HAND IF I WERE TO SUDDENLY DIE. THAT CAUSES SPASMS, RIGHT?
HONESTLY, I REALLY JUST WANT TO TALK. THE TWO OF YOU SEEM PRETTY HOT-HEADED.
IS THERE SOMEONE SLIGHTLY MORE CALM, WHO I COULD POSSIBLY HAVE A DISCUSSION WITH?
ACK!
WRAMM!
ASSHOLE.
KRAK!
DON'T PLAY WITH HIM--JUST GET OUT OF THE WAY!

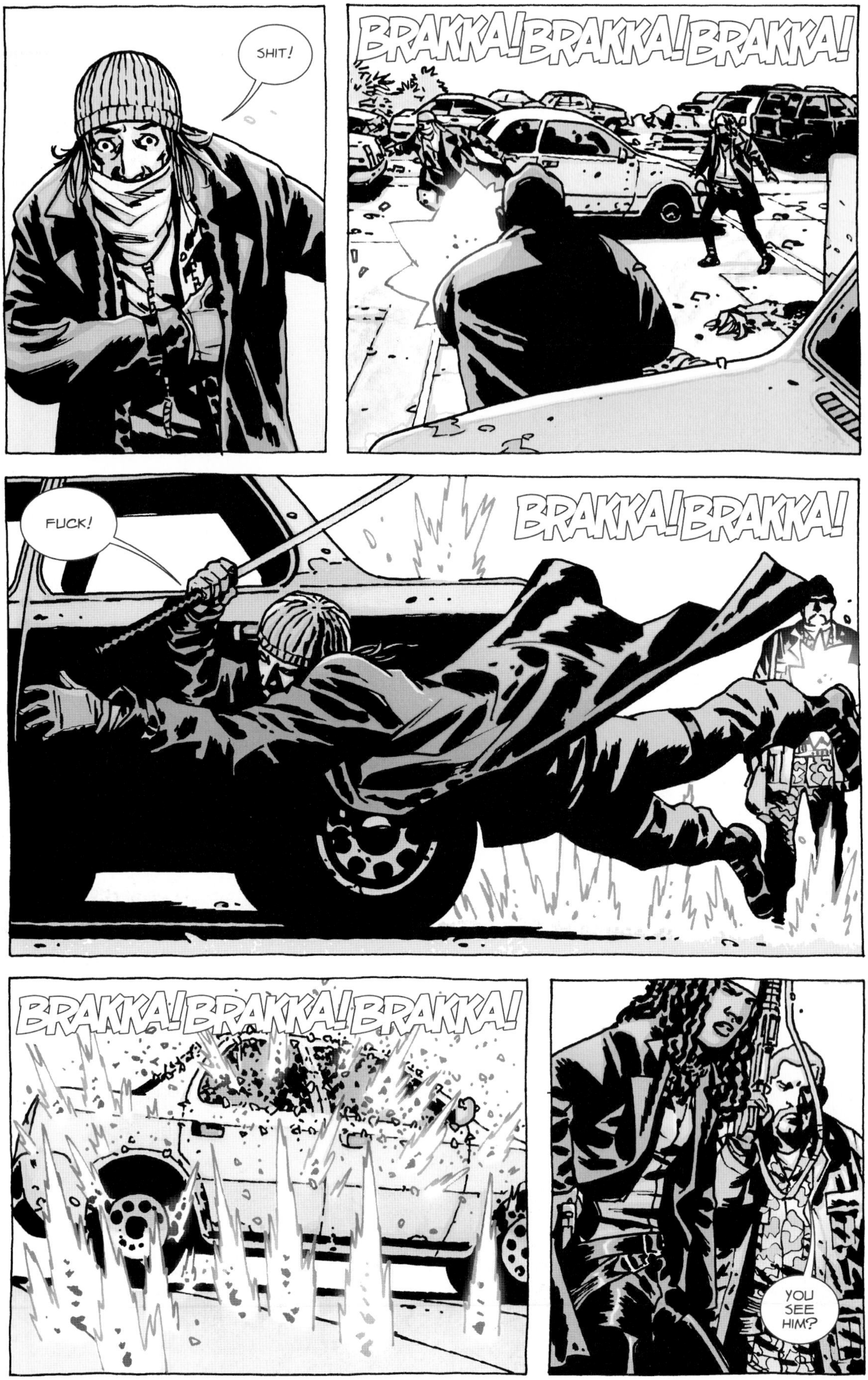
SHIT!
BRAKKA! BRAKKA! BRAKKA!
FUCK!
BRAKKA! BRAKKA!
BRAKKA! BRAKKA! BRAKKA!
YOU SEE HIM?

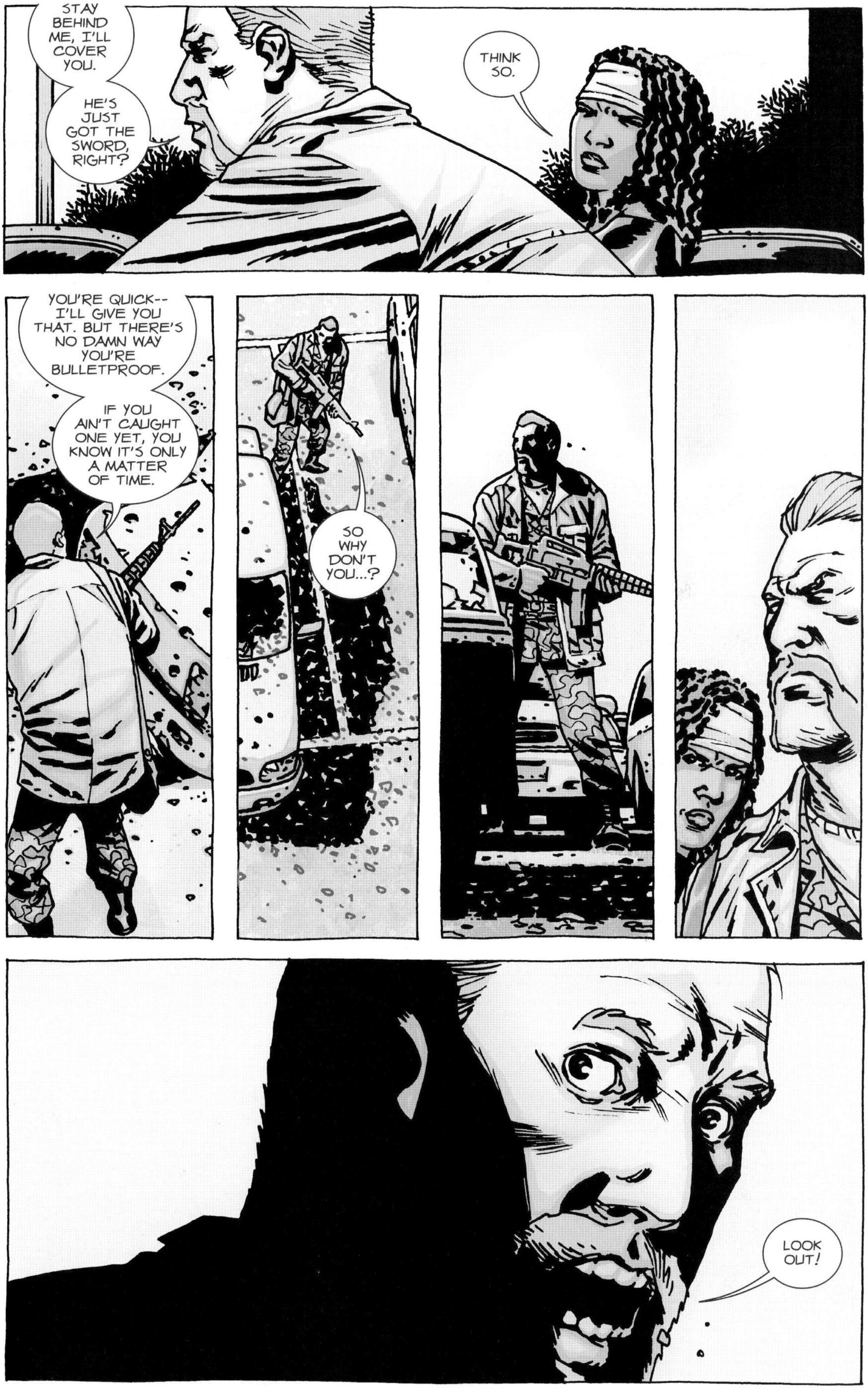
STAY BEHIND ME, I'LL COVER YOU.
HE'S JUST GOT THE SWORD, RIGHT?
THINK SO.
YOU'RE QUICK-- I'LL GIVE YOU THAT. BUT THERE'S NO DAMN WAY YOU'RE BULLETPROOF.
IF YOU AIN'T CAUGHT ONE YET, YOU KNOW IT'S ONLY A MATTER OF TIME.
SO WHY DON'T YOU...?
LOOK OUT!

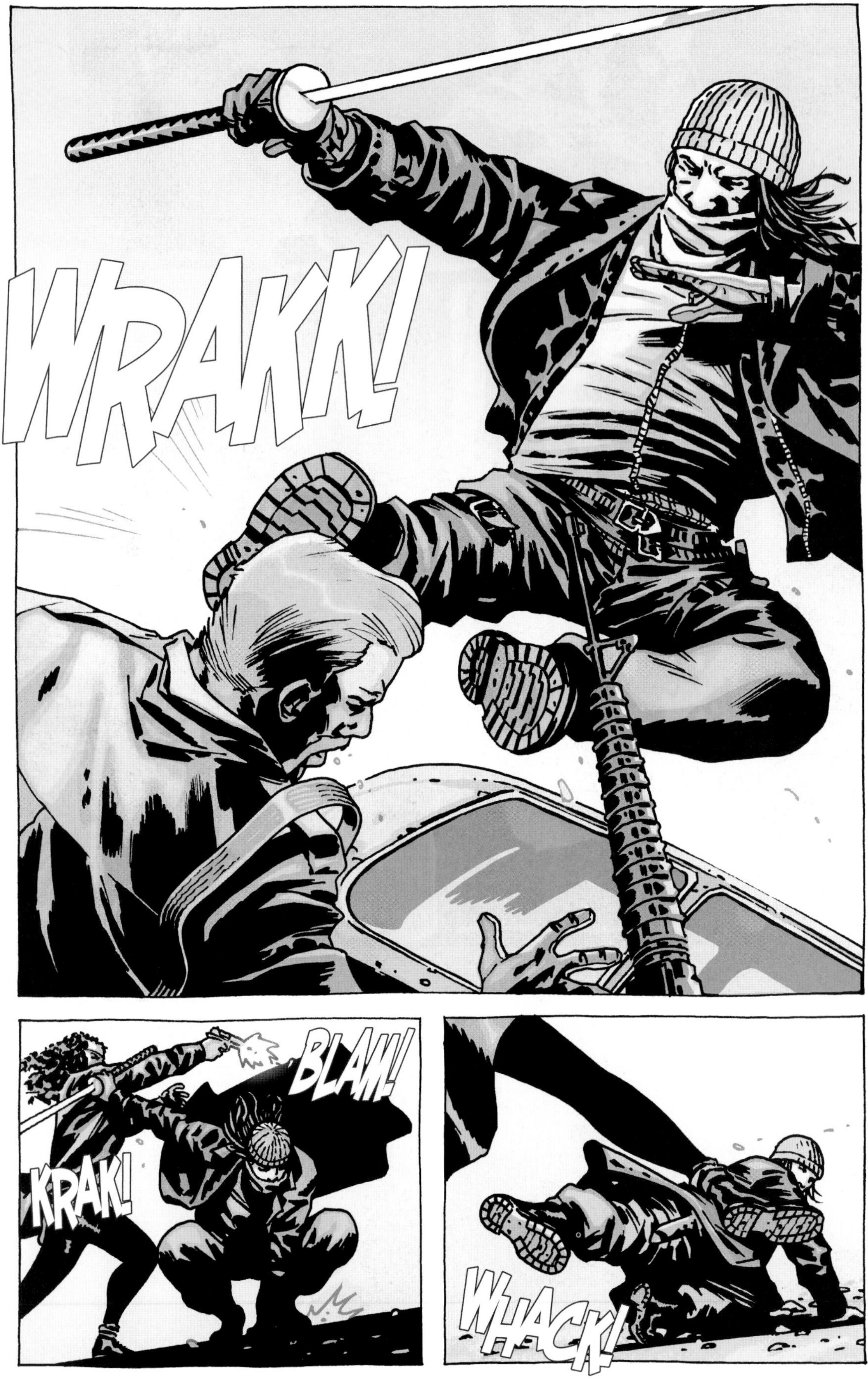
WRAKK!
BLAM!
KRAK!
WHACK!

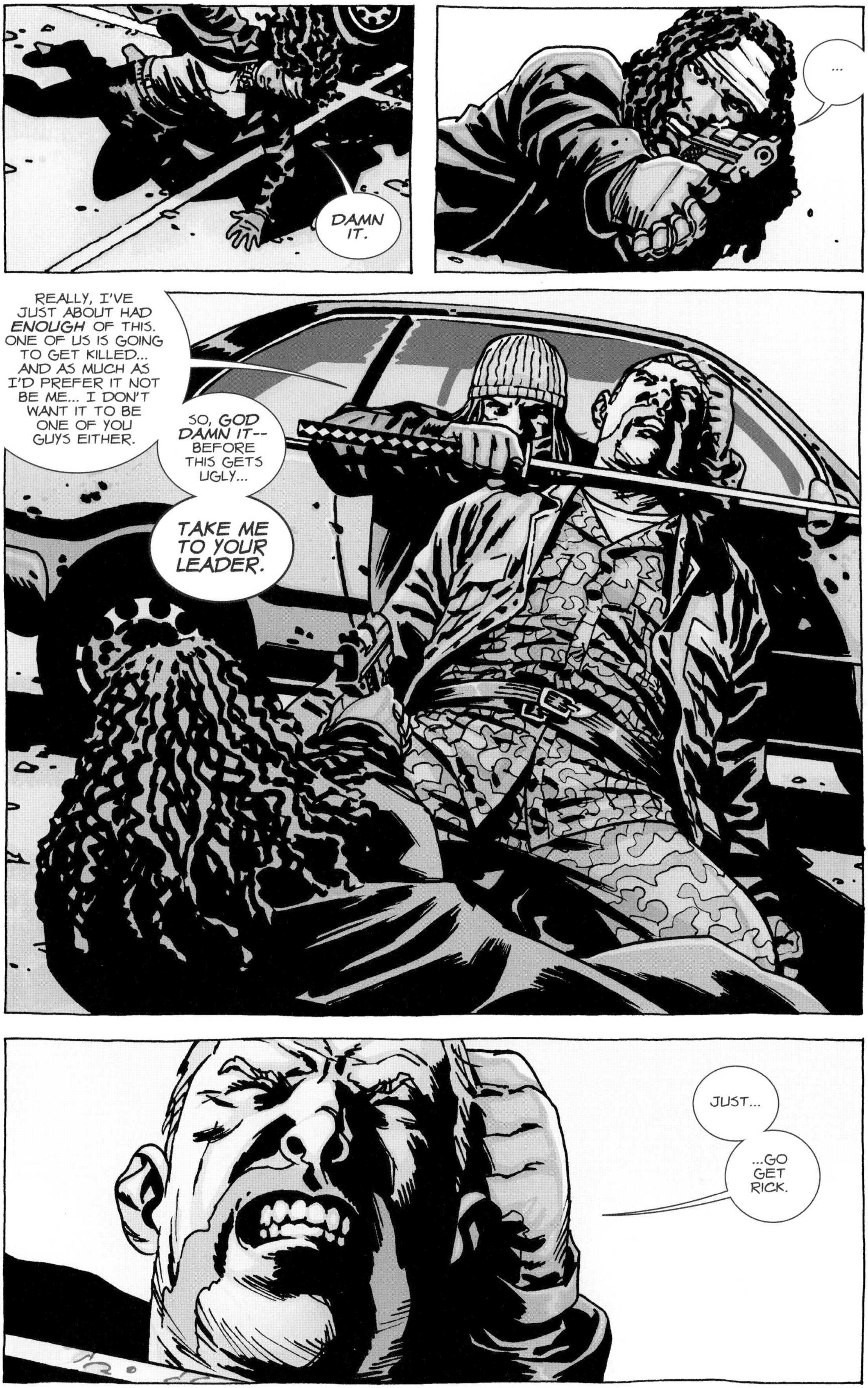
DAMN IT.
...
REALLY, I'VE JUST ABOUT HAD ENOUGH OF THIS. ONE OF US IS GOING TO GET KILLED... AND AS MUCH AS I'D PREFER IT NOT BE ME... I DON'T WANT IT TO BE ONE OF YOU GUYS EITHER.
SO, GOD DAMN IT-- BEFORE THIS GETS UGLY...
TAKE ME TO YOUR LEADER.
JUST...
...GO GET RICK.

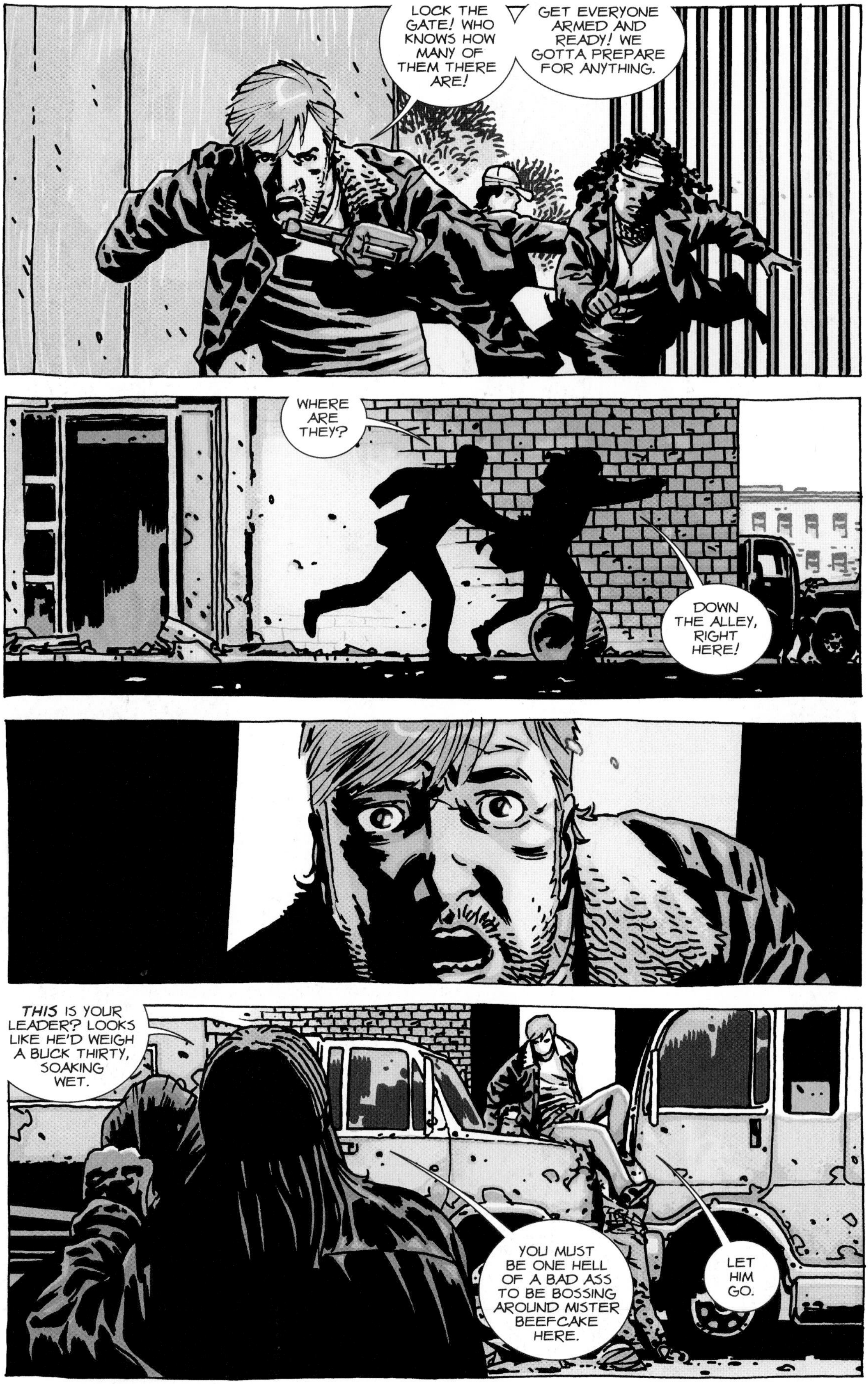
LOCK THE GATE! WHO KNOWS HOW MANY OF THEM THERE ARE!
GET EVERYONE ARMED AND READY! WE GOTTA PREPARE FOR ANYTHING.
WHERE ARE THEY?
DOWN THE ALLEY, RIGHT HERE!
THIS IS YOUR LEADER? LOOKS LIKE HE'D WEIGH A BUCK THIRTY, SOAKING WET.
YOU MUST BE ONE HELL OF A BAD ASS TO BE BOSSING AROUND MISTER BEEFCAKE HERE.
LET HIM GO.

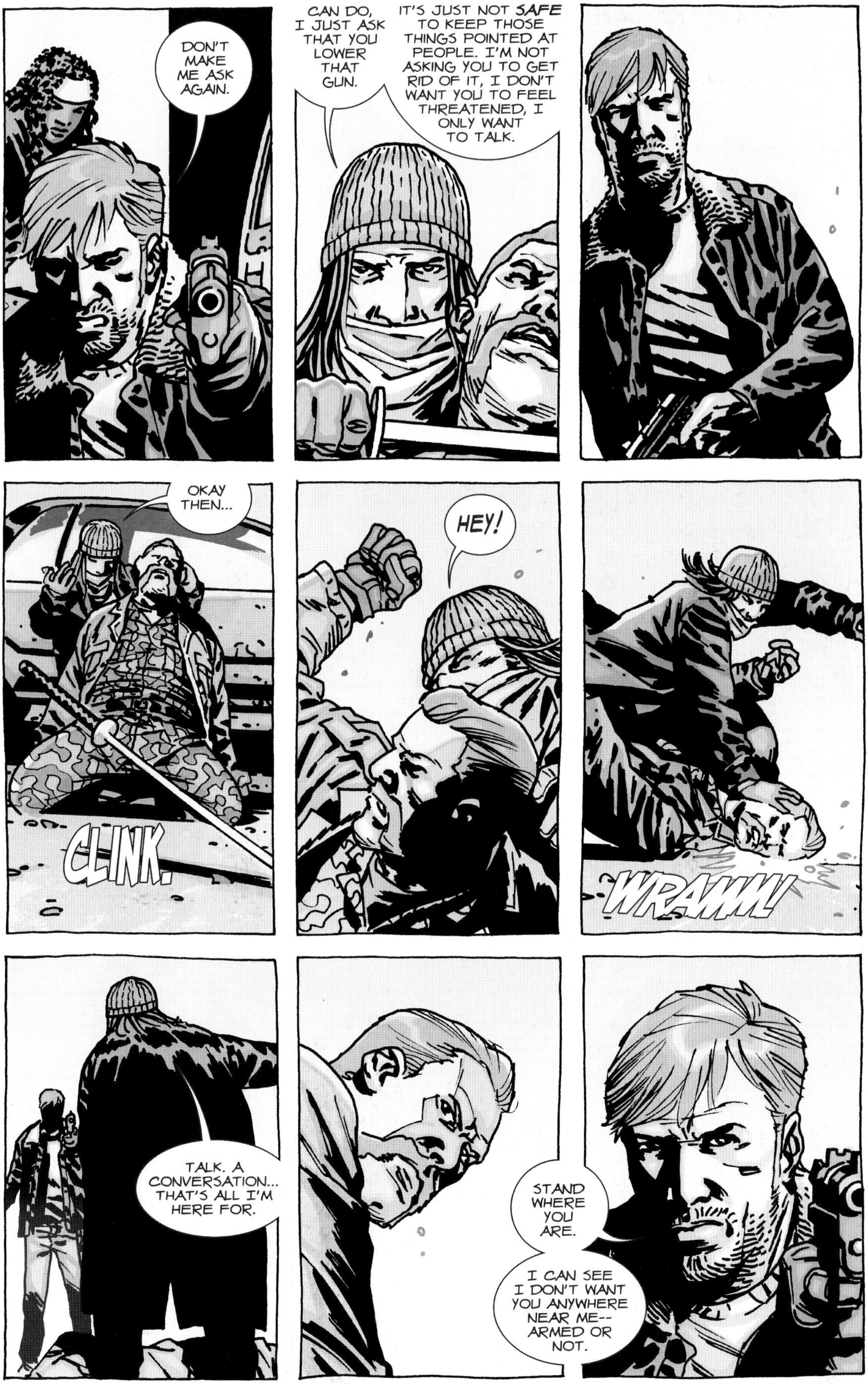
DON'T MAKE ME ASK AGAIN.
CAN DO, I JUST ASK THAT YOU LOWER THAT GUN.
IT'S JUST NOT SAFE TO KEEP THOSE THINGS POINTED AT PEOPLE. I'M NOT ASKING YOU TO GET RID OF IT, I DON'T WANT YOU TO FEEL THREATENED, I ONLY WANT TO TALK.
OKAY THEN...
CLINK.
HEY!
WRAMM!
TALK. A CONVERSATION... THAT'S ALL I'M HERE FOR.
STAND WHERE YOU ARE.
I CAN SEE I DON'T WANT YOU ANYWHERE NEAR ME-- ARMED OR NOT.

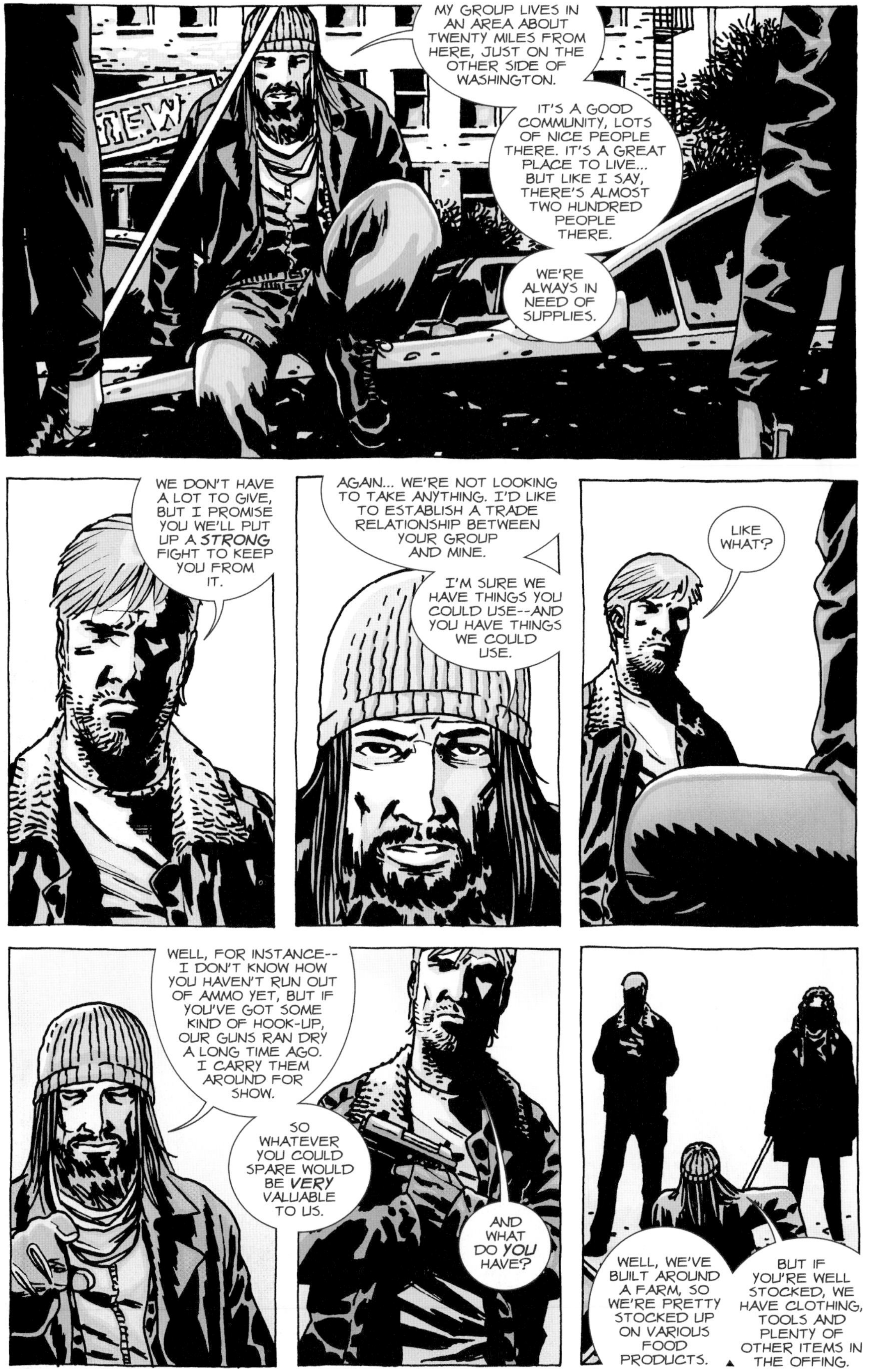
MY GROUP LIVES IN AN AREA ABOUT TWENTY MILES FROM HERE, JUST ON THE OTHER SIDE OF WASHINGTON.
IT'S A GOOD COMMUNITY, LOTS OF NICE PEOPLE THERE. IT'S A GREAT PLACE TO LIVE... BUT LIKE I SAY, THERE'S ALMOST TWO HUNDRED PEOPLE THERE.
WE'RE ALWAYS IN NEED OF SUPPLIES.
WE DON'T HAVE A LOT TO GIVE, BUT I PROMISE YOU WE'LL PUT UP A *STRONG* FIGHT TO KEEP YOU FROM IT.
AGAIN... WE'RE NOT LOOKING TO TAKE ANYTHING. I'D LIKE TO ESTABLISH A TRADE RELATIONSHIP BETWEEN YOUR GROUP AND MINE.
I'M SURE WE HAVE THINGS YOU COULD USE--AND YOU HAVE THINGS WE COULD USE.
LIKE WHAT?
WELL, FOR INSTANCE-- I DON'T KNOW HOW YOU HAVEN'T RUN OUT OF AMMO YET, BUT IF YOU'VE GOT SOME KIND OF HOOK-UP, OUR GUNS RAN DRY A LONG TIME AGO. I CARRY THEM AROUND FOR SHOW.
SO WHATEVER YOU COULD SPARE WOULD BE *VERY* VALUABLE TO US.
AND WHAT DO *YOU* HAVE?
WELL, WE'VE BUILT AROUND A FARM, SO WE'RE PRETTY STOCKED UP ON VARIOUS FOOD PRODUCTS.
BUT IF YOU'RE WELL STOCKED, WE HAVE CLOTHING, TOOLS AND PLENTY OF OTHER ITEMS IN THE OFFING.

YOU EXPECT ME TO BELIEVE ALL YOUR PEOPLE ARE INTERESTED IN... IS FINDING NEW *PARTNERS* TO TRADE WITH?

WELL, IT'S THE TRUTH-- SO YES.

AND YOU CAME ALL THE WAY HERE... JUST TO LET US KNOW ABOUT THIS?

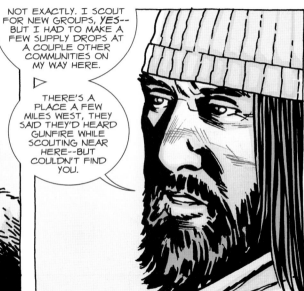

NOT EXACTLY. I SCOUT FOR NEW GROUPS, *YES*-- BUT I HAD TO MAKE A FEW SUPPLY DROPS AT A COUPLE OTHER COMMUNITIES ON MY WAY HERE.

THERE'S A PLACE A FEW MILES WEST, THEY SAID THEY'D HEARD GUNFIRE WHILE SCOUTING NEAR HERE--BUT COULDN'T FIND YOU.

DID YOU SAY TWO *OTHER* COMMUNITIES? THERE'S YOU AND TWO OTHERS?

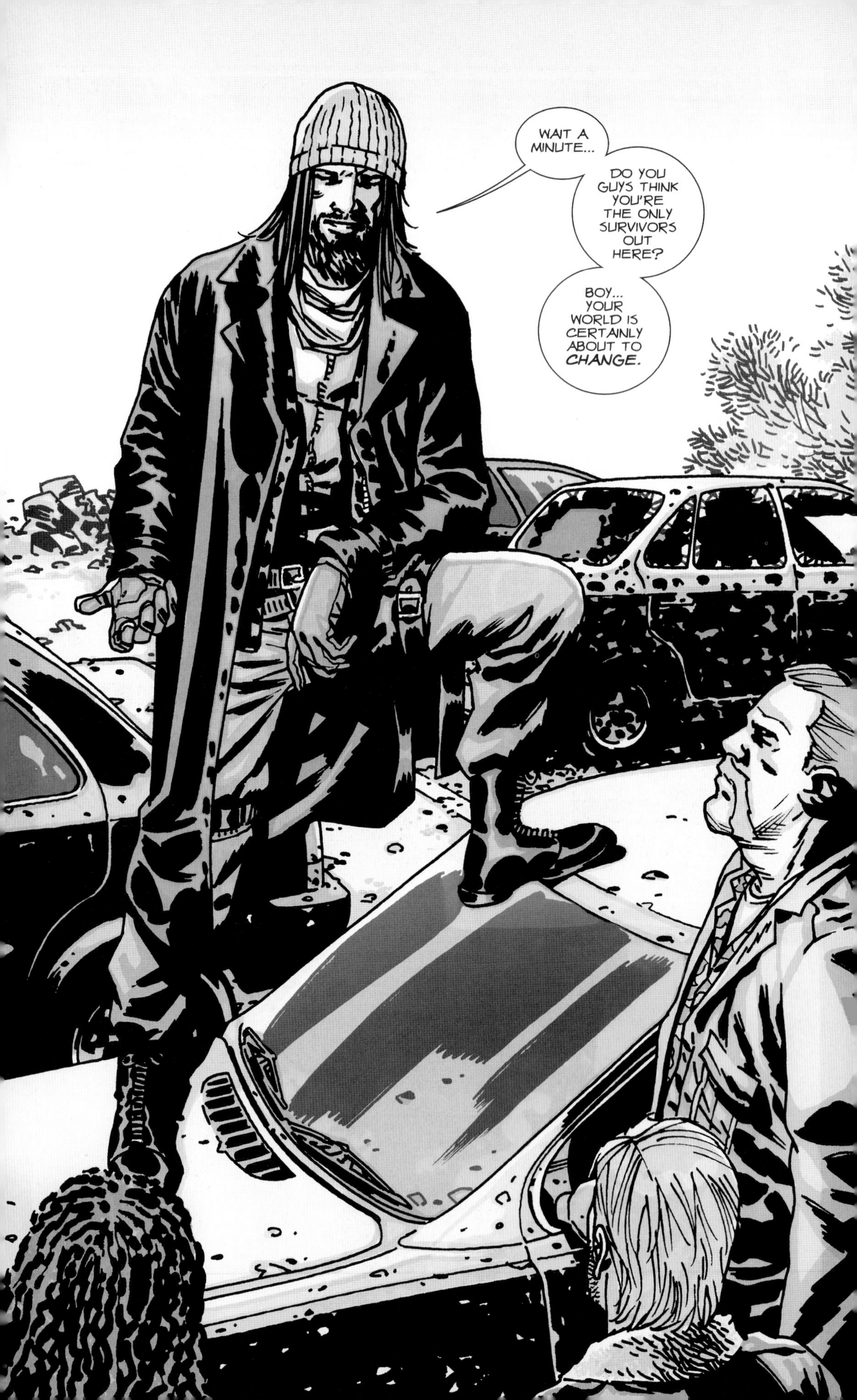
WAIT A MINUTE...
DO YOU GUYS THINK YOU'RE THE ONLY SURVIVORS OUT HERE?
BOY... YOUR WORLD IS CERTAINLY ABOUT TO *CHANGE.*

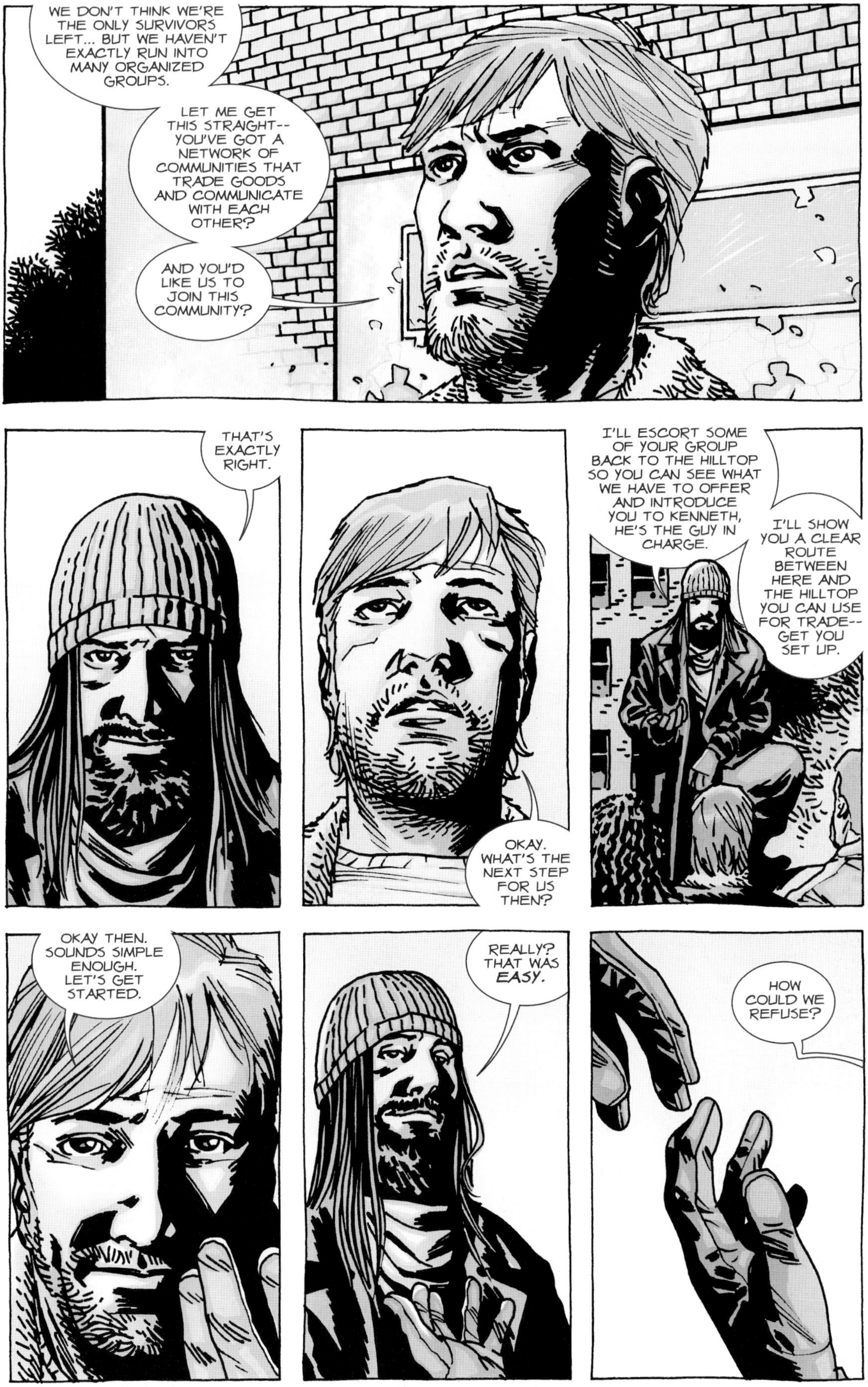
WE DON'T THINK WE'RE THE ONLY SURVIVORS LEFT... BUT WE HAVEN'T EXACTLY RUN INTO MANY ORGANIZED GROUPS.
LET ME GET THIS STRAIGHT-- YOU'VE GOT A NETWORK OF COMMUNITIES THAT TRADE GOODS AND COMMUNICATE WITH EACH OTHER?
AND YOU'D LIKE US TO JOIN THIS COMMUNITY?
THAT'S EXACTLY RIGHT.
OKAY. WHAT'S THE NEXT STEP FOR US THEN?
I'LL ESCORT SOME OF YOUR GROUP BACK TO THE HILLTOP SO YOU CAN SEE WHAT WE HAVE TO OFFER AND INTRODUCE YOU TO KENNETH, HE'S THE GUY IN CHARGE.
I'LL SHOW YOU A CLEAR ROUTE BETWEEN HERE AND THE HILLTOP YOU CAN USE FOR TRADE-- GET YOU SET UP.
OKAY THEN. SOUNDS SIMPLE ENOUGH. LET'S GET STARTED.
REALLY? THAT WAS *EASY.*
HOW COULD WE REFUSE?

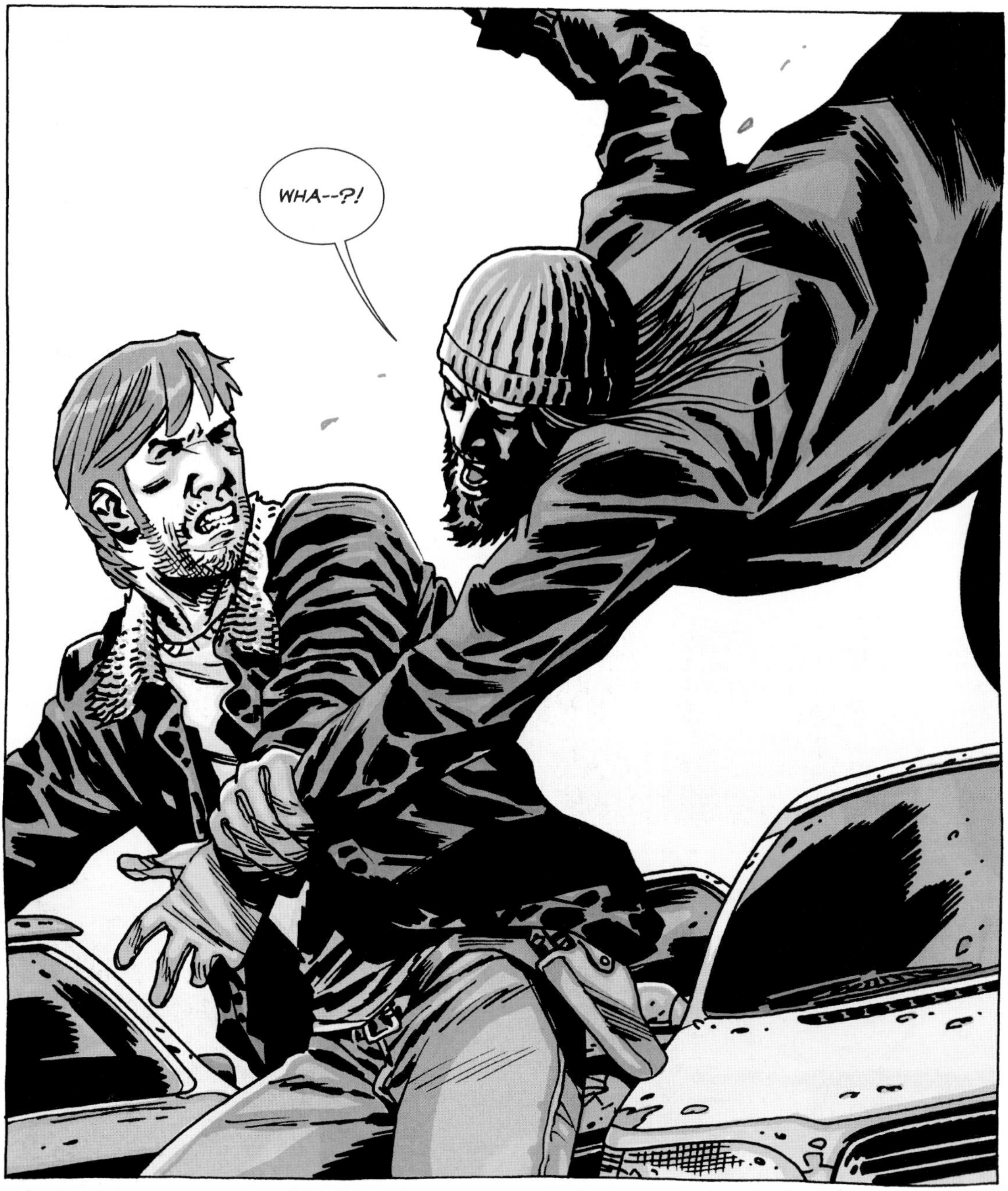
WHA--?!

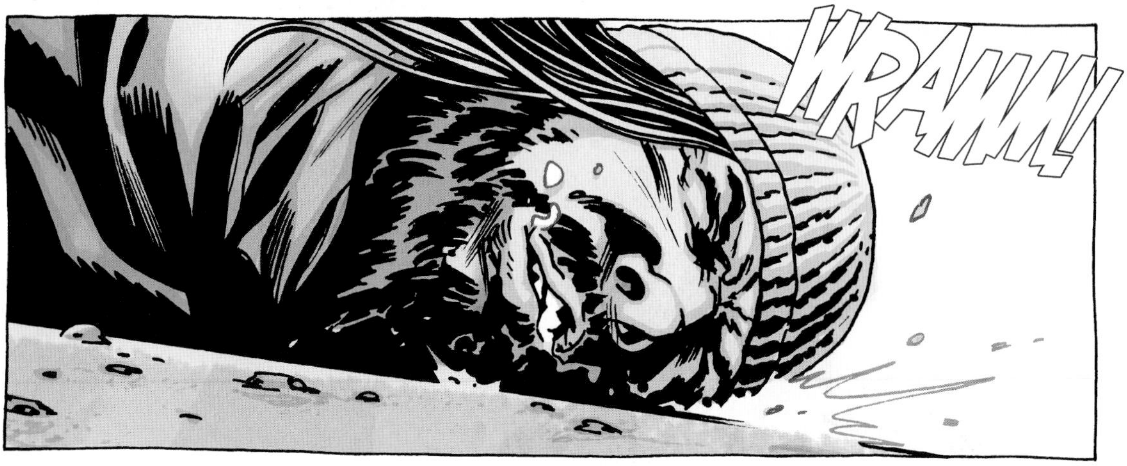
WRAMM!

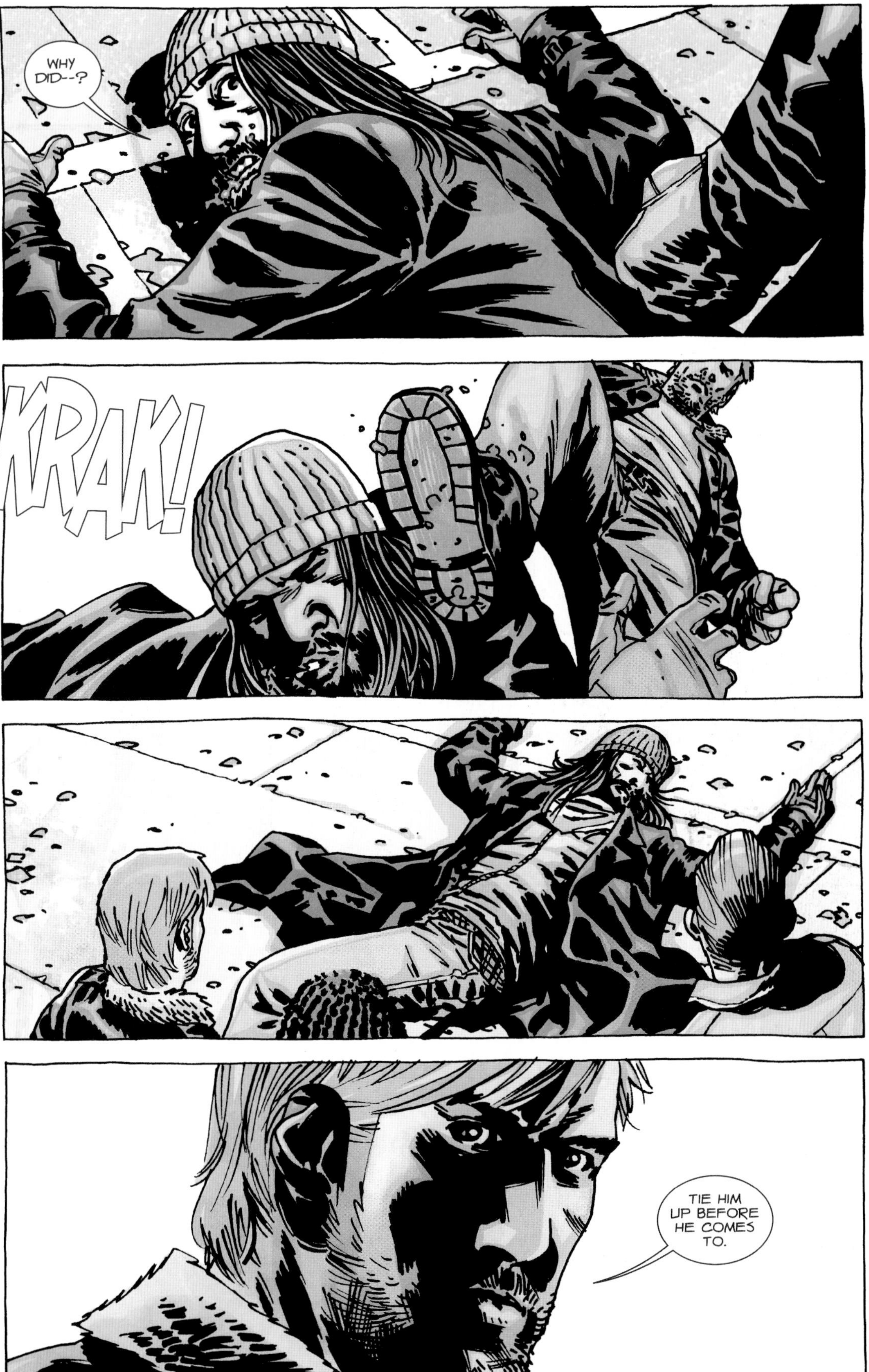
WHY DID--?
KRAK!
TIE HIM UP BEFORE HE COMES TO.

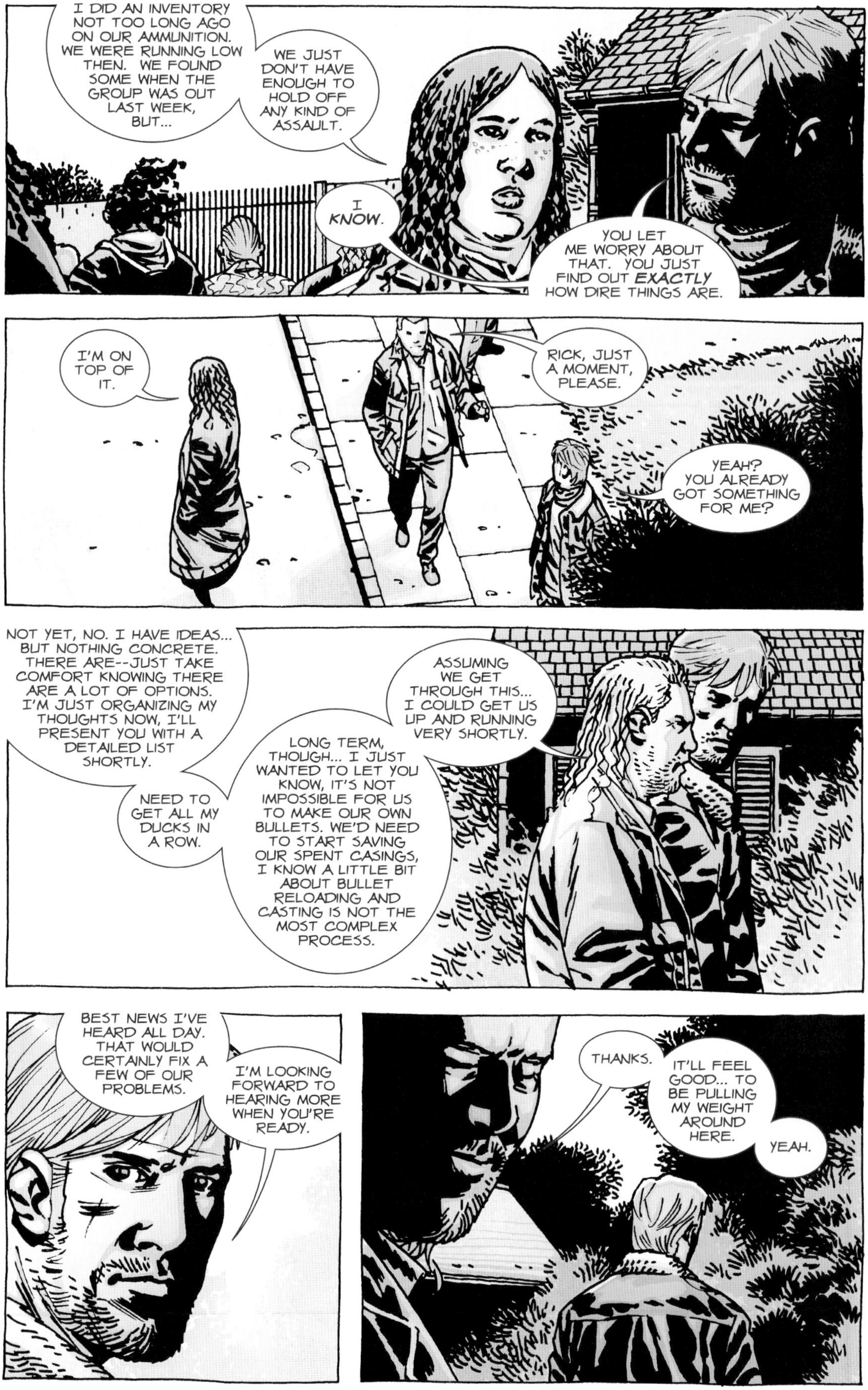
I DID AN INVENTORY NOT TOO LONG AGO ON OUR AMMUNITION. WE WERE RUNNING LOW THEN. WE FOUND SOME WHEN THE GROUP WAS OUT LAST WEEK, BUT...
WE JUST DON'T HAVE ENOUGH TO HOLD OFF ANY KIND OF ASSAULT.
I *KNOW*.
YOU LET ME WORRY ABOUT THAT. YOU JUST FIND OUT *EXACTLY* HOW DIRE THINGS ARE.
I'M ON TOP OF IT.
RICK, JUST A MOMENT, PLEASE.
YEAH? YOU ALREADY GOT SOMETHING FOR ME?
NOT YET, NO. I HAVE IDEAS... BUT NOTHING CONCRETE. THERE ARE--JUST TAKE COMFORT KNOWING THERE ARE A LOT OF OPTIONS. I'M JUST ORGANIZING MY THOUGHTS NOW, I'LL PRESENT YOU WITH A DETAILED LIST SHORTLY.
NEED TO GET ALL MY DUCKS IN A ROW.
LONG TERM, THOUGH... I JUST WANTED TO LET YOU KNOW, IT'S NOT IMPOSSIBLE FOR US TO MAKE OUR OWN BULLETS. WE'D NEED TO START SAVING OUR SPENT CASINGS, I KNOW A LITTLE BIT ABOUT BULLET RELOADING AND CASTING IS NOT THE MOST COMPLEX PROCESS.
ASSUMING WE GET THROUGH THIS... I COULD GET US UP AND RUNNING VERY SHORTLY.
BEST NEWS I'VE HEARD ALL DAY. THAT WOULD CERTAINLY FIX A FEW OF OUR PROBLEMS.
I'M LOOKING FORWARD TO HEARING MORE WHEN YOU'RE READY.
THANKS.
IT'LL FEEL GOOD... TO BE PULLING MY WEIGHT AROUND HERE.
YEAH.

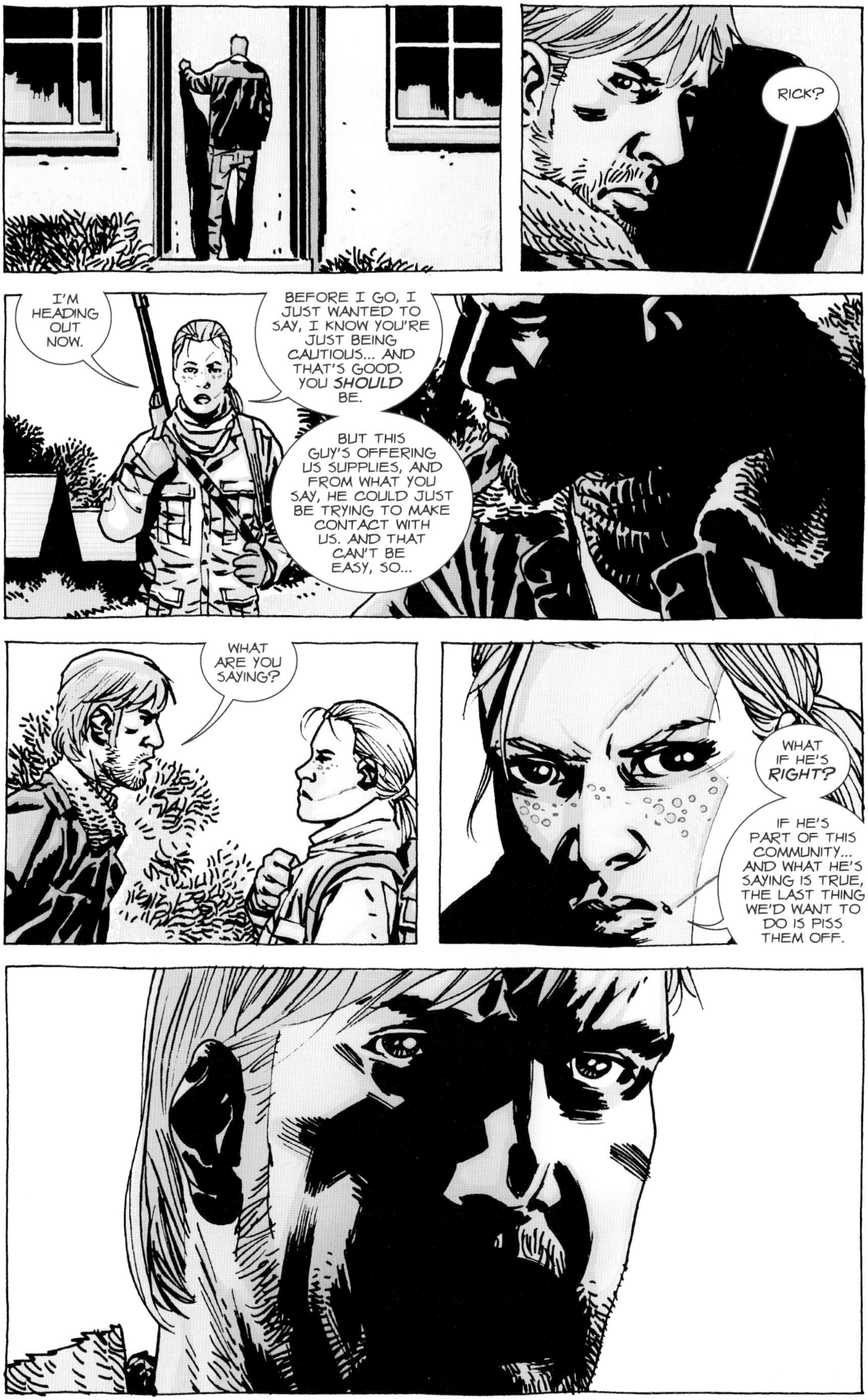
RICK?
I'M HEADING OUT NOW.
BEFORE I GO, I JUST WANTED TO SAY, I KNOW YOU'RE JUST BEING CAUTIOUS... AND THAT'S GOOD. YOU **SHOULD** BE.
BUT THIS GUY'S OFFERING US SUPPLIES, AND FROM WHAT YOU SAY, HE COULD JUST BE TRYING TO MAKE CONTACT WITH US. AND THAT CAN'T BE EASY, SO...
WHAT ARE YOU SAYING?
WHAT IF HE'S **RIGHT?**
IF HE'S PART OF THIS COMMUNITY... AND WHAT HE'S SAYING IS TRUE, THE LAST THING WE'D WANT TO DO IS PISS THEM OFF.

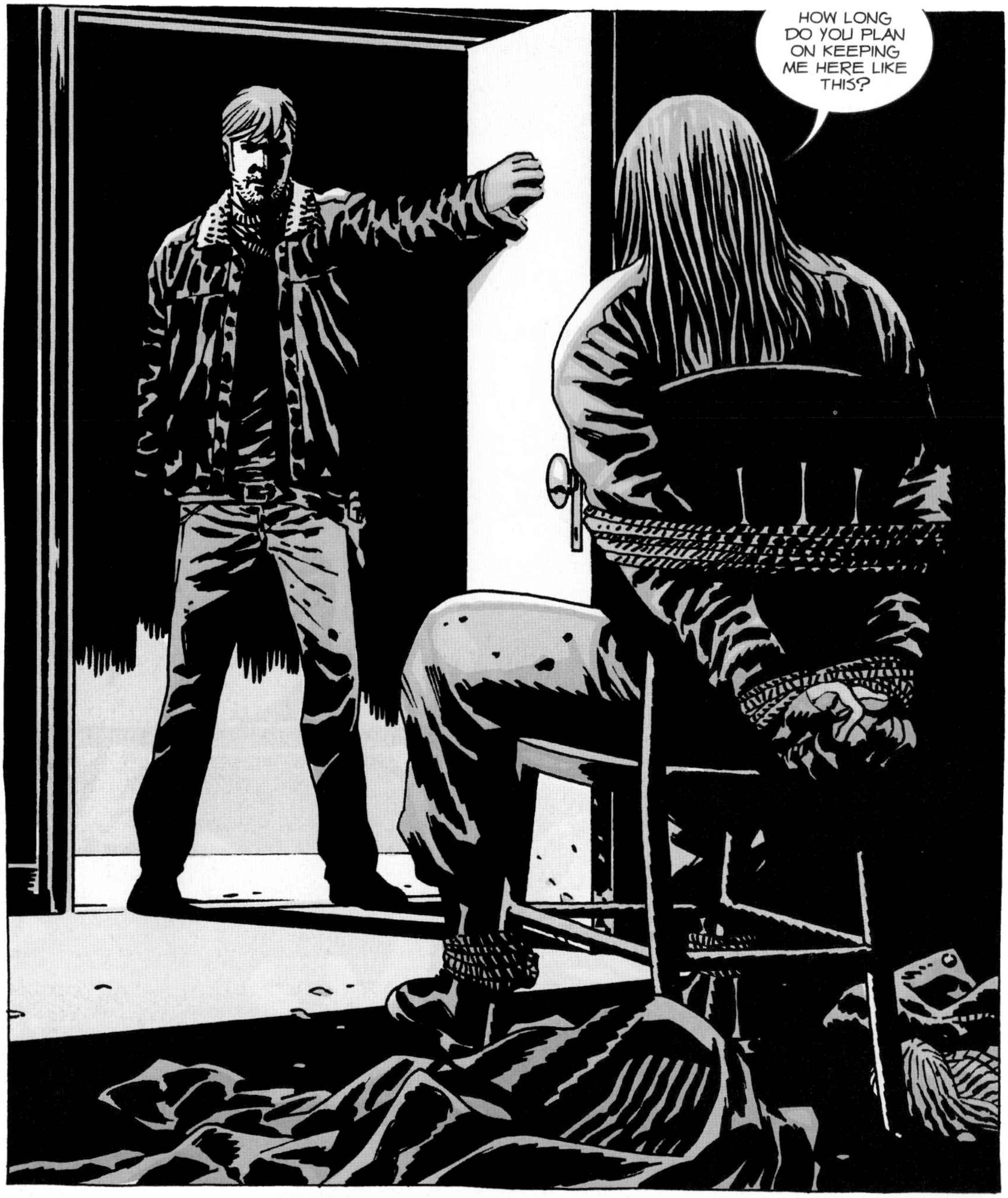
HOW LONG DO YOU PLAN ON KEEPING ME HERE LIKE THIS?

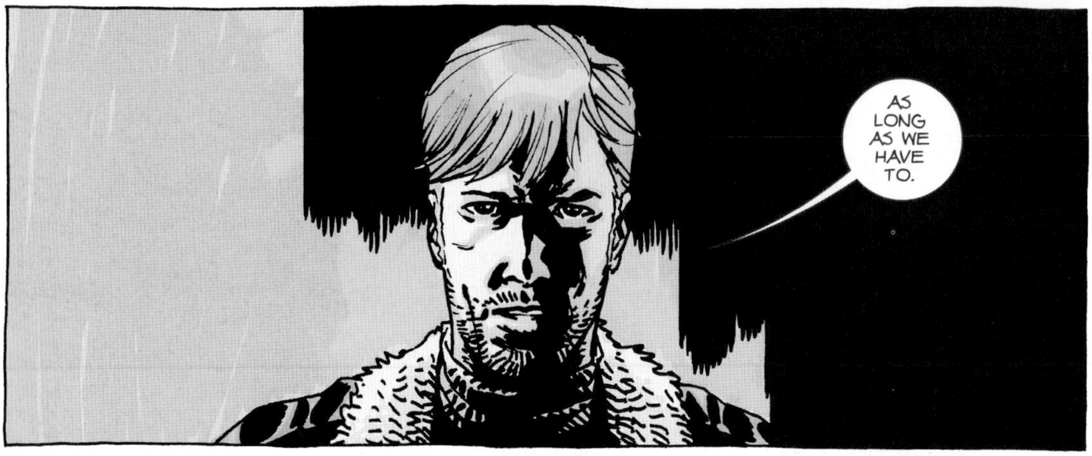
AS LONG AS WE HAVE TO.

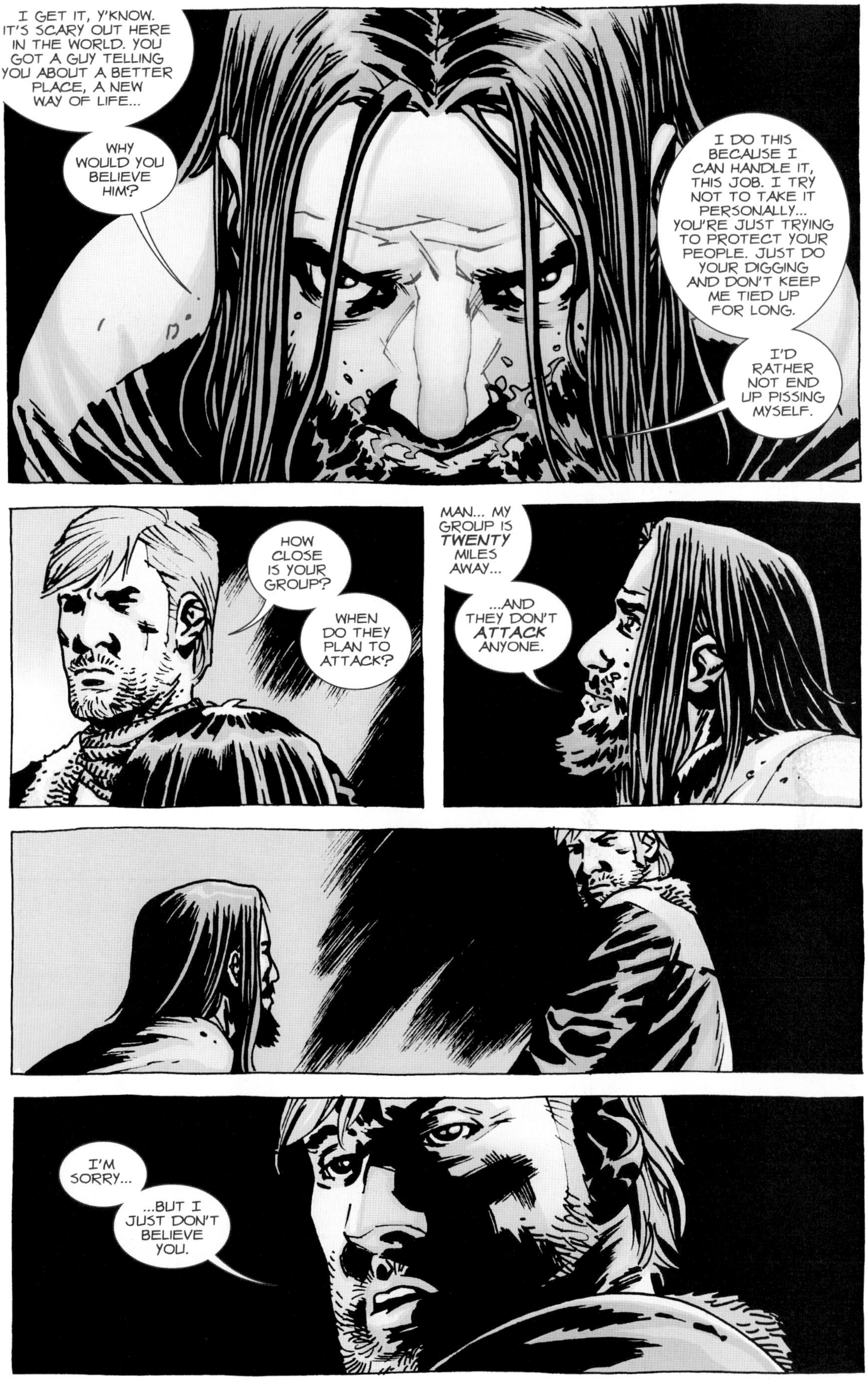
I GET IT, Y'KNOW. IT'S SCARY OUT HERE IN THE WORLD. YOU GOT A GUY TELLING YOU ABOUT A BETTER PLACE, A NEW WAY OF LIFE...
WHY WOULD YOU BELIEVE HIM?
I DO THIS BECAUSE I CAN HANDLE IT, THIS JOB. I TRY NOT TO TAKE IT PERSONALLY... YOU'RE JUST TRYING TO PROTECT YOUR PEOPLE. JUST DO YOUR DIGGING AND DON'T KEEP ME TIED UP FOR LONG.
I'D RATHER NOT END UP PISSING MYSELF.
HOW CLOSE IS YOUR GROUP?
WHEN DO THEY PLAN TO ATTACK?
MAN... MY GROUP IS TWENTY MILES AWAY...
...AND THEY DON'T ATTACK ANYONE.
I'M SORRY...
...BUT I JUST DON'T BELIEVE YOU.

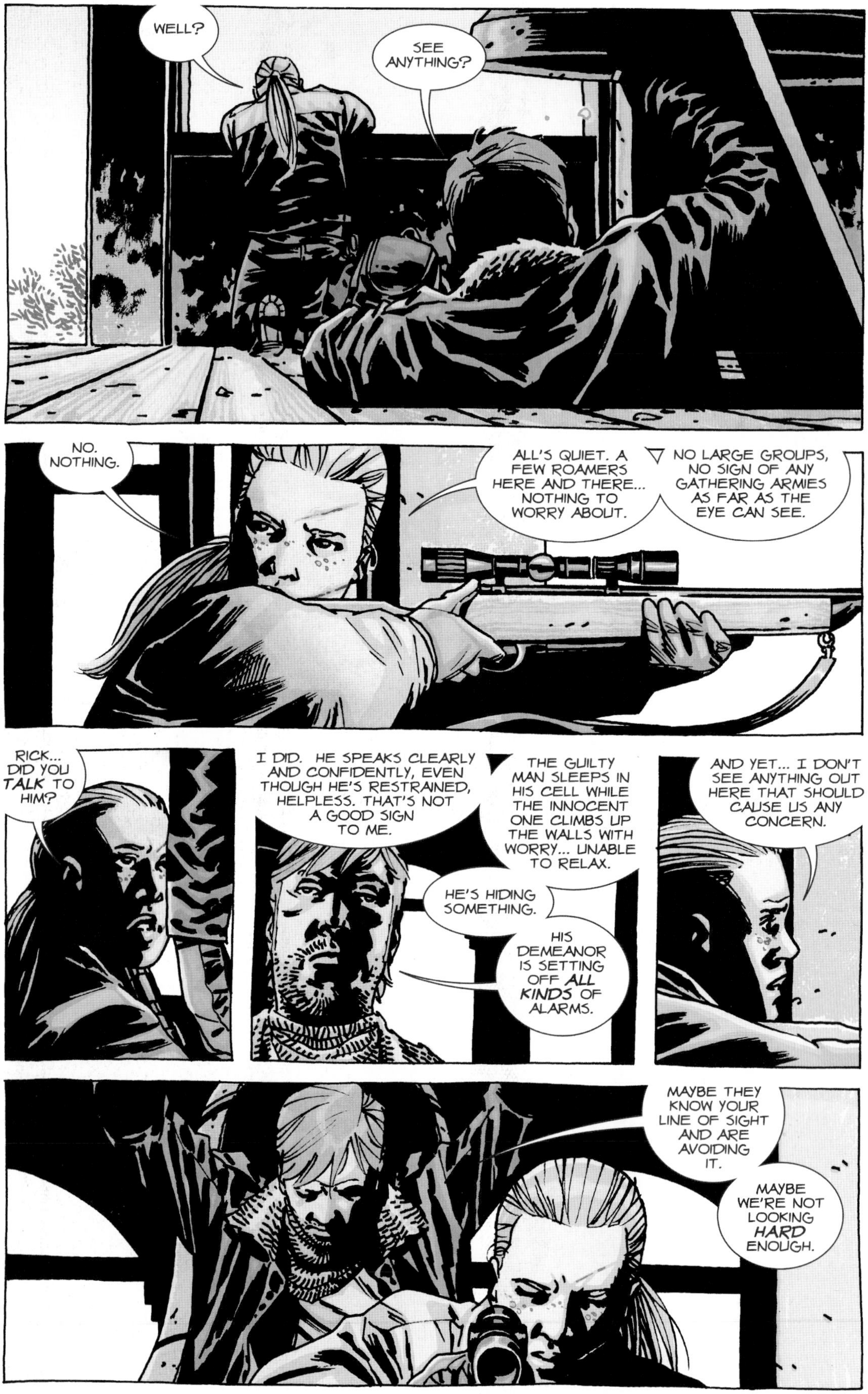
WELL?
SEE ANYTHING?
NO. NOTHING.
ALL'S QUIET. A FEW ROAMERS HERE AND THERE... NOTHING TO WORRY ABOUT.
NO LARGE GROUPS, NO SIGN OF ANY GATHERING ARMIES AS FAR AS THE EYE CAN SEE.
RICK... DID YOU *TALK* TO HIM?
I DID. HE SPEAKS CLEARLY AND CONFIDENTLY, EVEN THOUGH HE'S RESTRAINED, HELPLESS. THAT'S NOT A GOOD SIGN TO ME.
THE GUILTY MAN SLEEPS IN HIS CELL WHILE THE INNOCENT ONE CLIMBS UP THE WALLS WITH WORRY... UNABLE TO RELAX.
HE'S HIDING SOMETHING.
HIS DEMEANOR IS SETTING OFF *ALL KINDS* OF ALARMS.
AND YET... I DON'T SEE ANYTHING OUT HERE THAT SHOULD CAUSE US ANY CONCERN.
MAYBE THEY KNOW YOUR LINE OF SIGHT AND ARE AVOIDING IT.
MAYBE WE'RE NOT LOOKING *HARD* ENOUGH.

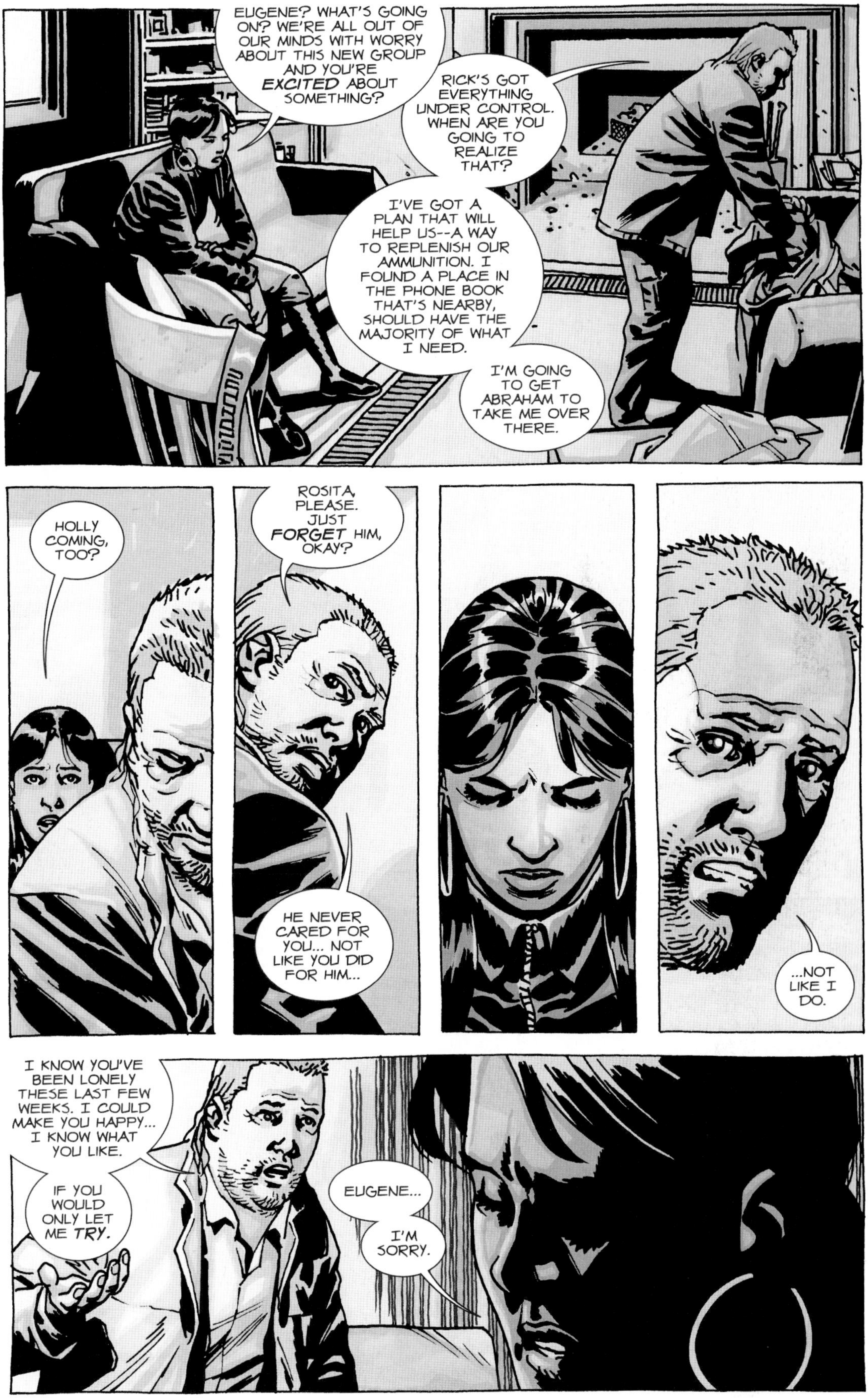
EUGENE? WHAT'S GOING ON? WE'RE ALL OUT OF OUR MINDS WITH WORRY ABOUT THIS NEW GROUP AND YOU'RE *EXCITED* ABOUT SOMETHING?
RICK'S GOT EVERYTHING UNDER CONTROL. WHEN ARE YOU GOING TO REALIZE THAT?
I'VE GOT A PLAN THAT WILL HELP US--A WAY TO REPLENISH OUR AMMUNITION. I FOUND A PLACE IN THE PHONE BOOK THAT'S NEARBY, SHOULD HAVE THE MAJORITY OF WHAT I NEED.
I'M GOING TO GET ABRAHAM TO TAKE ME OVER THERE.
HOLLY COMING, TOO?
ROSITA, PLEASE. JUST *FORGET* HIM, OKAY?
HE NEVER CARED FOR YOU... NOT LIKE YOU DID FOR HIM...
...NOT LIKE I DO.
I KNOW YOU'VE BEEN LONELY THESE LAST FEW WEEKS. I COULD MAKE YOU HAPPY... I KNOW WHAT YOU LIKE.
IF YOU WOULD ONLY LET ME *TRY*.
EUGENE...
I'M SORRY.

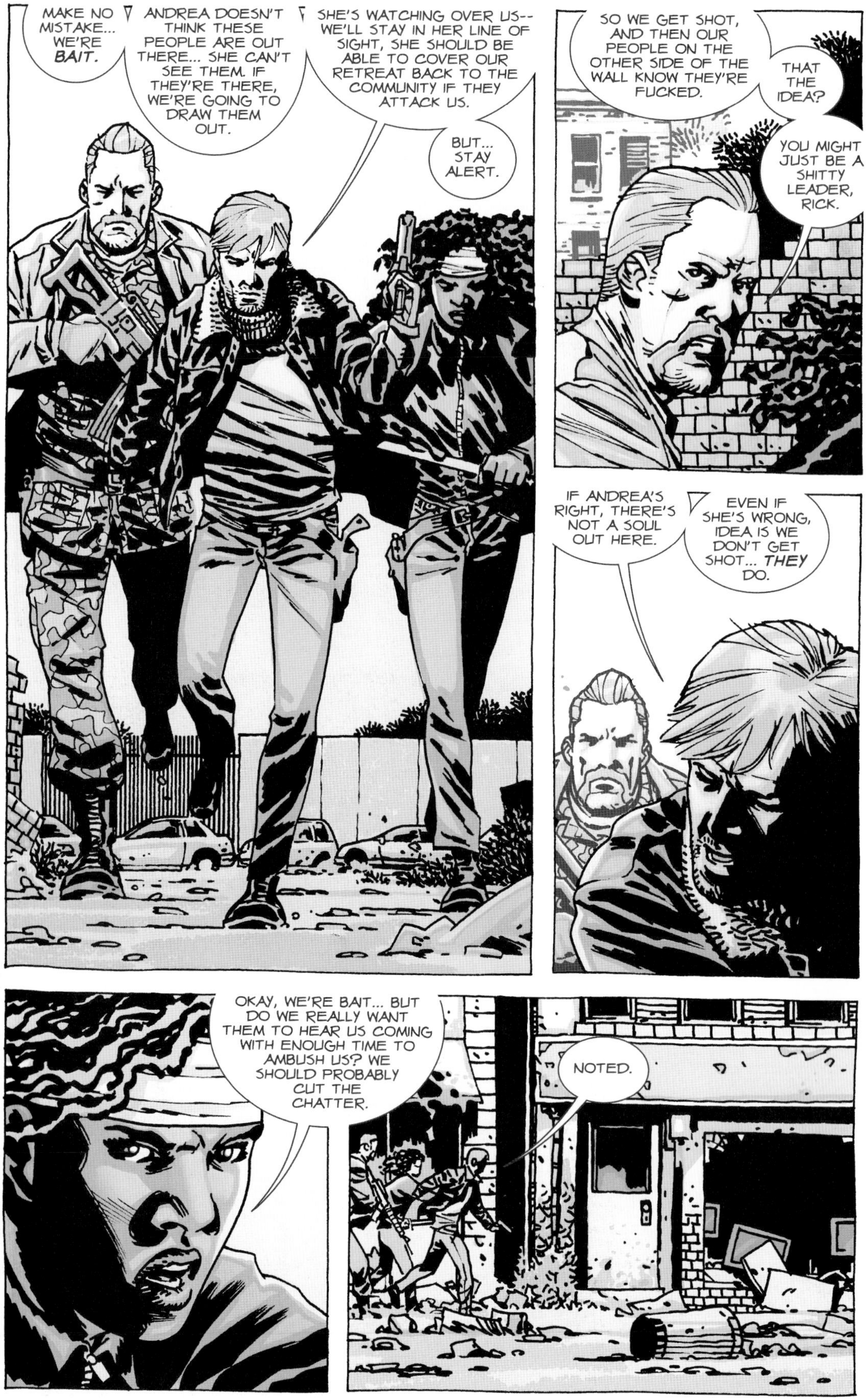
MAKE NO MISTAKE... WE'RE *BAIT.*
ANDREA DOESN'T THINK THESE PEOPLE ARE OUT THERE... SHE CAN'T SEE THEM. IF THEY'RE THERE, WE'RE GOING TO DRAW THEM OUT.
SHE'S WATCHING OVER US-- WE'LL STAY IN HER LINE OF SIGHT, SHE SHOULD BE ABLE TO COVER OUR RETREAT BACK TO THE COMMUNITY IF THEY ATTACK US.
BUT... STAY ALERT.
SO WE GET SHOT, AND THEN OUR PEOPLE ON THE OTHER SIDE OF THE WALL KNOW THEY'RE FUCKED.
THAT THE IDEA?
YOU MIGHT JUST BE A SHITTY LEADER, RICK.
IF ANDREA'S RIGHT, THERE'S NOT A SOUL OUT HERE.
EVEN IF SHE'S WRONG, IDEA IS WE DON'T GET SHOT... *THEY* DO.
OKAY, WE'RE BAIT... BUT DO WE REALLY WANT THEM TO HEAR US COMING WITH ENOUGH TIME TO AMBUSH US? WE SHOULD PROBABLY CUT THE CHATTER.
NOTED.

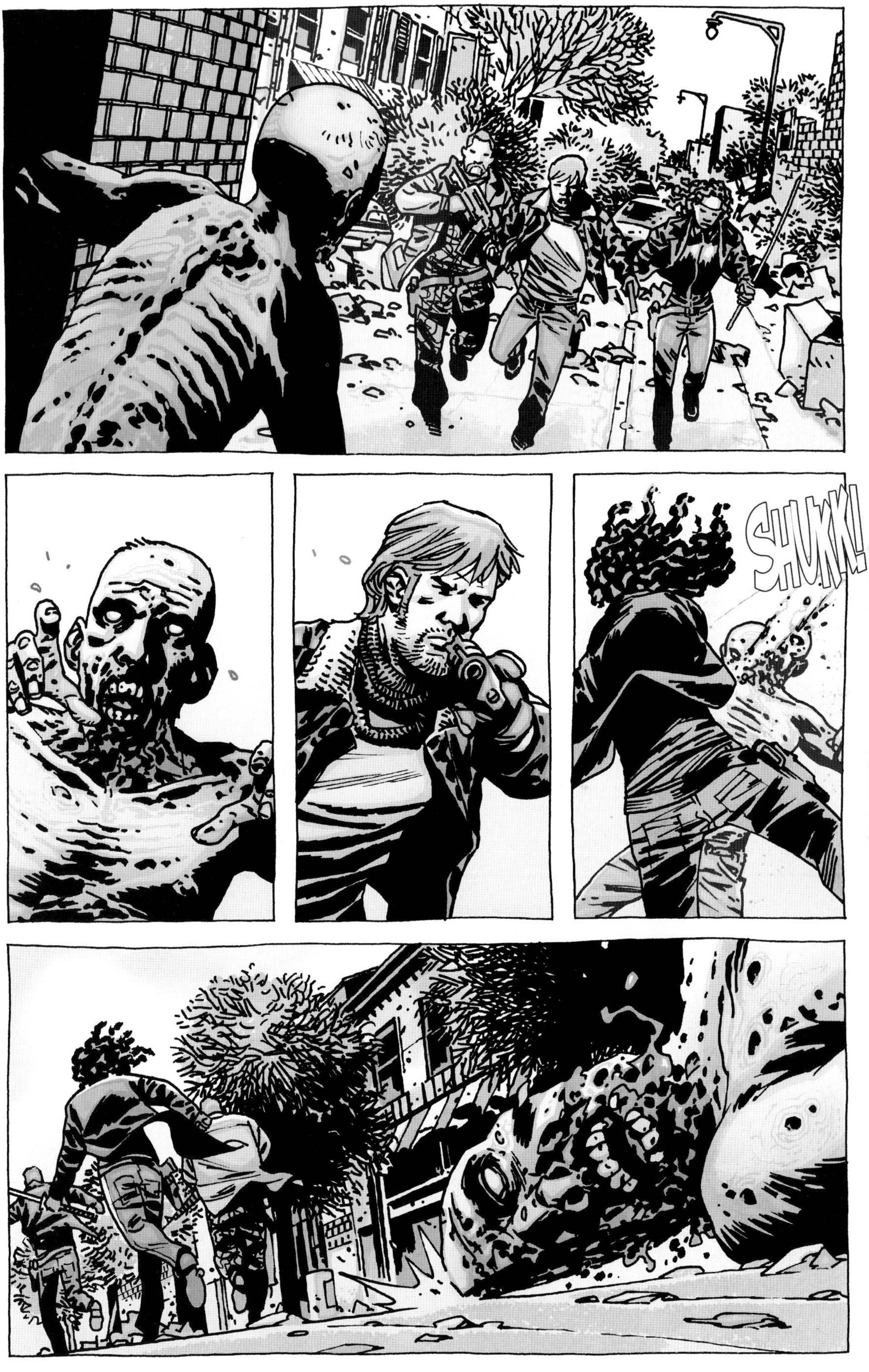
SHUKK!

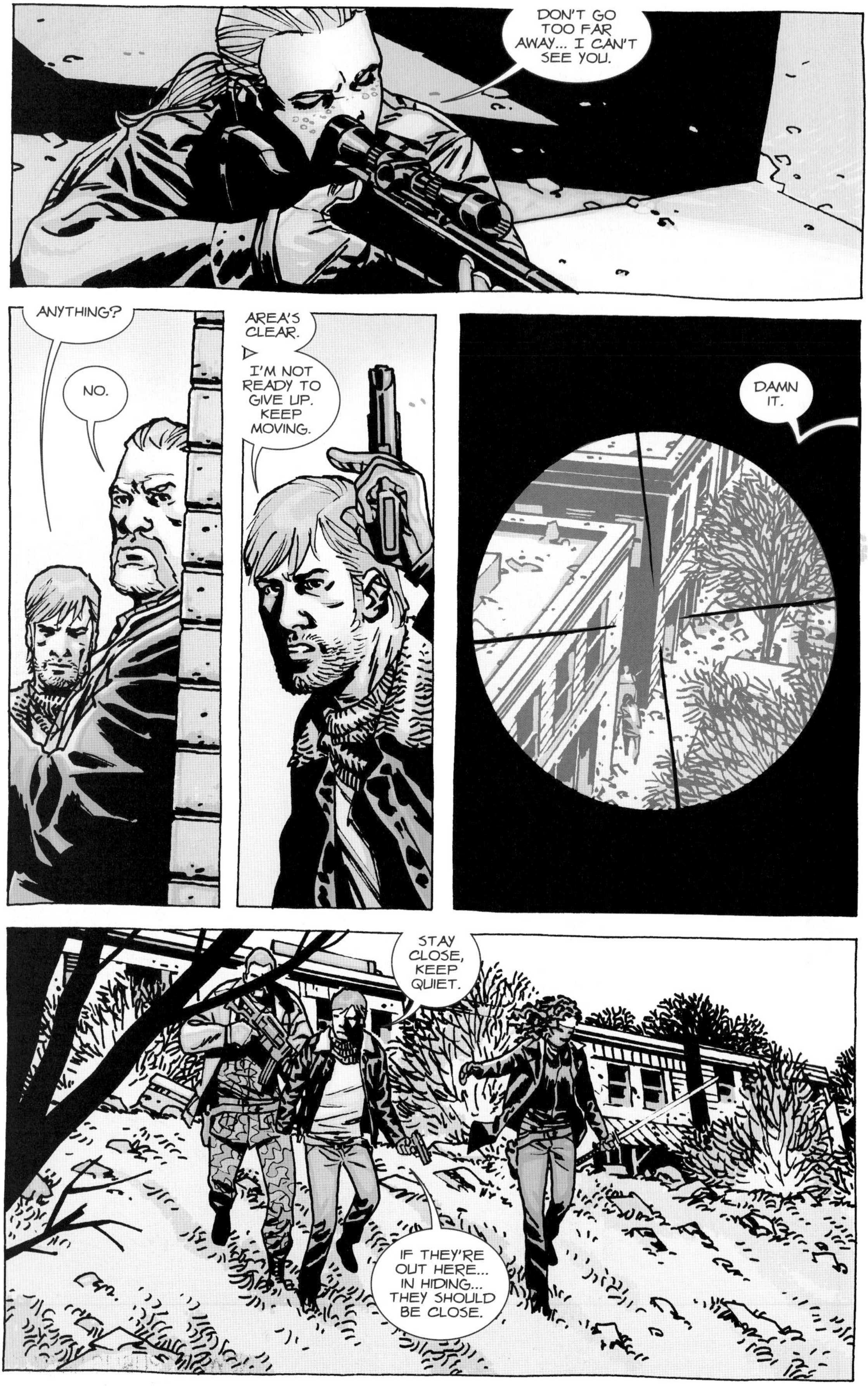

DON'T GO TOO FAR AWAY... I CAN'T SEE YOU.
ANYTHING?
NO.
AREA'S CLEAR.
I'M NOT READY TO GIVE UP. KEEP MOVING.
DAMN IT.
STAY CLOSE, KEEP QUIET.
IF THEY'RE OUT HERE... IN HIDING... THEY SHOULD BE CLOSE.

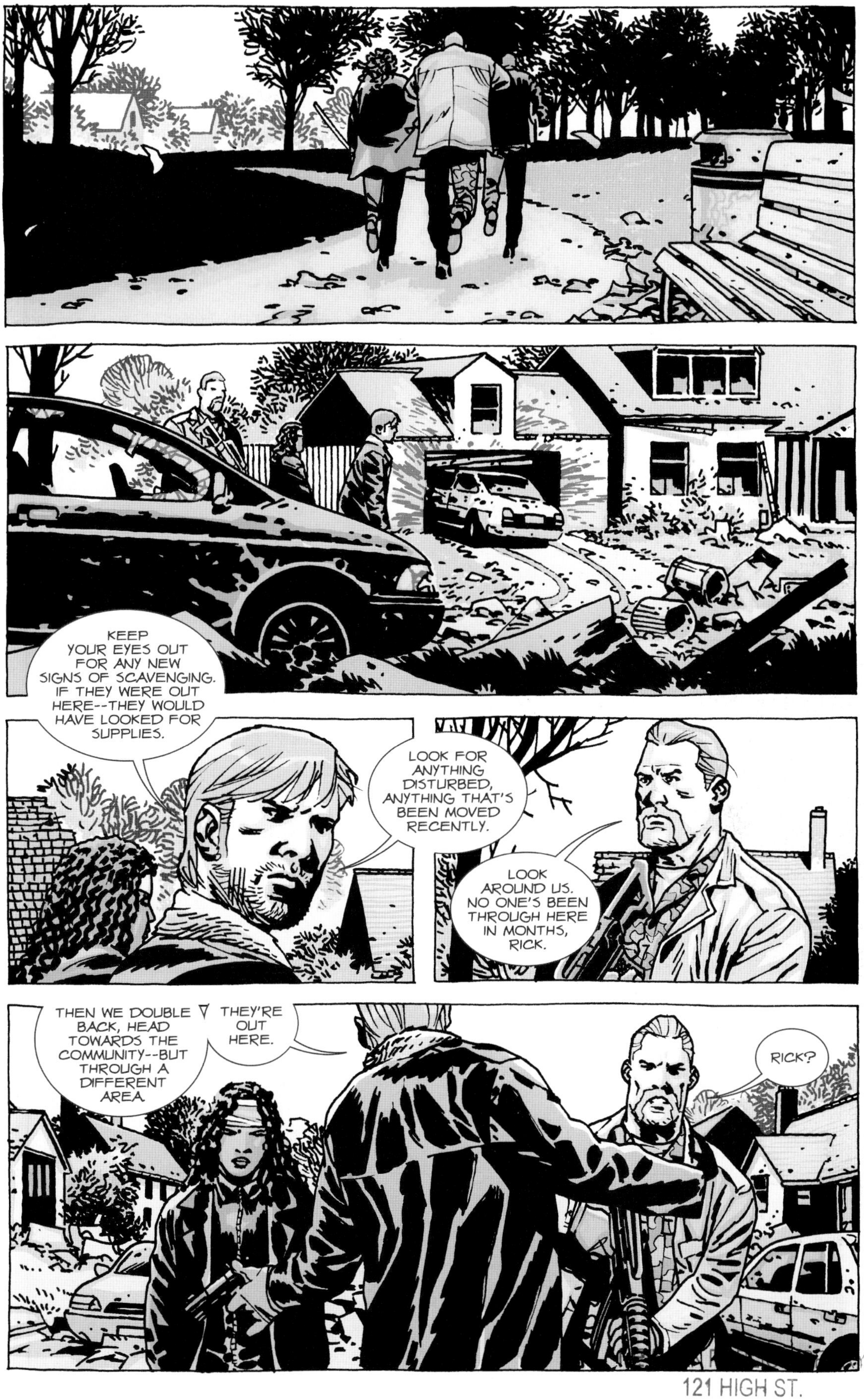
KEEP YOUR EYES OUT FOR ANY NEW SIGNS OF SCAVENGING. IF THEY WERE OUT HERE--THEY WOULD HAVE LOOKED FOR SUPPLIES.
LOOK FOR ANYTHING DISTURBED, ANYTHING THAT'S BEEN MOVED RECENTLY.
LOOK AROUND US. NO ONE'S BEEN THROUGH HERE IN MONTHS, RICK.
THEN WE DOUBLE BACK, HEAD TOWARDS THE COMMUNITY--BUT THROUGH A DIFFERENT AREA.
THEY'RE OUT HERE.
RICK?

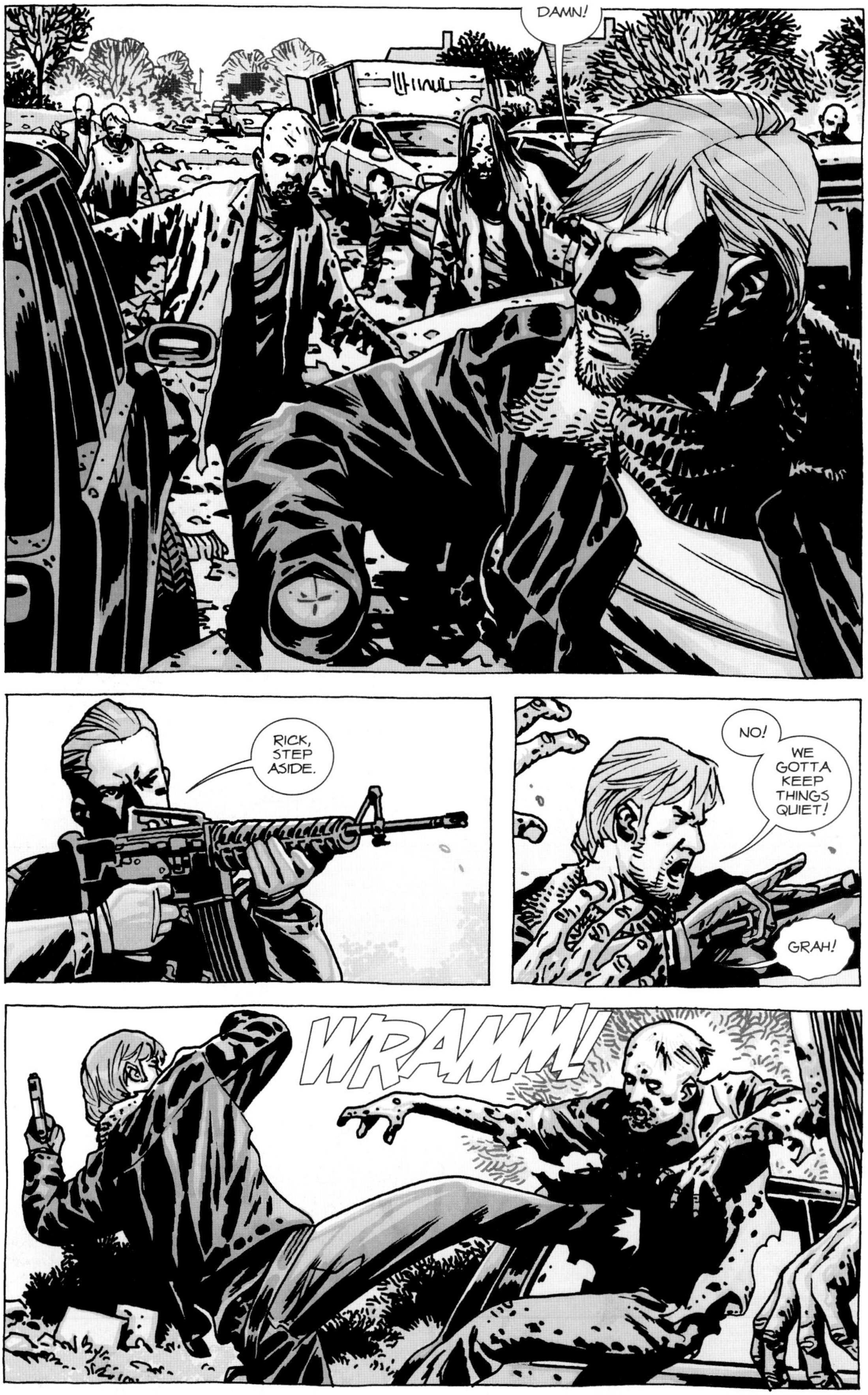
DAMN!
RICK, STEP ASIDE.
NO!
WE GOTTA KEEP THINGS QUIET!
GRAH!
WRAMM!

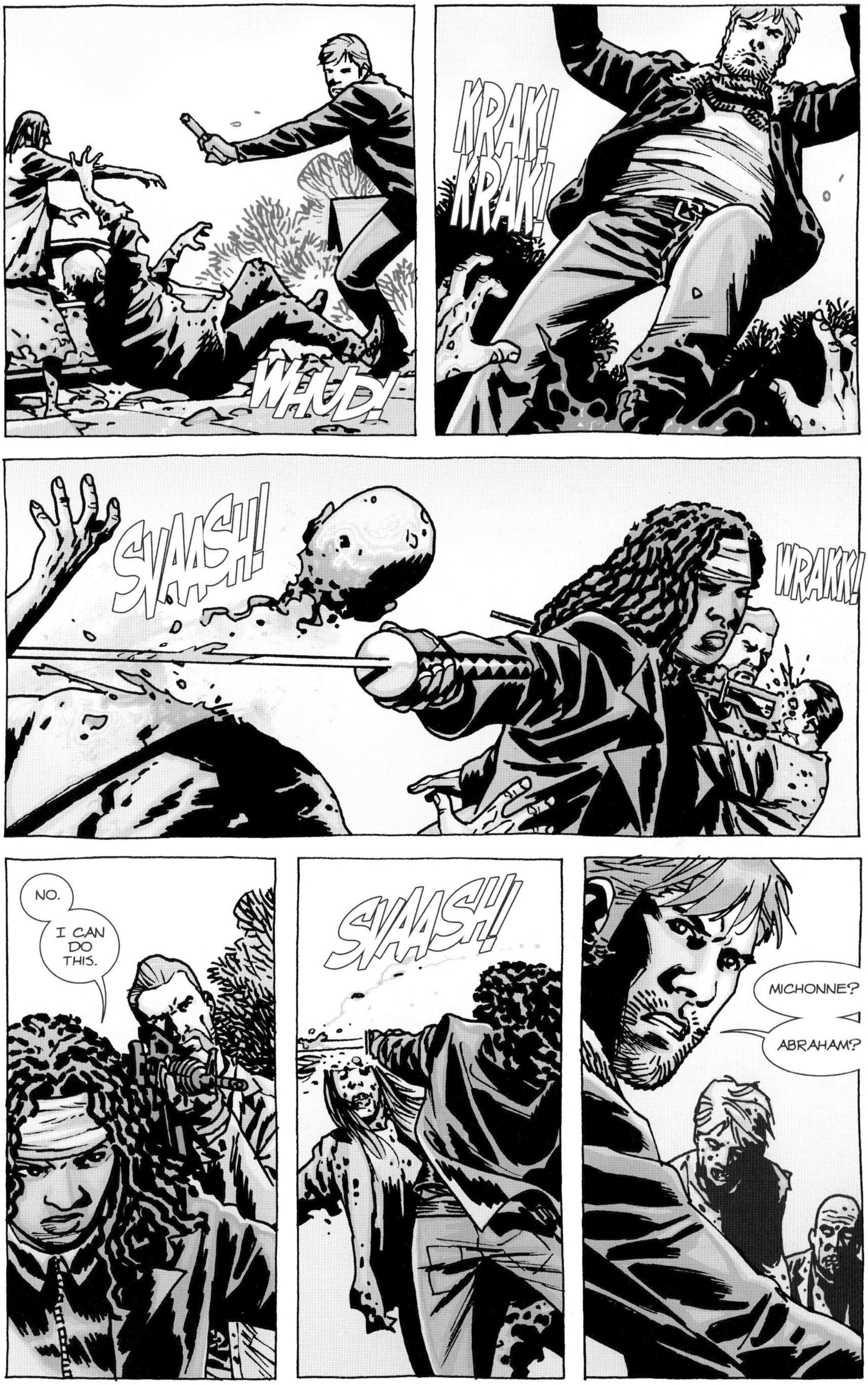
WHUD!
KRAK!
KRAK!
SVAASH!
WRAKK!
NO.
I CAN DO THIS.
SVAASH!
MICHONNE?
ABRAHAM?

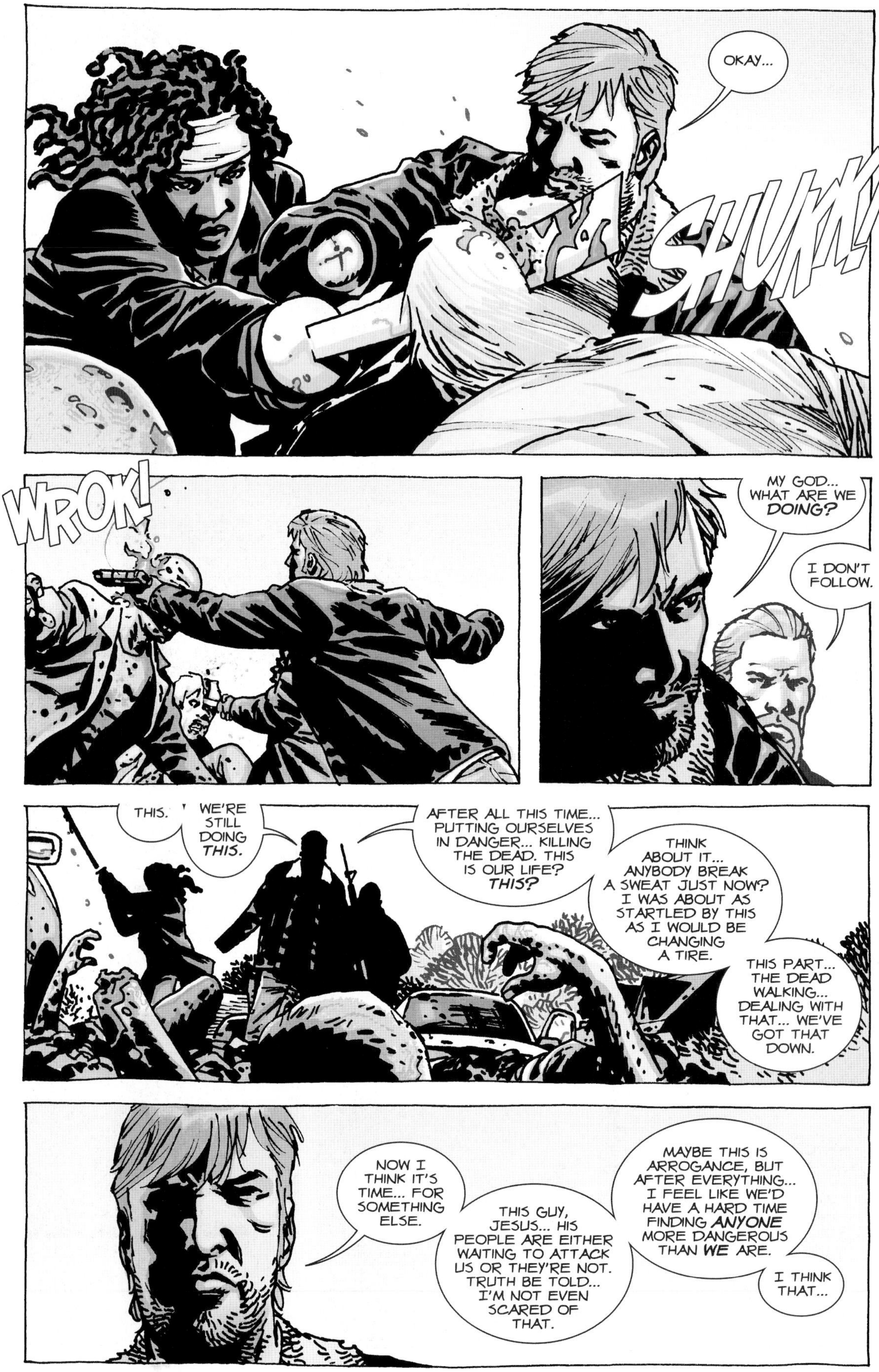
OKAY...
SHUKK!
WROK!
MY GOD... WHAT ARE WE DOING?
I DON'T FOLLOW.
THIS.
WE'RE STILL DOING THIS.
AFTER ALL THIS TIME... PUTTING OURSELVES IN DANGER... KILLING THE DEAD. THIS IS OUR LIFE? THIS?
THINK ABOUT IT... ANYBODY BREAK A SWEAT JUST NOW? I WAS ABOUT AS STARTLED BY THIS AS I WOULD BE CHANGING A TIRE.
THIS PART... THE DEAD WALKING... DEALING WITH THAT... WE'VE GOT THAT DOWN.
NOW I THINK IT'S TIME... FOR SOMETHING ELSE.
THIS GUY, JESUS... HIS PEOPLE ARE EITHER WAITING TO ATTACK US OR THEY'RE NOT. TRUTH BE TOLD... I'M NOT EVEN SCARED OF THAT.
MAYBE THIS IS ARROGANCE, BUT AFTER EVERYTHING... I FEEL LIKE WE'D HAVE A HARD TIME FINDING ANYONE MORE DANGEROUS THAN WE ARE.
I THINK THAT...

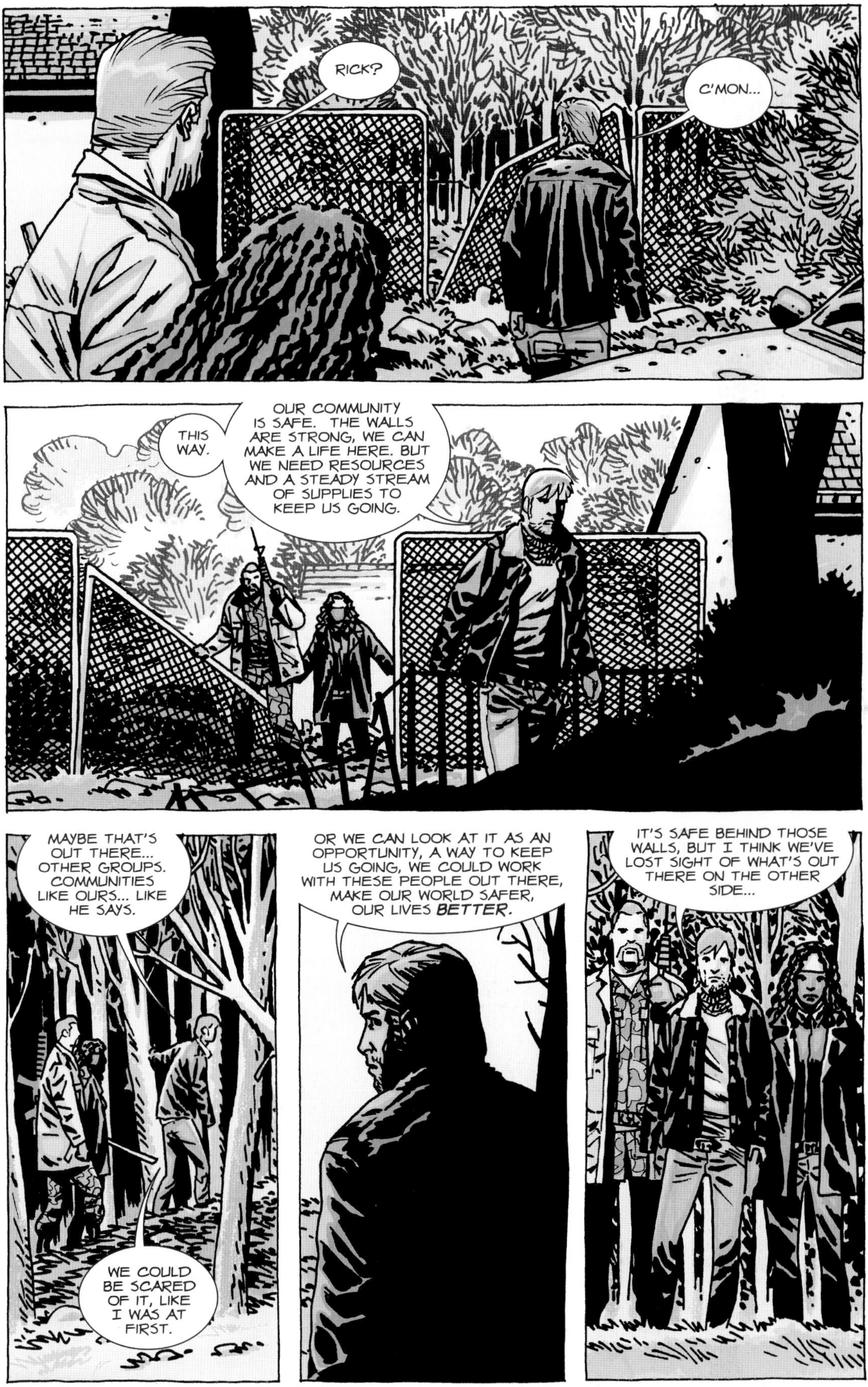
RICK?
C'MON...
THIS WAY.
OUR COMMUNITY IS SAFE. THE WALLS ARE STRONG, WE CAN MAKE A LIFE HERE. BUT WE NEED RESOURCES AND A STEADY STREAM OF SUPPLIES TO KEEP US GOING.
MAYBE THAT'S OUT THERE... OTHER GROUPS. COMMUNITIES LIKE OURS... LIKE HE SAYS.
WE COULD BE SCARED OF IT, LIKE I WAS AT FIRST.
OR WE CAN LOOK AT IT AS AN OPPORTUNITY, A WAY TO KEEP US GOING, WE COULD WORK WITH THESE PEOPLE OUT THERE, MAKE OUR WORLD SAFER, OUR LIVES BETTER.
IT'S SAFE BEHIND THOSE WALLS, BUT I THINK WE'VE LOST SIGHT OF WHAT'S OUT THERE ON THE OTHER SIDE...

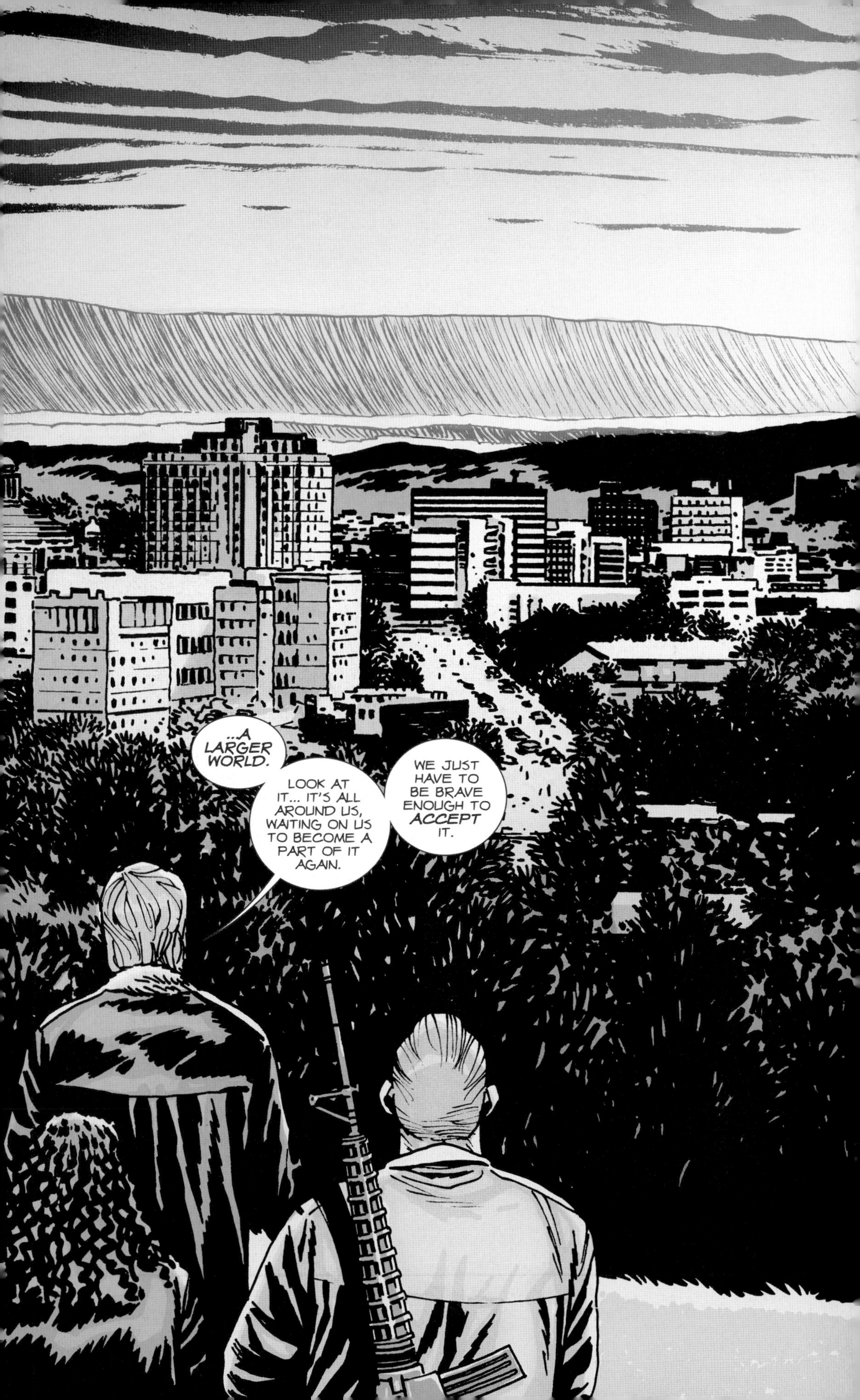
...A LARGER WORLD.
LOOK AT IT... IT'S ALL AROUND US, WAITING ON US TO BECOME A PART OF IT AGAIN.
WE JUST HAVE TO BE BRAVE ENOUGH TO ACCEPT IT.

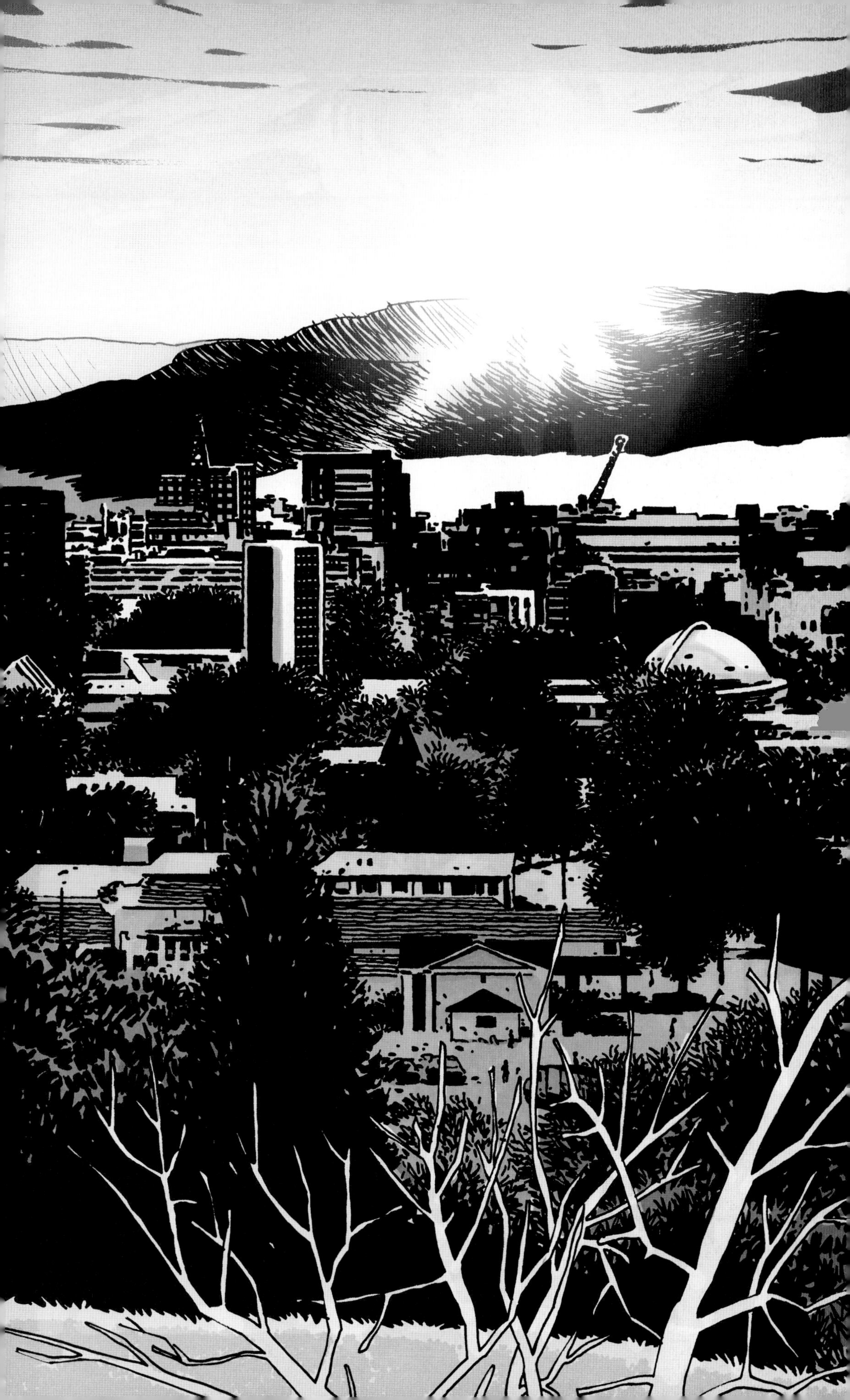

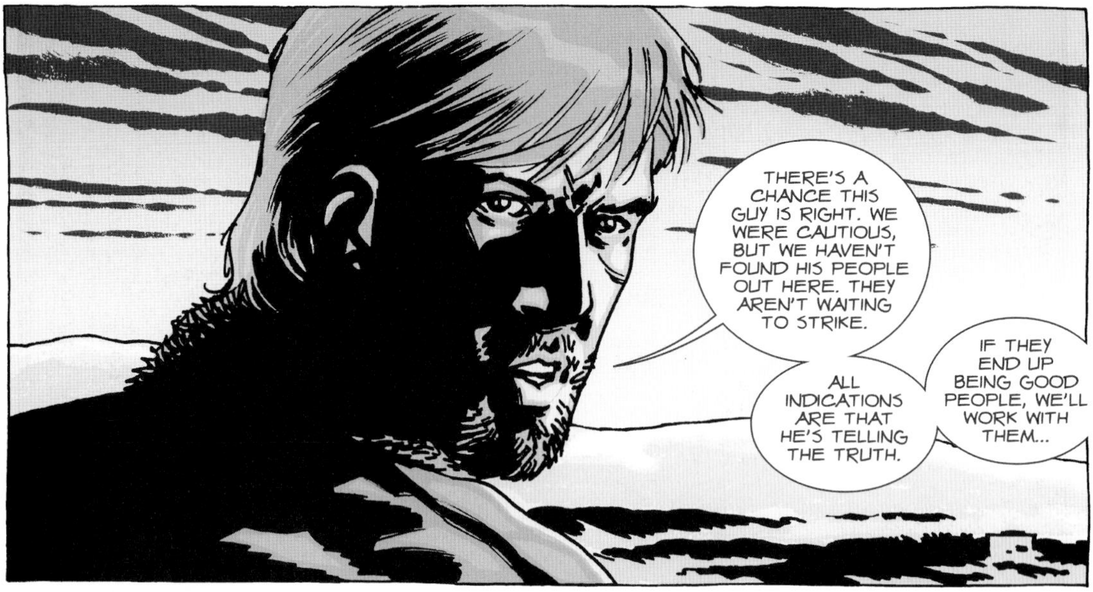
THERE'S A CHANCE THIS GUY IS RIGHT. WE WERE CAUTIOUS, BUT WE HAVEN'T FOUND HIS PEOPLE OUT HERE. THEY AREN'T WAITING TO STRIKE.
ALL INDICATIONS ARE THAT HE'S TELLING THE TRUTH.
IF THEY END UP BEING GOOD PEOPLE, WE'LL WORK WITH THEM...

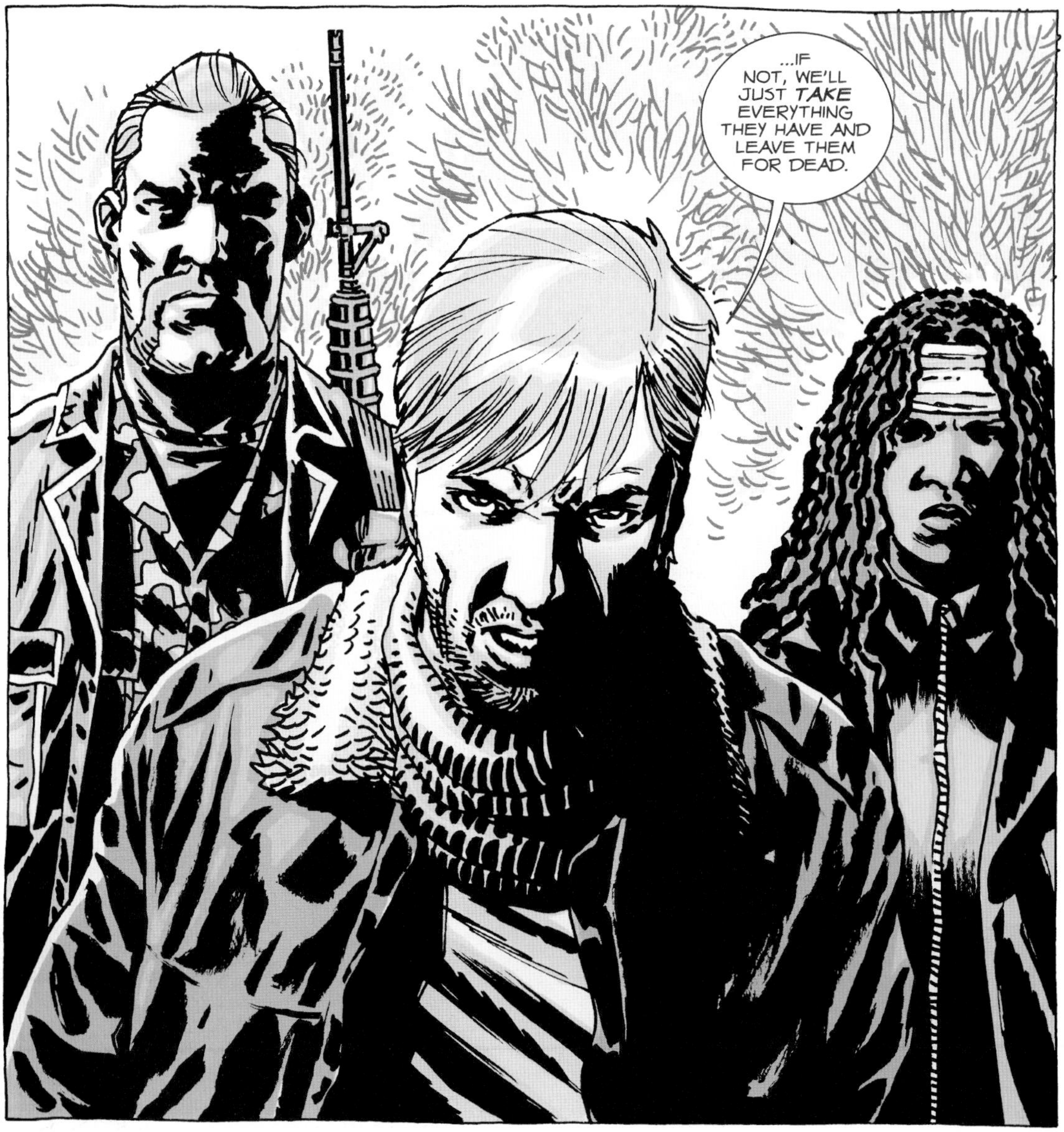
...IF NOT, WE'LL JUST TAKE EVERYTHING THEY HAVE AND LEAVE THEM FOR DEAD.

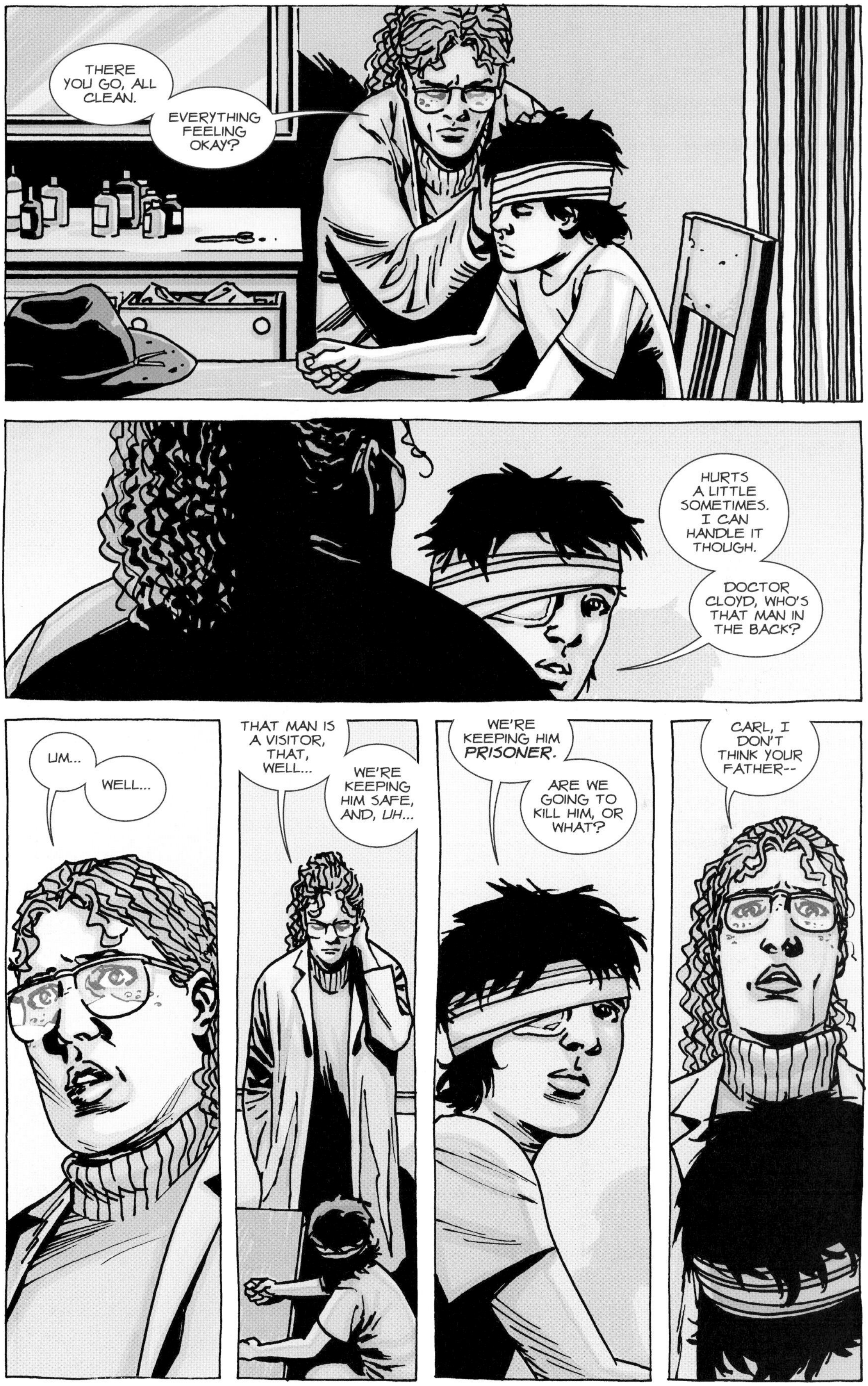

THERE YOU GO, ALL CLEAN.
EVERYTHING FEELING OKAY?
HURTS A LITTLE SOMETIMES. I CAN HANDLE IT THOUGH.
DOCTOR CLOYD, WHO'S THAT MAN IN THE BACK?
UM...
WELL...
THAT MAN IS A VISITOR, THAT, WELL...
WE'RE KEEPING HIM SAFE, AND, UH...
WE'RE KEEPING HIM PRISONER.
ARE WE GOING TO KILL HIM, OR WHAT?
CARL, I DON'T THINK YOUR FATHER--

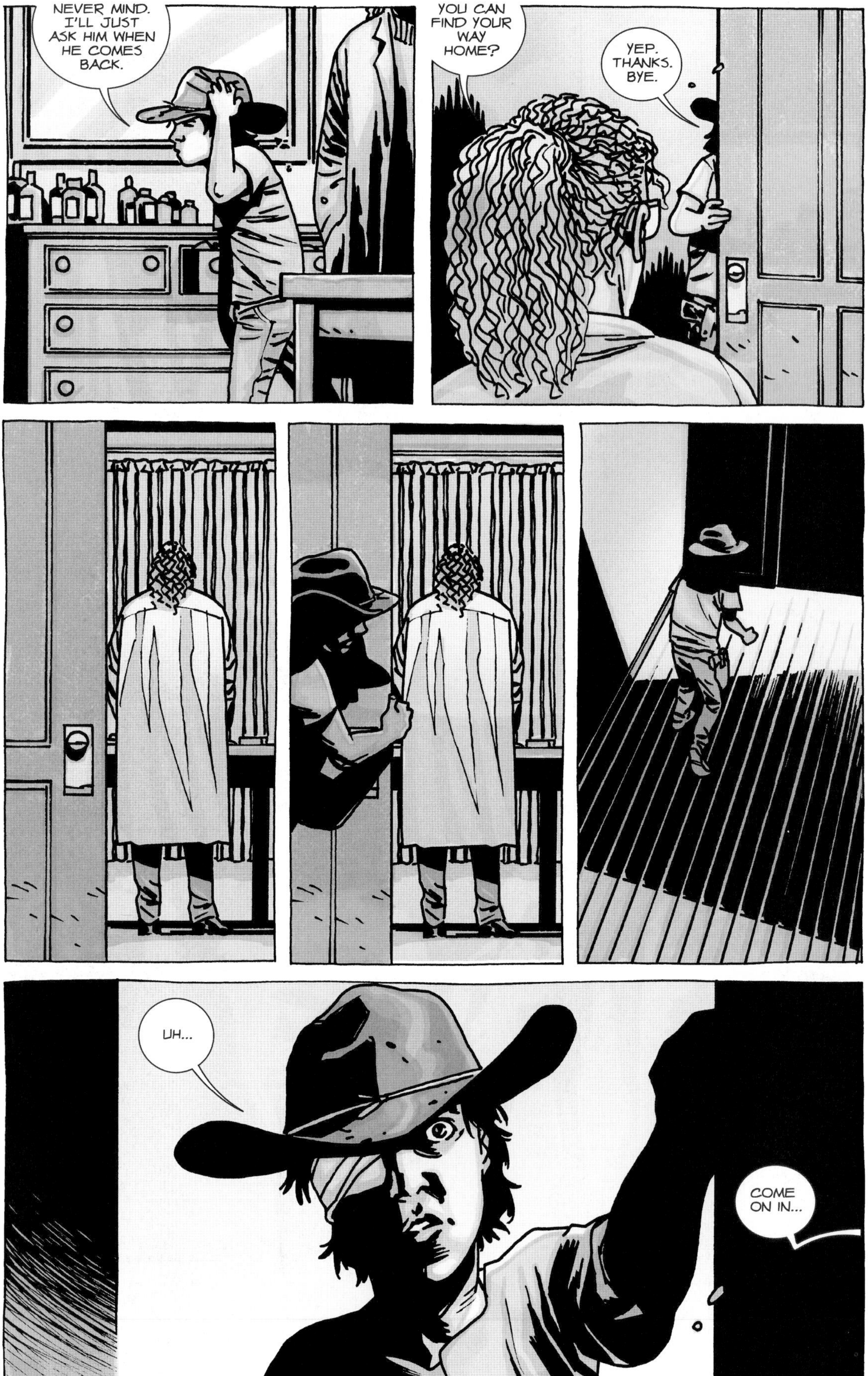
NEVER MIND. I'LL JUST ASK HIM WHEN HE COMES BACK.
YOU CAN FIND YOUR WAY HOME?
YEP. THANKS. BYE.
UH...
COME ON IN...

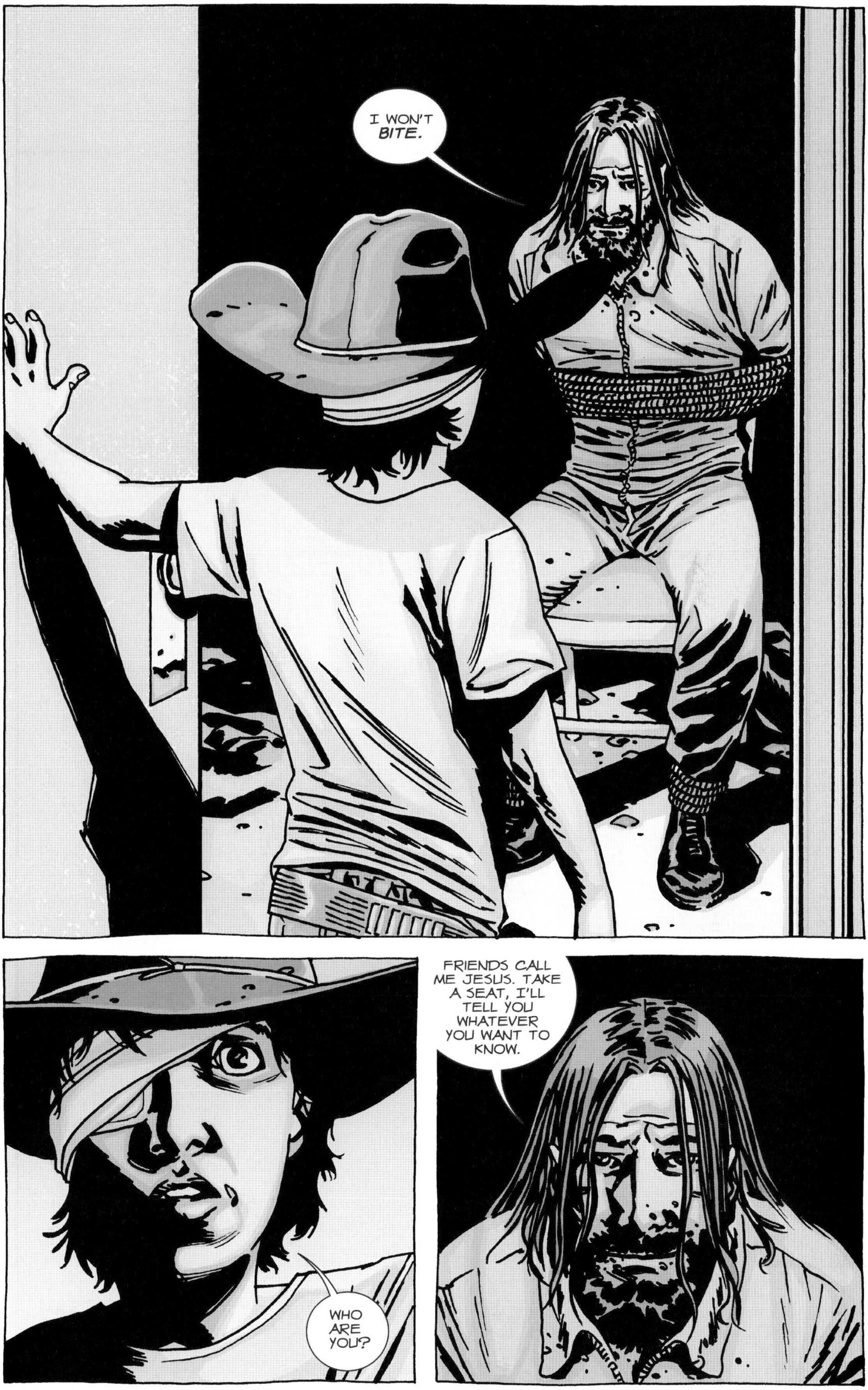
I WON'T *BITE.*
WHO ARE YOU?
FRIENDS CALL ME JESUS. TAKE A SEAT, I'LL TELL YOU WHATEVER YOU WANT TO KNOW.

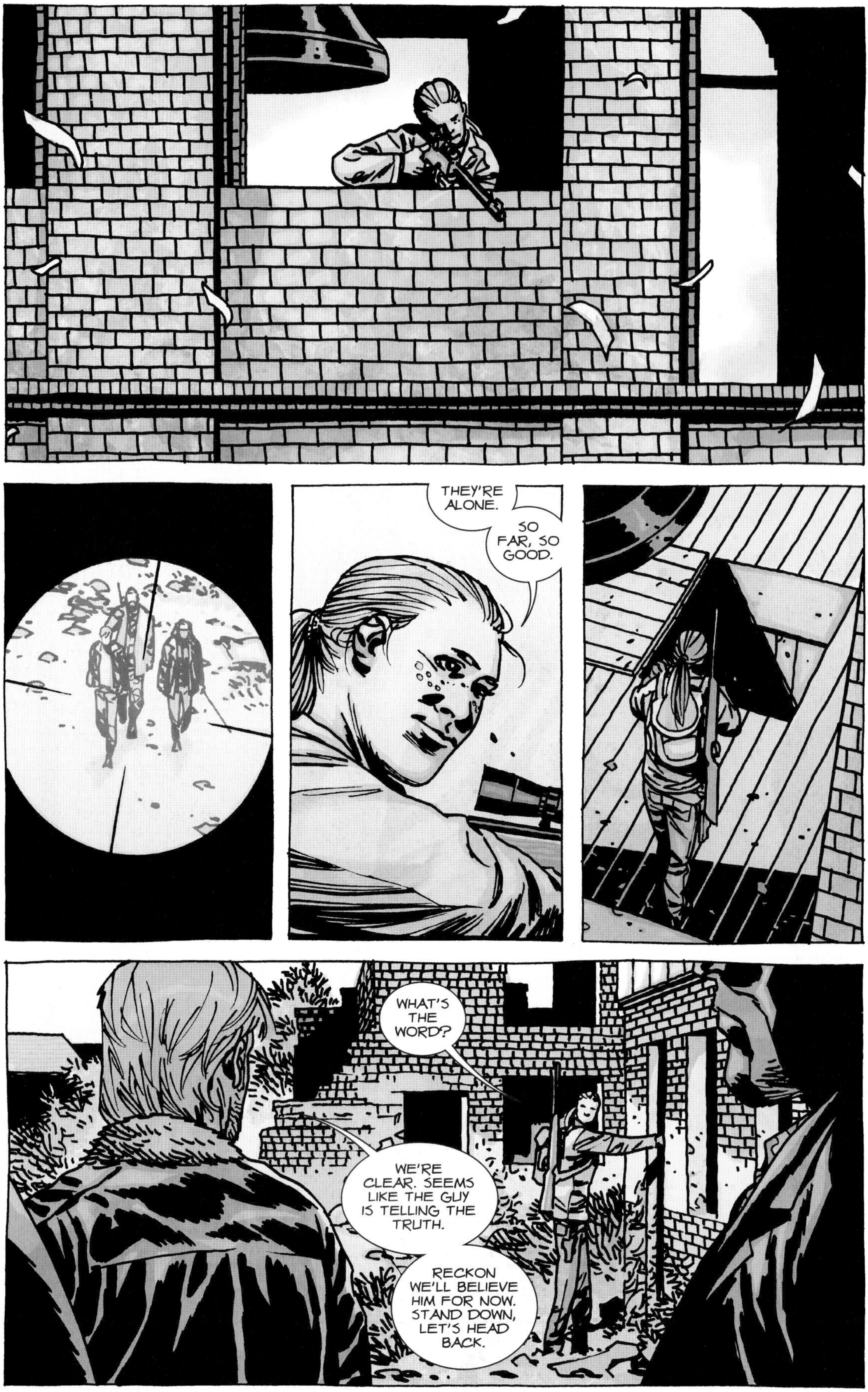
THEY'RE ALONE.
SO FAR, SO GOOD.
WHAT'S THE WORD?
WE'RE CLEAR. SEEMS LIKE THE GUY IS TELLING THE TRUTH.
RECKON WE'LL BELIEVE HIM FOR NOW. STAND DOWN, LET'S HEAD BACK.

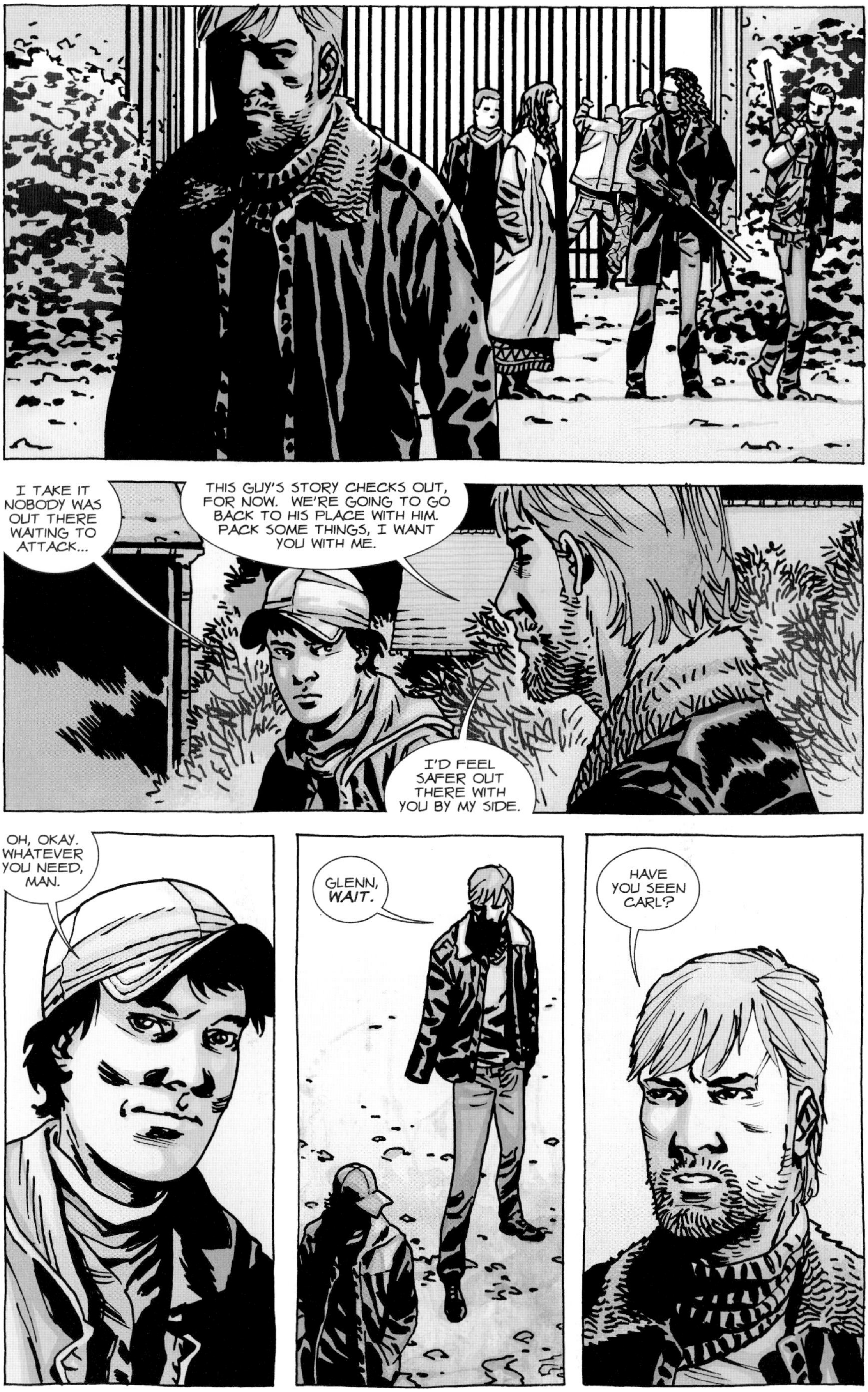
I TAKE IT NOBODY WAS OUT THERE WAITING TO ATTACK...
THIS GUY'S STORY CHECKS OUT, FOR NOW. WE'RE GOING TO GO BACK TO HIS PLACE WITH HIM. PACK SOME THINGS, I WANT YOU WITH ME.
I'D FEEL SAFER OUT THERE WITH YOU BY MY SIDE.
OH, OKAY. WHATEVER YOU NEED, MAN.
GLENN, *WAIT.*
HAVE YOU SEEN CARL?

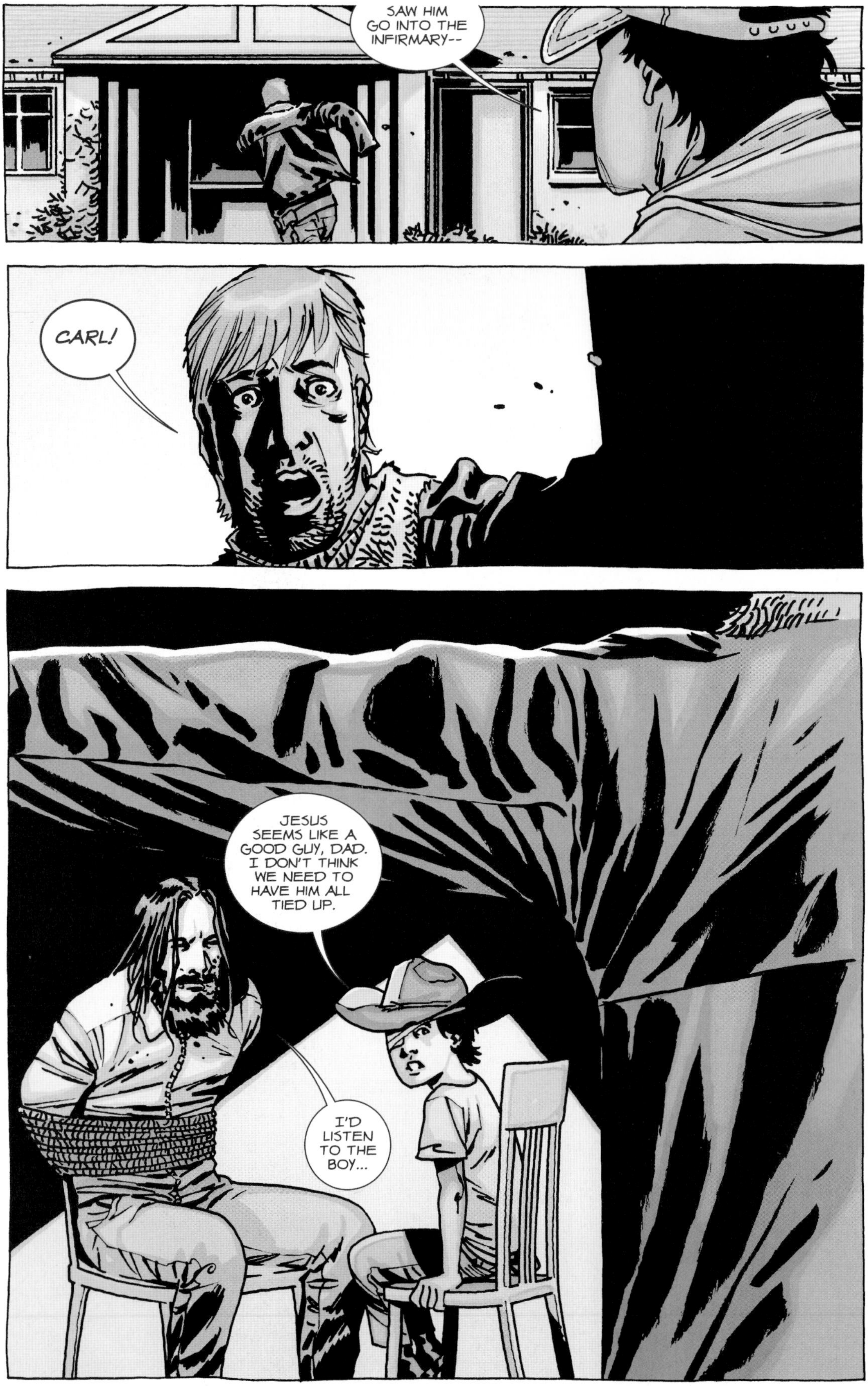
SAW HIM GO INTO THE INFIRMARY--
CARL!
JESUS SEEMS LIKE A GOOD GUY, DAD. I DON'T THINK WE NEED TO HAVE HIM ALL TIED UP.
I'D LISTEN TO THE BOY...

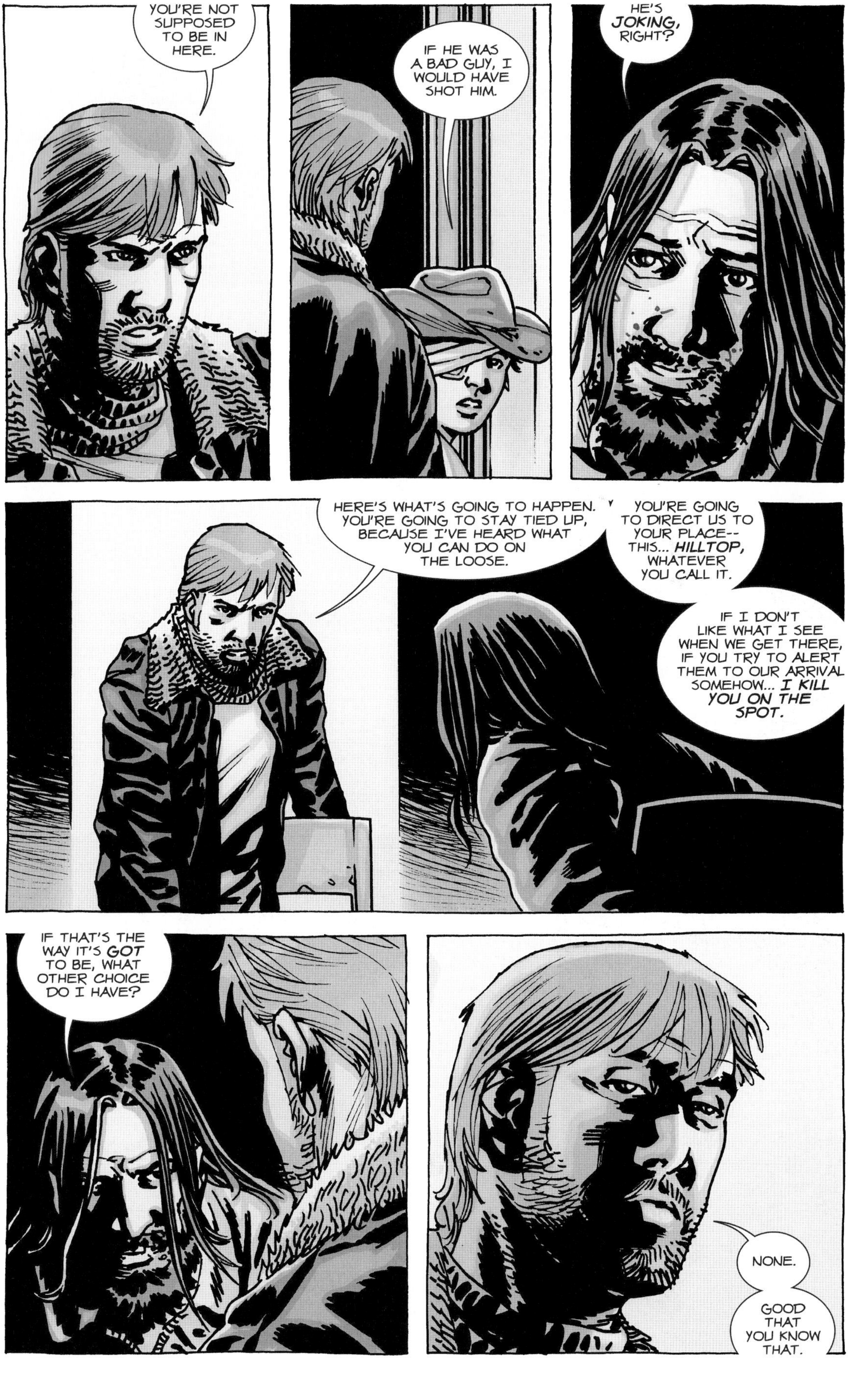
YOU'RE NOT SUPPOSED TO BE IN HERE.
IF HE WAS A BAD GUY, I WOULD HAVE SHOT HIM.
HE'S *JOKING,* RIGHT?
HERE'S WHAT'S GOING TO HAPPEN. YOU'RE GOING TO STAY TIED UP, BECAUSE I'VE HEARD WHAT YOU CAN DO ON THE LOOSE.
YOU'RE GOING TO DIRECT US TO YOUR PLACE-- THIS... *HILLTOP,* WHATEVER YOU CALL IT.
IF I DON'T LIKE WHAT I SEE WHEN WE GET THERE, IF YOU TRY TO ALERT THEM TO OUR ARRIVAL SOMEHOW... ***I KILL YOU ON THE SPOT.***
IF THAT'S THE WAY IT'S *GOT* TO BE, WHAT OTHER CHOICE DO I HAVE?
NONE.
GOOD THAT YOU KNOW THAT.

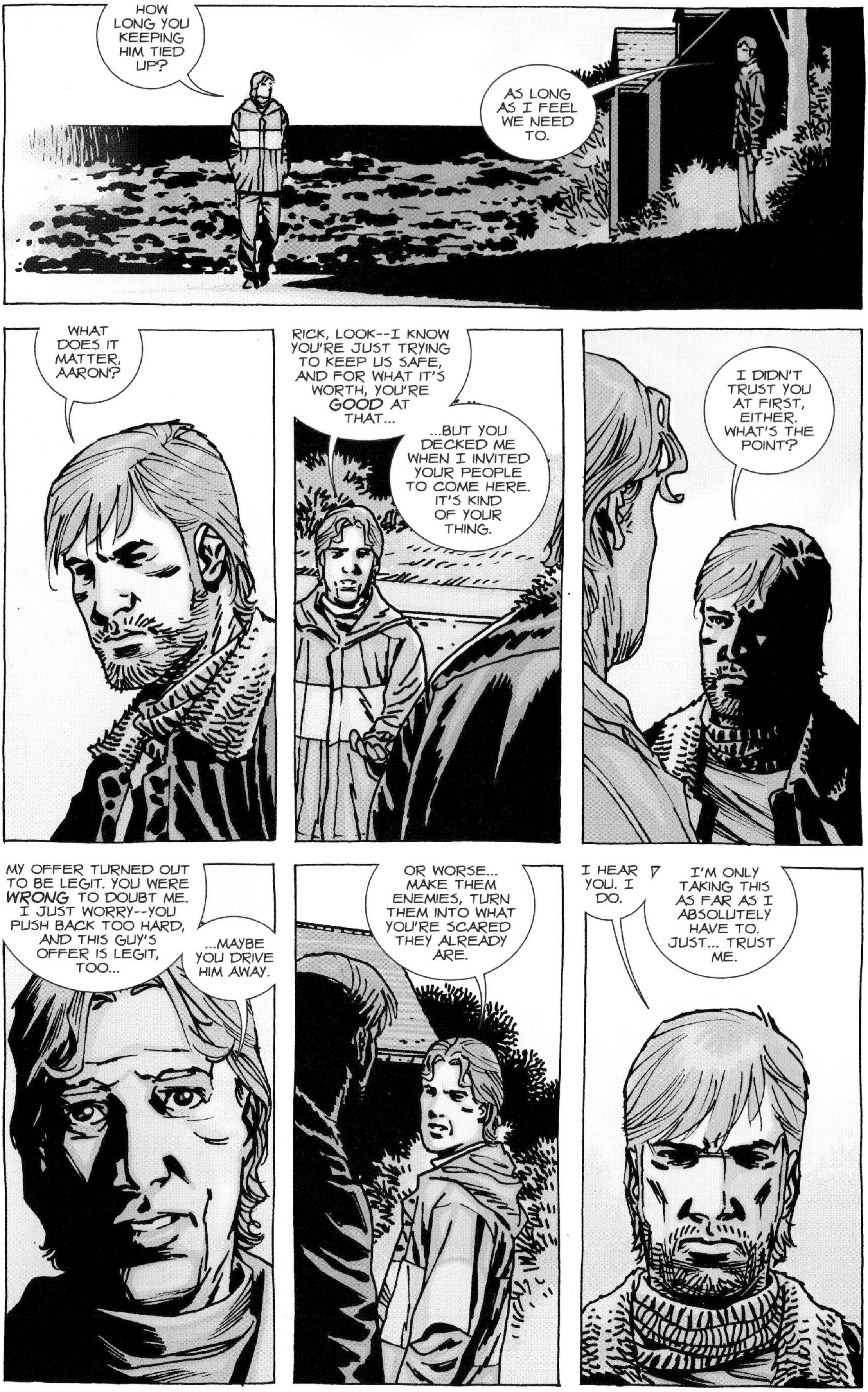
HOW LONG YOU KEEPING HIM TIED UP?
AS LONG AS I FEEL WE NEED TO.
WHAT DOES IT MATTER, AARON?
RICK, LOOK--I KNOW YOU'RE JUST TRYING TO KEEP US SAFE, AND FOR WHAT IT'S WORTH, YOU'RE GOOD AT THAT...
...BUT YOU DECKED ME WHEN I INVITED YOUR PEOPLE TO COME HERE. IT'S KIND OF YOUR THING.
I DIDN'T TRUST YOU AT FIRST, EITHER. WHAT'S THE POINT?
MY OFFER TURNED OUT TO BE LEGIT. YOU WERE WRONG TO DOUBT ME. I JUST WORRY--YOU PUSH BACK TOO HARD, AND THIS GUY'S OFFER IS LEGIT, TOO...
...MAYBE YOU DRIVE HIM AWAY.
OR WORSE... MAKE THEM ENEMIES, TURN THEM INTO WHAT YOU'RE SCARED THEY ALREADY ARE.
I HEAR YOU. I DO.
I'M ONLY TAKING THIS AS FAR AS I ABSOLUTELY HAVE TO. JUST... TRUST ME.

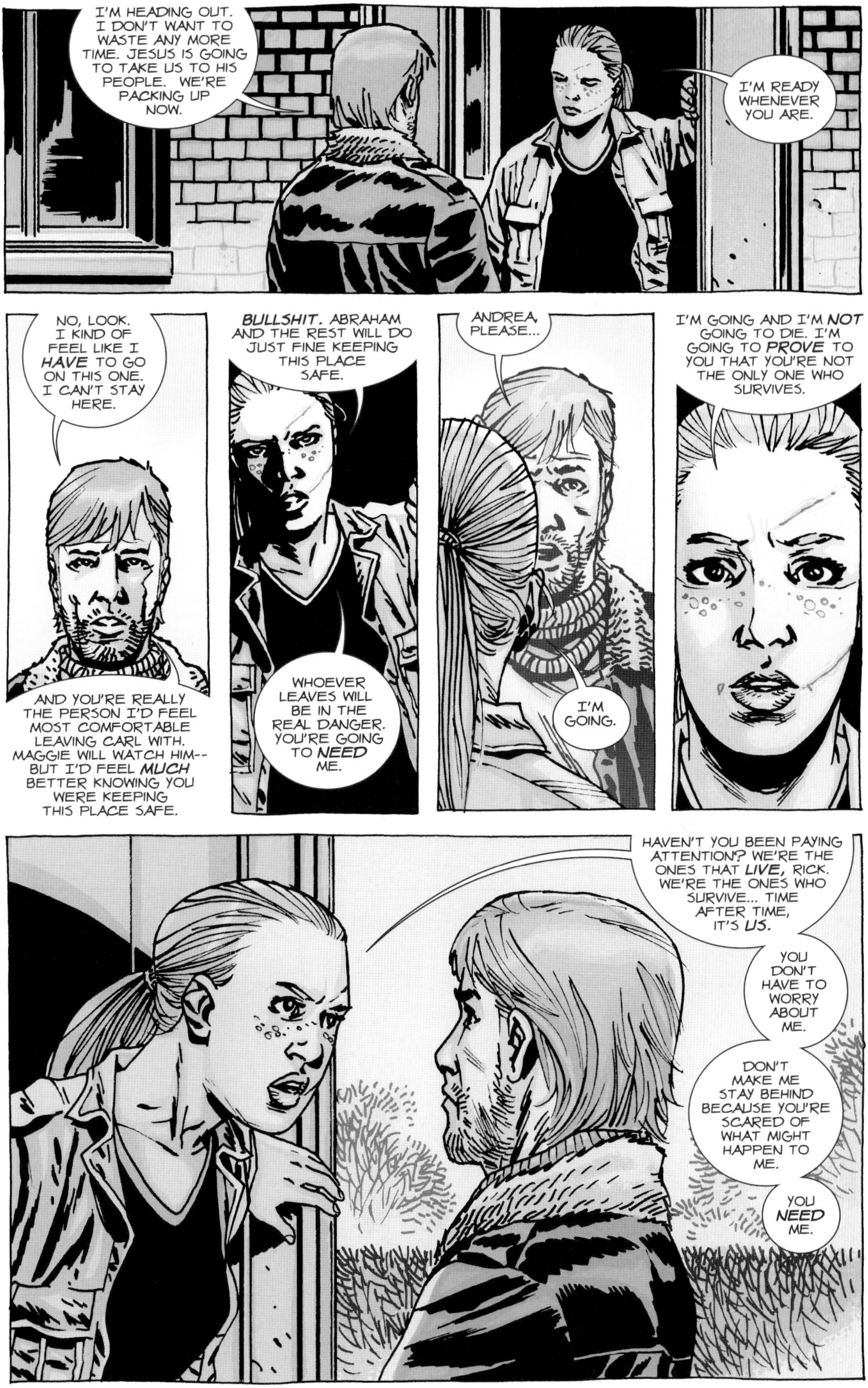

I'M HEADING OUT. I DON'T WANT TO WASTE ANY MORE TIME. JESUS IS GOING TO TAKE US TO HIS PEOPLE. WE'RE PACKING UP NOW.
I'M READY WHENEVER YOU ARE.
NO, LOOK. I KIND OF FEEL LIKE I HAVE TO GO ON THIS ONE. I CAN'T STAY HERE.
AND YOU'RE REALLY THE PERSON I'D FEEL MOST COMFORTABLE LEAVING CARL WITH. MAGGIE WILL WATCH HIM-- BUT I'D FEEL MUCH BETTER KNOWING YOU WERE KEEPING THIS PLACE SAFE.
BULLSHIT. ABRAHAM AND THE REST WILL DO JUST FINE KEEPING THIS PLACE SAFE.
WHOEVER LEAVES WILL BE IN THE REAL DANGER. YOU'RE GOING TO NEED ME.
ANDREA, PLEASE...
I'M GOING.
I'M GOING AND I'M NOT GOING TO DIE. I'M GOING TO PROVE TO YOU THAT YOU'RE NOT THE ONLY ONE WHO SURVIVES.
HAVEN'T YOU BEEN PAYING ATTENTION? WE'RE THE ONES THAT LIVE, RICK. WE'RE THE ONES WHO SURVIVE... TIME AFTER TIME, IT'S US.
YOU DON'T HAVE TO WORRY ABOUT ME.
DON'T MAKE ME STAY BEHIND BECAUSE YOU'RE SCARED OF WHAT MIGHT HAPPEN TO ME.
YOU NEED ME.

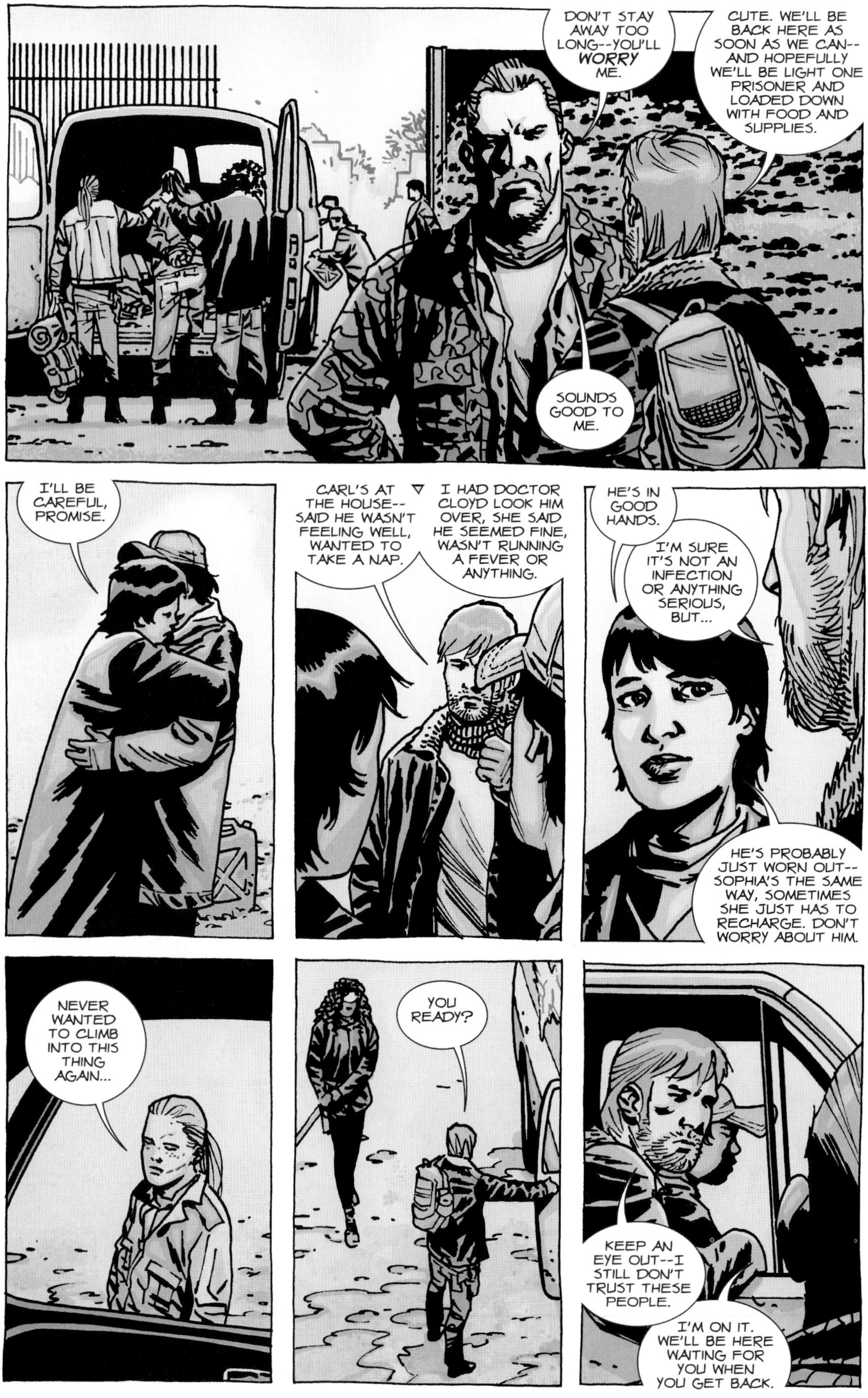
DON'T STAY AWAY TOO LONG--YOU'LL WORRY ME.
CUTE. WE'LL BE BACK HERE AS SOON AS WE CAN--AND HOPEFULLY WE'LL BE LIGHT ONE PRISONER AND LOADED DOWN WITH FOOD AND SUPPLIES.
SOUNDS GOOD TO ME.
I'LL BE CAREFUL, PROMISE.
CARL'S AT THE HOUSE--SAID HE WASN'T FEELING WELL, WANTED TO TAKE A NAP.
I HAD DOCTOR CLOYD LOOK HIM OVER, SHE SAID HE SEEMED FINE, WASN'T RUNNING A FEVER OR ANYTHING.
HE'S IN GOOD HANDS.
I'M SURE IT'S NOT AN INFECTION OR ANYTHING SERIOUS, BUT...
HE'S PROBABLY JUST WORN OUT--SOPHIA'S THE SAME WAY, SOMETIMES SHE JUST HAS TO RECHARGE. DON'T WORRY ABOUT HIM.
NEVER WANTED TO CLIMB INTO THIS THING AGAIN...
YOU READY?
KEEP AN EYE OUT--I STILL DON'T TRUST THESE PEOPLE.
I'M ON IT. WE'LL BE HERE WAITING FOR YOU WHEN YOU GET BACK.

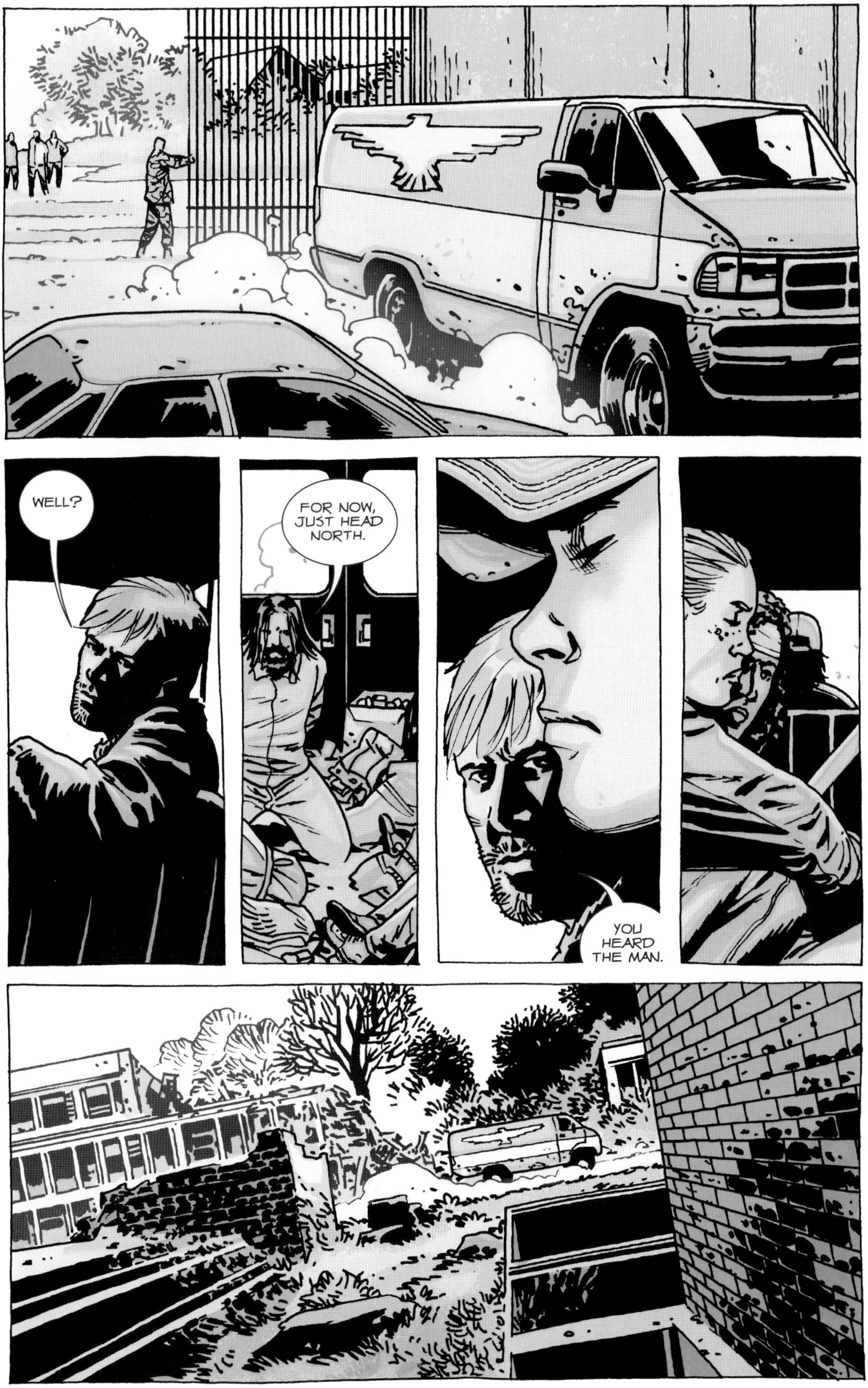
WELL?
FOR NOW, JUST HEAD NORTH.
YOU HEARD THE MAN.

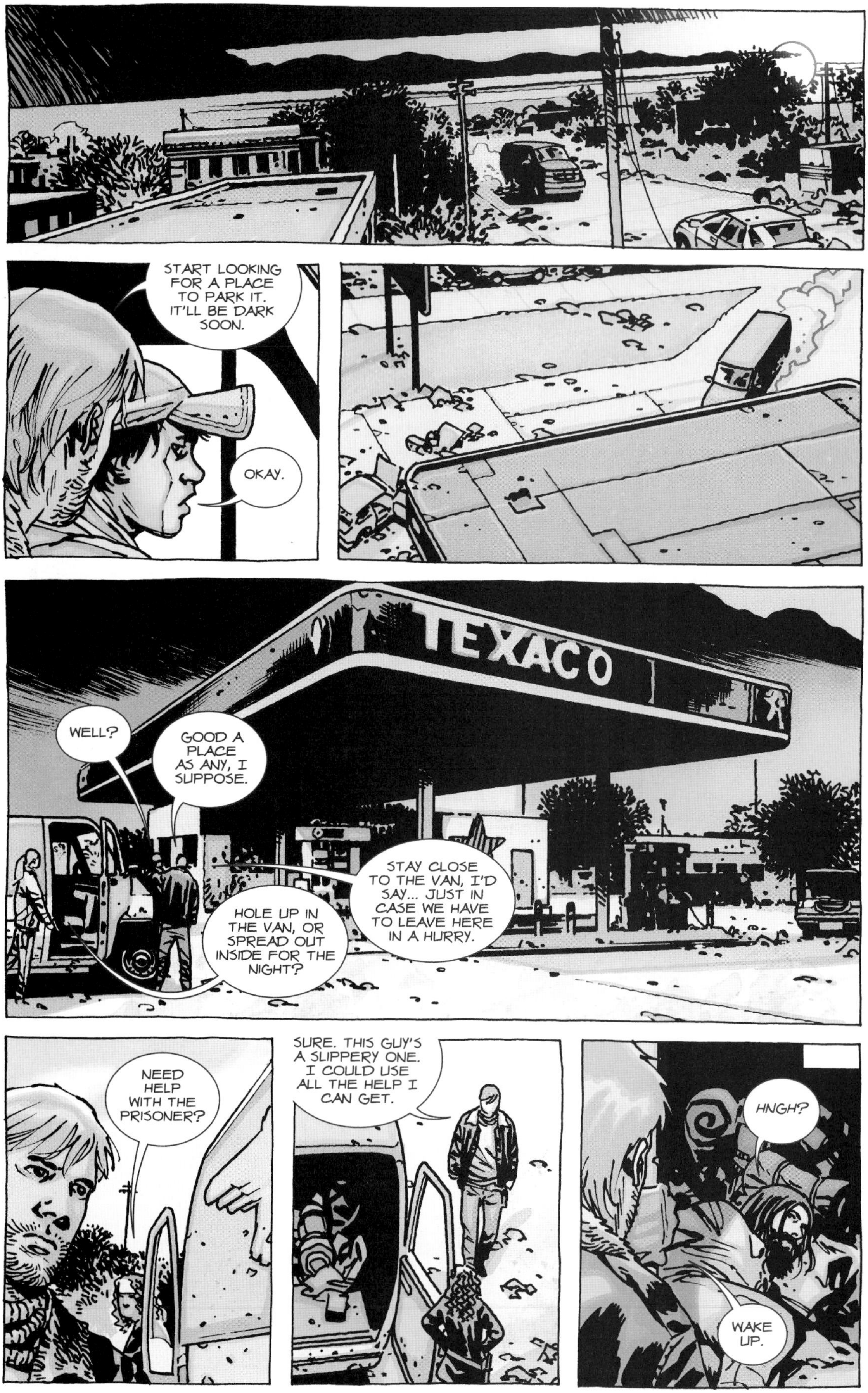
START LOOKING FOR A PLACE TO PARK IT. IT'LL BE DARK SOON.
OKAY.
TEXACO
WELL?
GOOD A PLACE AS ANY, I SUPPOSE.
HOLE UP IN THE VAN, OR SPREAD OUT INSIDE FOR THE NIGHT?
STAY CLOSE TO THE VAN, I'D SAY... JUST IN CASE WE HAVE TO LEAVE HERE IN A HURRY.
NEED HELP WITH THE PRISONER?
SURE. THIS GUY'S A SLIPPERY ONE. I COULD USE ALL THE HELP I CAN GET.
HNGH?
WAKE UP.

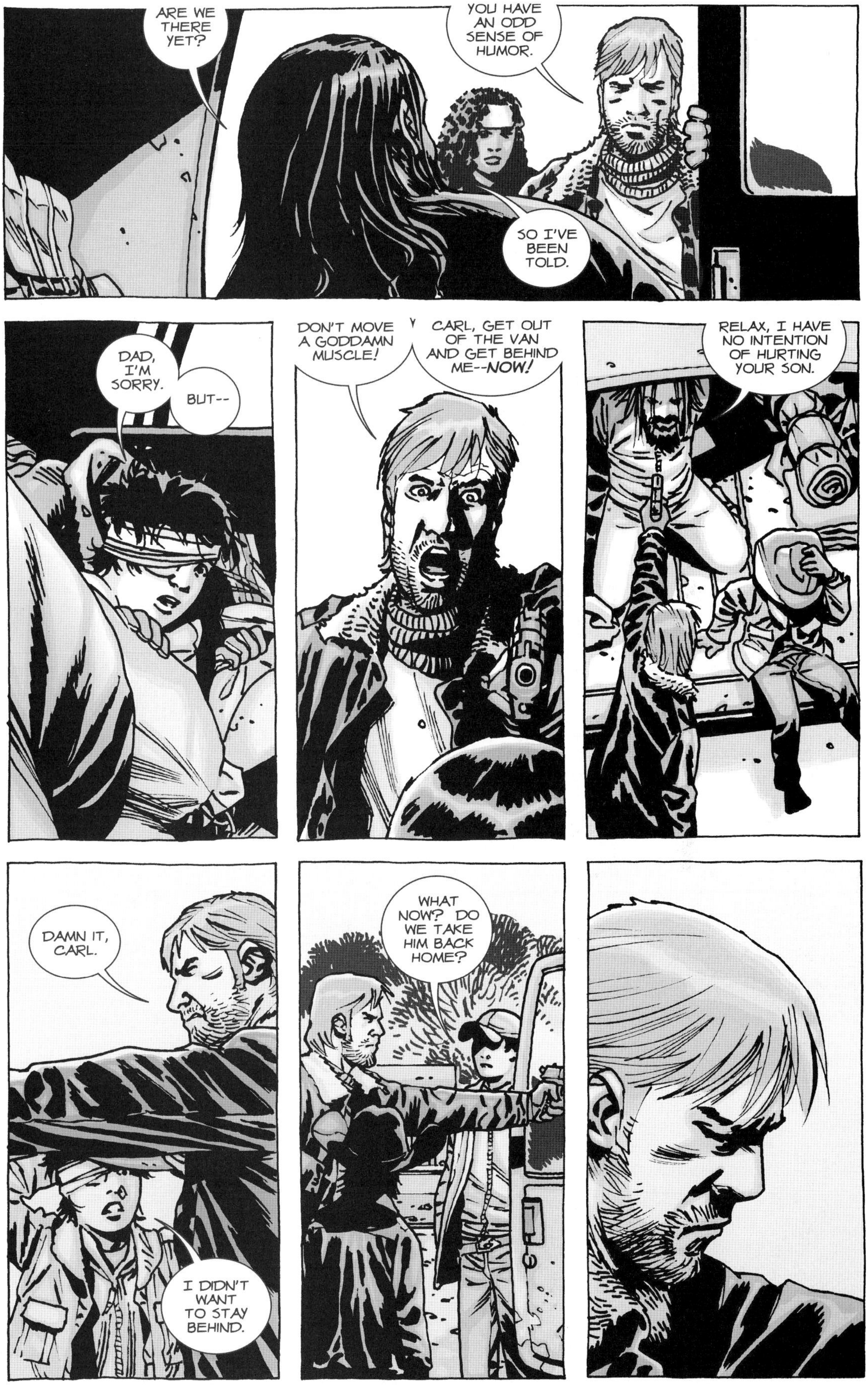
ARE WE THERE YET?
YOU HAVE AN ODD SENSE OF HUMOR.
SO I'VE BEEN TOLD.
DAD, I'M SORRY.
BUT--
DON'T MOVE A GODDAMN MUSCLE!
CARL, GET OUT OF THE VAN AND GET BEHIND ME--NOW!
RELAX, I HAVE NO INTENTION OF HURTING YOUR SON.
DAMN IT, CARL.
I DIDN'T WANT TO STAY BEHIND.
WHAT NOW? DO WE TAKE HIM BACK HOME?

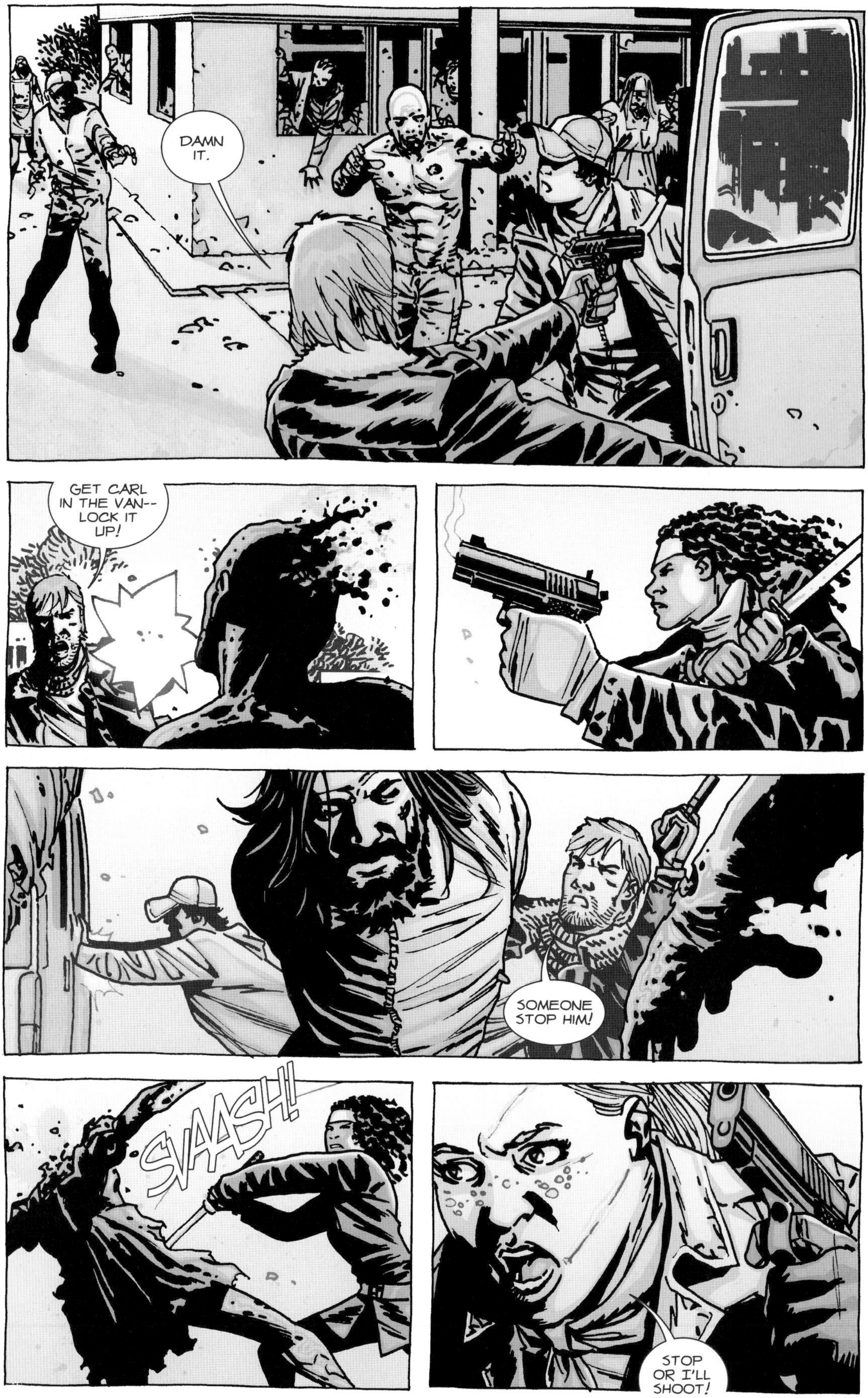
DAMN IT.
GET CARL IN THE VAN-- LOCK IT UP!
SOMEONE STOP HIM!
SVAASH!
STOP OR I'LL SHOOT!

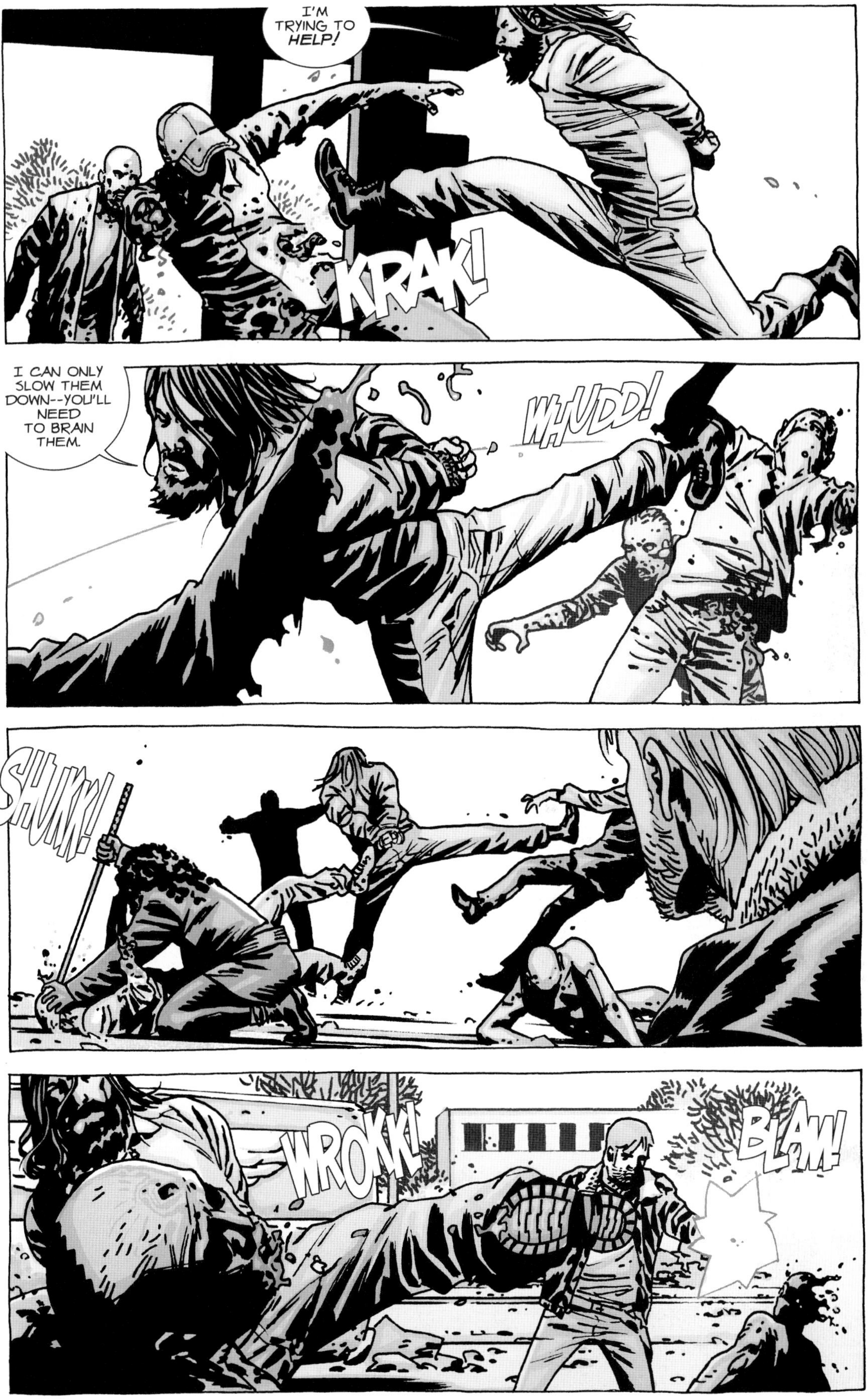
I'M TRYING TO HELP!
KRAK!
I CAN ONLY SLOW THEM DOWN--YOU'LL NEED TO BRAIN THEM.
WHUDD!
SHUKK!
WROKK!
BLAM!

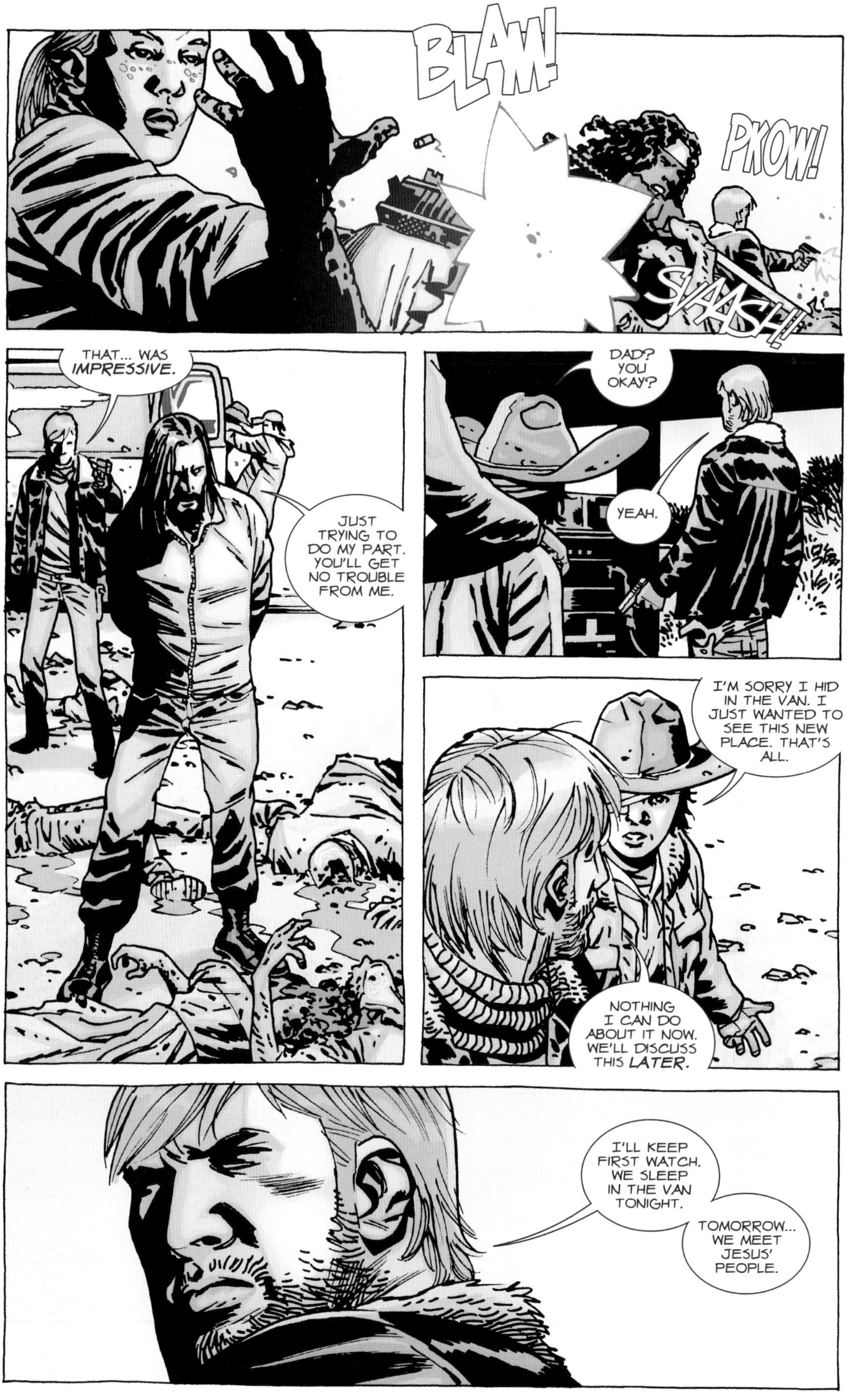
BLAM!
PKOW!
SHAASH!
THAT... WAS IMPRESSIVE.
JUST TRYING TO DO MY PART. YOU'LL GET NO TROUBLE FROM ME.
DAD? YOU OKAY?
YEAH.
I'M SORRY I HID IN THE VAN. I JUST WANTED TO SEE THIS NEW PLACE. THAT'S ALL.
NOTHING I CAN DO ABOUT IT NOW. WE'LL DISCUSS THIS LATER.
I'LL KEEP FIRST WATCH. WE SLEEP IN THE VAN TONIGHT.
TOMORROW... WE MEET JESUS' PEOPLE.

THIS ISN'T A GOOD SIGN.

SPENDING A NIGHT IN THE VAN WASN'T BAD ENOUGH? THIS *SUCKS*.

SHOULD TAKE NO MORE THAN HALF A DAY TO GET THERE FROM HERE.

THAT'S GOOD NEWS.

RIGHT?

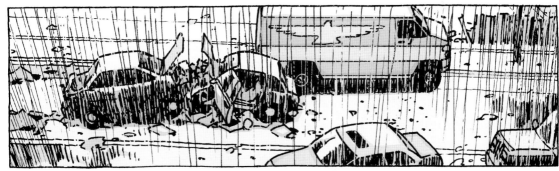

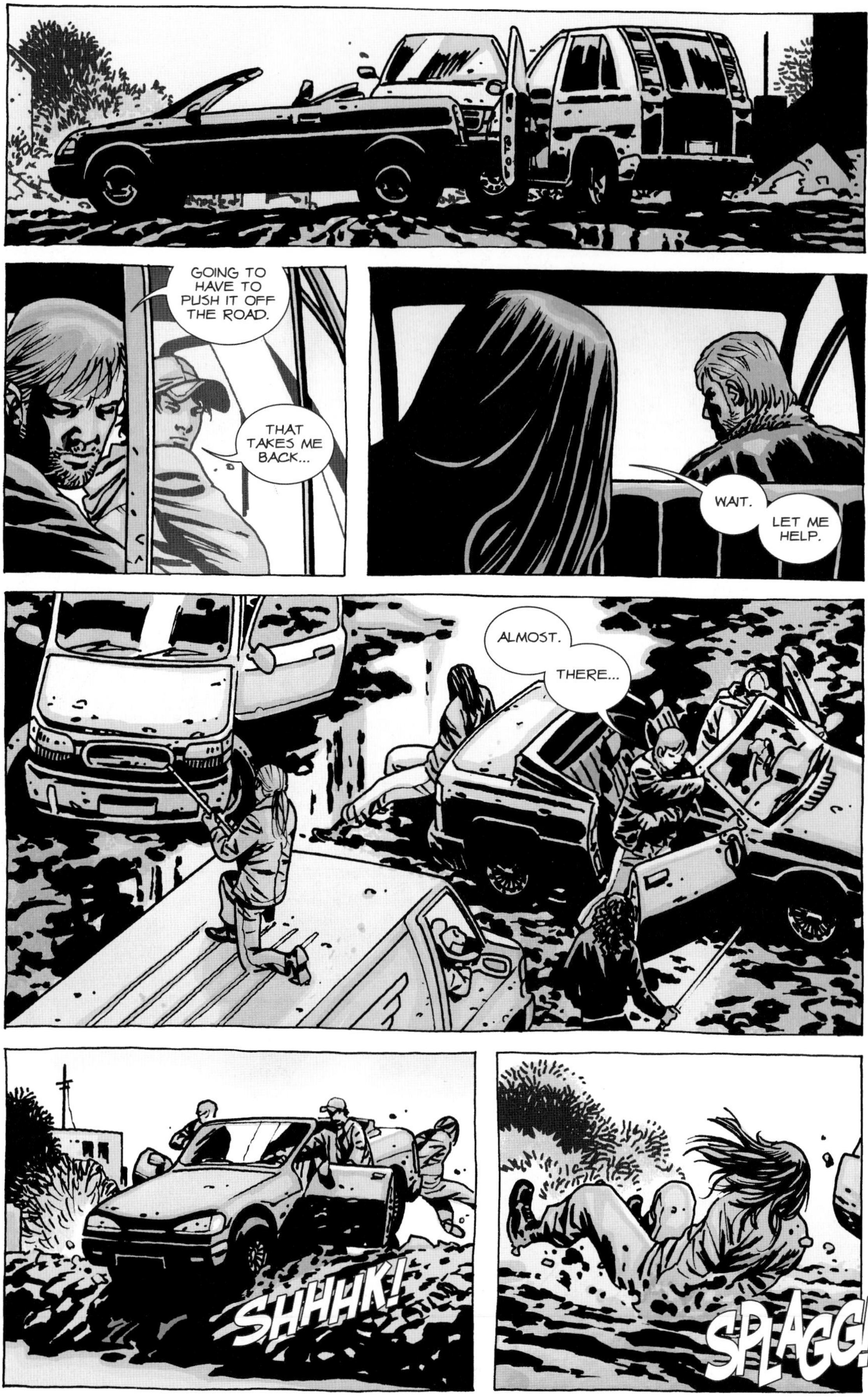
GOING TO HAVE TO PUSH IT OFF THE ROAD.
THAT TAKES ME BACK...
WAIT.
LET ME HELP.
ALMOST.
THERE...
SHHHK!
SPLAGG!

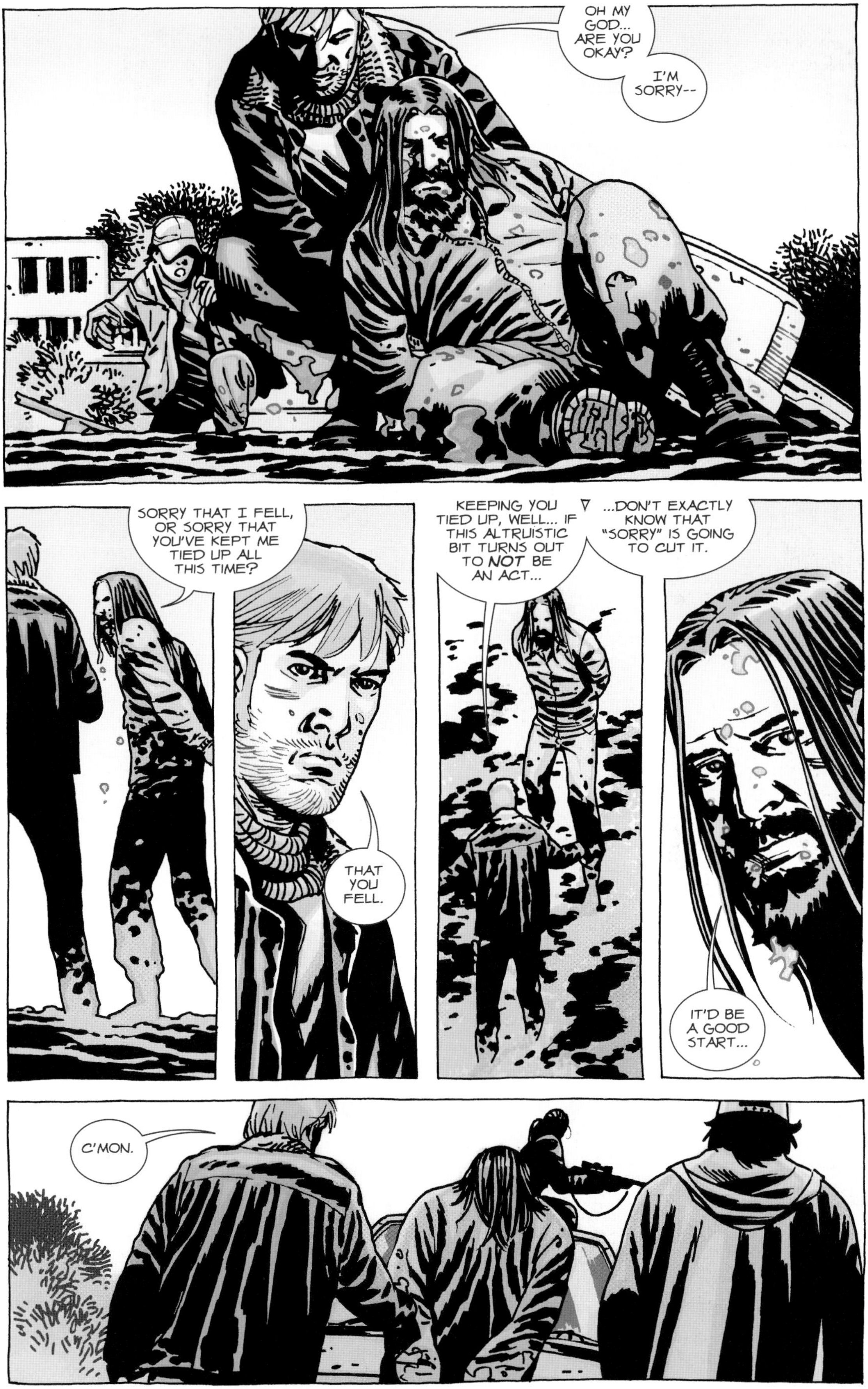
OH MY GOD... ARE YOU OKAY?
I'M SORRY--
SORRY THAT I FELL, OR SORRY THAT YOU'VE KEPT ME TIED UP ALL THIS TIME?
THAT YOU FELL.
KEEPING YOU TIED UP, WELL... IF THIS ALTRUISTIC BIT TURNS OUT TO NOT BE AN ACT...
...DON'T EXACTLY KNOW THAT "SORRY" IS GOING TO CUT IT.
IT'D BE A GOOD START...
C'MON.

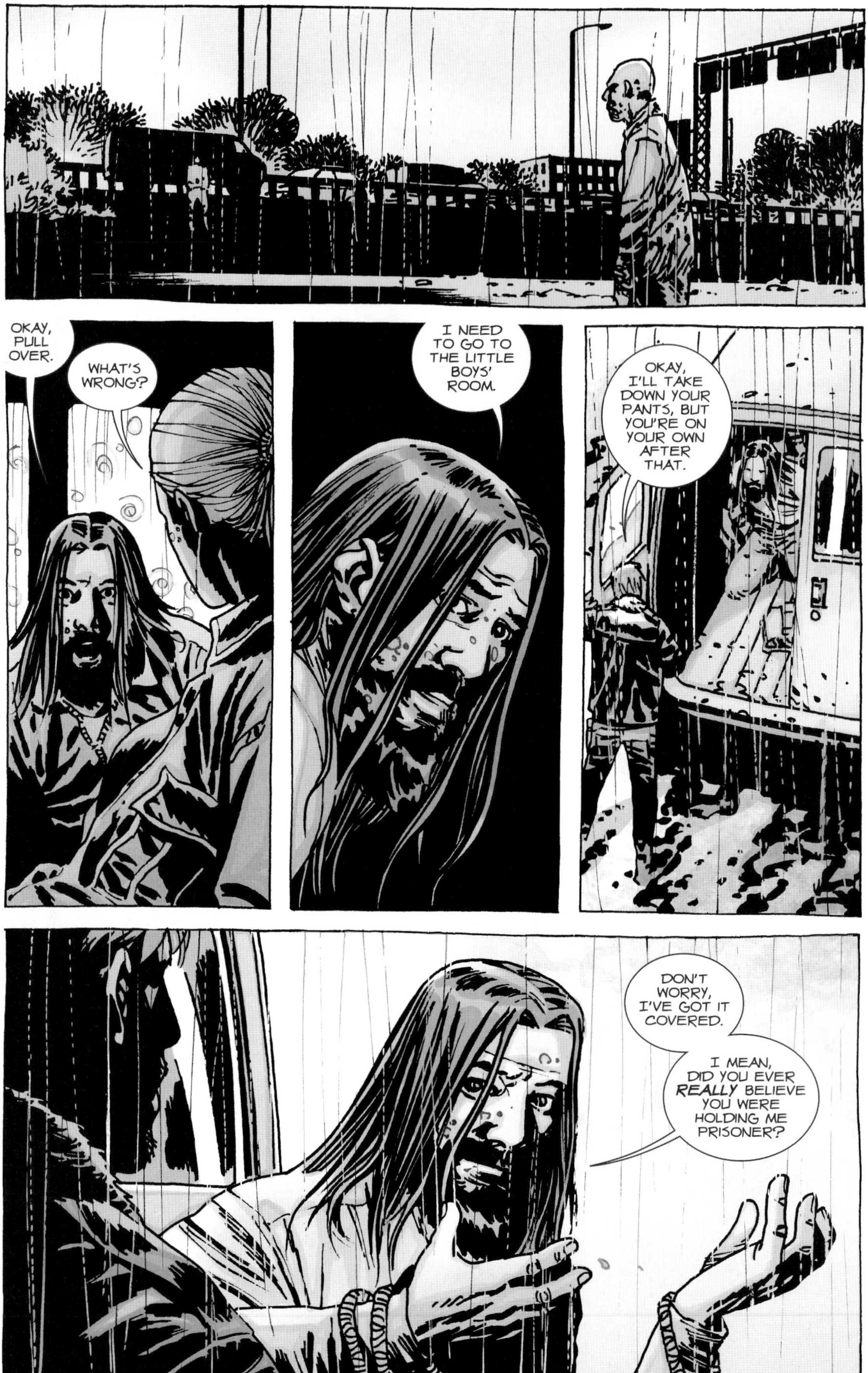
OKAY, PULL OVER.
WHAT'S WRONG?
I NEED TO GO TO THE LITTLE BOYS' ROOM.
OKAY, I'LL TAKE DOWN YOUR PANTS, BUT YOU'RE ON YOUR OWN AFTER THAT.
DON'T WORRY, I'VE GOT IT COVERED.
I MEAN, DID YOU EVER *REALLY* BELIEVE YOU WERE HOLDING ME PRISONER?

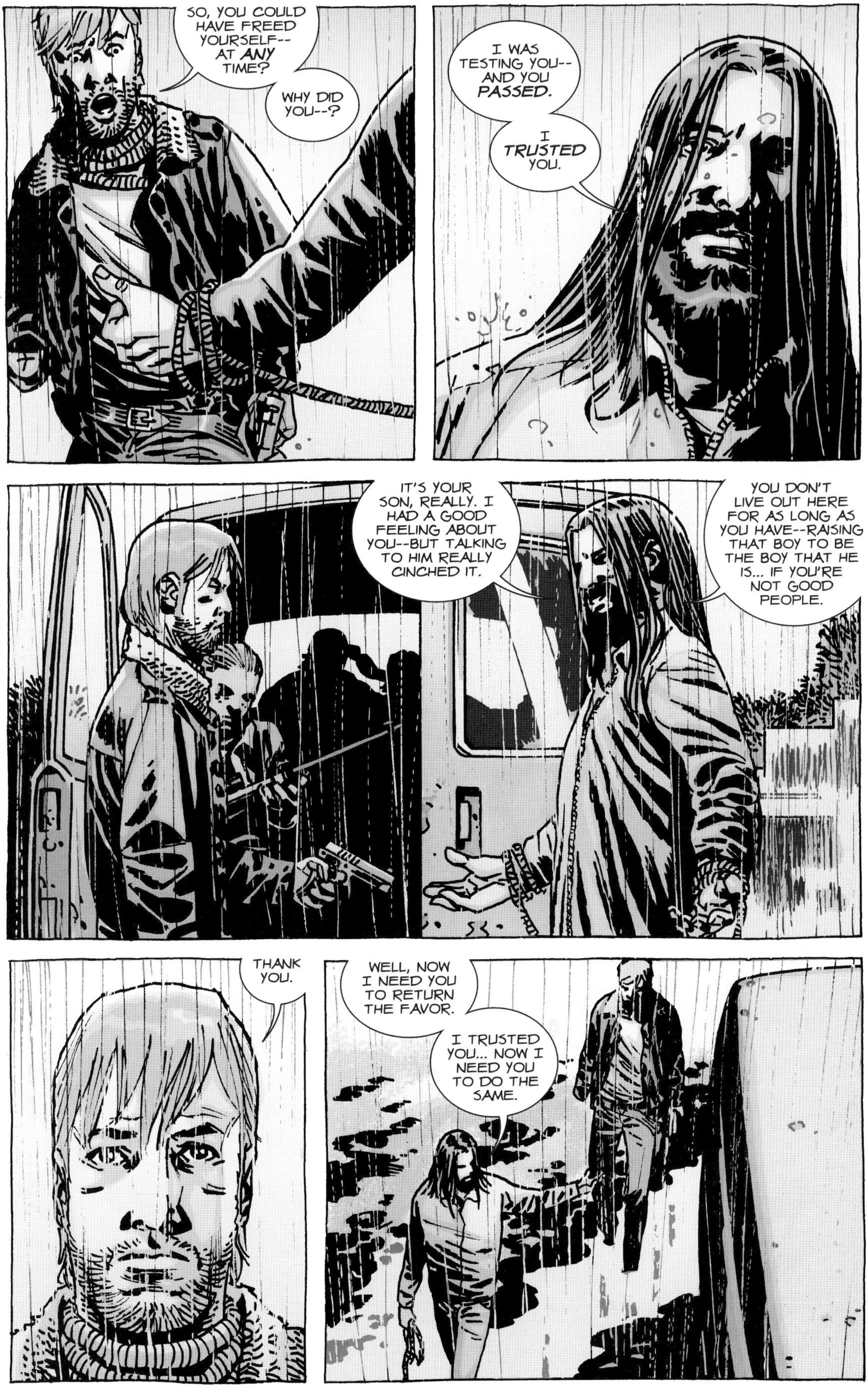
SO, YOU COULD HAVE FREED YOURSELF-- AT ANY TIME?
WHY DID YOU--?
I WAS TESTING YOU-- AND YOU PASSED.
I TRUSTED YOU.
IT'S YOUR SON, REALLY. I HAD A GOOD FEELING ABOUT YOU--BUT TALKING TO HIM REALLY CINCHED IT.
YOU DON'T LIVE OUT HERE FOR AS LONG AS YOU HAVE--RAISING THAT BOY TO BE THE BOY THAT HE IS... IF YOU'RE NOT GOOD PEOPLE.
THANK YOU.
WELL, NOW I NEED YOU TO RETURN THE FAVOR.
I TRUSTED YOU... NOW I NEED YOU TO DO THE SAME.

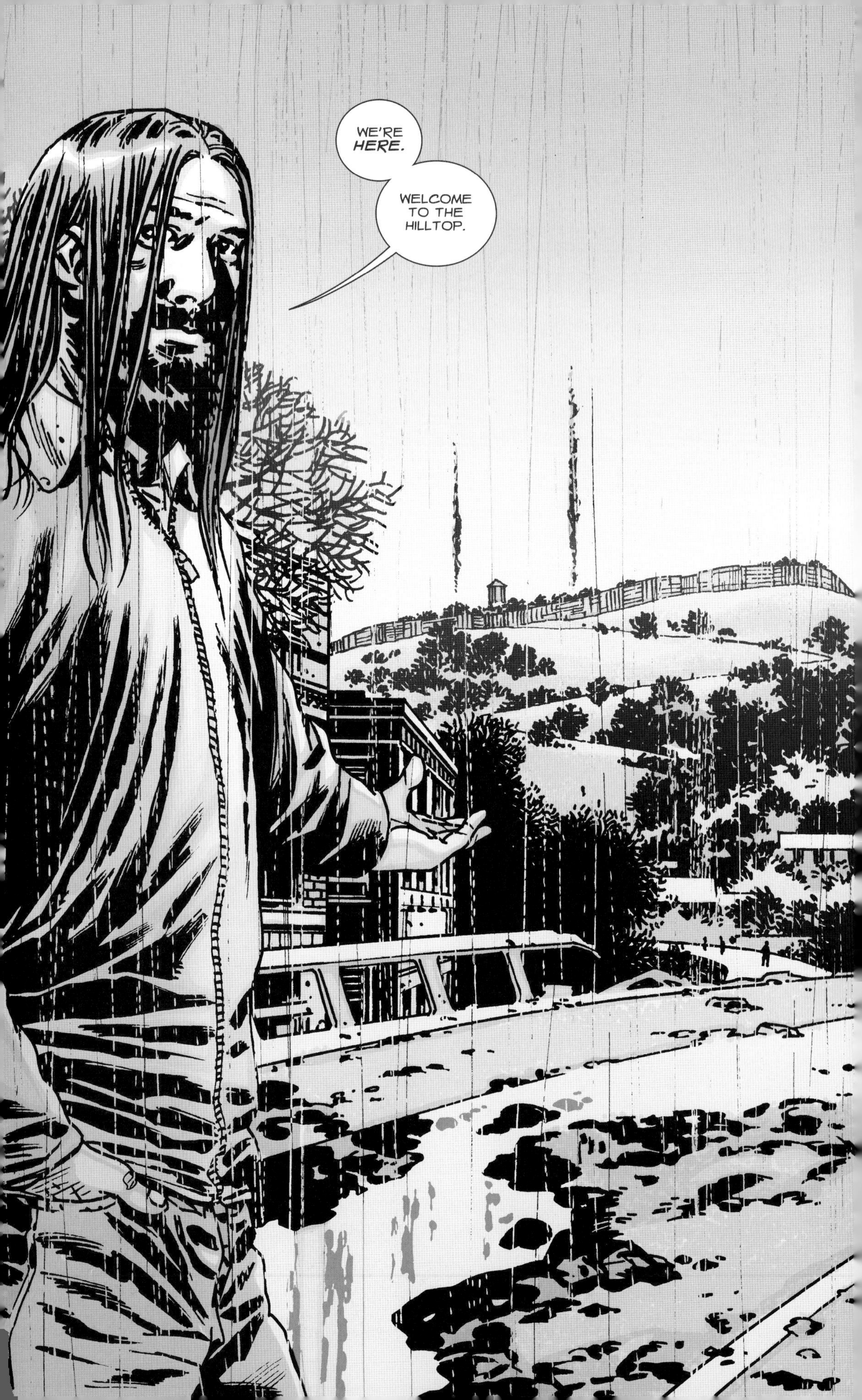
WE'RE HERE.
WELCOME TO THE HILLTOP.

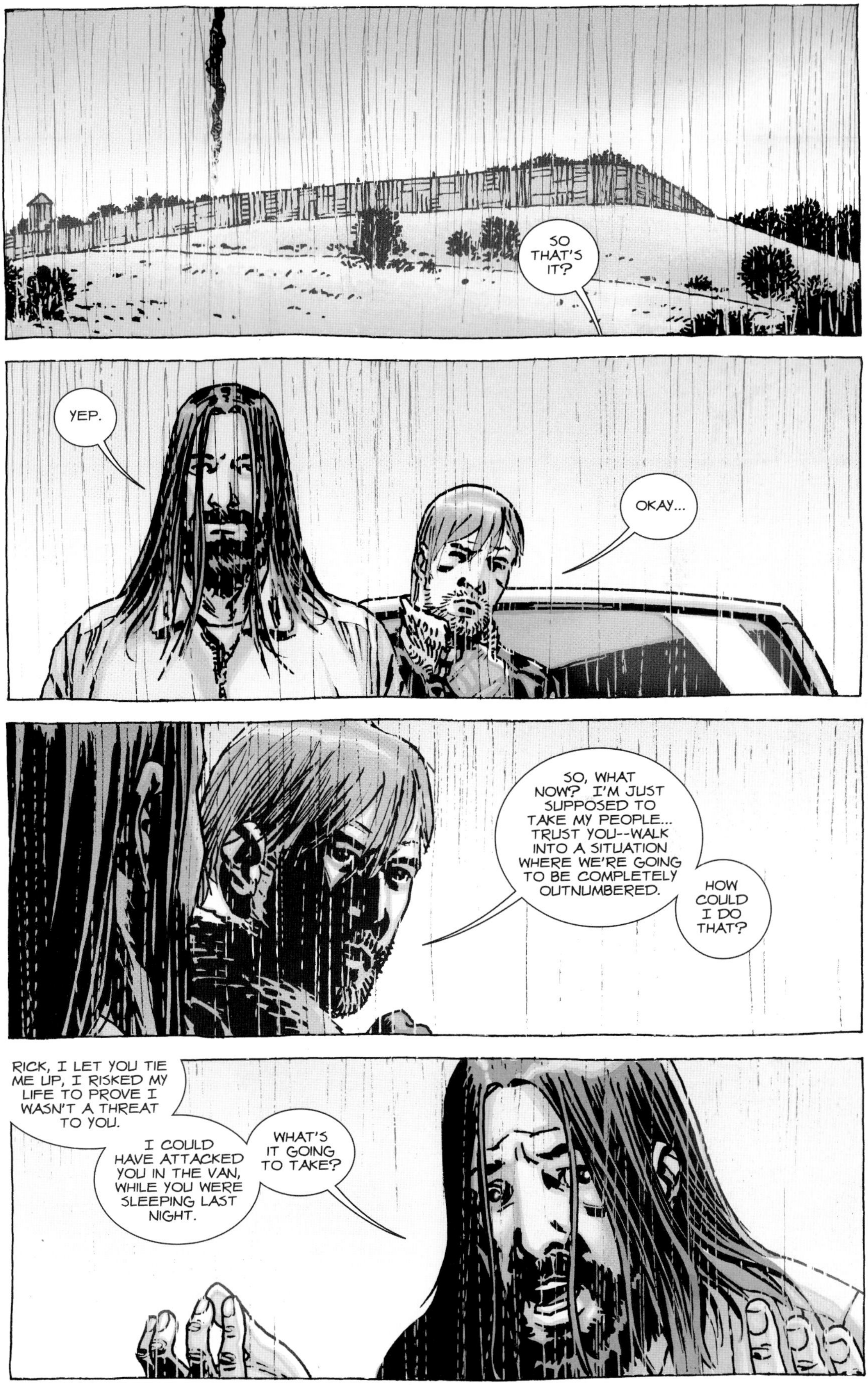
SO THAT'S IT?
YEP.
OKAY...
SO, WHAT NOW? I'M JUST SUPPOSED TO TAKE MY PEOPLE... TRUST YOU--WALK INTO A SITUATION WHERE WE'RE GOING TO BE COMPLETELY OUTNUMBERED.
HOW COULD I DO THAT?
RICK, I LET YOU TIE ME UP, I RISKED MY LIFE TO PROVE I WASN'T A THREAT TO YOU.
I COULD HAVE ATTACKED YOU IN THE VAN, WHILE YOU WERE SLEEPING LAST NIGHT.
WHAT'S IT GOING TO TAKE?

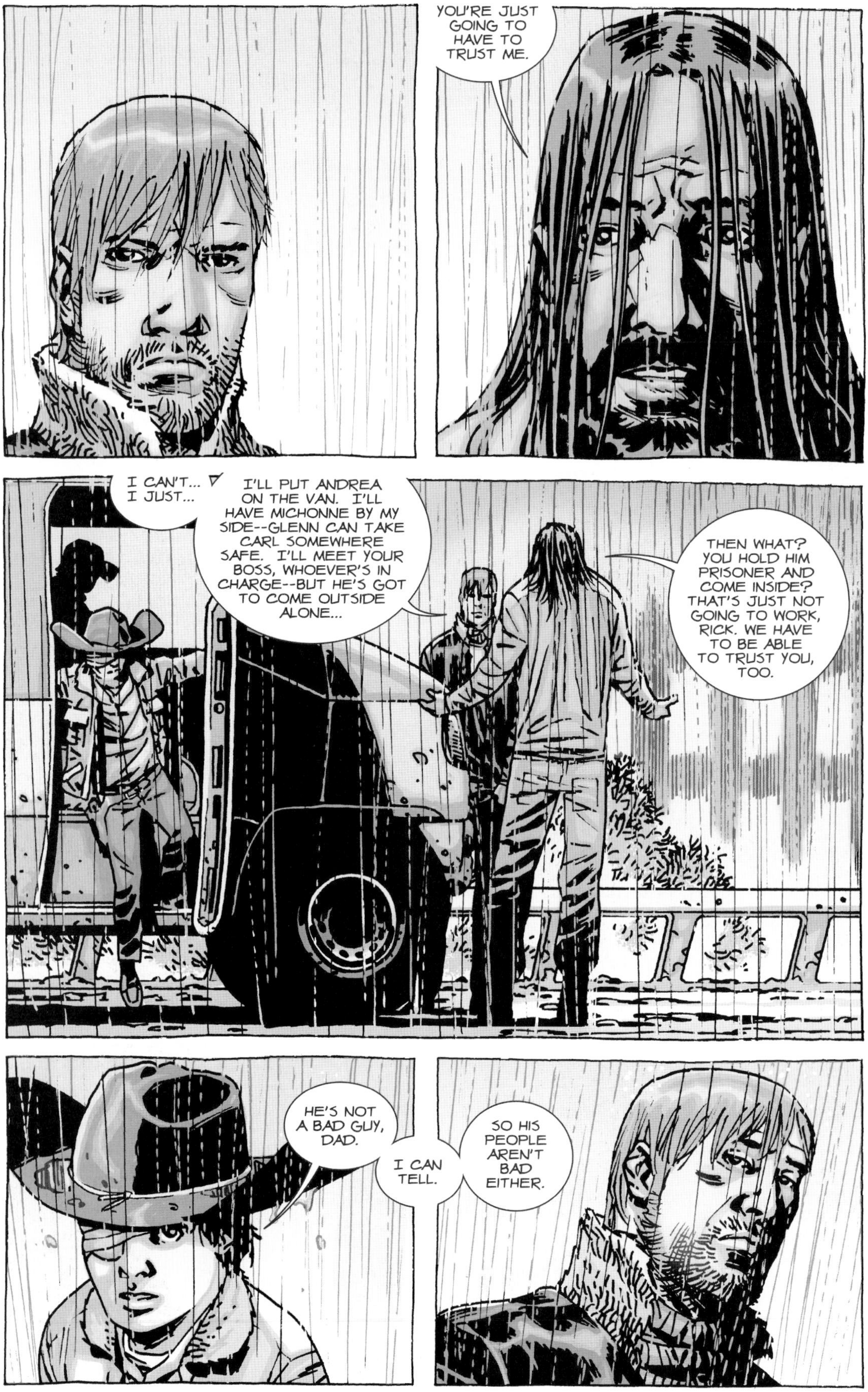
YOU'RE JUST GOING TO HAVE TO TRUST ME.
I CAN'T... I JUST...
I'LL PUT ANDREA ON THE VAN. I'LL HAVE MICHONNE BY MY SIDE--GLENN CAN TAKE CARL SOMEWHERE SAFE. I'LL MEET YOUR BOSS, WHOEVER'S IN CHARGE--BUT HE'S GOT TO COME OUTSIDE ALONE...
THEN WHAT? YOU HOLD HIM PRISONER AND COME INSIDE? THAT'S JUST NOT GOING TO WORK, RICK. WE HAVE TO BE ABLE TO TRUST YOU, TOO.
HE'S NOT A BAD GUY, DAD.
I CAN TELL.
SO HIS PEOPLE AREN'T BAD EITHER.

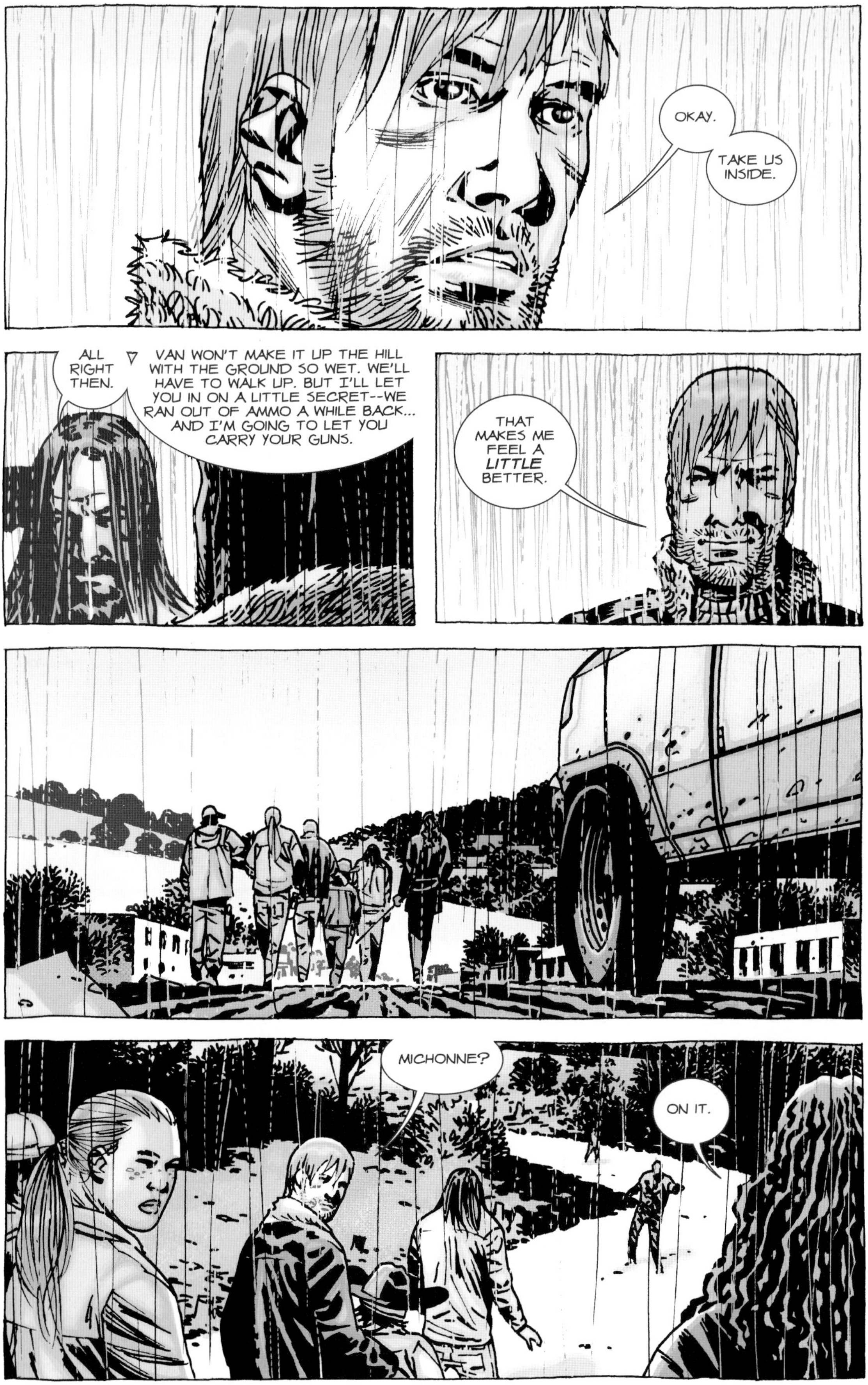
OKAY.
TAKE US INSIDE.
ALL RIGHT THEN.
VAN WON'T MAKE IT UP THE HILL WITH THE GROUND SO WET. WE'LL HAVE TO WALK UP. BUT I'LL LET YOU IN ON A LITTLE SECRET--WE RAN OUT OF AMMO A WHILE BACK... AND I'M GOING TO LET YOU CARRY YOUR GUNS.
THAT MAKES ME FEEL A *LITTLE* BETTER.
MICHONNE?
ON IT.

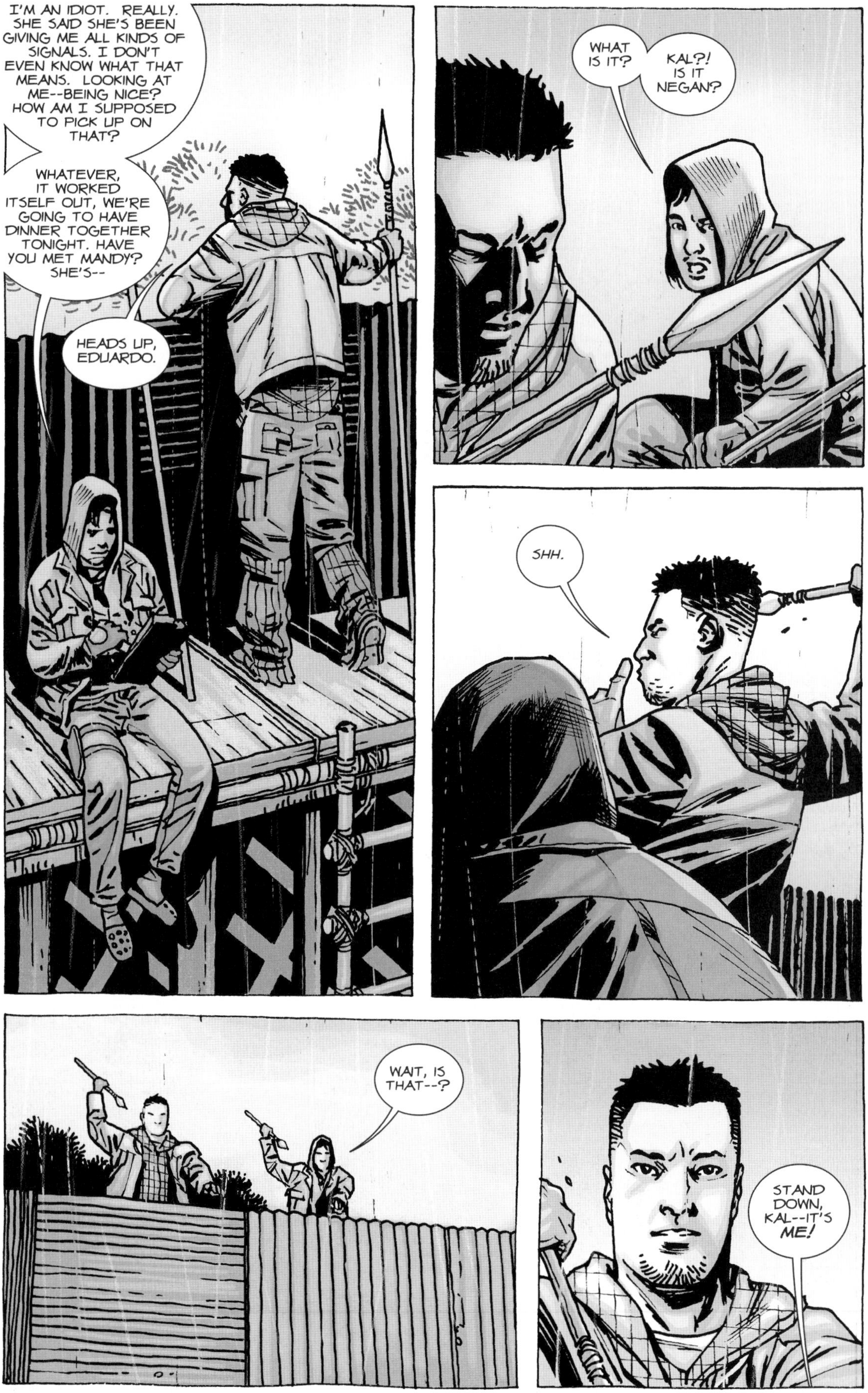
I'M AN IDIOT. REALLY. SHE SAID SHE'S BEEN GIVING ME ALL KINDS OF SIGNALS. I DON'T EVEN KNOW WHAT THAT MEANS. LOOKING AT ME--BEING NICE? HOW AM I SUPPOSED TO PICK UP ON THAT?
WHATEVER, IT WORKED ITSELF OUT, WE'RE GOING TO HAVE DINNER TOGETHER TONIGHT. HAVE YOU MET MANDY? SHE'S--
HEADS UP, EDUARDO.
WHAT IS IT?
KAL?! IS IT NEGAN?
SHH.
WAIT, IS THAT--?
STAND DOWN, KAL--IT'S *ME!*

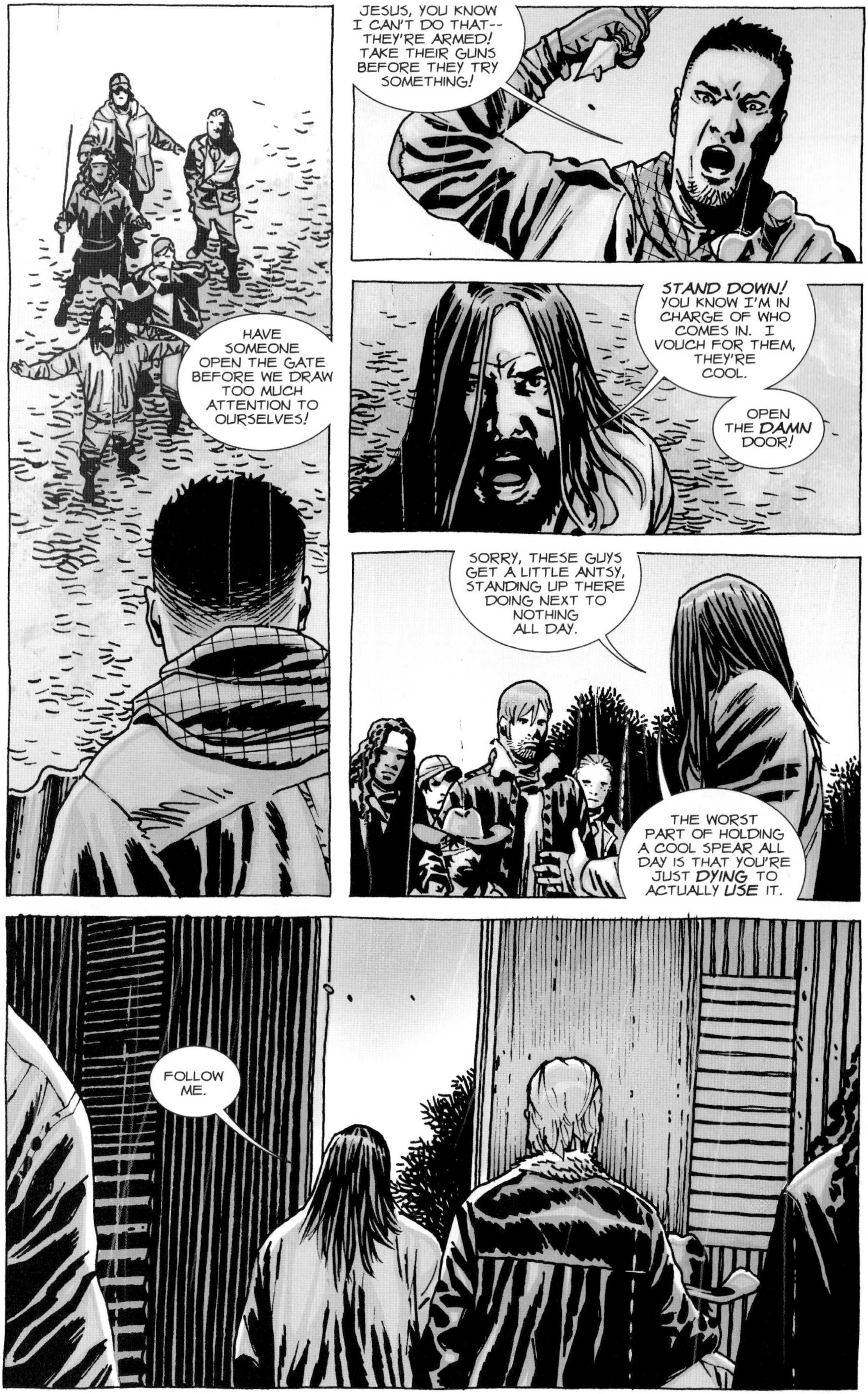
HAVE SOMEONE OPEN THE GATE BEFORE WE DRAW TOO MUCH ATTENTION TO OURSELVES!
JESUS, YOU KNOW I CAN'T DO THAT-- THEY'RE ARMED! TAKE THEIR GUNS BEFORE THEY TRY SOMETHING!
STAND DOWN! YOU KNOW I'M IN CHARGE OF WHO COMES IN. I VOUCH FOR THEM, THEY'RE COOL.
OPEN THE DAMN DOOR!
SORRY, THESE GUYS GET A LITTLE ANTSY, STANDING UP THERE DOING NEXT TO NOTHING ALL DAY.
THE WORST PART OF HOLDING A COOL SPEAR ALL DAY IS THAT YOU'RE JUST DYING TO ACTUALLY USE IT.
FOLLOW ME.

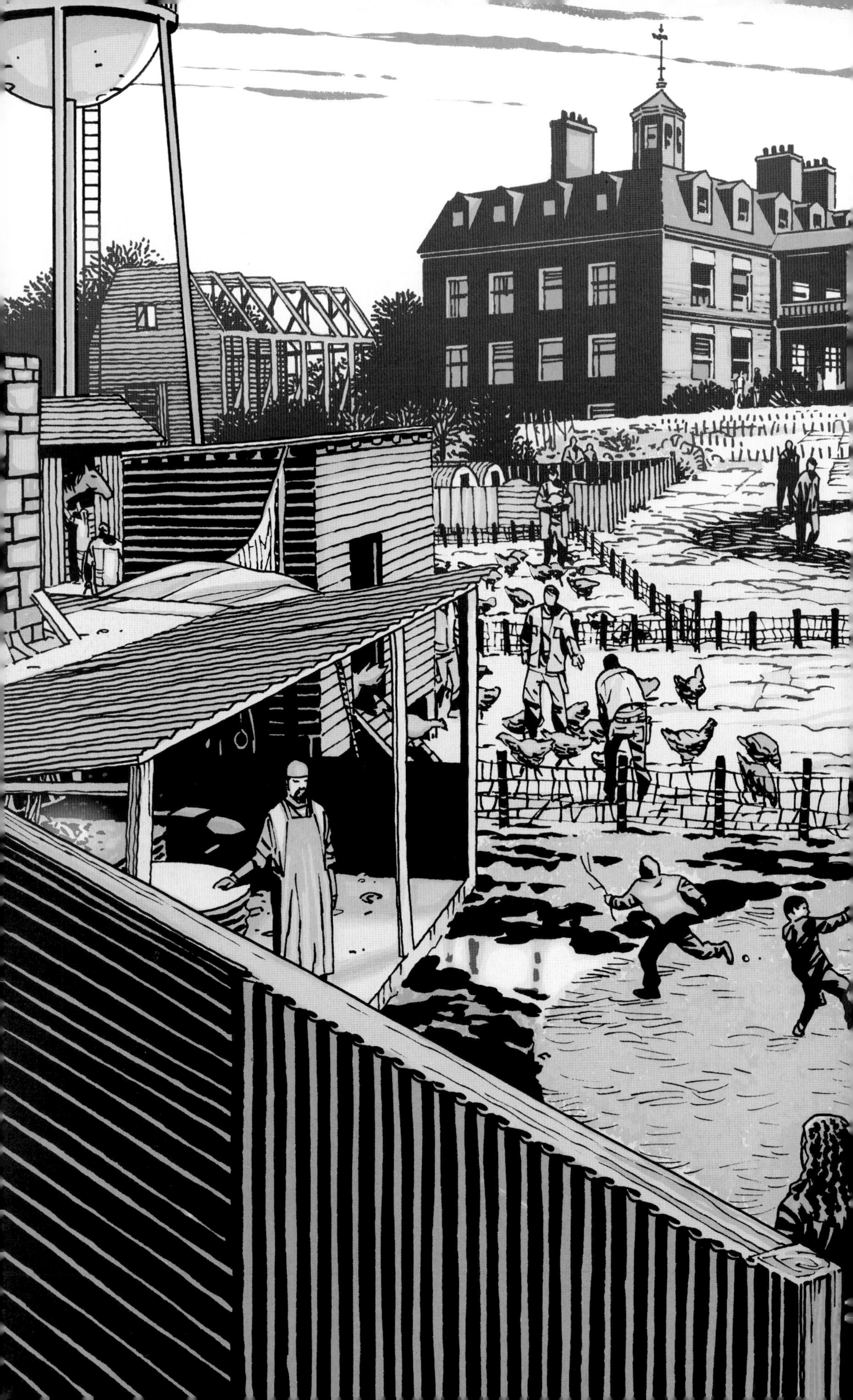

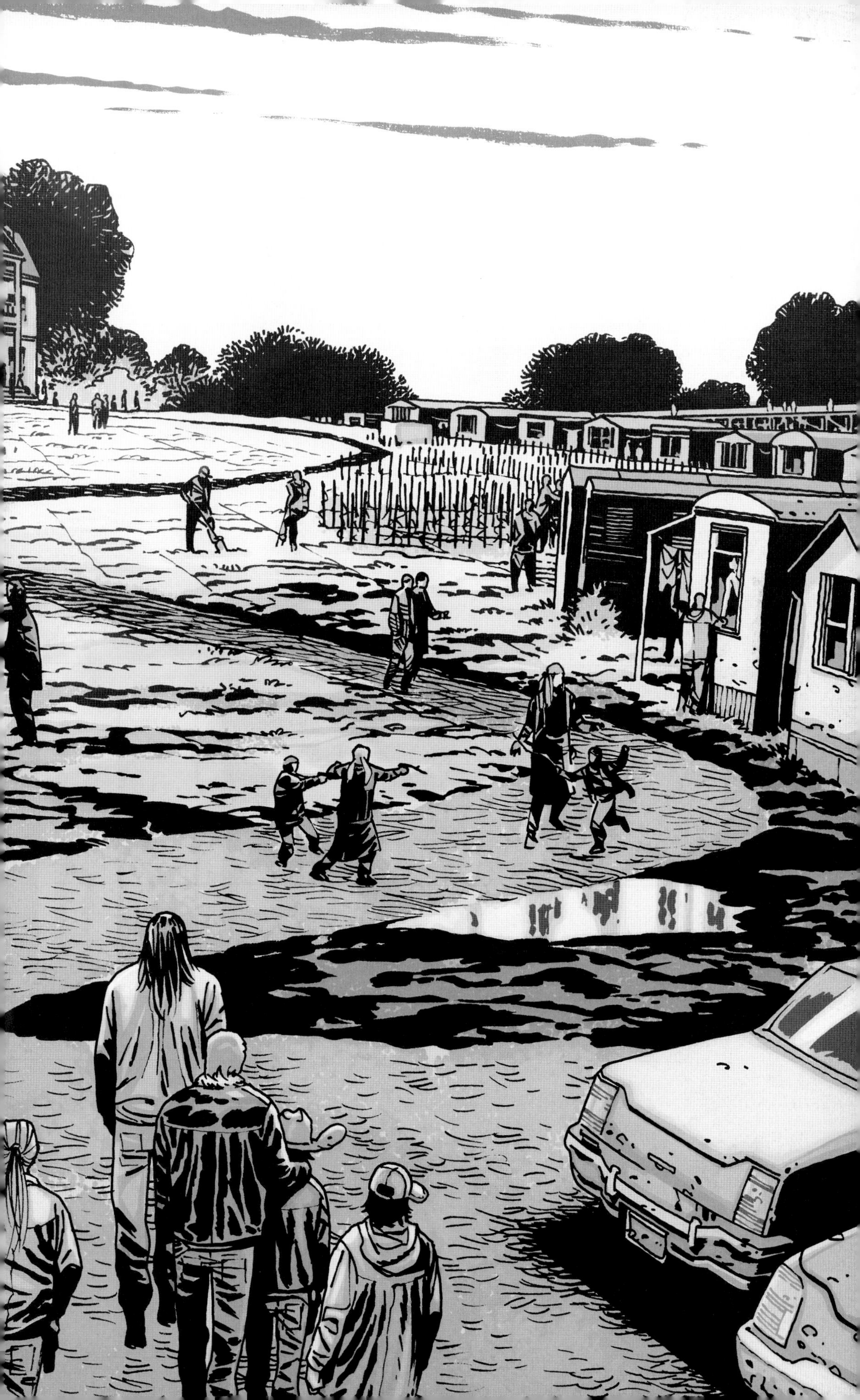

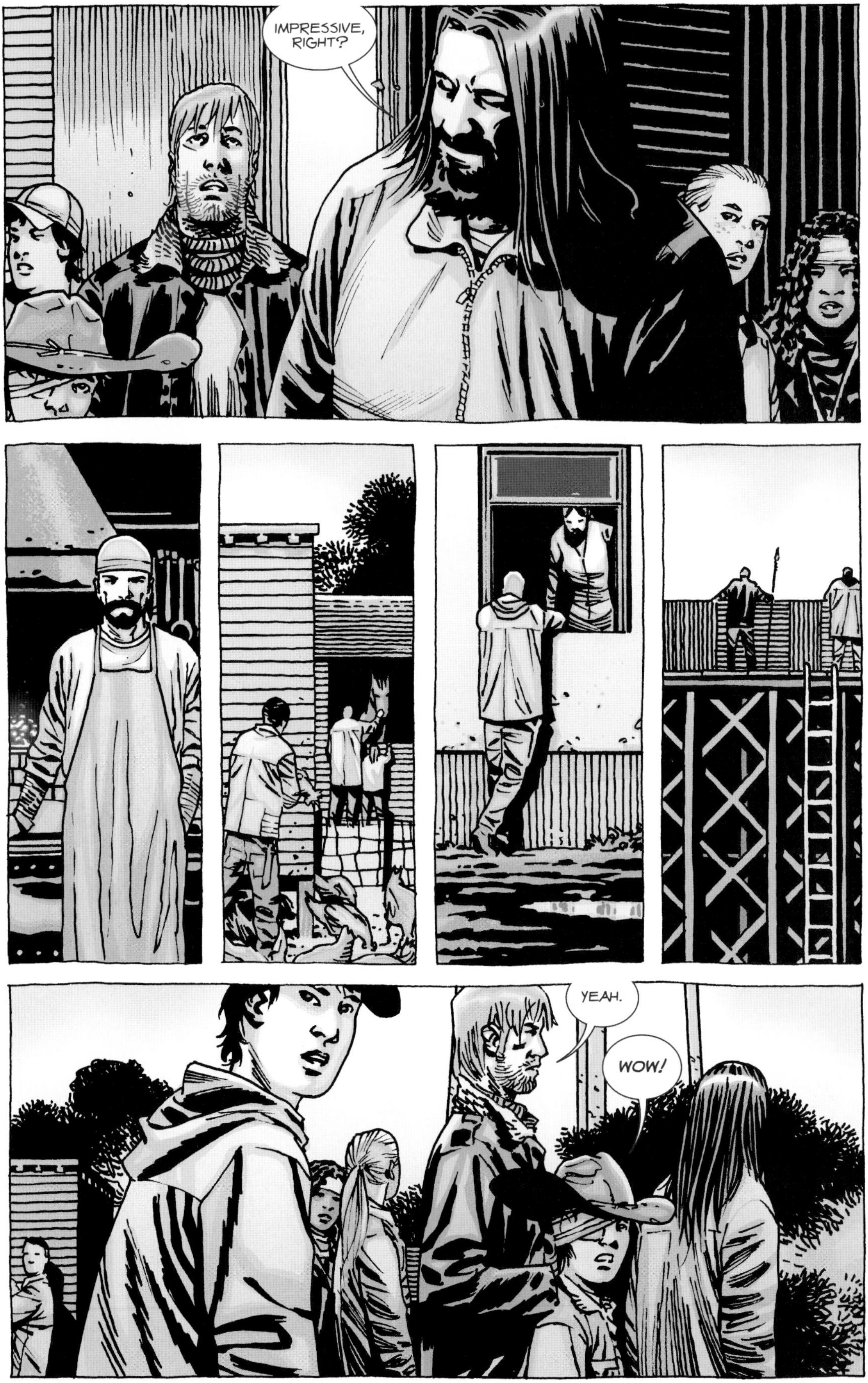
IMPRESSIVE, RIGHT?
YEAH.
WOW!

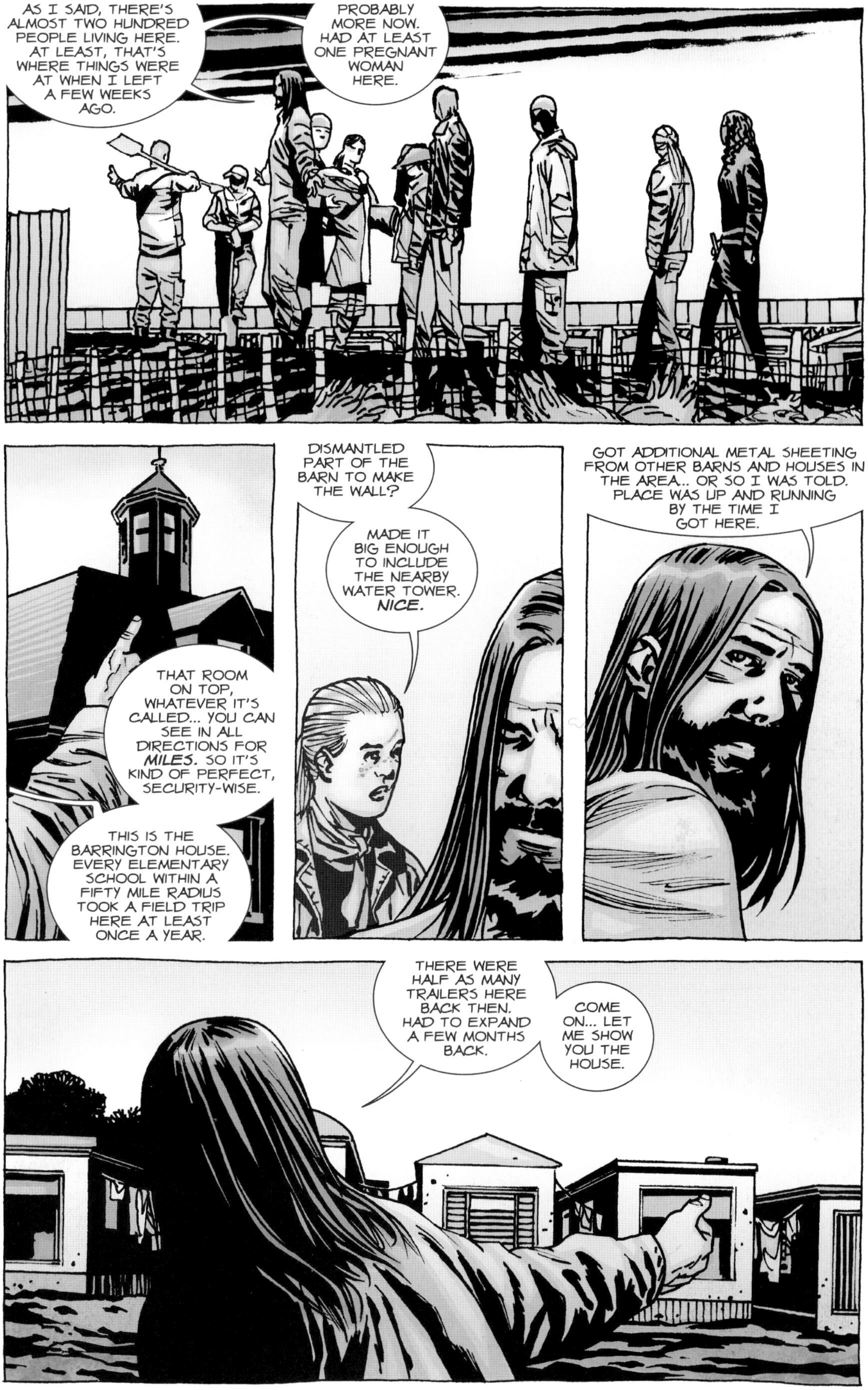
AS I SAID, THERE'S ALMOST TWO HUNDRED PEOPLE LIVING HERE. AT LEAST, THAT'S WHERE THINGS WERE AT WHEN I LEFT A FEW WEEKS AGO.
PROBABLY MORE NOW. HAD AT LEAST ONE PREGNANT WOMAN HERE.
THIS IS THE BARRINGTON HOUSE. EVERY ELEMENTARY SCHOOL WITHIN A FIFTY MILE RADIUS TOOK A FIELD TRIP HERE AT LEAST ONCE A YEAR.
THAT ROOM ON TOP, WHATEVER IT'S CALLED... YOU CAN SEE IN ALL DIRECTIONS FOR MILES. SO IT'S KIND OF PERFECT, SECURITY-WISE.
DISMANTLED PART OF THE BARN TO MAKE THE WALL?
MADE IT BIG ENOUGH TO INCLUDE THE NEARBY WATER TOWER. NICE.
GOT ADDITIONAL METAL SHEETING FROM OTHER BARNS AND HOUSES IN THE AREA.. OR SO I WAS TOLD. PLACE WAS UP AND RUNNING BY THE TIME I GOT HERE.
THERE WERE HALF AS MANY TRAILERS HERE BACK THEN. HAD TO EXPAND A FEW MONTHS BACK.
COME ON... LET ME SHOW YOU THE HOUSE.

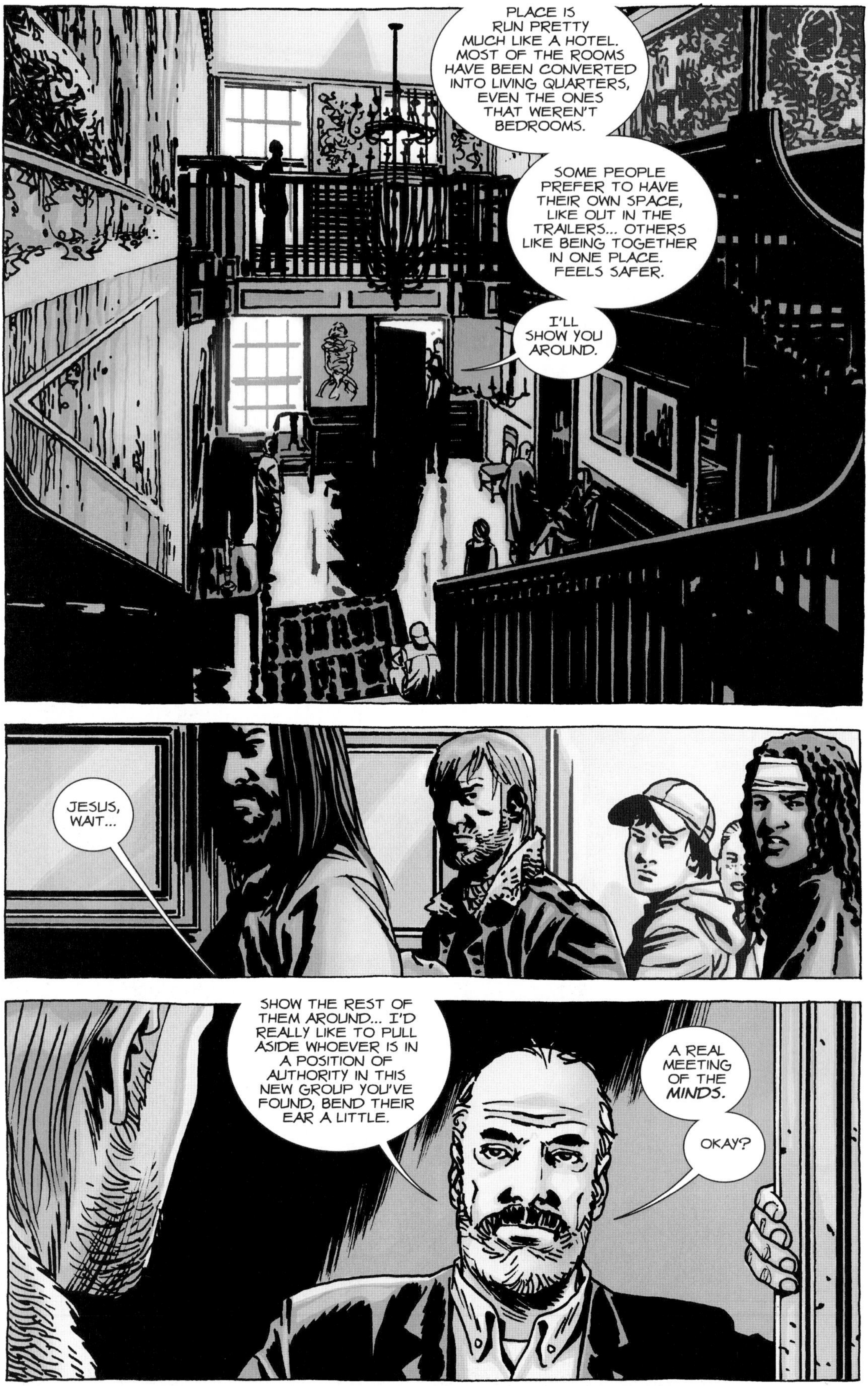
PLACE IS RUN PRETTY MUCH LIKE A HOTEL. MOST OF THE ROOMS HAVE BEEN CONVERTED INTO LIVING QUARTERS, EVEN THE ONES THAT WEREN'T BEDROOMS.
SOME PEOPLE PREFER TO HAVE THEIR OWN SPACE, LIKE OUT IN THE TRAILERS... OTHERS LIKE BEING TOGETHER IN ONE PLACE. FEELS SAFER.
I'LL SHOW YOU AROUND.
JESUS, WAIT...
SHOW THE REST OF THEM AROUND... I'D REALLY LIKE TO PULL ASIDE WHOEVER IS IN A POSITION OF AUTHORITY IN THIS NEW GROUP YOU'VE FOUND, BEND THEIR EAR A LITTLE.
A REAL MEETING OF THE *MINDS.*
OKAY?

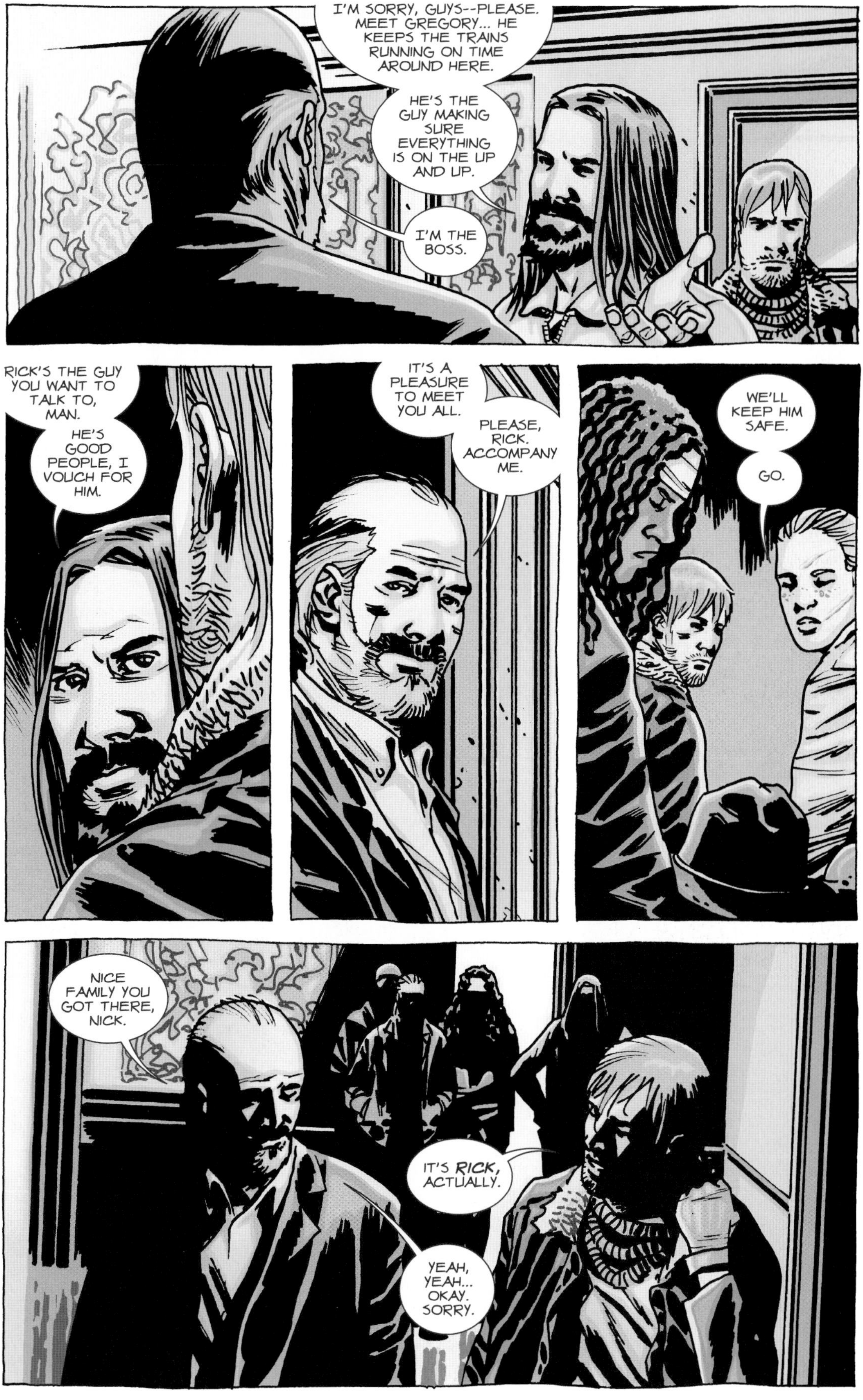

I'M SORRY, GUYS--PLEASE. MEET GREGORY... HE KEEPS THE TRAINS RUNNING ON TIME AROUND HERE.
HE'S THE GUY MAKING SURE EVERYTHING IS ON THE UP AND UP.
I'M THE BOSS.
RICK'S THE GUY YOU WANT TO TALK TO, MAN.
HE'S GOOD PEOPLE, I VOUCH FOR HIM.
IT'S A PLEASURE TO MEET YOU ALL.
PLEASE, RICK. ACCOMPANY ME.
WE'LL KEEP HIM SAFE.
GO.
NICE FAMILY YOU GOT THERE, NICK.
IT'S RICK, ACTUALLY.
YEAH, YEAH... OKAY. SORRY.

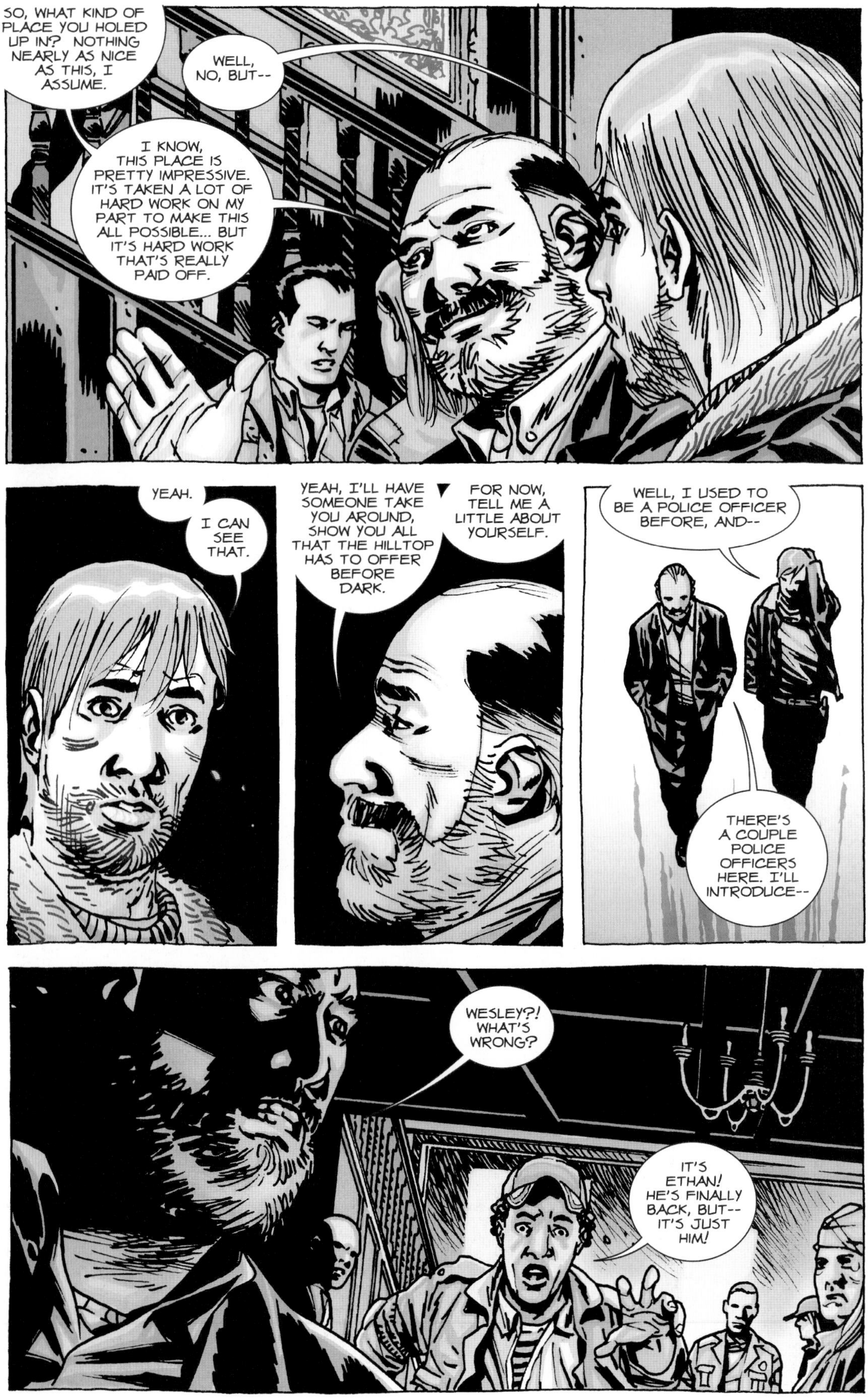
SO, WHAT KIND OF PLACE YOU HOLED UP IN? NOTHING NEARLY AS NICE AS THIS, I ASSUME.
WELL, NO, BUT--
I KNOW, THIS PLACE IS PRETTY IMPRESSIVE. IT'S TAKEN A LOT OF HARD WORK ON MY PART TO MAKE THIS ALL POSSIBLE... BUT IT'S HARD WORK THAT'S REALLY PAID OFF.
YEAH.
I CAN SEE THAT.
YEAH, I'LL HAVE SOMEONE TAKE YOU AROUND, SHOW YOU ALL THAT THE HILLTOP HAS TO OFFER BEFORE DARK.
FOR NOW, TELL ME A LITTLE ABOUT YOURSELF.
WELL, I USED TO BE A POLICE OFFICER BEFORE, AND--
THERE'S A COUPLE POLICE OFFICERS HERE. I'LL INTRODUCE--
WESLEY?! WHAT'S WRONG?
IT'S ETHAN! HE'S FINALLY BACK, BUT-- IT'S JUST HIM!

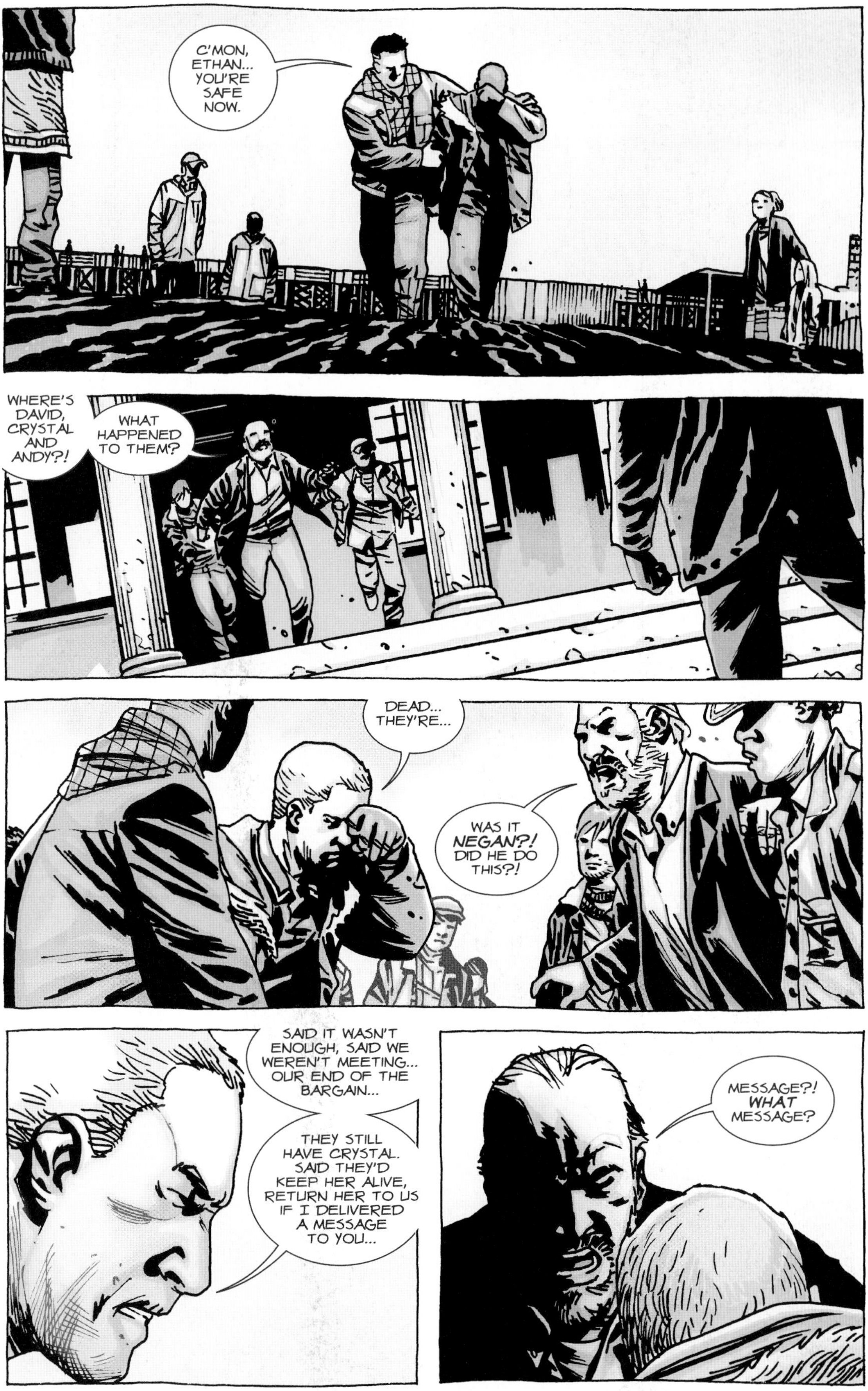
C'MON, ETHAN... YOU'RE SAFE NOW.
WHERE'S DAVID, CRYSTAL AND ANDY?!
WHAT HAPPENED TO THEM?
DEAD... THEY'RE...
WAS IT NEGAN?! DID HE DO THIS?!
SAID IT WASN'T ENOUGH, SAID WE WEREN'T MEETING... OUR END OF THE BARGAIN...
THEY STILL HAVE CRYSTAL. SAID THEY'D KEEP HER ALIVE, RETURN HER TO US IF I DELIVERED A MESSAGE TO YOU...
MESSAGE?! WHAT MESSAGE?

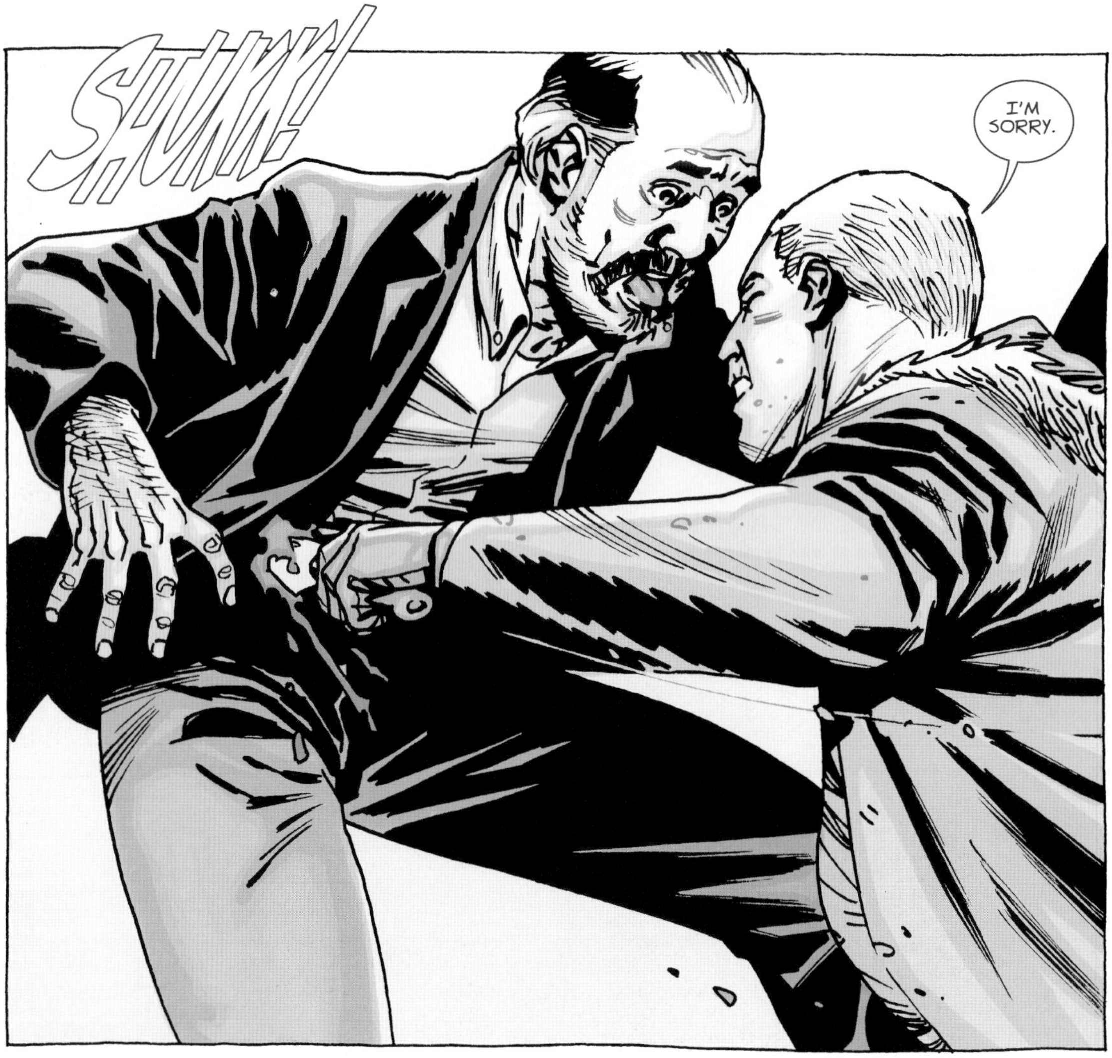
SHUNK!
I'M SORRY.

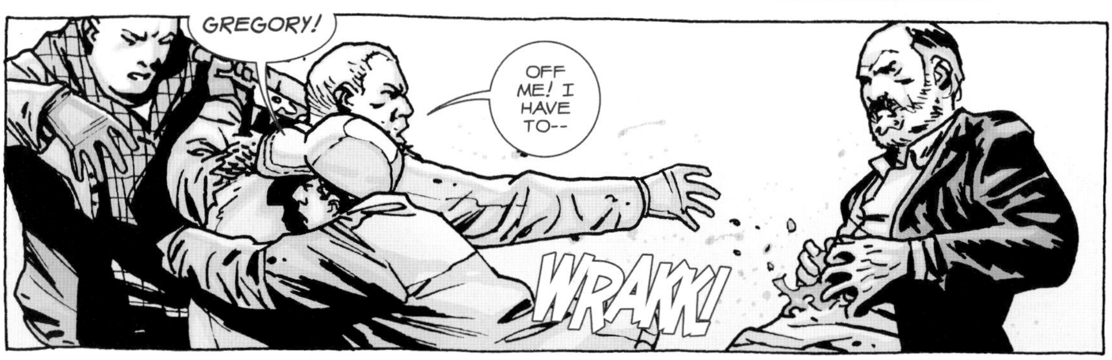
GREGORY!
OFF ME! I HAVE TO--
WRAKK!

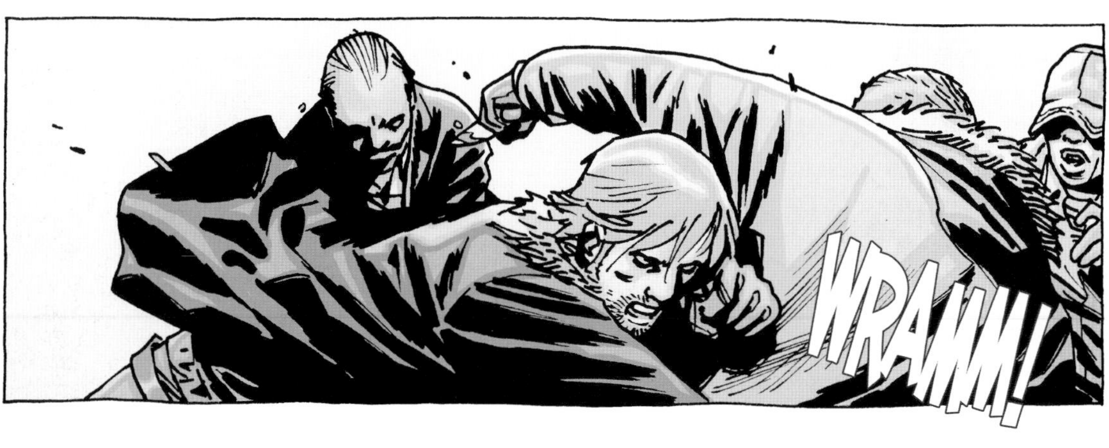
WRAMM!

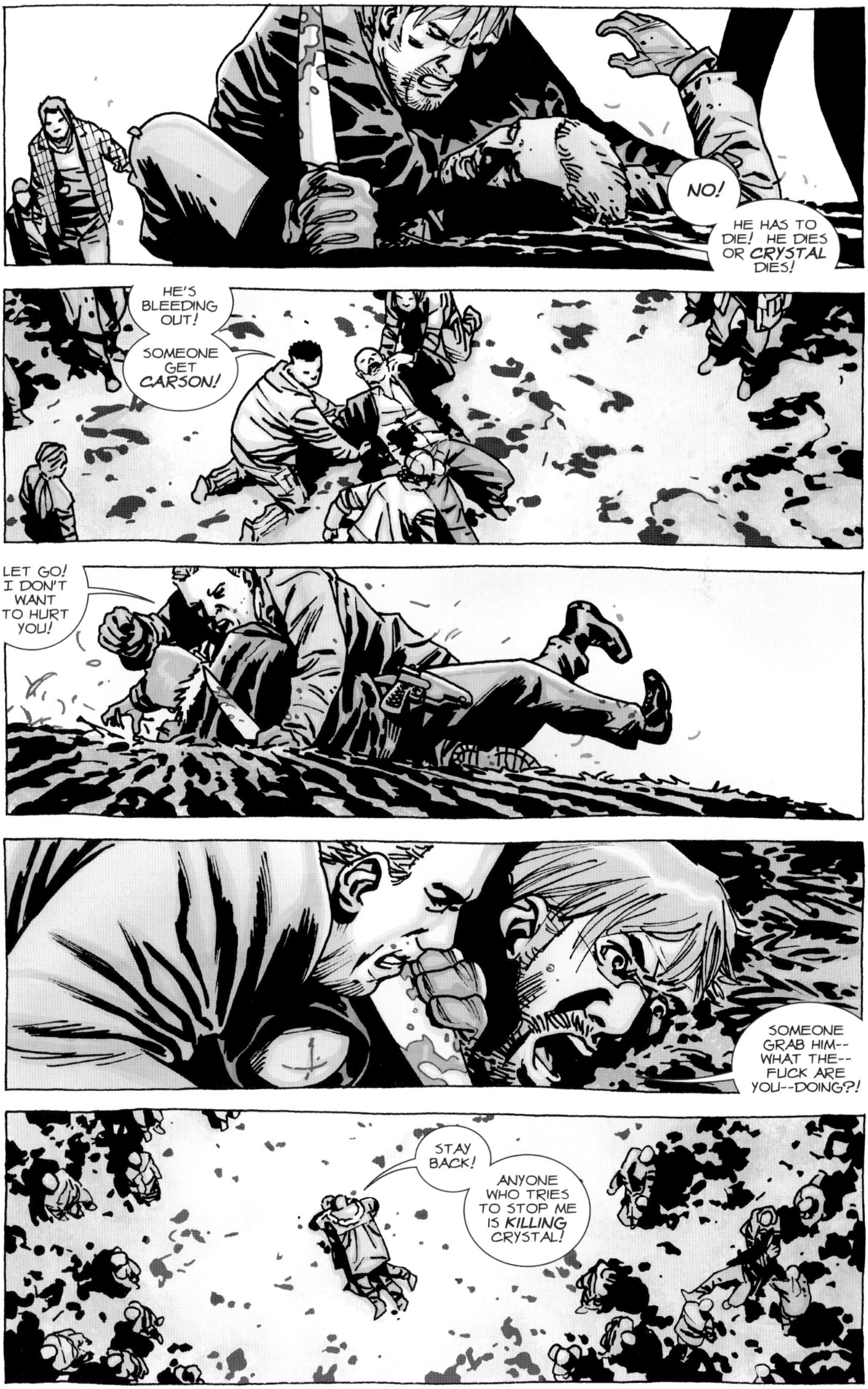
NO!
HE HAS TO DIE! HE DIES OR CRYSTAL DIES!
HE'S BLEEDING OUT!
SOMEONE GET CARSON!
LET GO! I DON'T WANT TO HURT YOU!
SOMEONE GRAB HIM-- WHAT THE-- FUCK ARE YOU--DOING?!
STAY BACK!
ANYONE WHO TRIES TO STOP ME IS KILLING CRYSTAL!

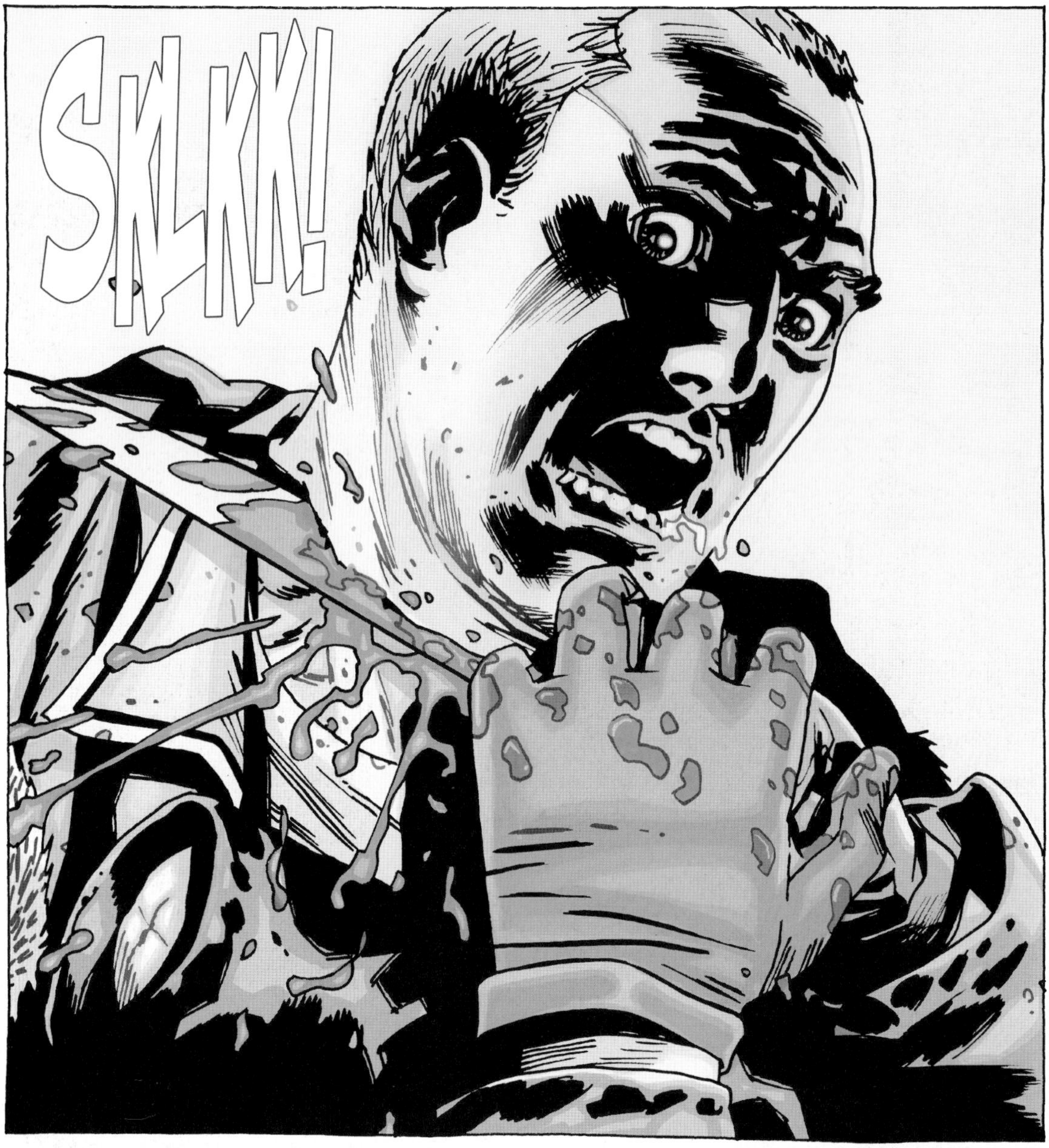
SKLKK!

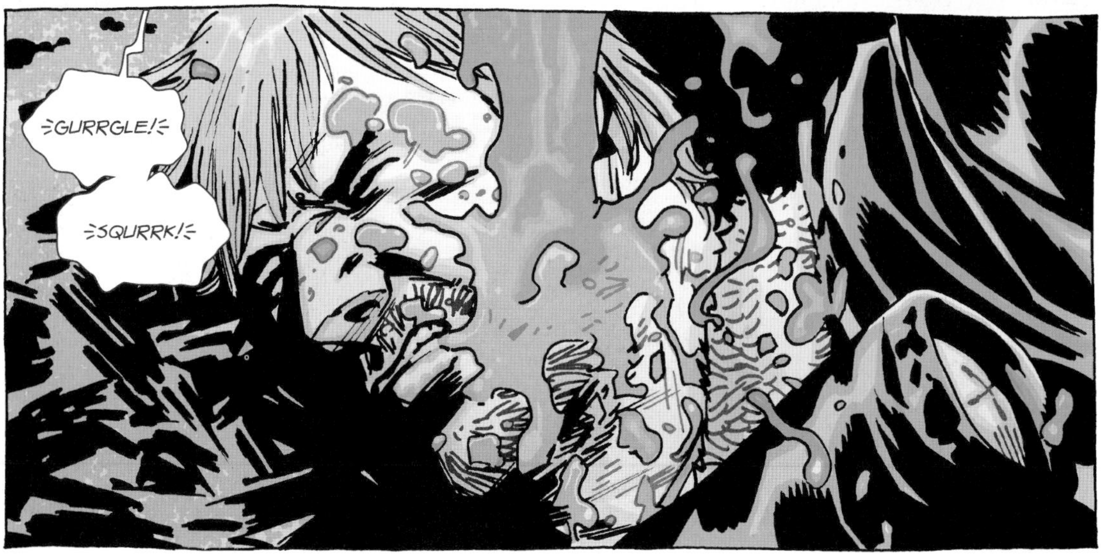
GURRGLE!
SQURRK!

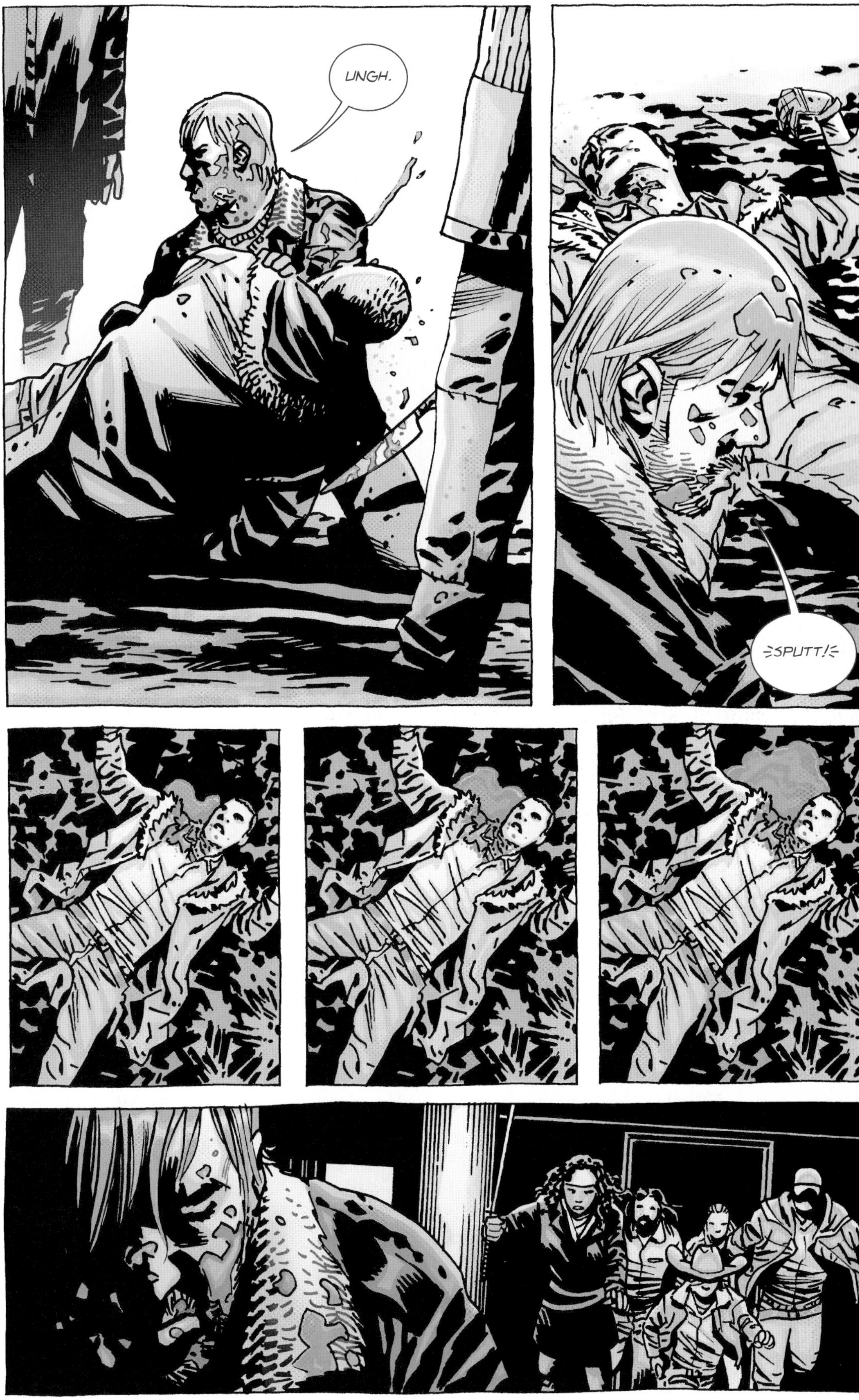
UNGH.
SPUTT!

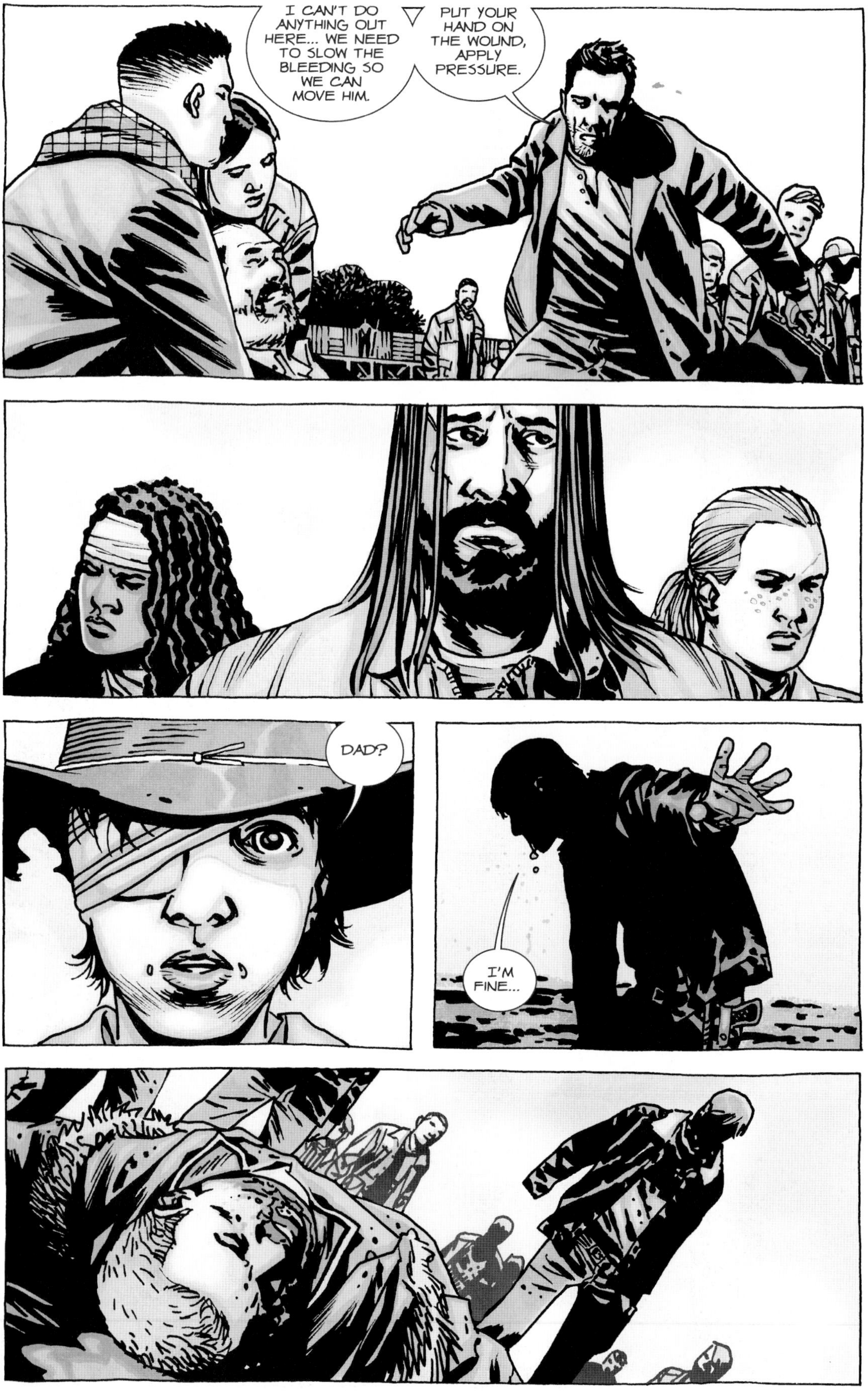
I CAN'T DO ANYTHING OUT HERE... WE NEED TO SLOW THE BLEEDING SO WE CAN MOVE HIM.
PUT YOUR HAND ON THE WOUND, APPLY PRESSURE.
DAD?
I'M FINE...

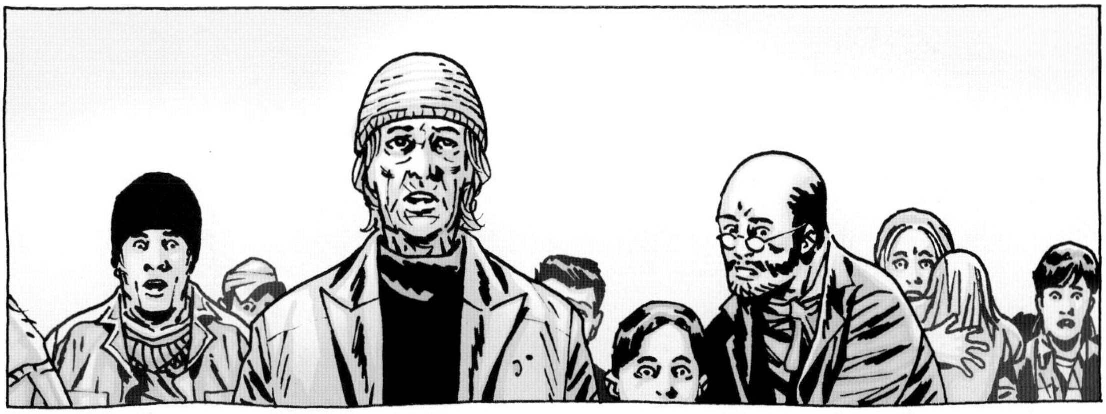
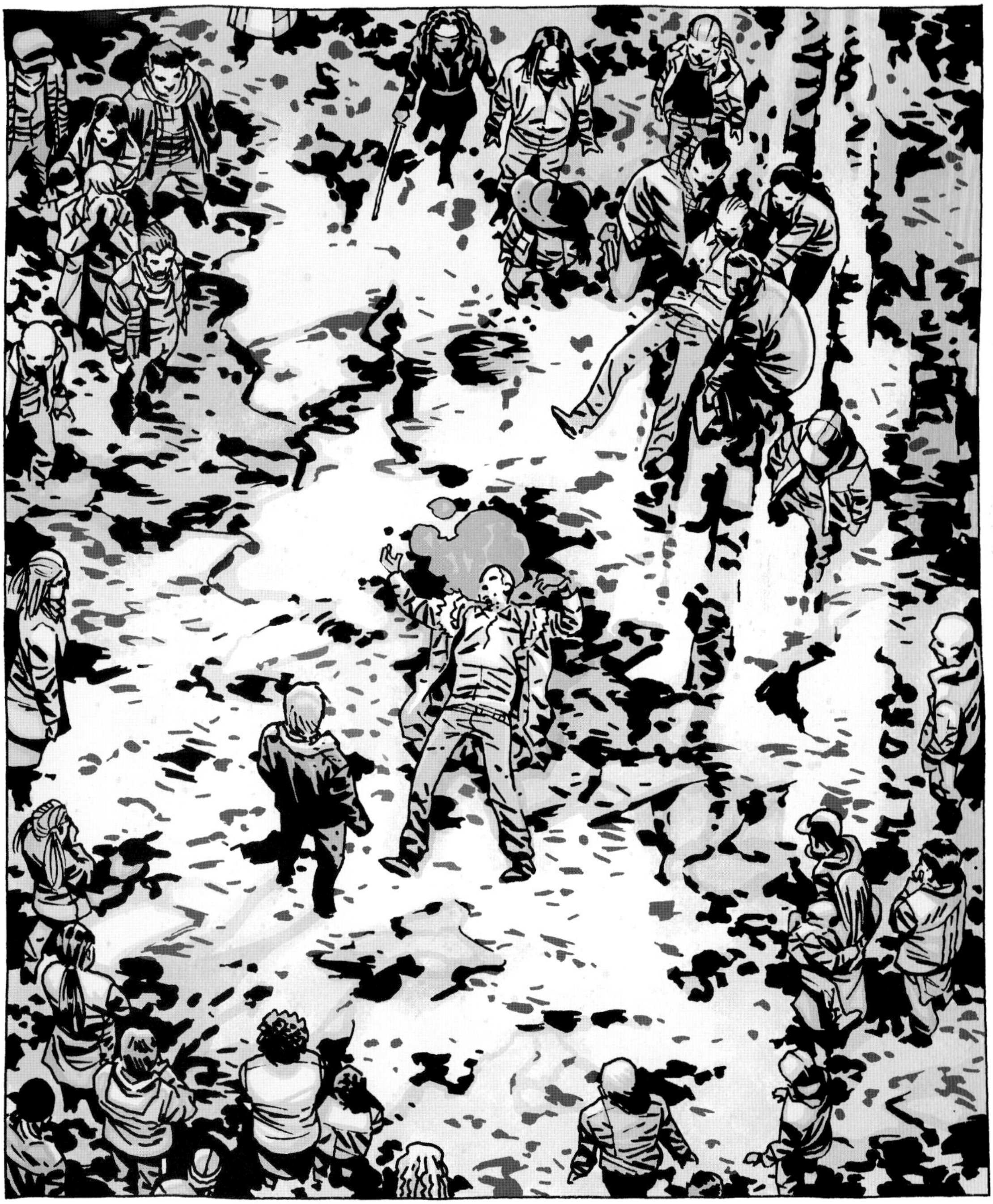

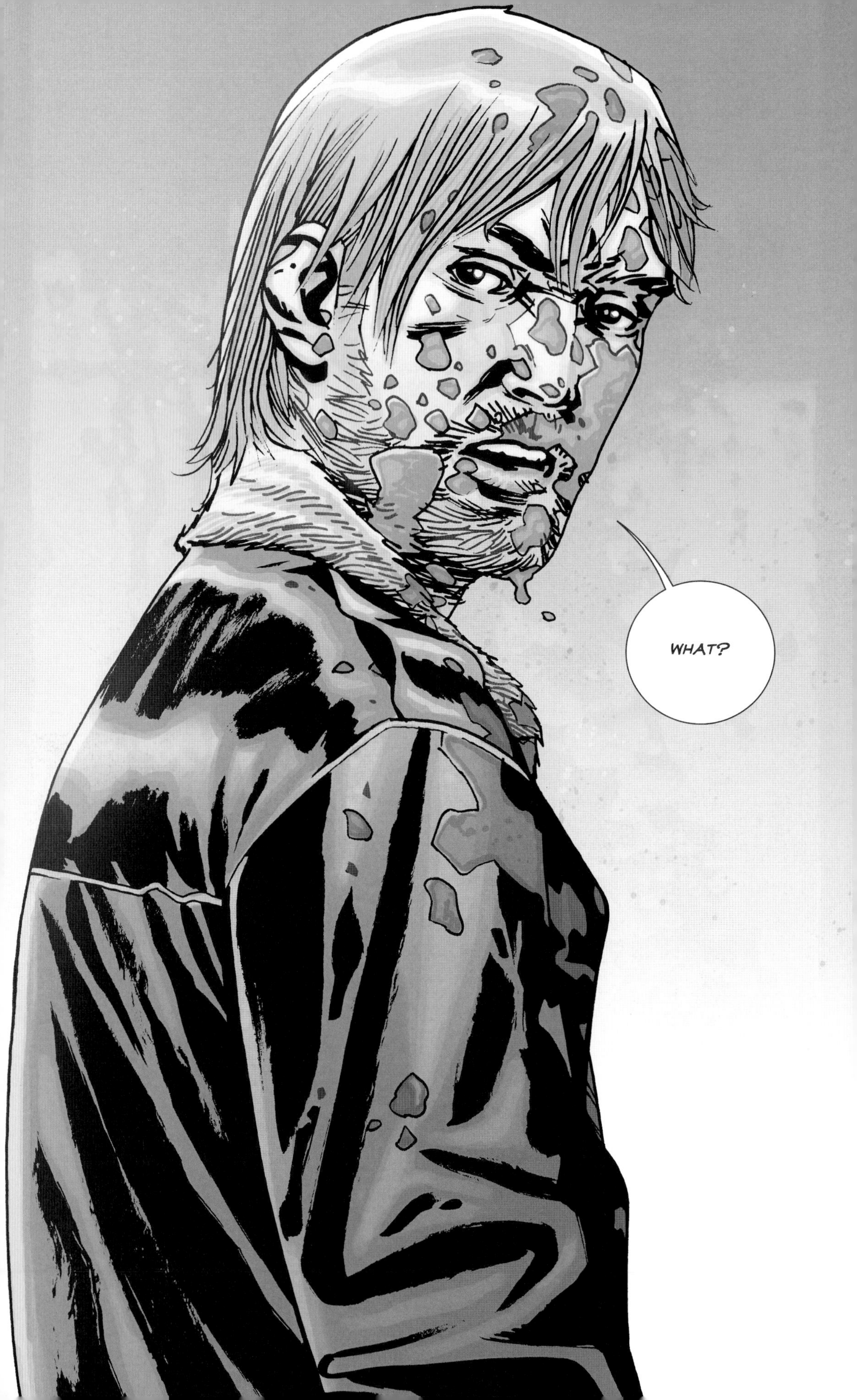
WHAT?

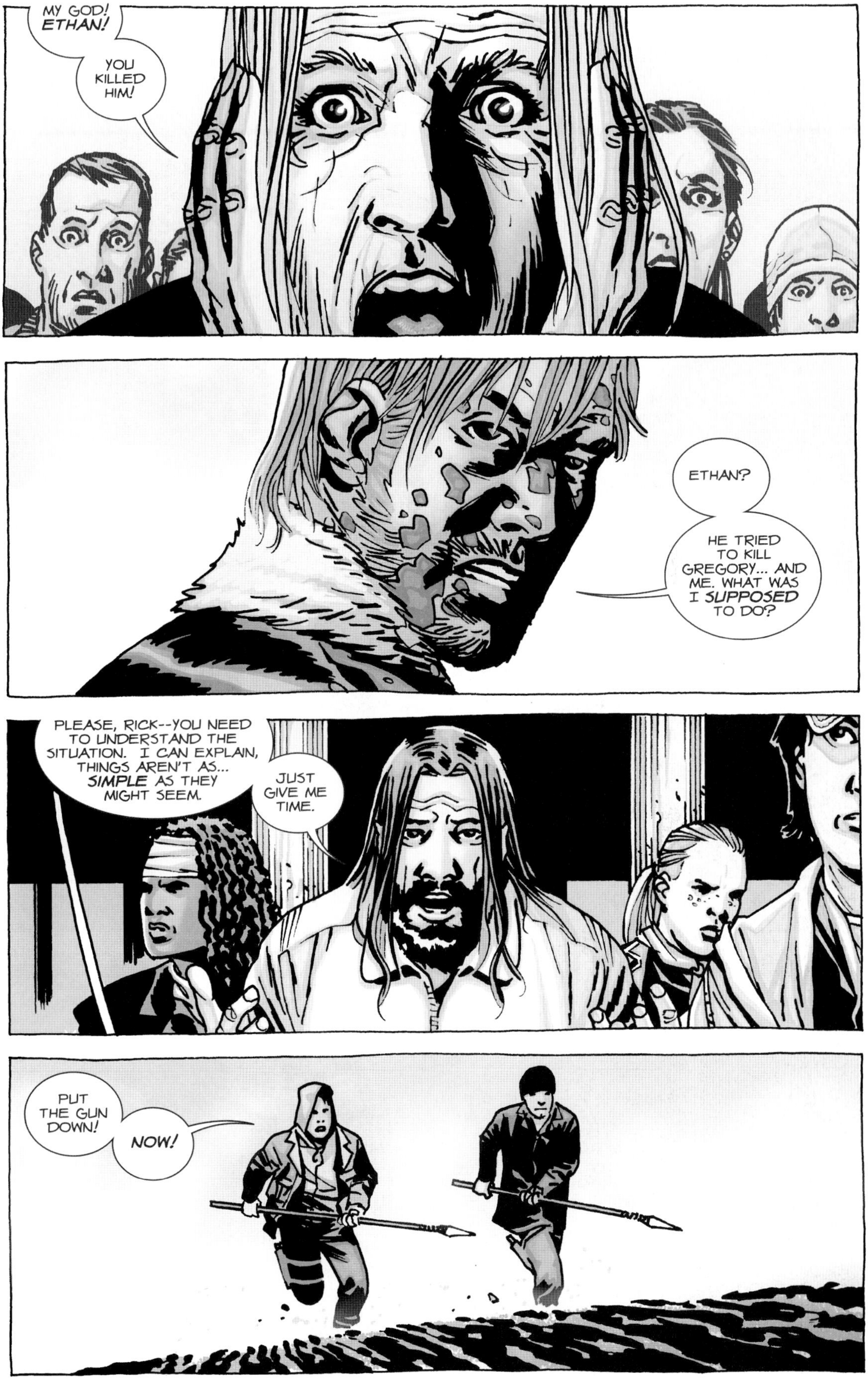
MY GOD! *ETHAN!*
YOU KILLED HIM!
ETHAN?
HE TRIED TO KILL GREGORY... AND ME. WHAT WAS I *SUPPOSED* TO DO?
PLEASE, RICK--YOU NEED TO UNDERSTAND THE SITUATION. I CAN EXPLAIN, THINGS AREN'T AS... *SIMPLE* AS THEY MIGHT SEEM.
JUST GIVE ME TIME.
PUT THE GUN DOWN!
NOW!

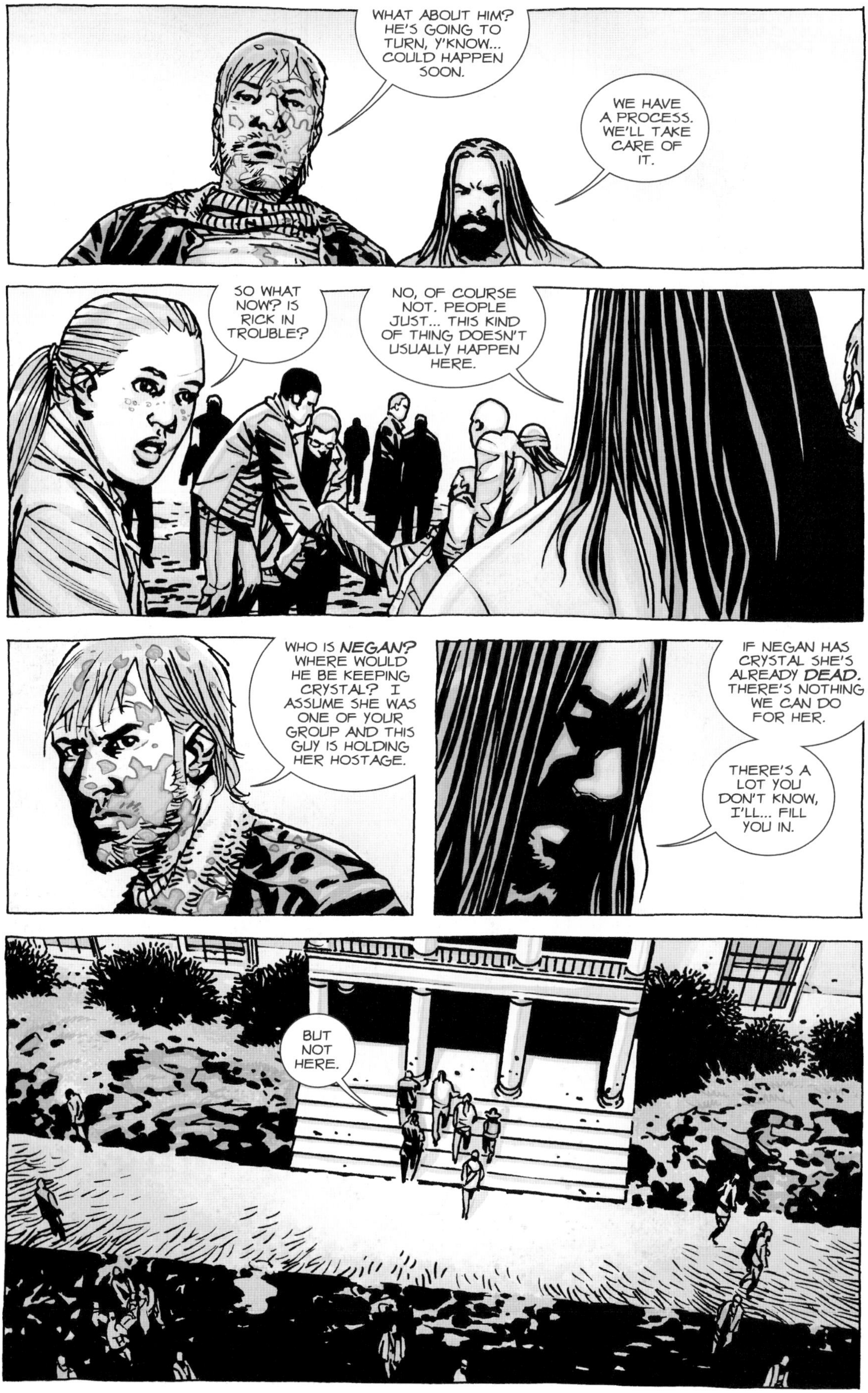
WHAT ABOUT HIM? HE'S GOING TO TURN, Y'KNOW... COULD HAPPEN SOON.
WE HAVE A PROCESS. WE'LL TAKE CARE OF IT.
SO WHAT NOW? IS RICK IN TROUBLE?
NO, OF COURSE NOT. PEOPLE JUST... THIS KIND OF THING DOESN'T USUALLY HAPPEN HERE.
WHO IS NEGAN? WHERE WOULD HE BE KEEPING CRYSTAL? I ASSUME SHE WAS ONE OF YOUR GROUP AND THIS GUY IS HOLDING HER HOSTAGE.
IF NEGAN HAS CRYSTAL SHE'S ALREADY DEAD. THERE'S NOTHING WE CAN DO FOR HER.
THERE'S A LOT YOU DON'T KNOW, I'LL... FILL YOU IN.
BUT NOT HERE.

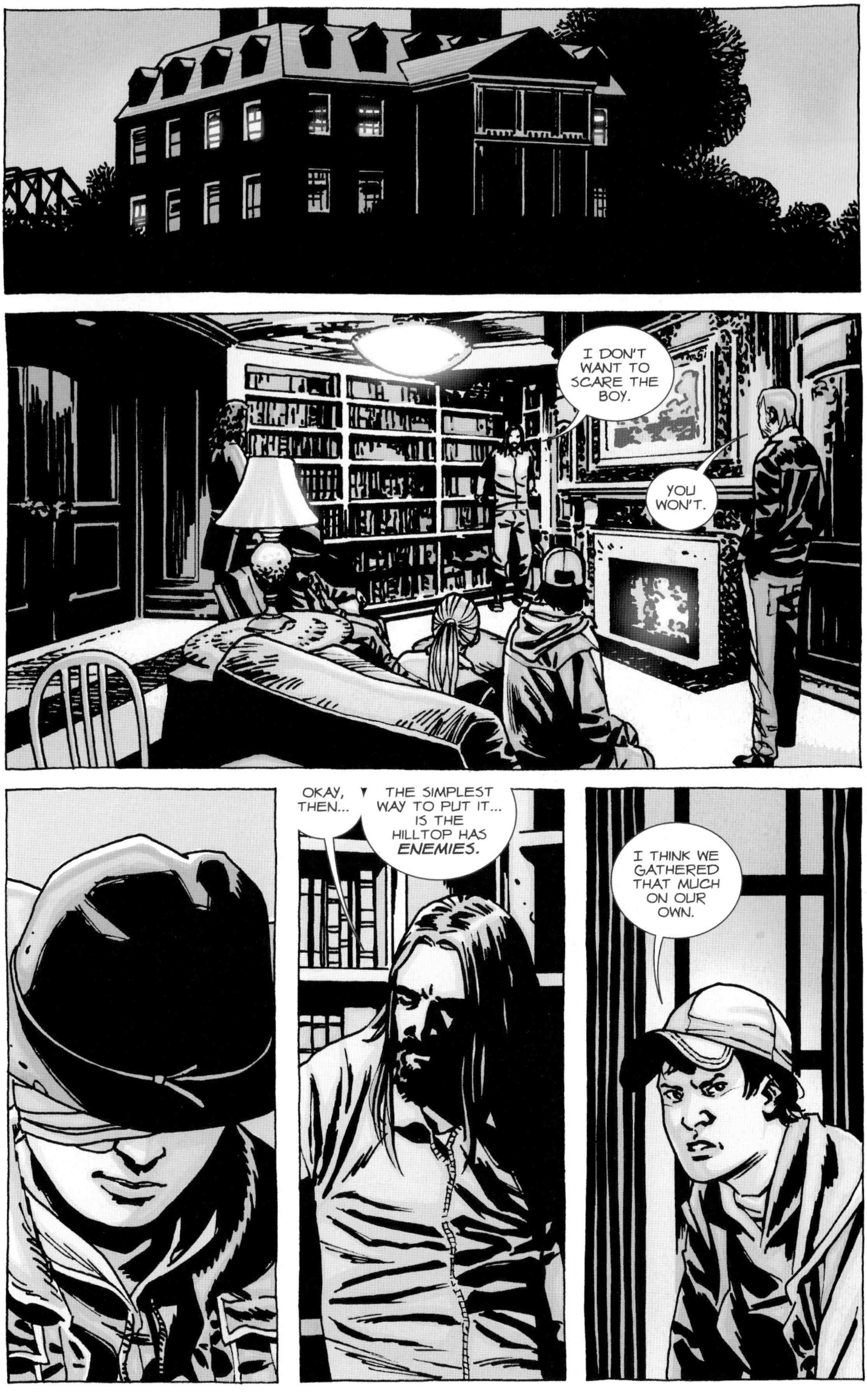
I DON'T WANT TO SCARE THE BOY.
YOU WON'T.
OKAY, THEN...
THE SIMPLEST WAY TO PUT IT... IS THE HILLTOP HAS *ENEMIES.*
I THINK WE GATHERED THAT MUCH ON OUR OWN.

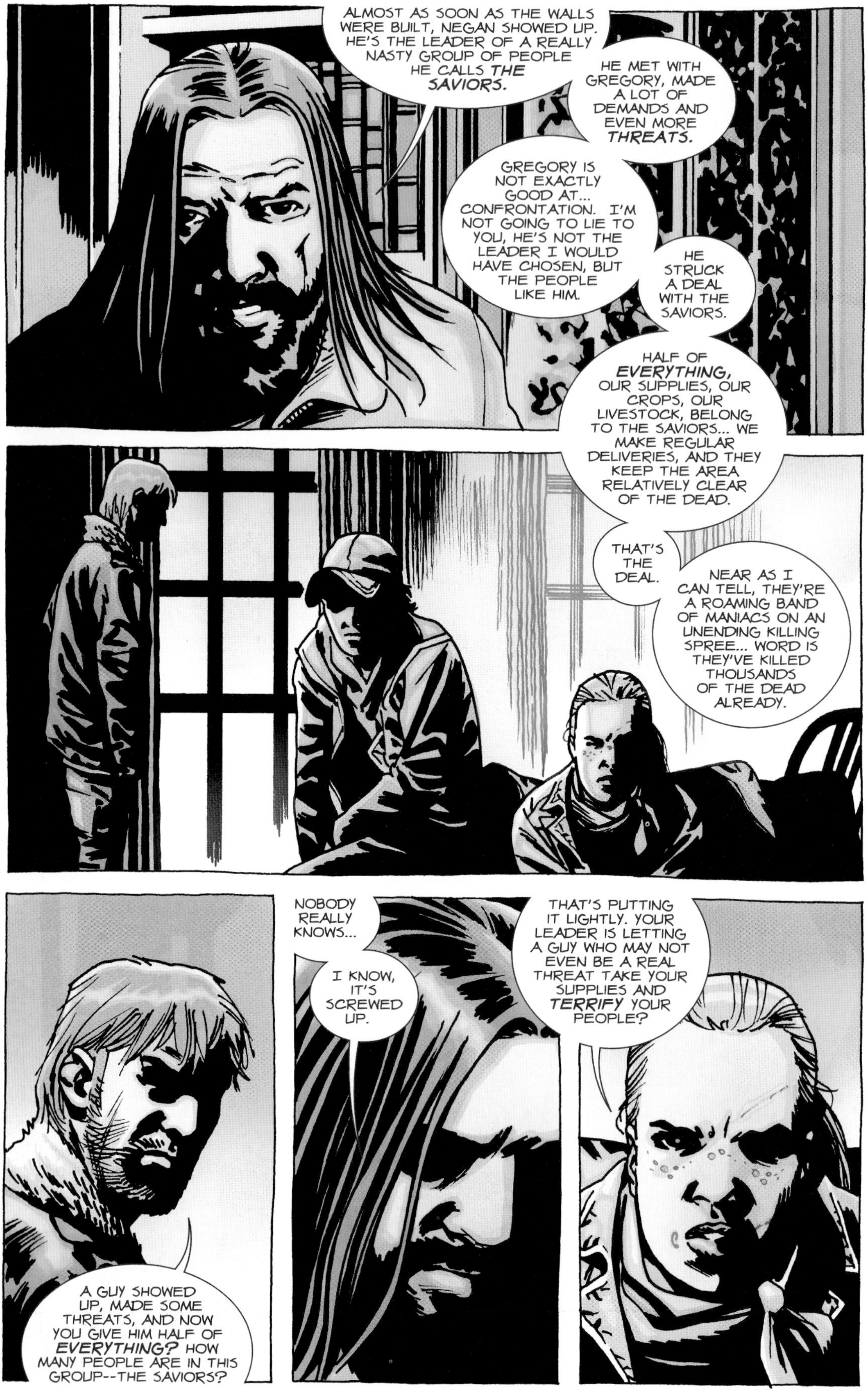
ALMOST AS SOON AS THE WALLS WERE BUILT, NEGAN SHOWED UP. HE'S THE LEADER OF A REALLY NASTY GROUP OF PEOPLE HE CALLS *THE SAVIORS.*
HE MET WITH GREGORY, MADE A LOT OF DEMANDS AND EVEN MORE *THREATS.*
GREGORY IS NOT EXACTLY GOOD AT... CONFRONTATION. I'M NOT GOING TO LIE TO YOU, HE'S NOT THE LEADER I WOULD HAVE CHOSEN, BUT THE PEOPLE LIKE HIM.
HE STRUCK A DEAL WITH THE SAVIORS.
HALF OF *EVERYTHING,* OUR SUPPLIES, OUR CROPS, OUR LIVESTOCK, BELONG TO THE SAVIORS... WE MAKE REGULAR DELIVERIES, AND THEY KEEP THE AREA RELATIVELY CLEAR OF THE DEAD.
THAT'S THE DEAL.
NEAR AS I CAN TELL, THEY'RE A ROAMING BAND OF MANIACS ON AN UNENDING KILLING SPREE... WORD IS THEY'VE KILLED THOUSANDS OF THE DEAD ALREADY.
A GUY SHOWED UP, MADE SOME THREATS, AND NOW YOU GIVE HIM HALF OF *EVERYTHING?* HOW MANY PEOPLE ARE IN THIS GROUP--THE SAVIORS?
NOBODY REALLY KNOWS...
I KNOW, IT'S SCREWED UP.
THAT'S PUTTING IT LIGHTLY. YOUR LEADER IS LETTING A GUY WHO MAY NOT EVEN BE A REAL THREAT TAKE YOUR SUPPLIES AND *TERRIFY* YOUR PEOPLE?

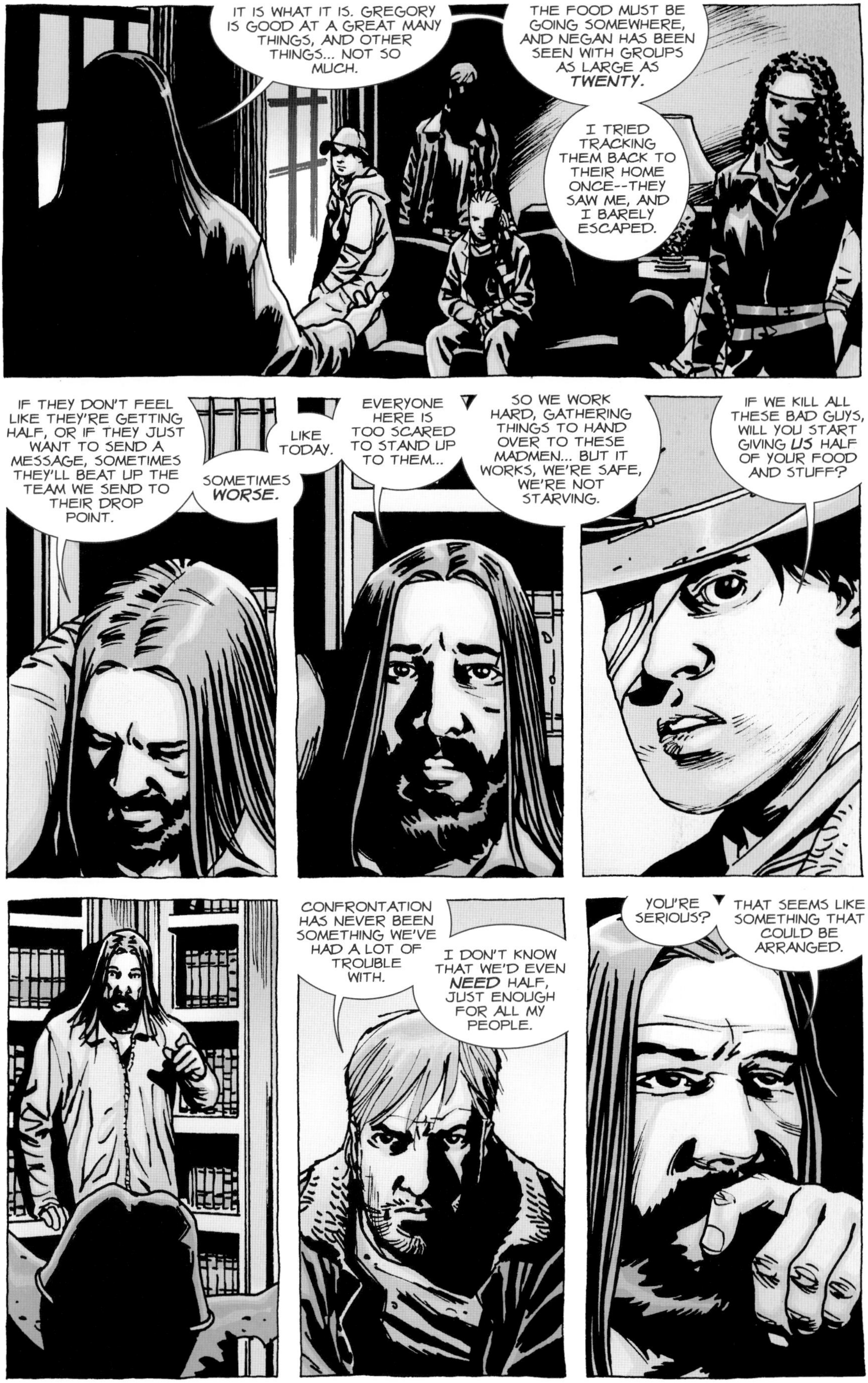
IT IS WHAT IT IS. GREGORY IS GOOD AT A GREAT MANY THINGS, AND OTHER THINGS... NOT SO MUCH.
THE FOOD MUST BE GOING SOMEWHERE, AND NEGAN HAS BEEN SEEN WITH GROUPS AS LARGE AS *TWENTY.*
I TRIED TRACKING THEM BACK TO THEIR HOME ONCE--THEY SAW ME, AND I BARELY ESCAPED.
IF THEY DON'T FEEL LIKE THEY'RE GETTING HALF, OR IF THEY JUST WANT TO SEND A MESSAGE, SOMETIMES THEY'LL BEAT UP THE TEAM WE SEND TO THEIR DROP POINT.
SOMETIMES *WORSE.*
LIKE TODAY.
EVERYONE HERE IS TOO SCARED TO STAND UP TO THEM...
SO WE WORK HARD, GATHERING THINGS TO HAND OVER TO THESE MADMEN... BUT IT WORKS, WE'RE SAFE, WE'RE NOT STARVING.
IF WE KILL ALL THESE BAD GUYS, WILL YOU START GIVING *US* HALF OF YOUR FOOD AND STUFF?
CONFRONTATION HAS NEVER BEEN SOMETHING WE'VE HAD A LOT OF TROUBLE WITH.
I DON'T KNOW THAT WE'D EVEN *NEED* HALF, JUST ENOUGH FOR ALL MY PEOPLE.
YOU'RE SERIOUS?
THAT SEEMS LIKE SOMETHING THAT COULD BE ARRANGED.

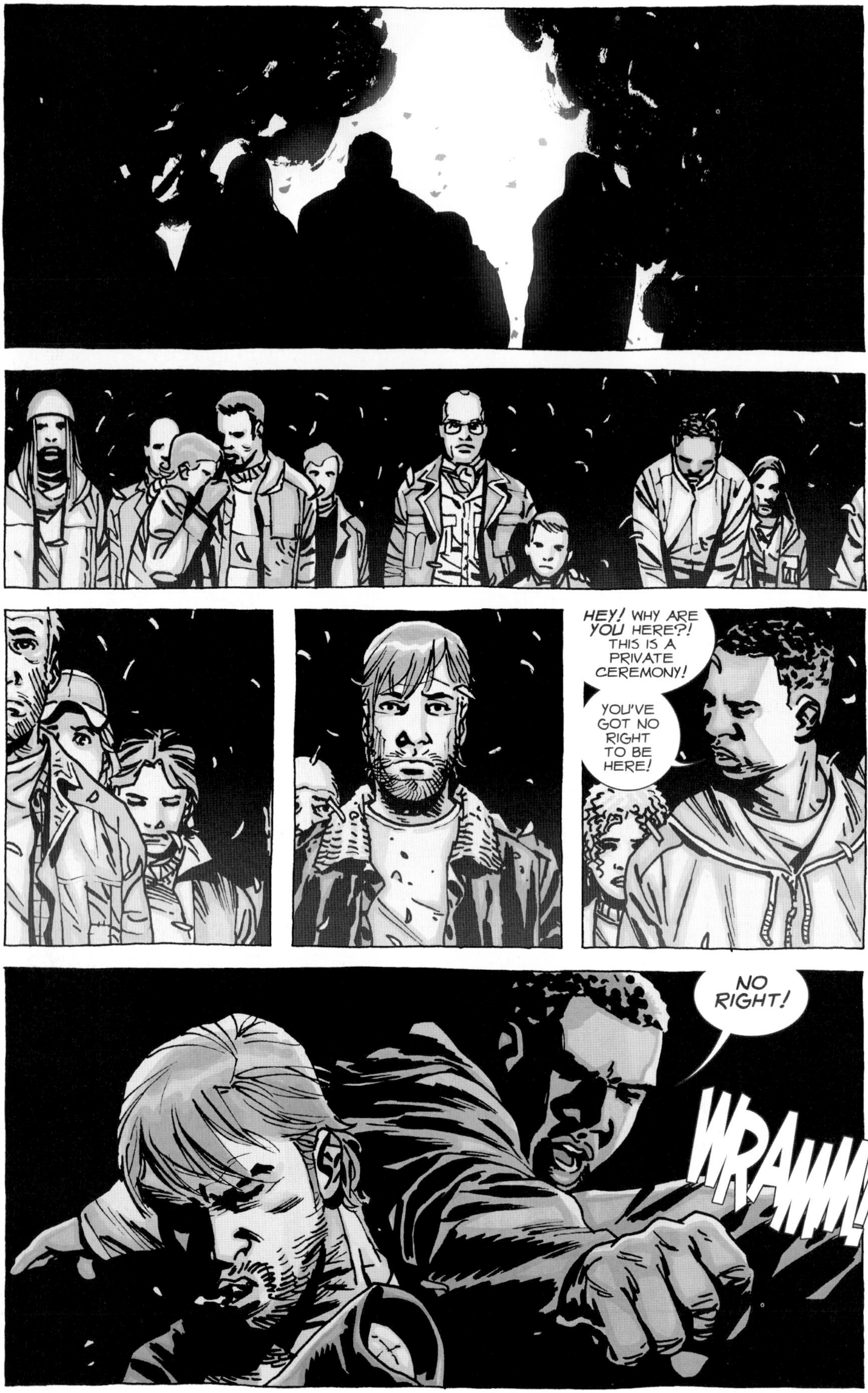
HEY! WHY ARE YOU HERE?! THIS IS A PRIVATE CEREMONY!
YOU'VE GOT NO RIGHT TO BE HERE!
NO RIGHT!
WRAMM!

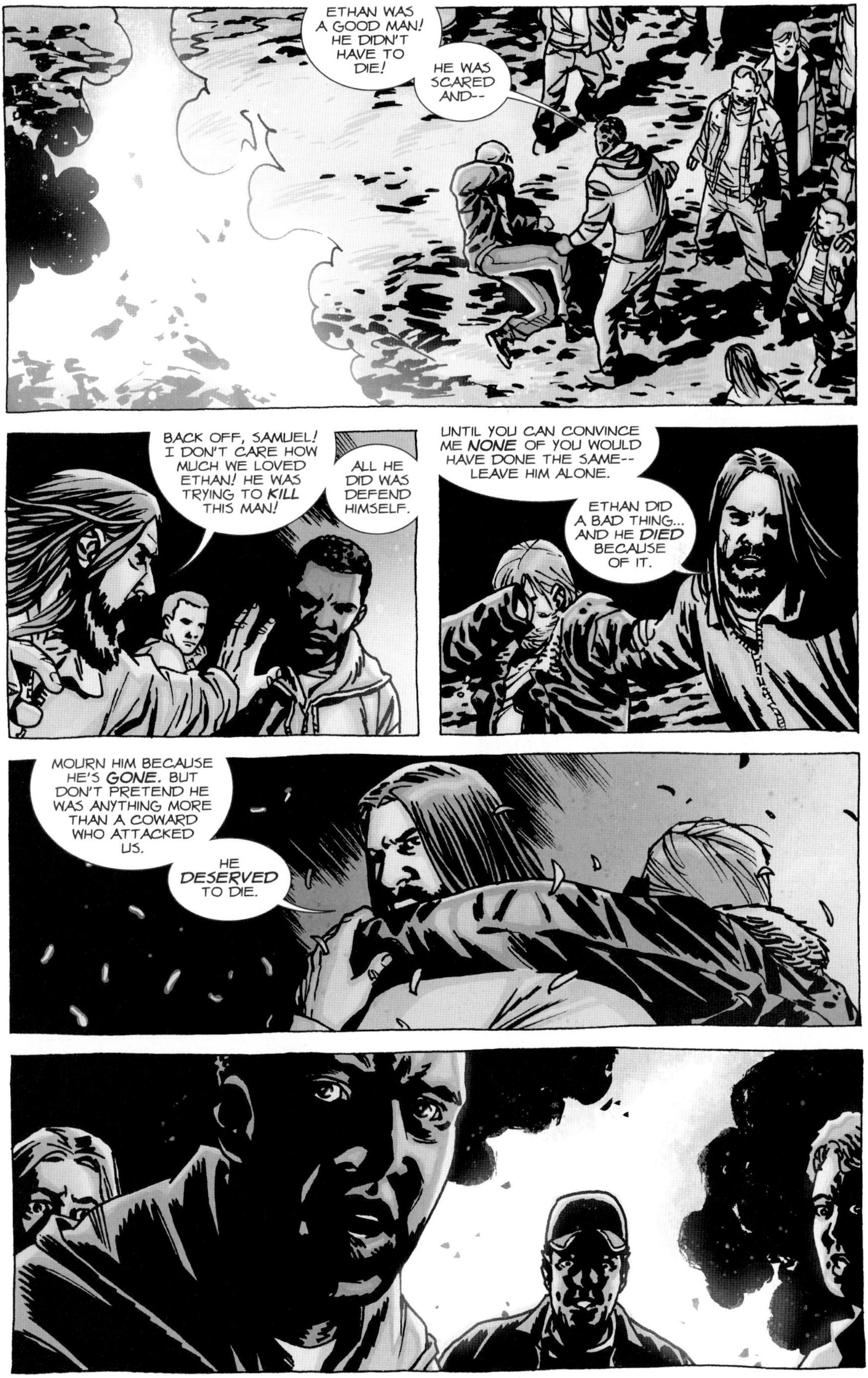
ETHAN WAS A GOOD MAN! HE DIDN'T HAVE TO DIE!
HE WAS SCARED AND--
BACK OFF, SAMUEL! I DON'T CARE HOW MUCH WE LOVED ETHAN! HE WAS TRYING TO KILL THIS MAN!
ALL HE DID WAS DEFEND HIMSELF.
UNTIL YOU CAN CONVINCE ME NONE OF YOU WOULD HAVE DONE THE SAME-- LEAVE HIM ALONE.
ETHAN DID A BAD THING... AND HE DIED BECAUSE OF IT.
MOURN HIM BECAUSE HE'S GONE. BUT DON'T PRETEND HE WAS ANYTHING MORE THAN A COWARD WHO ATTACKED US.
HE DESERVED TO DIE.

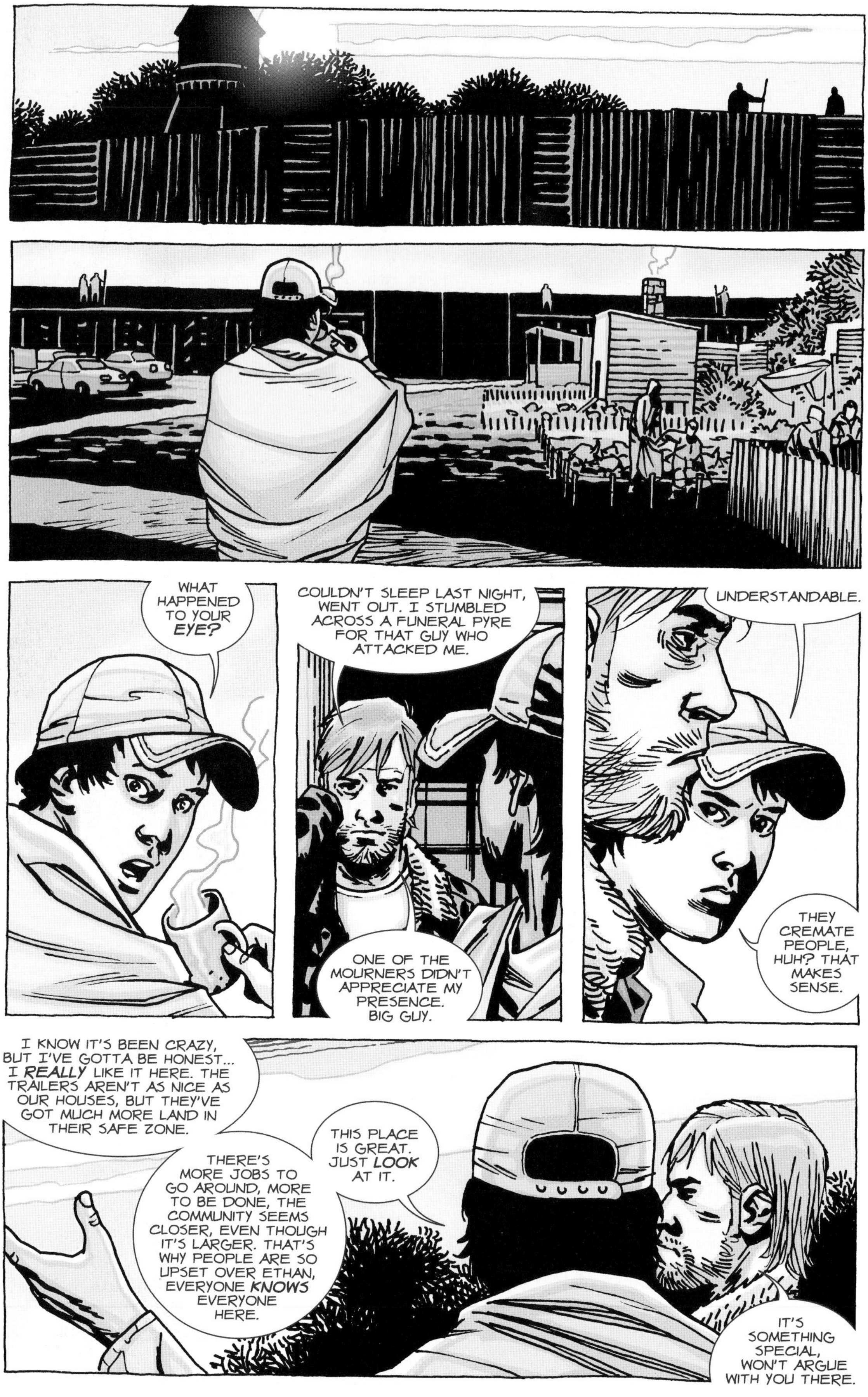
WHAT HAPPENED TO YOUR *EYE?*
COULDN'T SLEEP LAST NIGHT, WENT OUT. I STUMBLED ACROSS A FUNERAL PYRE FOR THAT GUY WHO ATTACKED ME.
ONE OF THE MOURNERS DIDN'T APPRECIATE MY PRESENCE. BIG GUY.
UNDERSTANDABLE.
THEY CREMATE PEOPLE, HUH? THAT MAKES SENSE.
I KNOW IT'S BEEN CRAZY, BUT I'VE GOTTA BE HONEST... I ***REALLY*** LIKE IT HERE. THE TRAILERS AREN'T AS NICE AS OUR HOUSES, BUT THEY'VE GOT MUCH MORE LAND IN THEIR SAFE ZONE.
THERE'S MORE JOBS TO GO AROUND, MORE TO BE DONE, THE COMMUNITY SEEMS CLOSER, EVEN THOUGH IT'S LARGER. THAT'S WHY PEOPLE ARE SO UPSET OVER ETHAN, EVERYONE ***KNOWS*** EVERYONE HERE.
THIS PLACE IS GREAT. JUST ***LOOK*** AT IT.
IT'S SOMETHING SPECIAL, WON'T ARGUE WITH YOU THERE.

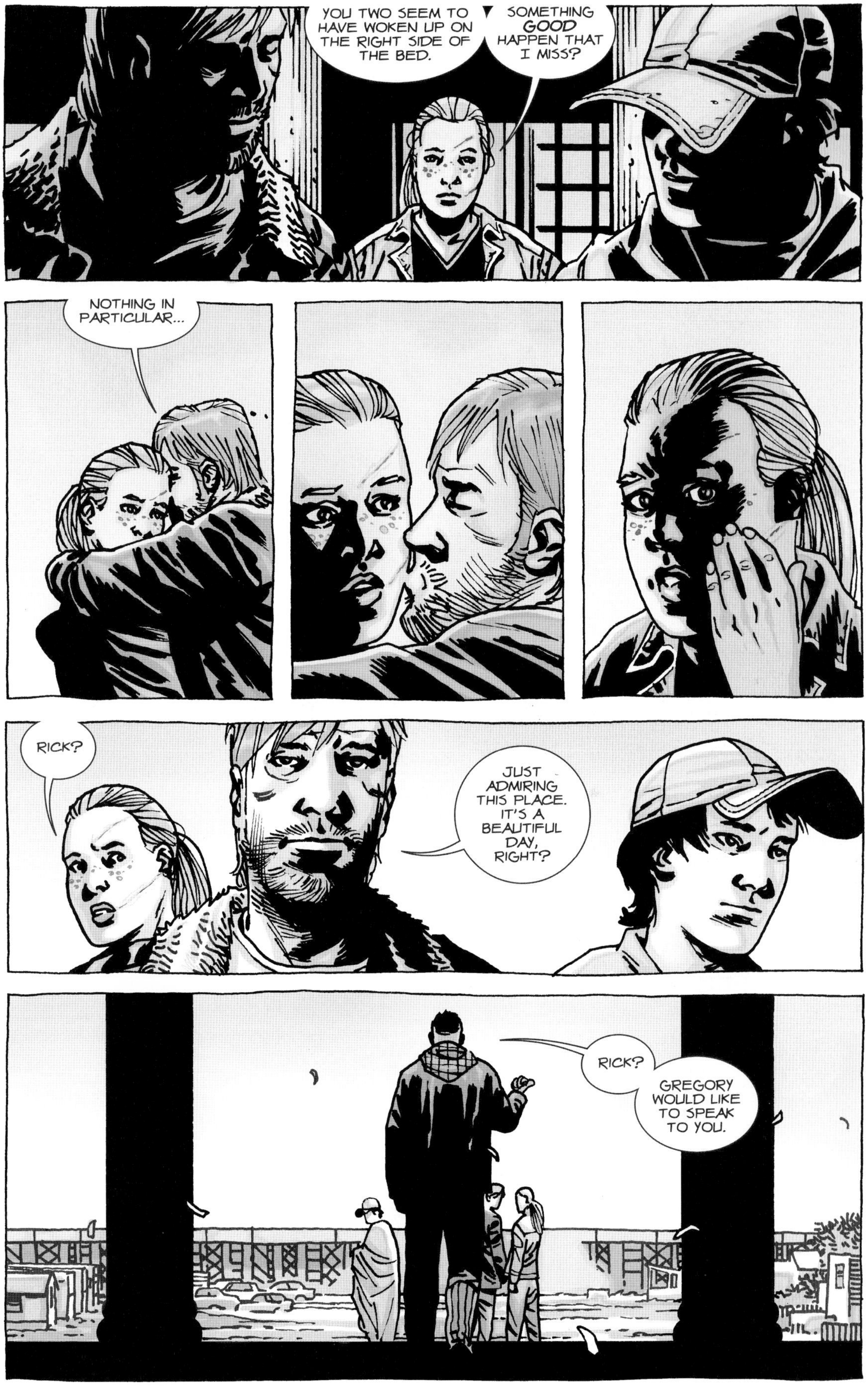
YOU TWO SEEM TO HAVE WOKEN UP ON THE RIGHT SIDE OF THE BED.
SOMETHING *GOOD* HAPPEN THAT I MISS?
NOTHING IN PARTICULAR...
RICK?
JUST ADMIRING THIS PLACE. IT'S A BEAUTIFUL DAY, RIGHT?
RICK?
GREGORY WOULD LIKE TO SPEAK TO YOU.

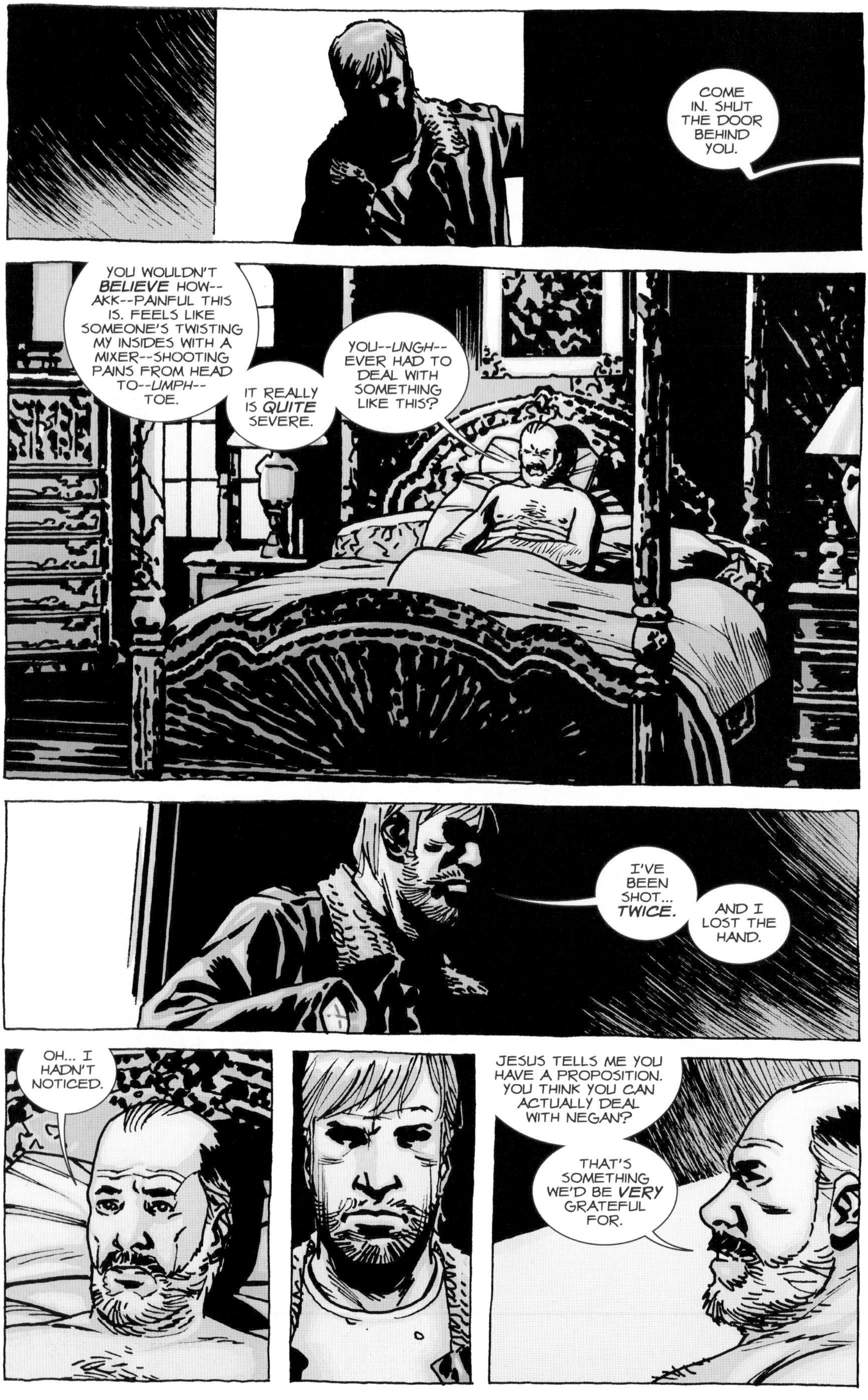
COME IN. SHUT THE DOOR BEHIND YOU.
YOU WOULDN'T BELIEVE HOW-- AKK--PAINFUL THIS IS. FEELS LIKE SOMEONE'S TWISTING MY INSIDES WITH A MIXER--SHOOTING PAINS FROM HEAD TO--UMPH-- TOE.
IT REALLY IS QUITE SEVERE.
YOU--UNGH-- EVER HAD TO DEAL WITH SOMETHING LIKE THIS?
I'VE BEEN SHOT... TWICE.
AND I LOST THE HAND.
OH... I HADN'T NOTICED.
JESUS TELLS ME YOU HAVE A PROPOSITION. YOU THINK YOU CAN ACTUALLY DEAL WITH NEGAN?
THAT'S SOMETHING WE'D BE VERY GRATEFUL FOR.

THE TRUTH OF THE MATTER IS THAT WE DON'T HAVE A LOT TO OFFER IN THE WAY OF SUPPLIES. WE'RE RUNNING LOW ON FOOD AS IT IS, WE DON'T HAVE *ANYTHING* TO SPARE.

SO THIS TRADE AGREEMENT THAT JESUS TOLD ME ABOUT PROBABLY WOULDN'T WORK, AT LEAST FOR NOW.

EVENTUALLY WE MAY BE ABLE TO CONTRIBUTE. BUT EVEN THEN, I DON'T KNOW HOW I'LL FEEL KNOWING HALF OF EVERYTHING I SEND HERE GOES TO A GROUP OF VIOLENT KILLERS.

NEGAN AND HIS PEOPLE HAVE BEEN A THORN IN OUR SIDE FOR SOME TIME NOW. I'VE ACCOMPLISHED AMAZING THINGS WITH THIS COMMUNITY, IT'S TRUE... BUT WE'VE NEVER BEEN STRONG ENOUGH TO FACE HIM.

ONE OF THE REASONS JESUS IS SO DILIGENT IN BRINGING NEW COMMUNITIES INTO THE FOLD IS TO LIGHTEN OUR BURDEN. MORE SOURCES OF SUPPLIES FOR THE OFFERING.

IT WAS A GOOD IDEA, BUT IT HASN'T SEEMED TO MAKE THINGS EASIER WITH NEGAN. OVER THE LAST FEW MONTHS... THINGS HAVE GOTTEN *WORSE*.

I'VE DEALT WITH HIS KIND BEFORE. MY PEOPLE LIVED ON THE ROAD MORE THAN OFF, FOR THE BETTER PART OF A YEAR.

WE KNOW HOW TO HANDLE PEOPLE LIKE THAT.

YOU SAYING YOU'LL FIGHT FOR US? THAT'D BE YOUR CONTRIBUTION?

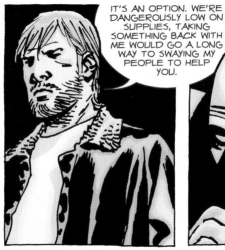

IT'S AN OPTION. WE'RE DANGEROUSLY LOW ON SUPPLIES, TAKING SOMETHING BACK WITH ME WOULD GO A LONG WAY TO SWAYING MY PEOPLE TO HELP YOU.

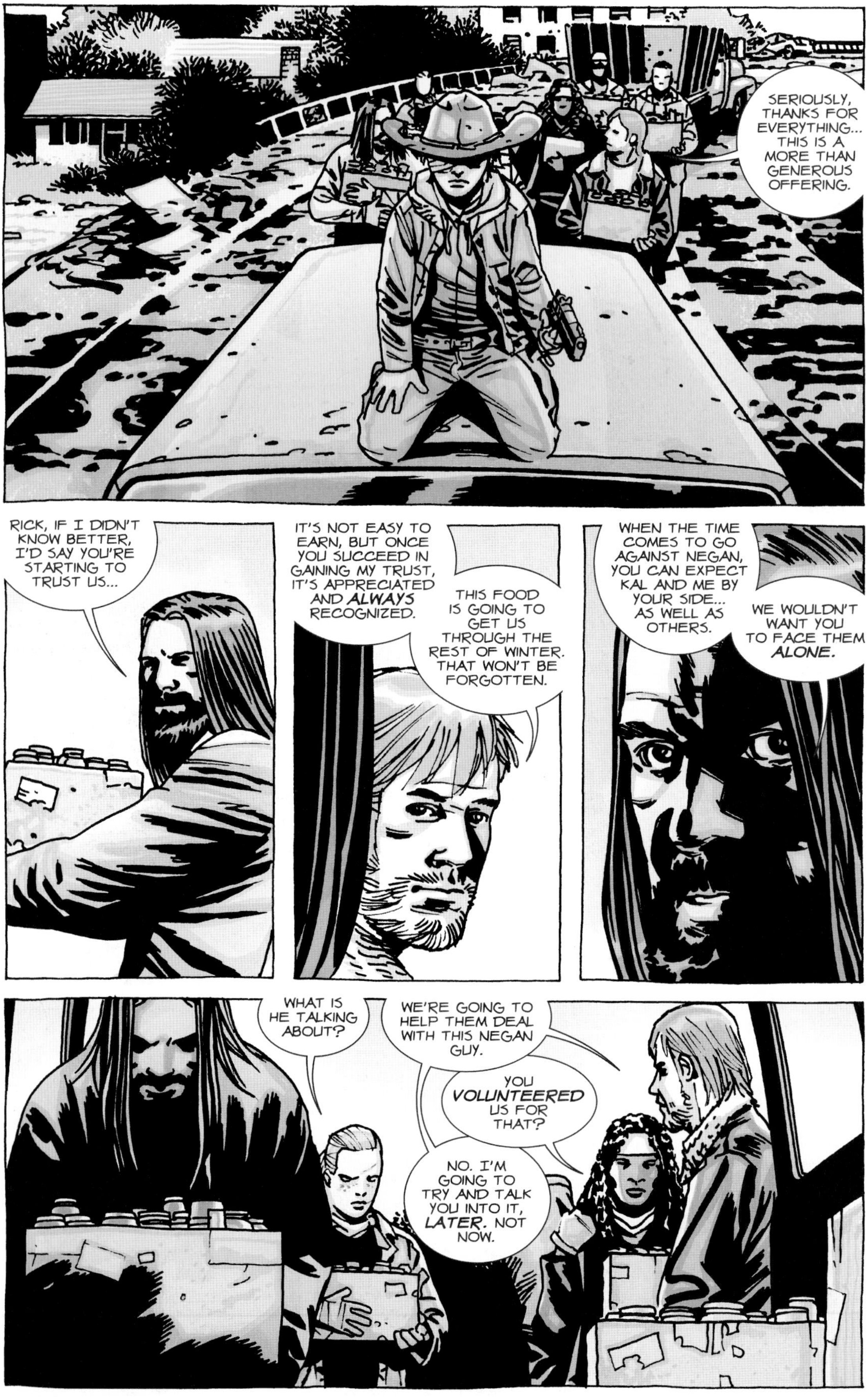
SERIOUSLY, THANKS FOR EVERYTHING... THIS IS A MORE THAN GENEROUS OFFERING.
RICK, IF I DIDN'T KNOW BETTER, I'D SAY YOU'RE STARTING TO TRUST US...
IT'S NOT EASY TO EARN, BUT ONCE YOU SUCCEED IN GAINING MY TRUST, IT'S APPRECIATED AND ALWAYS RECOGNIZED.
THIS FOOD IS GOING TO GET US THROUGH THE REST OF WINTER. THAT WON'T BE FORGOTTEN.
WHEN THE TIME COMES TO GO AGAINST NEGAN, YOU CAN EXPECT KAL AND ME BY YOUR SIDE... AS WELL AS OTHERS.
WE WOULDN'T WANT YOU TO FACE THEM ALONE.
WHAT IS HE TALKING ABOUT?
WE'RE GOING TO HELP THEM DEAL WITH THIS NEGAN GUY.
YOU VOLUNTEERED US FOR THAT?
NO. I'M GOING TO TRY AND TALK YOU INTO IT, LATER. NOT NOW.

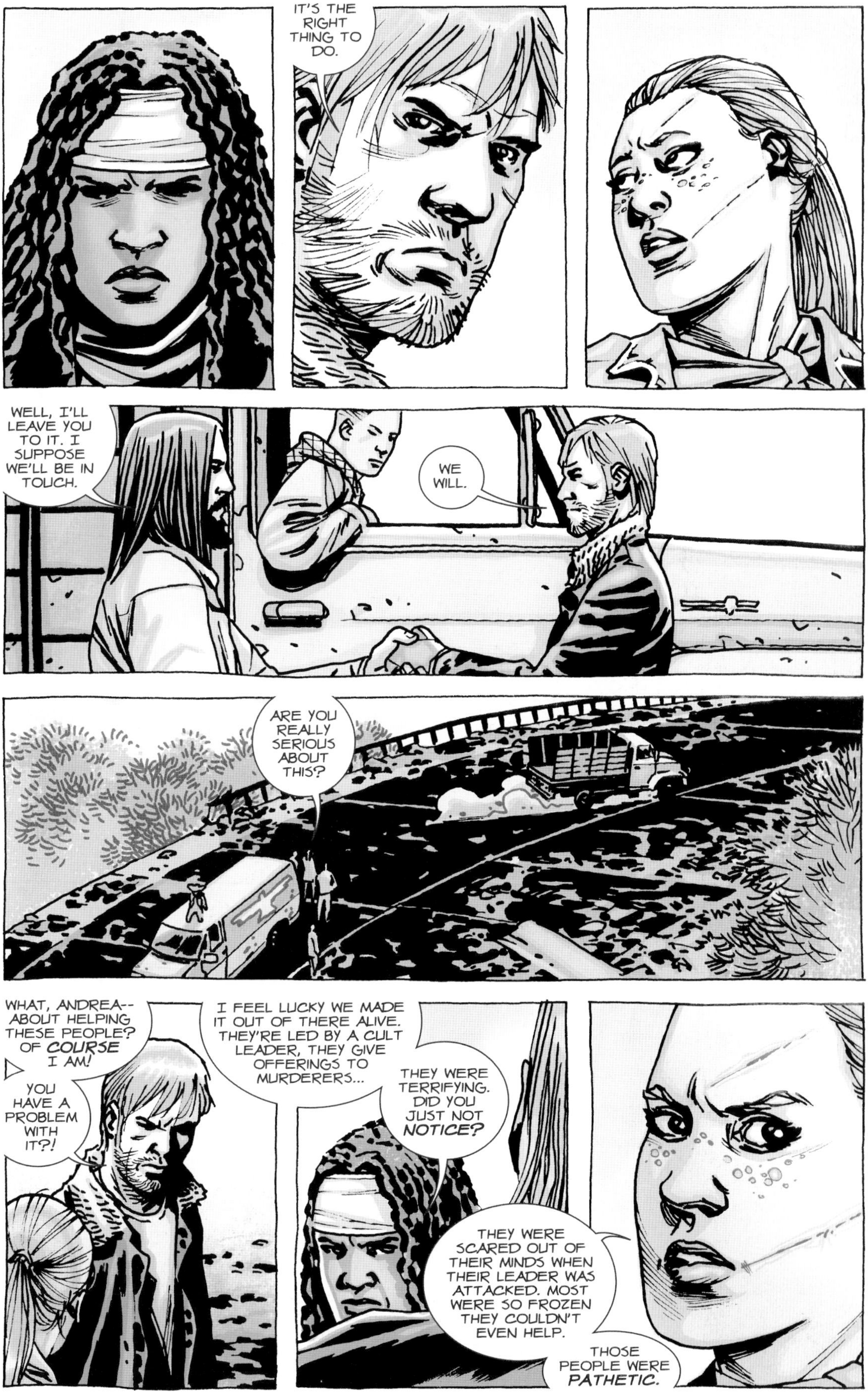

IT'S THE RIGHT THING TO DO.
WELL, I'LL LEAVE YOU TO IT. I SUPPOSE WE'LL BE IN TOUCH.
WE WILL.
ARE YOU REALLY SERIOUS ABOUT THIS?
WHAT, ANDREA-- ABOUT HELPING THESE PEOPLE? OF COURSE I AM!
YOU HAVE A PROBLEM WITH IT?!
I FEEL LUCKY WE MADE IT OUT OF THERE ALIVE. THEY'RE LED BY A CULT LEADER, THEY GIVE OFFERINGS TO MURDERERS...
THEY WERE TERRIFYING. DID YOU JUST NOT NOTICE?
THEY WERE SCARED OUT OF THEIR MINDS WHEN THEIR LEADER WAS ATTACKED. MOST WERE SO FROZEN THEY COULDN'T EVEN HELP.
THOSE PEOPLE WERE PATHETIC.

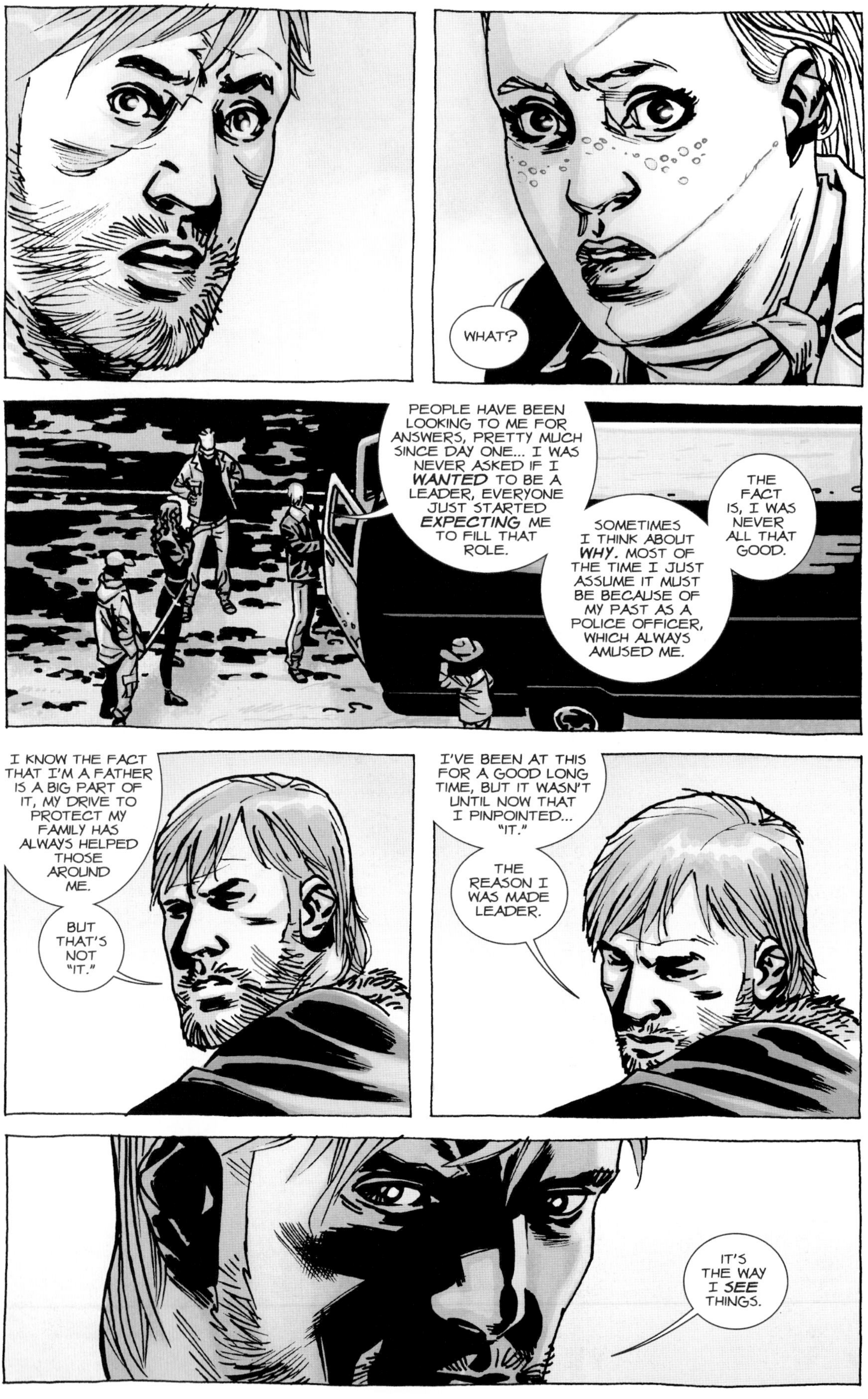
WHAT?
PEOPLE HAVE BEEN LOOKING TO ME FOR ANSWERS, PRETTY MUCH SINCE DAY ONE... I WAS NEVER ASKED IF I WANTED TO BE A LEADER, EVERYONE JUST STARTED EXPECTING ME TO FILL THAT ROLE.
SOMETIMES I THINK ABOUT WHY. MOST OF THE TIME I JUST ASSUME IT MUST BE BECAUSE OF MY PAST AS A POLICE OFFICER, WHICH ALWAYS AMUSED ME.
THE FACT IS, I WAS NEVER ALL THAT GOOD.
I KNOW THE FACT THAT I'M A FATHER IS A BIG PART OF IT, MY DRIVE TO PROTECT MY FAMILY HAS ALWAYS HELPED THOSE AROUND ME.
BUT THAT'S NOT "IT."
I'VE BEEN AT THIS FOR A GOOD LONG TIME, BUT IT WASN'T UNTIL NOW THAT I PINPOINTED... "IT."
THE REASON I WAS MADE LEADER.
IT'S THE WAY I SEE THINGS.

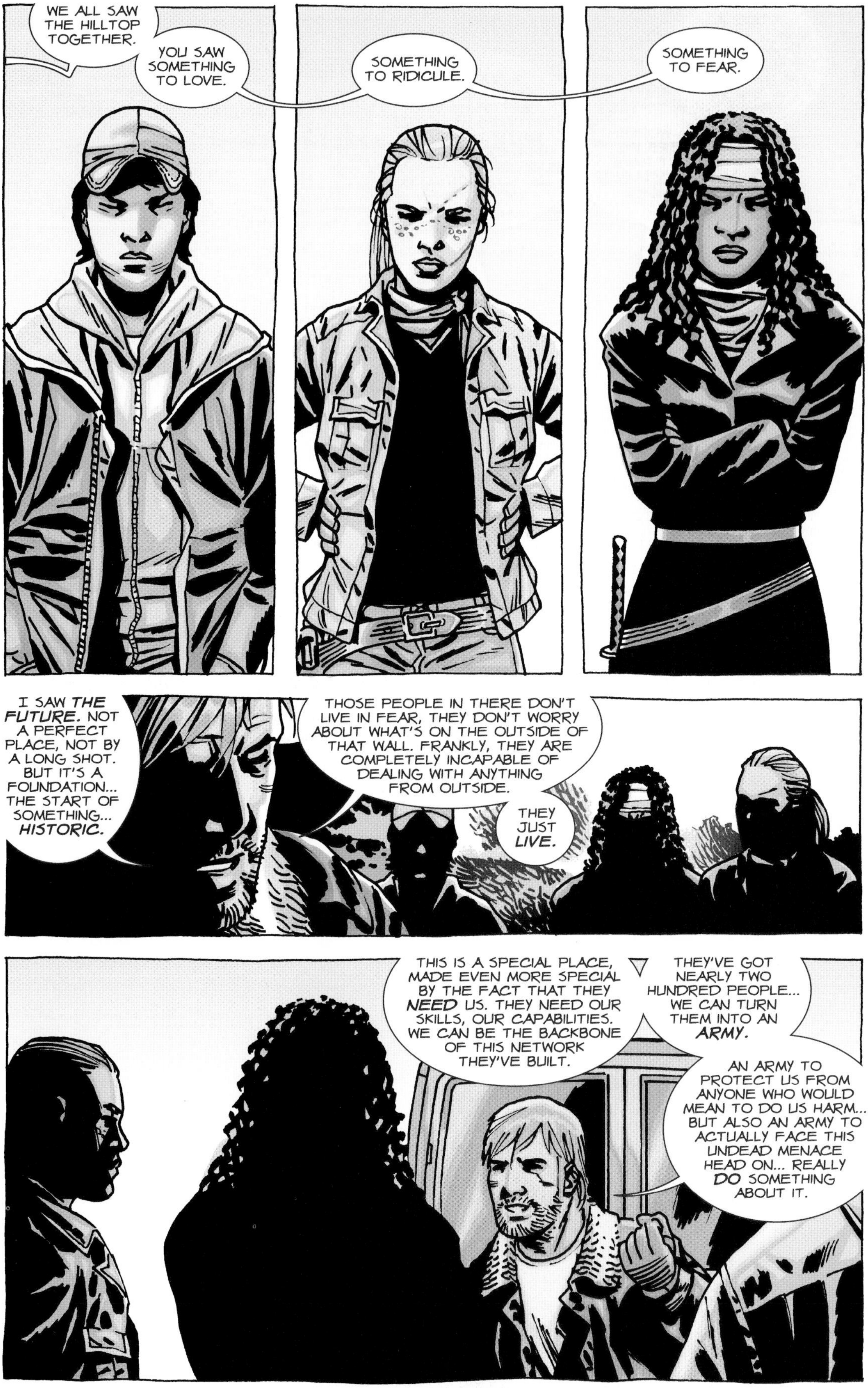
WE ALL SAW THE HILLTOP TOGETHER.
YOU SAW SOMETHING TO LOVE.
SOMETHING TO RIDICULE.
SOMETHING TO FEAR.
I SAW THE FUTURE. NOT A PERFECT PLACE, NOT BY A LONG SHOT. BUT IT'S A FOUNDATION... THE START OF SOMETHING... HISTORIC.
THOSE PEOPLE IN THERE DON'T LIVE IN FEAR, THEY DON'T WORRY ABOUT WHAT'S ON THE OUTSIDE OF THAT WALL. FRANKLY, THEY ARE COMPLETELY INCAPABLE OF DEALING WITH ANYTHING FROM OUTSIDE.
THEY JUST LIVE.
THIS IS A SPECIAL PLACE, MADE EVEN MORE SPECIAL BY THE FACT THAT THEY NEED US. THEY NEED OUR SKILLS, OUR CAPABILITIES. WE CAN BE THE BACKBONE OF THIS NETWORK THEY'VE BUILT.
THEY'VE GOT NEARLY TWO HUNDRED PEOPLE... WE CAN TURN THEM INTO AN ARMY.
AN ARMY TO PROTECT US FROM ANYONE WHO WOULD MEAN TO DO US HARM... BUT ALSO AN ARMY TO ACTUALLY FACE THIS UNDEAD MENACE HEAD ON... REALLY DO SOMETHING ABOUT IT.

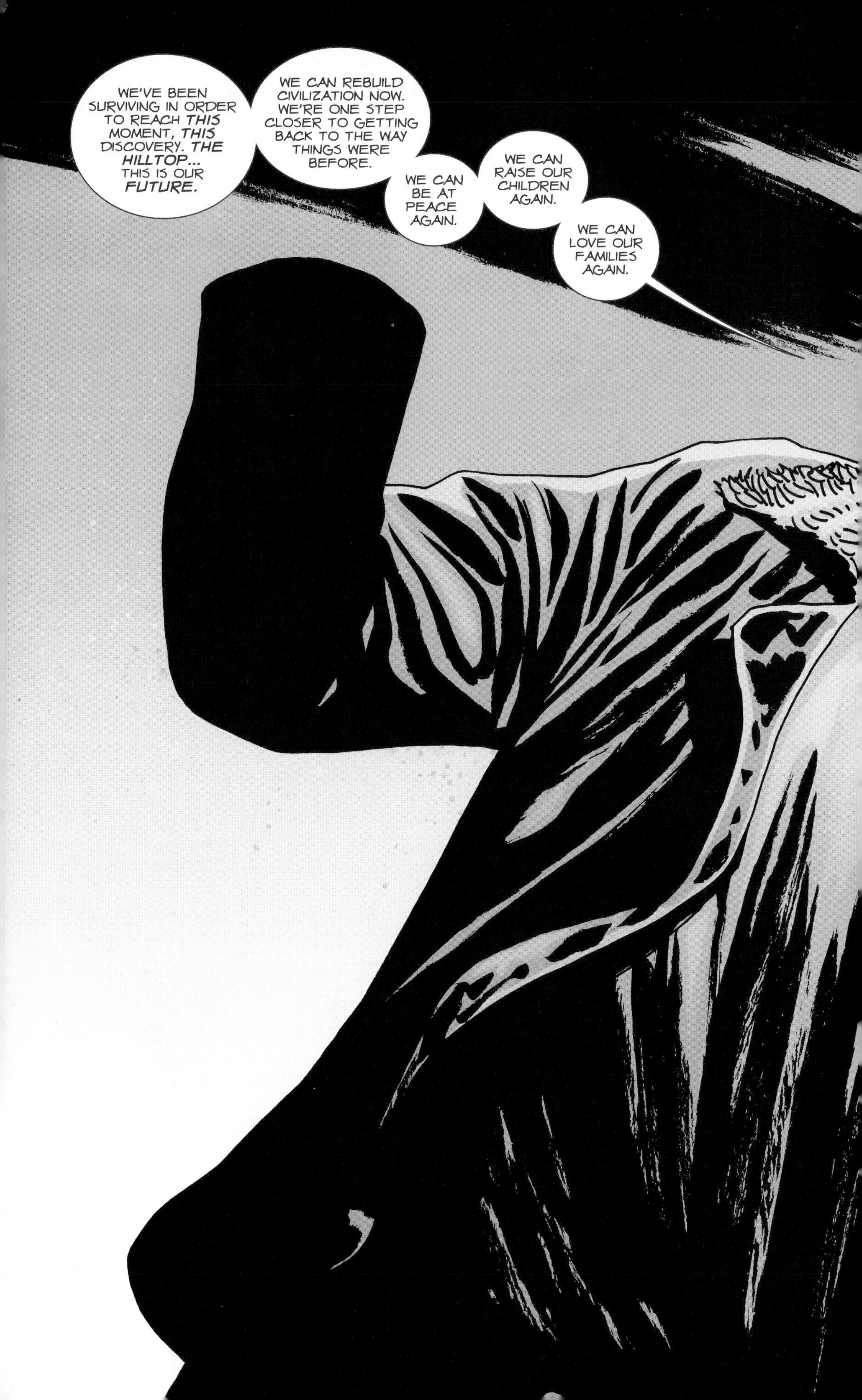
WE'VE BEEN SURVIVING IN ORDER TO REACH THIS MOMENT, THIS DISCOVERY. THE HILLTOP... THIS IS OUR FUTURE.
WE CAN REBUILD CIVILIZATION NOW. WE'RE ONE STEP CLOSER TO GETTING BACK TO THE WAY THINGS WERE BEFORE.
WE CAN BE AT PEACE AGAIN.
WE CAN RAISE OUR CHILDREN AGAIN.
WE CAN LOVE OUR FAMILIES AGAIN.

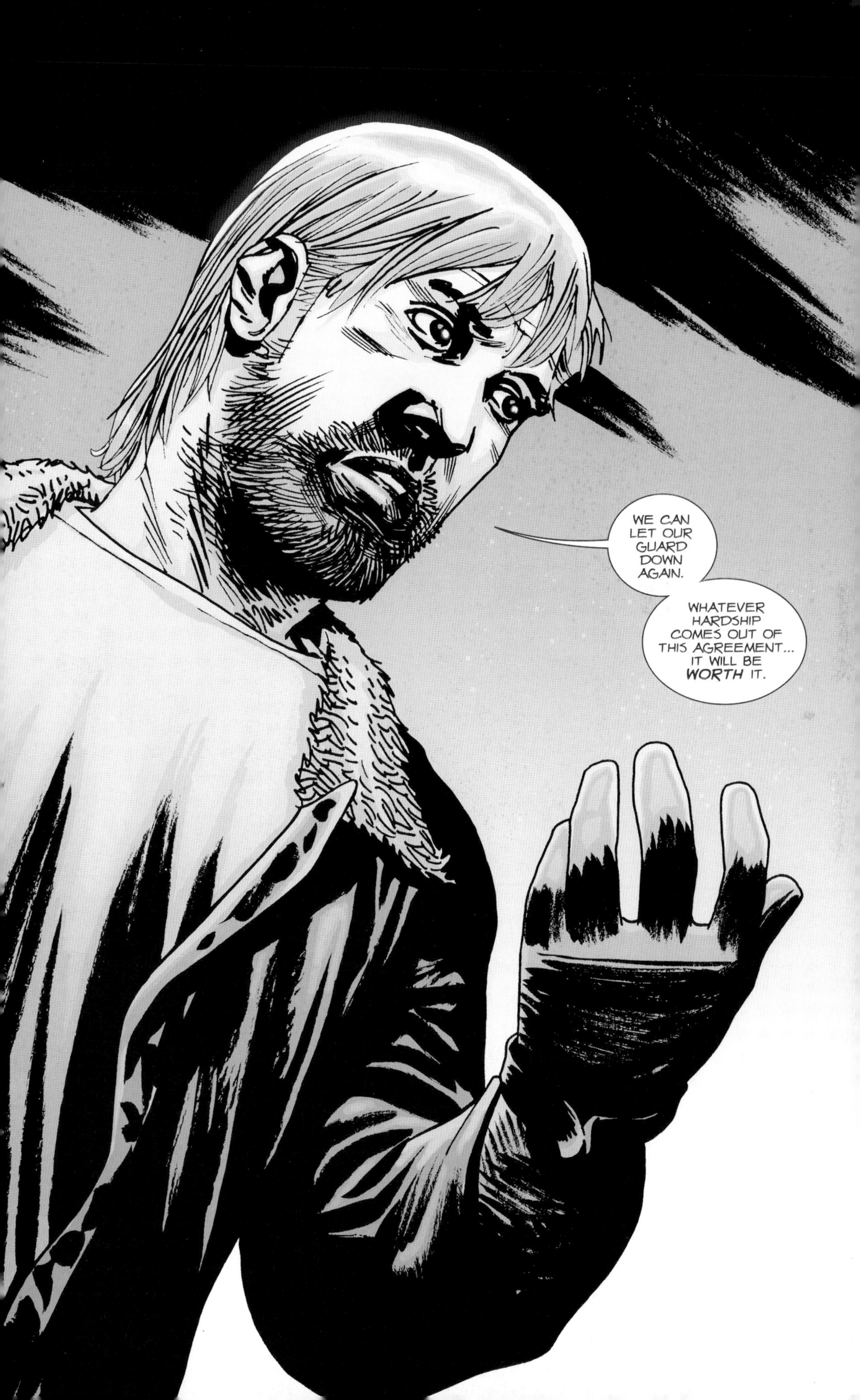
WE CAN LET OUR GUARD DOWN AGAIN.
WHATEVER HARDSHIP COMES OUT OF THIS AGREEMENT... IT WILL BE *WORTH* IT.

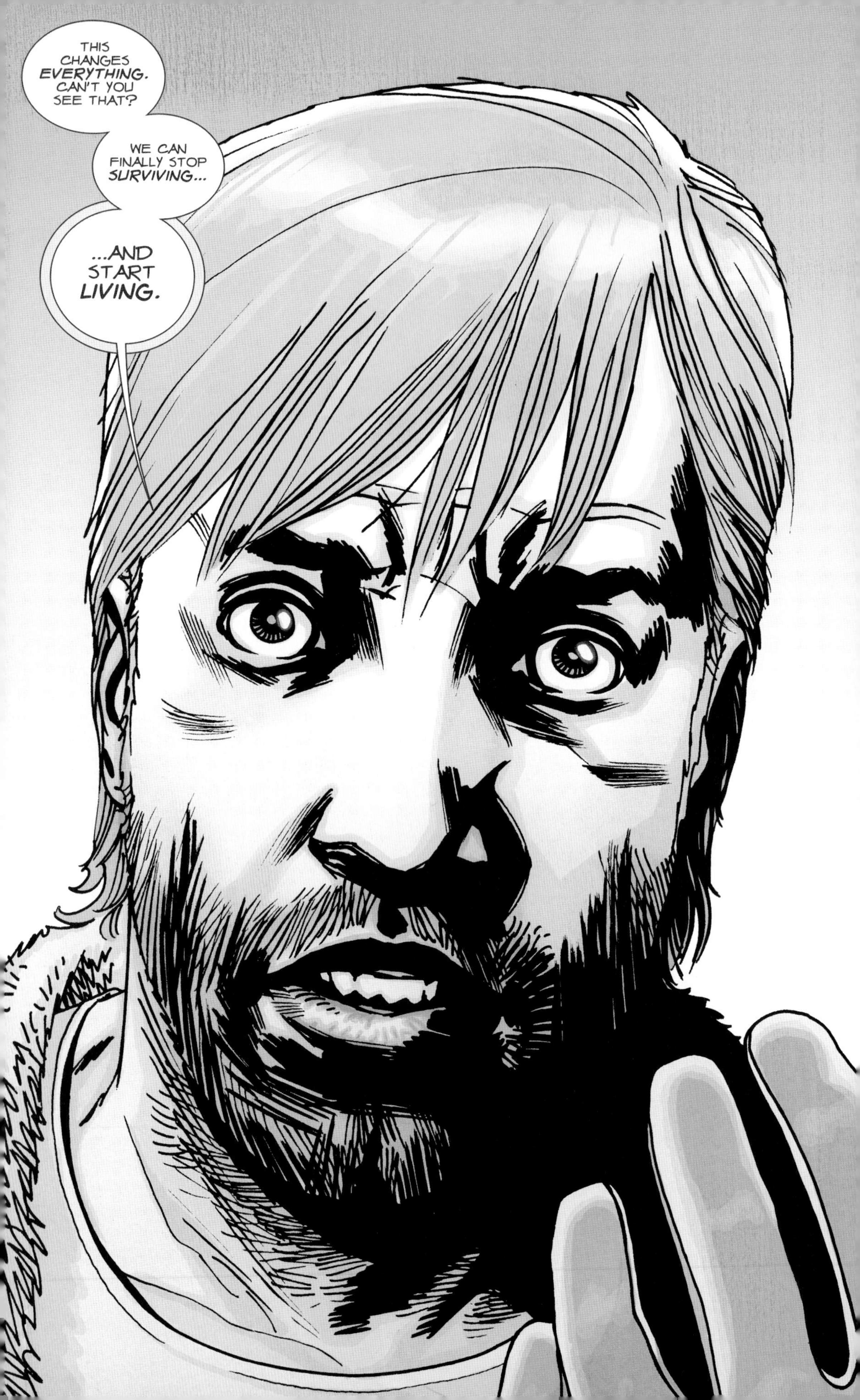
THIS CHANGES EVERYTHING. CAN'T YOU SEE THAT?
WE CAN FINALLY STOP SURVIVING...
...AND START LIVING.

TO BE CONTINUED...

MORE GREAT BOOKS FROM ROBERT KIRKMAN & IMAGE COMICS!

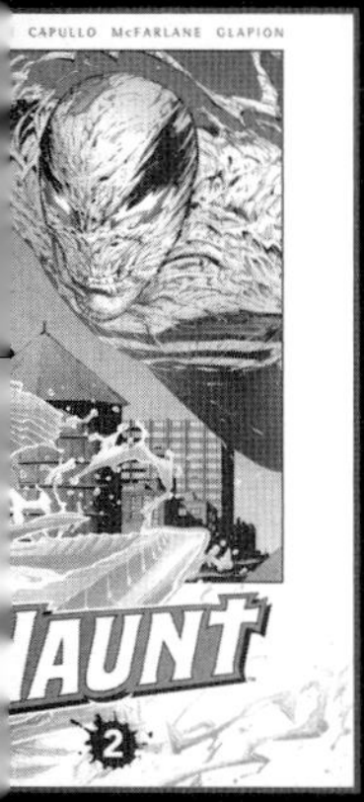
CAPULLO McFARLANE GLAPION
HAUNT
2

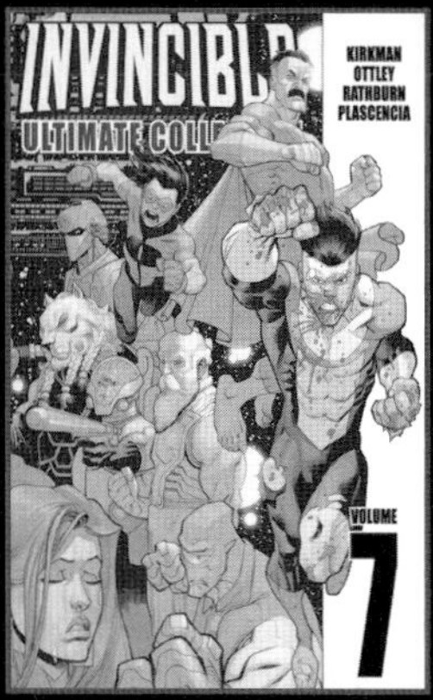
KIRKMAN
OTTLEY
RATHBURN
PLASCENCIA
VOLUME
7

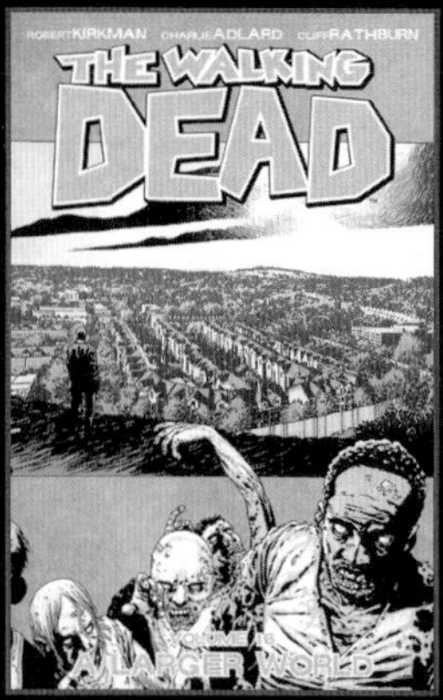
ROBERT KIRKMAN CHARLIE ADLARD CLIFF RATHBURN
THE WALKING DEAD

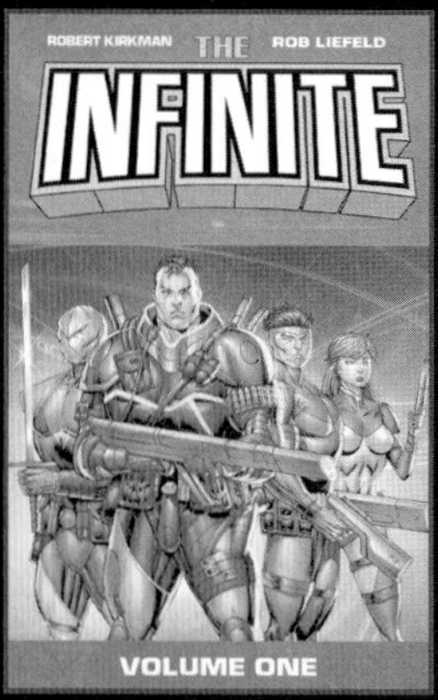
ROBERT KIRKMAN THE ROB LIEFELD
INFINITE
VOLUME ONE

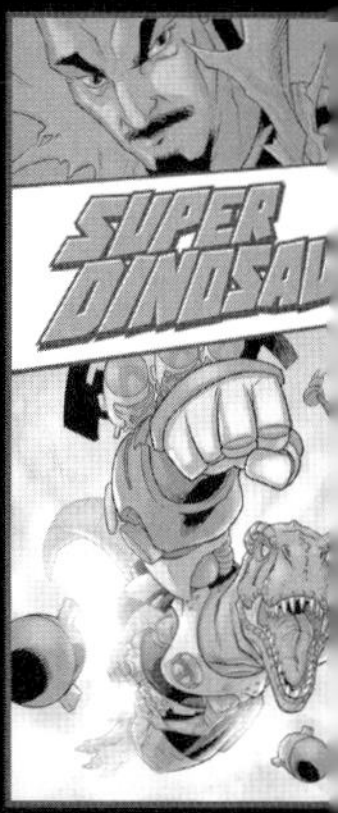

THE ASTOUNDING WOLF-MAN

VOL. 1 TP
ISBN: 978-1-58240-862-0
$14.99
VOL. 2 TP
ISBN: 978-1-60706-007-9
$14.99
VOL. 3 TP
ISBN: 978-1-60706-111-3
$16.99
VOL. 4 TP
ISBN: 978-1-60706-249-3
$16.99

BATTLE POPE

VOL. 1: GENESIS TP
ISBN: 978-1-58240-572-8
$14.99
VOL. 2: MAYHEM TP
ISBN: 978-1-58240-529-2
$12.99
VOL. 3: PILLOW TALK TP
ISBN: 978-1-58240-677-0
$12.99
VOL. 4: WRATH OF GOD TP
ISBN: 978-1-58240-751-7
$9.99

BRIT

VOL. 1: OLD SOLDIER TP
ISBN: 978-1-58240-678-7
$14.99
VOL. 2: AWOL
ISBN: 978-1-58240-864-4
$14.99
VOL. 3: FUBAR
ISBN: 978-1-60706-061-1
$16.99

CAPES

VOL. 1: PUNCHING THE CLOCK TP
ISBN: 978-1-58240-756-2
$17.99

HAUNT

VOL. 1 TP
ISBN: 978-1-60706-154-0
$9.99
VOL. 2 TP
ISBN: 978-1-60706-229-5
$16.99

THE INFINITE

VOL. 1 TP
ISBN: 978-1-60706-475-6
$9.99

INVINCIBLE

VOL. 1: FAMILY MATTERS TP
ISBN: 978-1-58240-711-1
$12.99
VOL. 2: EIGHT IS ENOUGH TP
ISBN: 978-1-58240-347-2
$12.99
VOL. 3: PERFECT STRANGERS TP
ISBN: 978-1-58240-793-7
$12.99
VOL. 4: HEAD OF THE CLASS TP
ISBN: 978-1-58240-440-2
$14.95
VOL. 5: THE FACTS OF LIFE TP
ISBN: 978-1-58240-554-4
$14.99
VOL. 6: A DIFFERENT WORLD TP
ISBN: 978-1-58240-579-7
$14.99
VOL. 7: THREE'S COMPANY TP
ISBN: 978-1-58240-656-5
$14.99
VOL. 8: MY FAVORITE MARTIAN TP
ISBN: 978-1-58240-683-1
$14.99
VOL. 9: OUT OF THIS WORLD TP
ISBN: 978-1-58240-827-9
$14.99
VOL. 10: WHO'S THE BOSS TP
ISBN: 978-1-60706-013-0
$16.99
VOL. 11: HAPPY DAYS TP
ISBN: 978-1-60706-062-8
$16.99
VOL. 12: STILL STANDING TP
ISBN: 978-1-60706-166-3
$16.99
VOL. 13: GROWING PAINS TP
ISBN: 978-1-60706-251-6
$16.99
VOL. 14: THE VILTRUMITE WAR TP
ISBN: 978-1-60706-367-4
$19.99
VOL. 15: GET SMART TP
ISBN: 978-1-60706-498-5
$16.99
ULTIMATE COLLECTION, VOL. 1 HC
ISBN 978-1-58240-500-1
$34.95
ULTIMATE COLLECTION, VOL. 2 HC
ISBN: 978-1-58240-594-0
$34.99
ULTIMATE COLLECTION, VOL. 3 HC
ISBN: 978-1-58240-763-0
$34.99
ULTIMATE COLLECTION, VOL. 4 HC
ISBN: 978-1-58240-989-4
$34.99
ULTIMATE COLLECTION, VOL. 5 HC
ISBN: 978-1-60706-116-8
$34.99
ULTIMATE COLLECTION, VOL. 6 HC
ISBN: 978-1-60706-360-5
$34.99
ULTIMATE COLLECTION, VOL. 7 HC
ISBN: 978-1-60706-509-8
$39.99
THE OFFICIAL HANDBOOK OF THE INVINCIBLE UNIVERSE TP
ISBN: 978-1-58240-831-6
$12.99
INVINCIBLE PRESENTS, VOL. 1: ATOM EVE & REX SPLODE TP
ISBN: 978-1-60706-255-4
$14.99
THE COMPLETE INVINCIBLE LIBRARY, VOL. 2 HC
ISBN: 978-1-60706-112-0
$125.00
THE COMPLETE INVINCIBLE LIBRARY, VOL. 3 HC
ISBN: 978-1-60706-421-3
$125.00
INVINCIBLE COMPENDIUM VOL. 1
ISBN: 978-1-60706-411-4
$64.99

THE WALKING DEAD

VOL. 1: DAYS GONE BYE TP
ISBN: 978-1-58240-672-5
$9.99
VOL. 2: MILES BEHIND US TP
ISBN: 978-1-58240-775-3
$14.99
VOL. 3: SAFETY BEHIND BARS TP
ISBN: 978-1-58240-805-7
$14.99
VOL. 4: THE HEART'S DESIRE TP
ISBN: 978-1-58240-530-8
$14.99
VOL. 5: THE BEST DEFENSE TP
ISBN: 978-1-58240-612-1
$14.99
VOL. 6: THIS SORROWFUL LIFE TP
ISBN: 978-1-58240-684-8
$14.99
VOL. 7: THE CALM BEFORE TP
ISBN: 978-1-58240-828-6
$14.99
VOL. 8: MADE TO SUFFER TP
ISBN: 978-1-58240-883-5
$14.99
VOL. 9: HERE WE REMAIN TP
ISBN: 978-1-60706-022-2
$14.99
VOL. 10: WHAT WE BECOME TP
ISBN: 978-1-60706-075-8
$14.99
VOL. 11: FEAR THE HUNTERS TP
ISBN: 978-1-60706-181-6
$14.99
VOL. 12: LIFE AMONG THEM TP
ISBN: 978-1-60706-254-7
$14.99
VOL. 13: TOO FAR GONE TP
ISBN: 978-1-60706-329-2
$14.99
VOL. 14: NO WAY OUT TP
ISBN: 978-1-60706-392-6
$14.99
VOL. 15: WE FIND OURSELVES TP
ISBN: 978-1-60706-392-6
$14.99
VOL. 16: A LARGER WORLD TP
ISBN: 978-1-60706-559-3
$14.99
BOOK ONE HC
ISBN: 978-1-58240-619-0
$34.99
BOOK TWO HC
ISBN: 978-1-58240-698-5
$34.99
BOOK THREE HC
ISBN: 978-1-58240-825-5
$34.99
BOOK FOUR HC
ISBN: 978-1-60706-000-0
$34.99
BOOK FIVE HC
ISBN: 978-1-60706-171-7
$34.99
BOOK SIX HC
ISBN: 978-1-60706-327-8
$34.99
BOOK SEVEN HC
ISBN: 978-1-60706-439-8
$34.99
DELUXE HARDCOVER, VOL. 1
ISBN: 978-1-58240-619-0
$100.00
DELUXE HARDCOVER, VOL. 2
ISBN: 978-1-60706-029-7
$100.00
DELUXE HARDCOVER, VOL. 3
ISBN: 978-1-60706-330-8
$100.00
THE WALKING DEAD: RISE OF THE GOVERNOR DELUXE SLIPCASE EDITION
ISBN: 978-1-60706-482-4
$74.99
THE WALKING DEAD: THE COVERS, VOL. 1 HC
ISBN: 978-1-60706-002-4
$24.99
THE WALKING DEAD SURVIVORS' GUIDE
ISBN: 978-1-60706-458-9
$12.99

REAPER

GRAPHIC NOVEL
ISBN: 978-1-58240-354-2
$6.95

SUPER DINOSAUR

VOL. 1
ISBN: 978-1-60706-420-6
$9.99
DELUXE COLORING BOOK
ISBN: 978-1-60706-481-7
$4.99

SUPERPATRIOT

AMERICA'S FIGHTING FORCE
ISBN: 978-1-58240-355-1
$14.99

TALES OF THE REALM

HARDCOVER
ISBN: 978-1-58240-426-0
$34.95
TRADE PAPERBACK
ISBN: 978-1-58240-394-6
$14.95

TECH JACKET

VOL. 1: THE BOY FROM EARTH TP
ISBN: 978-1-58240-771-5
$14.99

TO FIND YOUR NEAREST COMIC BOOK STORE, CALL: 1-888-COMIC-BOOK